Time Nin

Paul Barrett

Published by PBTS Ltd
A Publishing House in Kent

First published 2007

This paperback edition published 2007

Copyright © 2007 by Paul Barrett

The moral right of the author has been asserted

No part of this book may be used or reproduced in any manner whatsoever without written permission from the Publisher except in the case of brief quotations embodied in critical articles or reviews.

In this book, any similarity to actual persons, living or dead, is purely coincidental.

Published in Great Britain by PBTS Ltd
A Publishing House in Kent

A CIP catalogue for this book is available from the British Library

ISBN: 978-0-9556697-0-5

Printed in Great Britain by JEM Digital Print Services Ltd
Staplehurst Road, Sittingbourne, Kent, ME10 2NH

For Katie, Zachary and Luca

Time - he's waiting in the wings.
He speaks of senseless things.
His script is you and me...

Time
David Bowie

Time Ninety-Five

Saturday 19th August 2006
9.12am

The taking of someone's life is theft. Not killing as such – just theft. At least it is in my case. That's what happened to me. Someone – something - stole my life, and now they won't give it back, which is really sad.

I'm sitting in a café on a green chair, one of those cheap plastic ones, facing out to the street. I can see a few cars parked nearby – one of them has a sticker on the window which says 'Alarm Fitted'. It's a little white triangle, with a red border; a warning sign. I had a warning sign once, but I didn't realise what it was. I do now – but, of course, it's too late.
  Someone brought me a glass of lemonade, but now I can't find it. Perhaps I drank it; but I really can't remember now. I often forget things, near the end. I find it hard to focus; my mind is already looking ahead - looking beyond the Time I'm living in now. But, either way, my lemonade is gone, and that's also really sad.

I've only got two hours left this Time. Just two hours. That's enough time to find my lemonade, but not for much else. You're probably thinking 'Two hours is a long time – I could do a lot in two hours!' But you can't. You can't do much at all, really; especially when it's all you've got left.

* * * * * * * * * * * * * * *

I'm thirty-one years old, and I'm eighteen years old as well. Well, I'm thirty-one years old at the moment, but I'll be eighteen again in two hours time, just for a few minutes. And then I'll be thirty-one again – for a little while longer; for five months. But, I think I'm actually both ages at the same time, really.

It sounds ridiculous, doesn't it? It sounds ridiculous to me, anyway – but I'm kind of stuck with it. I hate saying things like 'kind of...' – I picked that up in America last Time, and it's stupid! Last Time – Austin, Texas! This Time – a crappy café opposite Kensington Gardens! Green plastic chairs and no lemonade! What a way to go! I wonder what happened to that lemonade?

* * * * * * * * * * * * * * * *

My name is Sandy - my mother was quite keen on Sandy Shaw. She met her at a party or something and thought she was quite nice. I met Kylie Minogue once, before all this started - and she seemed nice as well, but I don't think I'll ever name a child Kylie. Having said that, I quite like the name really - Sandy, that is. It reminds me of being on a beach – a nice white beach with palm trees and sunshine and lemonade. I like my name - it sounds friendly.

I'm going to leave this café now – abandon my lost lemonade – and walk across to Hyde Park. I'll just put the lemonade down as a mystery. I won't think about it anymore. I'll buy another one later – in a few minutes. I'm going to take a slow walk down Bayswater Road, see if there's anything interesting going on. I'm always looking out for interesting things – things I can remember, things I can learn from. It's amazing what you can learn just from looking at things.

Sometimes, I book onto these six-week college courses – I've studied cookery and astronomy and carpentry and loads of other stuff. I even studied Spanish once – I think it was Time Sixty-Five – and I was hopeless at it! It's a stupid language – a bit like French, only worse!

I need to tell you how it all started – how it always starts. I hate the way it starts. It was terrifying the first Time, but now, in many ways, it's even worse. It was my eighteenth birthday, and I was waiting for Julie. Julie is always late, so I turned up five minutes after we agreed to meet, but she still wasn't there.

I'm standing outside Tottenham Court Road Tube station – the entrance opposite MacDonald's. There's a man on a bike, a pushbike – a courier. He keeps looking at me – not at my body or anything – but at my face. That's exactly what he's doing. He's not even looking me in the eyes, not really – he's just staring at my face. He's smiling at me as well. He's wearing a black jacket with loads of pockets. Nine pockets, in fact. I've counted them. There's also a small skull and crossbones on his right shoulder, like on a pirate flag. He smiles at me all the time…all the time. He knows something, that man. He knows something is going to happen. The first Time – the Time I'm telling you about – he *knew* something was going to happen. This is a clue; clue number one.

So, I'm waiting for Julie, and she's late as usual. The man on the bike is still watching me, smiling, always smiling. A little boy comes up the steps of the tube with his mum. It's a boiling hot day. It's July – July 6th, my birthday - but he's wearing a woolly jumper and a bobble hat with little snowmen on it. He's also wearing a pair of snow boots, and I think 'poor kid! He must be baking! Why would his mum dress him up like that in the middle of July?' He gets to the top of the stairs with his mum, and then suddenly they both stop right in front of me. The little boy smiles at me and points up at the sky. This is also a clue; clue number two. But, more than that, this is also the beginning.

Suddenly, in a second, everything turns to blood. Everything is soaked in blood. The sky, the buildings, the little boy, the man on the bike – everything is the colour of blood. And I *know* it is blood. Not red dye, or a trick of the light, or a nuclear holocaust or something like that – I just realise somehow that it's blood. I actually feel my heart stop for a second, I'm that scared. I'm terrified.

I stand there like a statue for, well, a few seconds, but it feels like ages. Then – clue number three – a girl appears on the other side of the road. She's about my age (when I am eighteen), she has long dark hair, and she's holding up a placard. My name is on it. It says, in big black letters (or dark red because of the blood), 'Sandy Glover'. That's all. She doesn't smile – she looks cross! But what can I do? I don't know what I should do next – run away? But where would I run? Everything is different – everything is saturated in blood. The pavement is like an ink-pad, squishy and oozing blood when I apply pressure with my feet. I remember thinking over and over again, 'This is a dream! This is a dream!'. But I knew it wasn't.

So I cross the road to the girl. People are still moving around me, but slowly now - more slowly than people normally move. A pigeon flies past me and drops blood in my hair, which runs down between my eyes. I stand facing the girl, but say nothing. She says nothing. Then, in an instant, she grabs me hard by the shoulders, twists me around, and pushes me under a passing car. I remember her hurting me; holding my shoulders, and I remember the pain of the car on my ribs and arm; but that's all. I remember nothing else at all. No more clues.

I always wake the same way – with the song in my head. It's a crazy song – like a jazz tune of some kind. There's a saxophone, and drums, and I only ever remember a tiny part. There's a tune played on the saxophone, and the words 'Please paint my heart...'

This is all I hear, every Time. And it's not even clear. It's muffled and kind of far away. It's distant. Like my life. It's best viewed from a distance. And that's the strange thing – I don't really feel like I'm part of my own life; if you can call it a life. I'm not sure I have a life, really – not in the traditional sense.

I think I need to tell you what happens to me – what happens to me each Time. I can't really explain anything - if I understood more, perhaps I could do something about it. I don't know what I would do, what I would practically do to escape. But perhaps if I understood more, it would help in some way.

Well, I always wake the same way, and in the same place. I'm in a BUPA hospital - in a white room with a vase of pretty purple flowers, and a picture of a field of corn on the wall opposite my bed. I think it's a Van Gogh, and I believe it's supposed to be uplifting. I don't find it very uplifting. I feel really, really terrible – the song is playing between my ears, and I feel sick. Sick like when you know you're going to actually be sick in a moment - there's nothing you can do about it - and you just have to make a run for the toilet. Like on an aeroplane – like in the back of a car.

Apart from this, I have a headache and my eyes hurt. I can't move my legs or arms, so I'm just staring around the room waiting to be sick and then, hopefully, feel a bit better. At first, it was really horrible and pretty scary as well. Hospitals are scary anyway – and I know I'm in hospital. The room I'm in looks a bit like a hotel room – like a room at a Travel Inn, but I know it's a hospital room. I'm used to being here now – I'm used to the picture of the corn and the flowers and the headache and the sickness. I've done this ninety-five times.

After a few minutes, a nurse comes in and calls the doctor. A few minutes more, and the doctor walks in. He's completely bald, and very tall. He looms over me and smiles. He feels my pulse and says something to the nurse. She rushes off somewhere.

'So, Sandy, you're awake... Can you see me?' The doctor speaks to me quietly. He always says this.

'Yes.' I reply. I always say that.

'That's good. You've been asleep for a long time.'

After this, the conversation varies depending on what I say

next. However, basically what happens after this is they bring me a glass of water and some tablets, and a bit later an apple chopped up into little bits. Actually it's a kind of apple puree – like baby food. I always get the water and apple. I tried saying stupid things once – like making stupid answers when the doctor asked me questions. I still got the water and apple, but I did get some different tablets. I didn't like that – I wanted the same tablets as always. I like to know where I am at this stage.

The next few days are spent building up the muscles in my legs and arms. I fall asleep on my eighteenth birthday, and wake up when I am thirty-one. I've been asleep for thirteen years, and that's why I can't move my arms and legs. I should take ages to recover from this, for my legs and arms to work again – but I can manage it in six days now. It took about two weeks at first, but now I try harder and I'm better at it. I'm better at getting better!

The medical staff are always astonished at my recovery. They treat it as if it's a miracle. They write unbelievable amounts of notes and create folders full of paperwork all about me. They call in experts to study me and watch me work on my muscles. I work like there's no tomorrow, which, in a way, is true for me. Or, at least, there's always the same tomorrow. But, I'm the only expert on this. If I told them the truth, they'd think I'd gone crazy – sustained some kind of brain damage – and that would hinder my escape from BUPA.

This is the truth. Each Time I live for five months. Actually, five months and one day. I wake up at 11.35am on March 18th 2006 and I go back, I am taken back, at 11.12am on August 19th 2006. That's five months and one day, minus twenty-three minutes. Both days are Saturdays. 'Going back' means that I return to Tottenham Court Road to get pushed under the same car again – then I wake up in the same hospital. Always the same; there's the man on the bike, the little kid in the woolly hat - no variation.

But there is one difference... every Time now that I'm inside my body, my eighteen year old body, I can't make it move. When I'm back at Tottenham Court Road each Time, I can't make it move at all.

Well, that's not totally true. I can move my eyes and even my head a little bit - from one side to the other. But I can't run off – far from it. I can't even make my feet move forward. I've tried, many times, but I don't try anymore. The effort makes me feel like I've run a mile, two miles – it makes me feel sick with tiredness. I feel as if I'm being punished for trying to move, trying to change what's happening to me. When I started to think I was being punished, I fought harder – tried to move my hands, to turn around. But it was too painful. That's it, really. It was just too painful.

I still cross the road to the girl with the placard, but it's not me moving my feet. If I try to stand still at this point, then I feel the same pain; feel as if I am being punished in the same way. I have to just let it all happen. I don't struggle any more.

* * * * * * * * * * * * * * * *

Now I discharge myself after six days. The doctors try to persuade me to stay. I think they would like to study me more, but I also think they are genuinely worried about me. They can't understand how I've recovered so quickly. I can walk now – well, at least I can shuffle forward fairly rapidly - and I can hold a cup of water and drink it without spilling any. These things are still an effort, but I don't really feel weak any more – just tired and a bit weird. Weirdness I can live with – I've grown used to weird.

Well, actually, I haven't. I haven't grown used to it. Everything in my life is strange and normal at the same time. It's like living with a terminal illness. That's what it's like. It's not like that film 'Groundhog Day'. I saw that on DVD. It's nothing like that at all. Anyway, the man in the film escapes by falling in love; like in a fairy story. But it's not that simple. If it were that simple, then I'd fall in love with some bloke, and I'd be free. And, anyway, I am in love with someone. But I don't think love will help me here. Love is not one of the clues.

* * * * * * * * * * * * * * * *

These are the clues I have:

1) It's my birthday when it all starts. It could be a clue, but maybe not.
2) My recovery – because it's so quick.
3) There is no media interest in me at all. I'm a young girl, in a coma for thirteen years, and I suddenly wake up. Surely that's a story for someone – even a local paper.
4) The man on the bike who looks at me. He is definitely up to something, but now I can't talk to him.
5) The little boy in the hat and coat. He's in on it as well. Somehow. Anyway, he's a clue, I'm certain of it.
6) All the blood.
7) The girl with my name on the placard.
8) The song.

I think the song is the biggest clue. I've tried to find out where it's from, but I can't find any trace of it. I can hear it in my head, but that's where it stays – inside my head. I need to hear it somewhere else; somewhere outside of my head.

I can hum it as well. And I can sing the words 'Please paint my heart...' Perhaps it's called that. I don't know. I've tried looking it up everywhere. I've asked in loads of record shops, always with the same response. No one has heard of it. I've tried Googling it, of course – the best bet is Dave Tompkins' CD database, which lists 'Piece of my heart' by Janis Joplin.

This, needless to say, is not the right song. If you can hear me, Dave Tompkins, you are no help at all.

Time Ninety

Friday 4th August 2006
1.30pm

I was looking up at the ceiling - there were lights; bright lights above my head. I remember this; the lights. I remember all this quite well, but it was not so long ago; not so very long. I remember that I closed my eyes for a second, but the lights were still there, beneath my eyelids. At least the impression was there, and whether I closed or opened my eyes, it made no difference. I could still see them either way, either outside or inside of me.

I was at the airport - at Gatwick Airport - sitting in the departure lounge. We - my fellow travellers and I - were waiting to board our flight, a British Airways flight. I was thinking: Where am I going - and why?
 I opened my eyes, trying to remember. Edinburgh. I am going to Edinburgh. And I am going to save a little boy's life, a little boy who falls over a barrier. A different boy – not my boy, not my baby – this was a different boy.

I looked down at my watch - 1.30pm. Early in the afternoon, but already I felt tired. Not just tired, but worn out. I slowly looked around me, looking at all the people. I don't understand everything around me. I don't understand them, all these people. They are not like me; not at all. They are not me, but I am them. Just here, just for now, I am them.
 I am the man in the black tie, opposite me, staring into space. I am the man beside me, reading the newspaper - seemingly transfixed. I am the girl and the boy, watching each other - possessive - loving each other with eyes and hands. I am them both, and then I am each one alone, holding the

other's hand. Then I am them both again.

I am the baby in the pushchair, bemused, bewildered. I am the lady in the headscarf, alone. I am the child with the blue bag; excited just to be here.

I look beyond them, out onto the runway, and I am the bird flying past the window, high into the air. Just for a moment I am the bird. I have its mind, and it is vacant; terrifying in its emptiness.

I am so many people. I am the check-in staff, sharing a joke, and I am all the others - the passengers - waiting; just waiting. I am all of them, but they are not me. So who am I? Who am I if they are not me? Who am I? I am different. I am, in many ways, detached from them; as if I have been peeled away.

They cannot touch me. I will board the plane with them, but they will not be near me; not really. Only the madness now - that is all that is close to me, all that can touch me, sit next to me on the flight, serve me drinks, and help me with my bag. And it is the madness that is these other people, not me. I can see that now. I should have always seen it, right from the beginning.

It is this madness, this appalling madness, which is in their faces, in the colours of their clothes, in their voices and hands. This is who they are; what they really are.

I looked up at the ceiling again, at the lights (still burning above me), and these thoughts drifted away, becoming nothing. And that is how I felt, at that moment, as if I am nothing.

I must escape the madness - its pursuit for me is relentless. It will not give in. Like the people, it is all around me, closing in. I must escape.

But, each day, it is all that I can do to stay sane. And it is such a struggle, such an effort; such a terrible effort.

Time Ninety-Five

Saturday 19th August 2006
9.49am

I'm walking through Hyde Park now. There is one hour and twenty-three minutes left this Time. This is Time Ninety-Five. The sun is shining today, and it's very warm. It's the middle of August, and families are out in the park enjoying the summer weather. It's a beautiful day - today is always a beautiful day. Children stand on tip-toes to buy ice creams from a van parked beside one of the gates along Bayswater Road. The police will be along soon, and ask him to move on. He's trying to unload as many ice creams as he can before he gets moved. He knows, as well as me, that he's going to be moved. This is London. It's inevitable.

His name is Nedim, and he's married with a small son. He's from Istanbul, and most of his family are still in Turkey. Not his immediate family - they live with him in Walthamstow. He told me there are lots of Turks living in Walthamstow, and he is one of them. I bought an ice cream from him once, and we got talking. I didn't learn much about him or his family. We only spoke for a few minutes, but he seemed like a nice bloke.

I'm not going to buy an ice cream on this occasion – I'm going to buy a can of lemonade when I get to the other side of Hyde Park. Also, I'm going to have a look around Harrods. I still enjoy shopping, even though there's not that much point in buying anything. Well, not to keep, anyway. They say 'You can't take it with you...'

Whoever they are, they are right.

This is true for me especially. I can't take things with me, not

from one Time to the next. I can't write anything down, because I can't take the book with me. I wasn't always sure of that. I once tried taking a book with me – as an experiment.
This is what I did.

Time Fourteen

Saturday 19th August 2006

It was Time Fourteen, and I was still discovering more and more. In some way, the initial shock had worn off, and it had become a bit exciting. There was about one hour to go before the Time I was living in ended, and I suddenly had an idea. I was passing the big Waterstones bookshop at Bluewater Shopping Centre in Kent, and I saw a window display full of books stacked up on top of each other. There was an offer of some kind – 'Buy two, get one free!' – or something similar to that. I stood looking at the piles of books for a few seconds, and an idea started to take shape. It was a stupid idea, but I didn't know that at the time.

Actually, I did know – on some level – that it was a stupid idea. I know a lot of things that I didn't know before this all happened; but they're all buried inside me somewhere. They help me live day to day – it's a kind of instinct, but it's made up of facts and ideas. I am good at using my instinct now, but during the first few Times, I didn't know how to sort these ideas out – they just seemed like random feelings. I had a feeling that buying these books was pointless, but I ignored it.

I walked into the shop and picked up three copies of the same book – it was 'The Broker' by John Grisham. I've read it since and it is quite good. I gave the three books to the man at the till and paid for them, taking advantage of the 'Three for Two' offer. I handed over the money and took the bag of books from Chris. Chris was the man at the till – I knew this because it said so on his badge. Chris had a kind face, a friendly face, so I grinned and braced myself for the difficult bit of the transaction.

'Chris,' I said, nodding to his badge. 'Would you do me a favour?'

'Of course,' said Chris in reply.

'Would you look after one of my books for me?' I said, as brightly as possible.

'What do you mean…look after it here?' Chris replied, uncertainty creeping into his voice.

'If you don't mind - you can just put it under the counter, with my name on it. You could put a little ticket on it.'

'Oh – alright; I don't mind doing that. But I don't have any tickets.'

'You could use a bit of paper…'

'Oh, right. I'll do that. I'll write on this…' He produced a small slip of paper from under the counter. It looked a bit like a ticket. 'What name shall I put on it?'

'You can put my name. Sandy Glover.'

Chris wrote my name on the paper, and slipped it in the front of the book. The book then disappeared under the counter.

'Thank you,' I said with a big smile.

'That's fine,' Chris said, smiling back. I could tell from his eyes he was starting to think that his morning was about to get off to a winning start. He cleared his throat. 'So…when will you be back to pick it up?'

'Soon, I hope. Thanks very much for your help,' I said with a smile. 'See you soon.'

I picked up my remaining two books and walked out of the shop.

After this I walked through the food court, past the giant bottle of Coke, and out to the lake. The lake was glistening in the sun, and one or two people were already aboard little pedaloes, trying to build up speed in a craft for which speed is impossible. As I strolled around the lake, I remember thinking that my life was a bit like a pedalo – sometimes I am furiously peddling, but not really getting anywhere. I often have these kinds of thoughts – even now. Given the circumstances, I suppose it's no real surprise. 'Sandy the Pedalo' - it has a nice ring to it.

I walked right around the lake and through the underpass at the back. Lots of people don't realise there's another lake at the back, more 'natural' than the one at the front. I strolled all the way around this lake as well, and I found myself alone. I walked into a big clump of bushes, and dug a shallow hole with my hands. I took one of the books out of the bag, and put it on the ground. The other I wrapped in the plastic, and buried it as well as I could in the little hole. I stood up, and committed to memory as best as I could the scene around me. I remember it struck me as a beautiful place, quiet and peaceful. I closed my eyes and stood for a moment, enjoying the shade and the silence. I could hear cars in the distance, and ducks that seemed even further away. Perhaps they were. I can't remember now.

I looked at my watch - 10.59am. Thirteen minutes left. I started walking back around the lake. I remember that I couldn't decide where to go, so I just walked back through the underpass, and sat on a grass bank looking out over the water. I held the last book close to my skin, under my t-shirt, so that it was tight against my tummy. There was just a minute left now – it was 11.11am; just fifty-five seconds.

I stared out over the lake. Thoughts flooded into my mind. Shit. This is all shit. I felt sick, afraid. I hated this bit. I hate it now. I remember thinking just how much I hate this bit; I hated the lake and the boats and the people in the boats. But most of all, more than anything, I hated myself.

I pushed the book closer against my skin. Involuntarily, I pulled my knees up under my chin – crash position. Twelve seconds left. Everything seemed wrong, tainted. I felt alone; completely alone. Impossible to concentrate on anything, my thoughts and emotions flooded out of me. 'What have I done to deserve this? I've been thinking it's exciting, but it's not at all - it's just shit.' Five seconds left. I started to cry. 'Why is this happening? What is the point of this? When will

Time Eighty-Nine

Saturday 5th August 2006
8.22pm

'Billy! Come off of there now, ya wee bastard! You'll fall and break ya neck! Come down now!'
   'I canna come down, Ma! I canna see ma spacegun!'
   'Billy! Come down now! I mean it, son! I'll kill ye myself, I will!'
   'But Ma...I dropped it down here - just here. I canna see it! I dinna ken where it is!'
   'Billy, down ya come now! We'll find it later - now come down. I'll not tell ye again!'

This was Edinburgh, and there were fireworks that evening. It was cold, and people were pressed around me, not for warmth, but for the view. Everyone wanted to see the fireworks. Clouds were overhead, as crowded as us - fighting for space in the sky.
   'It's going to rain,' I had said to the man beside me.
   'No,' he replied. 'It's no gonna rain...'
   We had both looked up at the sky, looking for clues to support our different views.

Billy was ten years old, and he'd dropped, or rather accidentally thrown, his plastic gun over the edge of the barrier. It had fallen over the other side of a large, stone wall. The barrier, like the gun, was also made of some kind of plastic, and it had a flat edge - about three inches wide. It was orange, and stood about five feet high. There was a smaller barrier between us and it (he had stepped over that earlier) – and so he stood, balanced on the larger barrier, a little way in front of us; as if on display. He was looking over the wall. He was looking for his gun.

His mum was calling for him to get down. Before it happened, a number of other people joined in - calling at him to get off the barrier. Then he spotted the gun, and by impulse, he leant out towards it.

'Billy! You're gonna fall!' his mum cried.

He wobbled about a bit, and then seemed to steady himself. A man standing near him (he was about four feet from reach) leant across to get him.

'Come on now, son,' he said. 'You're gonna hurt yourself...'

Meaning well, he reached out and took the boy's leg, to draw Billy towards him. But, in an instant, Billy lost his balance, the man couldn't hold him, and he fell backwards over the barrier and tumbled over the wall to the other side. The drop was about thirty feet.

People screamed as he fell. I heard voices - shouting for the stewards, some just shouting. People were pressing out of the crowd to run down the stairs to the side; down to where the boy lay, only six feet from his gun, now dead.

But I didn't run or shout. I didn't try to push forward to see over the wall. I just looked up at the sky, saw not just the black and grey, but the hundreds of colours - beautiful colours - that made up the sky that evening. Droplets of water fell onto my face; at first just a few, but then a steady flow, coating my face and hair as if with a fine spray.

I turned to the man beside me. He was still there, leaning towards the barrier, trying to catch a glimpse of this disaster; this horror.

'See,' I said to him. 'I told you it would rain.'

* * * * * * * * * * * * * * * *

An hour later, and I was still there. The ambulance had come and gone, and so had the fireworks. Few people, apart from those around us, realised that anything had happened.

The man beside me had gone as well – he didn't stay to see the fireworks. That was a shame – for him, because they were very good.

After a few minutes staring over the wall – looking down at where it happened – I turned around and sat down on the pavement. I tried to decide, in a logical way, what I felt about the boy's death. I knew what I didn't feel…not sad, not upset, not shocked. As he wobbled about at the end, it was almost a relief to see him fall. I had wanted to cry out to him, to the crowd, to his mum, 'He's going to fall. There's nothing we can do! Let's just turn our heads away, not look. Let's just wait for it to happen, and then get on with things. What's the point in getting upset? We can't help him now'.

But I didn't say anything at all. I knew what would happen – I think lots of us did – and I felt as though it was inevitable. It was obvious, and there was no escape from it.

To have saved him would have taken time - forethought and planning.

* * * * * * * * * * * * * * * *

I looked around me, up and down the street. I felt stiff and I was getting cold. I think I had been cold for a while, but I had just realised it at that moment. Somebody appeared in front of me, as if from nowhere. It was a policeman, about my age. He had obviously thought I was sleeping rough, but on closer inspection of my appearance, he had changed his mind.

'Are you alright, miss?' he asked.

I looked up at him, trying to get his face into focus. 'Yes,' I replied. 'I'm fine.'

'It's a wee bit cold to be sitting here…are you sure you're OK? Have you had a few drinks this evening, maybe?'

'No. I'm OK, really.' I stood up, steady on my feet. 'I don't drink.'

'Oh? That's good. I see too much trouble here.' He waved up and down the street. 'Too many people who've had too much to drink…'

'I know…I saw a boy this evening. He fell just there by the wall. He fell and he died.'

'Oh! I heard about that. A wee lad, messing about on the barrier.'

'He wasn't messing about. He'd lost something – it was important to him. His mum didn't realise how important it was. Nobody did. He was just trying to get it back.'

As I said those last words I felt a lump in my throat, and tears starting forming in my eyes. Then I was crying.

'Let's go and sit down,' said the policeman, his voice now sounding concerned. 'I think you've had a wee shock, a bit much for one evening…'

His voice suddenly became distant. Not fading away, but as if someone had turned the volume down really quickly.

'I don't feel well…' I said. I felt his hands on my shoulders, holding me up as I passed out.

Time Ninety

Saturday 5th August 2006
8.18pm

He fell at 8.22pm last Time – at least it was 8.22pm on the big church clock. I remember, as I looked up at the sky after he fell, seeing the time on the clock. It was 8.22pm, and, this Time, he will fall in four minutes.

He climbed up onto the barrier, as before. His mum started to shout at him – telling him to get down. The same people were around me, the man who thought it wouldn't rain – he was there. I didn't speak to him this Time – I was just focused on the task in hand.

I waited until 8.20pm, and then I made my move.

I stepped over the barrier – the smaller one – and then moved across to where Billy was standing. He was above me; looking down at me. My head was level with the bottom of his legs.

'Billy,' I said, smiling up at him. 'Come down now. Take my hand, and come down.'

He looked at me, unsure. I think I made him nervous, perhaps because I spoke with authority; with confidence.

'I canna come down,' he said. 'I'm trying to see ma gun.'

'I know. But we can walk along here, and down the steps. Then we can get your gun and come back. Your mum will come as well. Now, come down, or you will die.'

He smiled at me, his face suddenly one of confidence.

'I'm no gonna die,' he said.

'Yes, you are going to die, in just one minute, if you don't take my hand.'

I stared into his eyes, and he saw I was serious. His mum was still calling to him, but he just looked at me.

'You're weird!' he said, and held his right hand out to me. I pulled him towards me, and caught him as he dropped the right side of the barrier; the safe side - the side where he would be alive, and not dead.

His mum thanked me for getting him down, and swore at him for ignoring her warnings.
 'Can I get me gun, ma? The lady said I could go and get me gun.'
 'You'll miss the fireworks…' his mum replied.
 'The steps are just there,' I pointed. 'Let's just go down and get the gun, and we'll all be back in a minute.'
 Billy's mum looked at me strangely, sizing me up, and then gave a little shrug.
 'Go down with the lady, then,' she said, as much to me as to him.
 'Thanks, Ma!' he said.

We walked along behind the crowd, and pushed our way to the stairs. Once clear of the people, we trotted down the stone steps and along to path below to the plastic gun, just a few feet from where he had died. I stared for a moment at where his body had been, and then at him, alive.
 Which one was real? I had no idea.

I took him back to his mum, and said that I hoped they enjoyed the fireworks.
 'Are you no staying?' she said. 'They'll start in a minute…'
 'No,' I replied. 'Not this Time.' And I walked off, away from the crowds, in the direction of my hotel.
 As I walked back, I heard the fireworks exploding in the sky behind me. It was as if they were miles away; miles and miles in the distance.

Time Fifteen

Saturday 19th August 2006

It was the last day of Time Fifteen. This was the Time following on from where I'd buried the book and met Chris. I remember this Time well.

Much of it had been enjoyable - I'd been to Greece and spent a month walking in the Highlands of Scotland. The trip to Scotland was great. I met a girl called Kathy – she's a student in Edinburgh and lives with three other girls in a flat in Musselburgh. She's only nineteen, and of course I'm thirty-one most of the time, but we had a lot in common and she was fun. Anyway, I think that I'm still eighteen really, in a lot of ways; in my head.

Fun is something often missing from my life. I try to do 'fun things', but usually they're not much fun. Fun isn't so much what you do, it's how you feel. And mostly, I don't feel fun – not inside, anyway. But Kathy was fun, and some of it rubbed off on me.

But, whatever I was doing, I was always aware of the last day looming. I'm always aware of it – the last day - but this Time I knew I had a couple of jobs to do.

I remember waking in the hospital room, and I was aware straight away that the book I'd been holding to my skin had gone. I didn't hold out much hope for that book – all my clothes are taken each Time, so I didn't suppose that the book would be any different. Still, you never know.

So, on this last day I was back at Bluewater; Saturday morning at 9.45am. I knew I'd given Chris the book at about ten-twenty in the morning last Time, so I thought it would be best to wait until about ten-thirty before trying to get it back. So, I walked around the ground floor looking in the shop windows and wandering in and out of the clothes shops.

There was not much point in buying anything – especially not now, so I was strictly window shopping. I sat for a while on one of the little chairs, watching the first shoppers passing back and forth and from shop to shop. A giant fibreglass white bird was suspended high above my head from the ceiling. It looked down on me accusingly, asking me why I was here at all.

I looked at my watch, and it was 10.28am. I stood up and walked to the bookshop, which was just around the next corner. The same offer was still in the windows - the same piles of books. I stood in the opening to the shop and looked to see if Chris was standing at the counter. He was. This was a good sign, I thought. I could see the pile of John Grisham books to my left, the same pile I picked up three books from last Time. I can't remember how many books were in the pile – or whether the books I picked up were still sitting on that same pile. It was now 10.33am. I walked across to Chris, who smiled a welcome.

'Can I help you?' He said cheerfully.

'Yes,' I said with a smile, but feeling the hopelessness of this creeping over me already. 'I wonder if you can. I left a book here a while ago – in fact, I left it with you. You put a little note in it with my name on. I'm Sandy Glover. It's called 'The Broker', by John Grisham.'

'You left it with me?'

'Yes – with you. You put it under the counter there.'

I pointed down to beneath the counter where he was standing. He was starting to look a little confused, but he bent down to have a look for my book. I resisted the urge to just run out of the shop; to just forget the whole thing. Chris reappeared from beneath the counter.

'Sorry, I can't seem to find it. How long ago did you leave it here? Did we order it for you?'

Suddenly I felt like I needed to cry. I started to fight back the tears. I knew if I spoke then the tears would start. So I just shook my head in answer to his question. He could see something was wrong, but instead of looking embarrassed, he looked concerned.

'Are you alright?' He asked.

'Yes,' I replied quickly, but the words came out as a half-sob. I felt stupid and ashamed. I'd been so stupid. Stupid! Stupid! How could I just leave a book under a counter – turn up next Time, and someone would say 'Oh! Here it is!' As if that would ever happen! Not ever.

I could see myself now; imagine myself digging with my hands in the soil, clawing and feeling for a book that wasn't there - couldn't be there. I could see myself, digging down and down; further and further down. I could feel tears on my face. I needed to get out of the shop, but I felt sick, and I suddenly knew that I was going to faint. I looked across the counter to Chris, my eyes pleading for help. But he was gone.

In fact, he hadn't gone, but he'd run around the counter to catch me. He obviously knew a 'girl about to faint' when he saw one, and he was standing beside me as I started to fall. He lifted me into a leather chair which was just a few feet behind me, resting against a post. 'Stay there,' he said firmly, and he disappeared again. He came back with a glass of water, and I drank it and started to feel a lot better. I think I was still crying a bit, but I can't remember for certain.

I looked at my watch, it was 10.38am. I still had over half an hour left. A girl had joined Chris; her name was Rebecca, and she was the store supervisor. She crouched down beside me and asked if I was alright. I said that I was, but asked if I could just sit for a few minutes. She said that was fine, and that I could sit for as long as I wanted. She was very kind, but not as kind as Chris, who disappeared once more and returned with another glass of water. It was actually another glass, because I was still holding the first one.

'How are you feeling now?' He asked.

'Much better,' I replied - my voice now even again. I smiled at him, and he smiled back. 'Look, I'm sorry...' I continued.

'Don't be sorry. No harm done,' he said with a smile.

'You don't have to stay with me. I'll be alright in a minute. If you need to work...'

'It's alright. No customers. See...' He pointed back to the counter, just a few feet in front of me. He was right, there were no customers. 'It's a bit early yet,' he added, almost by way of apology.

I laughed, as I thought he was trying to make a joke. He laughed back, trying to be friendly - trying to make me feel better.

'Thank you very much for helping me...' I started to say.

'I didn't help you; not really, I didn't have your book.'

'Oh, that's OK. You did help me. I need you to follow me around to catch me in case I fall again,' I said this with a smile, but inside I thought it was a totally stupid thing to say. Chris looked embarrassed.

'Oh, I can't,' he said. 'Much as I'd love to, I have to work.' As he said this he looked at me closely, searching my eyes, smiling.

'Never mind,' I said. 'I'll just have to manage on my own.'

I stood up slowly and he held my arm for me, to steady me. He looked again into my eyes.

'Are you sure you're alright?' He said, this time searching my face for something.

I gave him a little smile, a shy smile. I knew he was going to say something else.

'I'm fine now,' I said, but I stood and waited.

'Oh, well – that's good. I can't follow you around; you know...my job, and all that. But, if you'd like a cup of tea or something; if you're still here...I go to lunch at one o'clock.'

'I'd love to,' I smiled.

Chris seemed surprised by the immediate and positive nature of my reaction.

'Oh, right. That's great! Where shall I meet you?' he said.

I looked at my watch. 10.45am – just over twenty-five minutes left. I smiled a big smile at him - a happy smile.

'I'll meet you here,' I replied. 'I'll come back.'

Time Ninety-Five

Saturday 19th August 2006
10.12 am

I make my way across Hyde Park in the sun, and walk out over the grass on the south side; onto South Carriage Drive. Harrods is just a five-minute walk from here. I check my watch. It's 10.12am - exactly one hour left.

I'm walking down towards Harrods now, and I can see a man and a woman kissing. They are standing at a bus-stop, and everyone else is getting on a bus. They are going to be left behind, but perhaps it's not their bus. Perhaps they don't mind. Sometimes, I think, it's alright to be left behind. I never get left behind; I just leave everyone else behind.

Harrods is big. It's a big shop. It's too big when you've only got fifty minutes left. You could spend a day in Harrods, looking at things; making decisions. I try walking from place to place, but I can't focus on anything. This is what I'm like, with an hour or less to go. I'm just treading water – waiting for the next Time to begin.

Sometimes, during the last hour, I think about my life before it all started. This is the worst time to think like this, when I'm feeling so vulnerable, but I can't help it. Against my will, I try to remember details and people, things from a life I have lost - but it is so hard. Every time, it is harder and harder, but it seems so necessary; so important. It's like searching for an anchor - one I can throw down and be rooted to the spot.

But my past - my 'real' past - is like an island. I used to be able to reach it, at one time I lived on it, but now it seems far away and inaccessible. I've lost my connection to it - that life I had before I was eighteen. I know it happened - that it was real - but it's so removed from me now that it seems like a dream. Having said that, sometimes I remember things as if they had happened yesterday; I feel the memories, the vibrations, and they ripple through my mind when I least expect them.

It's as if there's a long piece of string - running right from when I was born (still tied to my umbilical cord) and all the way through to now - with each Time marked out in equal lengths. And occasionally, but not very often, the vibrations I mentioned travel up the string to me now, shaking me, and I remember something from my impossible past, my childhood, my time before.

My dad died before I was two years old, so I don't remember him at all. He worked for a sportswear company, arranging meetings between potential clients and his firm. My mum told me that he liked his job, although sometimes he would have to travel - which he hated. He hated being away from the home - from us - and my mum plied me with hundreds of stories about his kindness and his love for us both. I grew to love him in his absence - his eternal absence - and strangely the lack of all of him, past, present and future, made the memories my mum created for me seem more real.

Sometimes, as a little girl, perhaps just five or six years old, I would dream that he was with us still - just sitting at breakfast or in the front of the car. The second-hand memories became first-hand, and, although I knew he was dead, in a way, he had never been alive, and the stories told by my mum became the reality for me.

And again, in this way, he influenced me, growing up, without the solidity of his presence. Although he was not physically there, I carried him with me in my mind everywhere, and held those memories like a precious toy.

He died in a car accident in France - a large crash involving over twenty cars. He was thirty-five.

My mum brought me up by herself. Her family had a fair

amount of money, something to do with sugar, and they helped support us - just the two of us now - in our four-bedroomed house in Bexley.

The thing I remember best of all is that house. It seemed incredibly old and rambling when I was a little girl, but it shrunk as I grew. It finally became a good sized semi-detached house on a fairly quiet road. I recall with some detail the furniture and décor - the stairs leading up to the landing, my room at the top, to the right. We had pale blue carpets, magnolia walls - also lots of pink, especially in the bathroom. I spent a lot of time in that bathroom, lying in the bath. Even then I loved lying in the bath, surrounded by bubbles, cocooned from the world.

I had, I think, a happy childhood. I was, in most ways, an average child. I never did well or badly at school. I was not especially pretty, but I was not ugly. I was OK at sports and drama and art. In this way, both the bullies and the 'super-popular' girls failed to notice me, and I happily sailed along the river of childhood towards adolescence aboard a boat of mediocrity.

My school reports told my mum that I had 'great potential', and that hard work would lead me to greater things. But we all knew - my teachers, my mum, and me - that I was already as I would be later, an average girl, and it would be best if I simply stayed that way. And for myself, I was happy - content to be average. After all, most people are, even if they think they are not.

I had a few good friends along the way, all as average as me, and they changed between schools and between interests. Chloe and Julie and Melinda; each of them had their own little likes, their own secrets. I can't remember their faces now; not one of them.

My mum liked my friends, and she was pleased by my normality; she was secretly afraid that I would turn out 'bad', and that she would not be able to handle me on her own. By the time I was seventeen, I was starting to think about leaving school and going to college. Although this would still be a year away, I saw its possibilities on the horizon - the freedom and independence that it would bring. I was growing in confidence as a person - I had my whole life stretching ahead, and I was looking forward to what the world had to offer me.

Boys liked me now, and my interest in them - which had been steadily rising for years - was in full bloom. And I still remember them - those boys - but only at the very edges of my vision; Jamie, Peter… not just their faces, but their whole existence is just a blur.

When I reached eighteen, that milestone in a girl's life, I discovered quickly that the world had decided to offer me nothing. I wasn't even eighteen for a single day, never went to my own party, never got to open all my presents.

Instead, my birthday present from the world is the life I have now. And it wasn't even wrapped.

* * * * * * * * * * * * * * * *

I leave Harrods, and walk back to the bus stop to see if the couple are still there. They've gone. Perhaps they just decided to walk. It's a strange sensation now – waiting to go back; waiting to be taken. When you have less than an hour left, it's almost like a mixture of nervousness and boredom. It's just like waiting in a dentist's waiting room. You don't want to go in to see the dentist, but you can't bear just sitting there waiting.

There are only forty-five minutes left, and I need to find something to do.

I walk along a couple of side streets, and find a small café with a green and yellow canopy. It's called 'Edward's.' It looks nice and bright, so I walk in and sit down in a little yellow wooden chair. It one of those folding ones that you could possibly see in a garden. There's a menu lying flat on the table. It looks up at me in French. I flip it over and it talks to me – the words now have meaning. A man in an apron comes over and stands beside me. I ask for an orange juice and a cup of tea (there's no lemonade). He nods and moves away towards the counter. The inside of the café is painted yellow and blue. There are pictures of mermaids and sea serpents around the walls. These are for sale. I stand up and wander around looking at each one. The café is almost empty. It's a bit early, but not for me. For me, it's late.

The pictures are very good. The man behind the counter smiles at me. He nods at one of the pictures.

'Do you like them?' He asks.

'I do - very much. Did you paint them?' I reply.

'No, my wife - she's the artistic one. I just serve up the drinks.'

'Oh, well – they're very good.' I see a sign for the toilets to the right of where he is standing. 'Excuse me,' I say, and wander towards the sign.

The toilet sign is next to a big velvet curtain hanging on the wall. It is deep purple, with hundreds of little silver sequins sewn on to it. The sequins are like tiny eyes, each one staring out at me. I pull it to one side, and find a door behind.

'That's just hanging there,' says the man, without further explanation.

I just smile and open the door. A tiny green toilet is inside. It has seen better days. I sit down and pee, then wash my hands in a small enamel sink. Above the sink is a round mirror. I look up at my reflection. I stare for a long time. I smile at myself.

These are the things that make me pretty:

1) My face. I have a pretty face.
2) My hair. I have long auburn hair, parted in the middle. I also have a fringe. It goes well with my face.

3) My breasts. When I'm eighteen, my breasts are a D-cup. At thirty-one, as a result of the coma, they shrink to a B-cup. But they recover quickly, and settle on C. I'm very comfortable with them.
4) My figure. I'm quite tall - five feet eight inches – and fairly slim. This is because of the coma, and the fact that I don't have much of an appetite. The slimness makes my breasts look bigger – which I think is a good thing.

My appearance seems to have survived the coma extremely well. To be honest, I look almost dead when I first wake up, but within days I can walk, my face has colour again - as opposed to shades of grey – and the rest of me is well on the road to recovery. This is unnatural - I know this. This is, as I've mentioned, another clue.

All in all, I would say that I am quite pretty in a classic sense. Not in an 'eye of the beholder' sense, but in a 'really' sense. That's how pretty I am; quite pretty.

Saying that I'm pretty does not make me bad, does not make me proud; it just makes me honest. I like to be honest. Honest with myself. I gave up lying ages ago.

* * * * * * * * * * * * * * * *

When I return to my table my orange juice and tea are there waiting for me. I smile across at the man, and he smiles back. I drink the orange juice and stir sugar into my tea. I sit and drink my tea slowly. The café begins to fill up, and I become worried that someone will ask to sit at my table. There is an empty chair in front of me. I look at my watch, eight minutes left. I hate the thought of spending the last few minutes with someone else – with anyone.

I need to be on my own, and this is because I can never cope with it; cope with going back. Dealing with it is bad enough, without having to deal with someone else - to have to make small talk, discuss the weather or listen to someone tell me about their job, or tell me about anything at all. That I couldn't stand – that would make me feel sick. I feel sick.

It's 11.07am – five minutes left. I'm obsessed with someone taking the seat in front of me – sitting down and smiling at me. I can't stand the thought, and I'm starting to feel like I really am going to be sick. I have to leave.

I fumble in my purse for money – I leave a twenty pound note on the table. It's the first note I find. As I stand up the man behind the counter shouts across to me.

'Thanks for coming in! Did you see any pictures that you liked? They're very reasonable...'

But I'm already heading out the door. I don't look back and pass through into the small street. It's sunny with a light breeze, and I can feel the wind blowing in my hair; touching my skin. I just start walking, counting down the seconds in my mind...

This is my dream.

I'm sitting on a big wheel at a fairground; it's evening and there are coloured lights on all over the fair. We are at the top of the wheel, and the lights are like little stars; twinkling and shining beneath us. I'm sitting in one of those swinging seats, like on the old style big wheels. I'm on the left, and Jack is sitting next to me. He's about 3 years old. Jack is my little boy. Jack is my son.

We are going round and round on the wheel – the seat is swinging and Jack is smiling and waving. I'm smiling and waving too. We are happy. The wind is blowing in our hair and we are laughing. Jack looks at me and says 'Mummy, I'm falling!' I smile and say 'You won't fall, darling - Mummy's holding on to you.'

Suddenly, in an instant, the bar holding us in swings open. We are still at the top of the ride, and Jack slips out of his seat. I grab his coat and try to hold on, but the coat is like oil, like butter. He slips away and out of the car. He falls into the air, down through the big wheel and towards the grass below.

I scream and scream after him, my screams growing louder, following him through the air.

'Jack! Jack! My little boy! My baby! My baby!'

Time One

When I look back now and think about the first Time, I remember it as being the strangest Time of all. Of course, it was also the least strange Time; I didn't realise then what was coming, what lay ahead of me. I had no idea. But it was strange because of the feelings I had – it was during this Time I had to first come to terms with the coma. And it was the only Time that I felt, despite all that had happened – the coma and everything - that my life would go on into the future; that I would have a future at all.

Now I know better, but then I didn't. When I awoke from my coma, the first Time, I was totally bewildered. I thought that I'd been asleep for a few hours, maybe a few days. After all, I still felt tired – I felt as if I still needed more sleep, more time to lie down. When I discovered that I'd been asleep for thirteen years, it was as though someone had kicked me. I stared at the doctor, disbelieving, wondering what I could do to get all that time back. My twenty-first birthday, my whole twenties; they were all gone, forgotten. They never happened.

But at the same moment I knew even then – straight away – that I would never get them back. I felt an incredible sense of loss – a very real sense of grief. My whole awakening was clouded by these feelings; I couldn't sleep because of them. Anyway, I knew more sleep would just rob me of more time, so I tried to stay awake. This was difficult, because, as I said, I felt tired all the time.

The doctors were very excited by my recovery, as they are every Time. But I remember their excitement more clearly for some reason during my first Time. I can see them rushing about, calling colleagues; and my room being filled with people in white coats and suits and bow-ties. Everyone wanted to talk to me, to ask me questions, to give me advice.

They told me that I had not simply been in a 'persistent

vegetative state' (which is bad enough), but that I had been in a 'hopeless vegetative state', which I suppose requires little or no explanation. I was, in every sense, a hopeless case. My chances of recovery were zero.

I had 'lived' at an NHS hospital in Cambridgeshire for nearly seven years; but there had been moves to have me 'switched off'. Having no voice of my own, my mum intervened and paid for me to be moved to a nearby BUPA hospital, just a few miles away. The care would be expensive, she was told, but this did not deter her.

Shortly after I was moved, my mum died of a heart attack. Literally within weeks, I was told. I was not told that the strain of my coma on her life almost certainly contributed to her early death, but I worked that out quickly for myself. This increased my sense of loss, and added to it a spoonful of guilt.

* * * * * * * * * * * * * * * *

Although everyone around me seemed excited, I did not feel the same way. I actually felt awful, both in my mind and all over my body. I was locked into a body I no longer knew – I couldn't move properly, couldn't walk at all without help, and I was really skinny and pale. I appeared as a shadow of myself, my mind trapped inside a walking corpse.

They avoided giving me a mirror – they knew what a shock it would be. But after three days in bed I decided that I would take a look at myself in the mirror hanging in the disabled toilet across the corridor from my room. My room had a toilet in it, but they had removed the mirror on the day I awoke - they did this with an electric screwdriver. I knew the disabled toilet had a mirror, because I'd caught a glimpse of it when they were carrying me to my toilet during day two of my recovery.

I remember lying in my bed, plucking up the courage and physical energy to get myself across to the toilet. I was wondering how I could possibly get there, and thought that perhaps I should just roll out of bed and crawl as best I could. I was scared of getting caught, and I wondered if it was a pointless task.

Suddenly, as I was almost ready to give it a try, I became aware that I could walk. This was the first experience of my new found instinct, and I didn't recognise it as that at the time, but I just knew that I could do it – that I could walk.

Moments passed, and then I sat up in bed. It was easy. It hurt, and I felt a bit dizzy; but it was easy. I swung my legs – slowly – over the side of the bed, and gingerly placed my feet on the floor. I waited a couple of minutes, and then put the meagre weight of my emaciated body onto my feet. I was standing up.

My trip to the disabled toilet took a minute or two to complete, and it was both a triumph and a disaster. It was a triumph because I felt amazed that I had done it – they had told me I would not be able to walk for weeks. But when I looked at myself, what I had become, in the mirror, I put my hand to my mouth and stared – wide eyed – with tears rolling down my cheeks.

I looked barely alive – I was grey, not white, a horrible pale grey. My eyes were sunk into my face – I had lines where none had been before, around my eyes and cheeks, and the corners of my mouth. My arms and legs were as thin as I could have ever thought possible. My breasts had shrunk at least two sizes, in fact they had shrunk from a D to a B, but I didn't care about those details at the time. They had shrunk, and so had I. I had shrunk as a person.

I looked worse than I could have ever imagined, much worse. I turned and made my way back to my room. Nobody saw me, and I lay in the bed that night – no longer eighteen, no longer a girl – feeling as though my life had truly ended, not begun again.

However, the trip to the toilet turned out to be a catalyst in my recovery. Within a few more days I was up and about. I was feeling better each day, and able to eat and drink and take short walks up and down the corridor. The doctors could not believe their luck. They had a miracle on their hands, and they were writing articles on their laptops and in their heads, each dreaming of seeing their findings and discoveries published in eminent medical journals.

I, on the contrary, was getting bored. I felt I had lost enough of my life, and I was ready to get out. However, the first Time, I stayed for over three weeks before I asked to leave. I was told that would not be possible – I was simply not ready. It would be dangerous.

But I knew I would be alright. I looked at myself in the mirror that evening. I was getting back to normal. In fact, I looked almost like myself again, just a bit older. I was still thin, still looked a bit frail, but my colour was back and my breasts were growing. Alarmingly, it seemed as though one (the right one) was growing faster than the other. I spent a good few minutes locked in the bathroom of my room (they had replaced the mirror by now) carefully studying this bizarre but potentially terrible occurrence. After some time, I concluded that it was a kind of optical illusion, and that everything was alright. I smiled at myself, my first smile in three weeks.

I was ready to leave.

* * * * * * * * * * * * * * * *

The doctors tried and tried to persuade me to stay, but I left. I had been bequeathed my family's money in a trust; I had a debit card and a cheque book. BUPA had cleared out a fair chunk of my bank account, but there was a sizable amount left.

In the days following my departure from the hospital, I tried to get my life back into some kind of order. I made an attempt to track down some of my friends from the past. I called the telephone numbers I had used when I was eighteen, but I couldn't get in contact with any of them. They had not been to visit me in hospital since my recovery, not one of them – not once. It was as if I was forgotten, as if I'd never been eighteen at all. My mum had died years ago, I had no other family. Once I left the hospital – apart from returning for check-ups and tests – nothing else was familiar to me. I was truly, and absolutely, alone.

I looked for a support group of some kind, but there were none that I would want to join. My parents' house, my house, had been sold after my mum's death, and the proceeds had been added to my trust. I had no home - my previous life had disappeared.

Now, of course, I don't look for that previous life, and the fact that it has all vanished now seems completely weird – it is a clue. But, back then, it didn't seem weird at all. At least, it didn't seem any stranger than anything else that was happening to me. It was all weird – everything was weird.

I had been thrust into a situation that, in reality, I had no idea how to cope with. And the loss of my past was just another thing to add to the pile of things to deal with. But, at least then, I still thought there was a future. No past, but still a future.

* * * * * * * * * * * * * * * *

As I know now, I have no past, and there is no future - just the same five months. But then I had no idea about that. I carried on with my life, rebuilding it bit by bit. I rented a flat, fully furnished, in Greenwich – just a five minute walk from the park and the river. It was nice, but I've never rented it since. I planned to enrol in an English Literature course in September, at the University of Kent. They had buildings in Greenwich, and I thought this would be convenient. It would have been - convenient - except for the small detail that there is no September.

I also started jogging, and I would run miles around Greenwich Park some mornings. I was full of energy, and I couldn't understand, nor could my doctors understand how my recovery had been so complete. I was becoming happy again. I was coming to terms with being thirty-one. I had my life back, and I felt that I needed to make the best of it.

* * * * * * * * * * * * * * * *

In the last few weeks before Time One came to an end, I began to feel as though something strange was happening. I was aware of some change in myself, something beyond anything I could understand. I put it down to the after-effects of the coma, and I even mentioned it to the doctors who, religiously, were still checking me out.

They asked if I was feeling depressed or lonely or sad, and I said that I wasn't. I suppose I was feeling all three a little, but I was sure that any sense of depression or loneliness had nothing to do with this growing, powerful sensation.

I tried to explain the feeling I had, but other than to describe it as 'strange', I could think of no suitable title to give it. I told them that it was like I was waiting for something – like standing at a bus stop, peering down the road to catch a glimpse of something big and red; waiting for the bus to come into view. The bus would then stop and take me to my destination. Not home – just to a destination.

The analogy of the bus stop was the best I could do. Of course, now I know what I am waiting for; it is the end of each Time. But then, I was just aware of my new situation on some subconscious level. The doctors could make nothing of my explanations, other than to make more notes. These, I felt, were for their benefit, not mine.

During this time, during the last four weeks, I made a friend. She was called Helen, and she lived in the flat across from me. Her parents were rich, and she was studying French Art and History at the University in Greenwich. She was only twenty-one, but she acted as if she were much older. I suppose she was what you would call sensible. She was very nice, and she liked me – so I liked her. For me, that had always been the case, I always liked people who seemed to like me.

I mention her only because one of the strangest things that happened during Time One was when I was with her. Just ten days before the end of my first Time, on August 9th, we went on a trip to London Zoo. I can't even remember why we decided to go; I remember it was Helen's idea, but I'm not sure where the idea came from. It was a Wednesday, a beautiful sunny day, and we set out early on a bus into the centre of London.

We had packed tuna and cucumber sandwiches, which we'd made together the evening before, in my flat. Helen had talked about love a lot that evening – I remember that; and I also remember that I felt that she had somehow made a pass at me – in the vaguest possible terms, but a pass nonetheless. I had ignored it, and it – or the shadow of it – had not intruded upon our trip to the zoo.

However, I do recall watching her closely from time to time during the day, studying her conversation and facial expressions, almost as though you would study a laboratory animal that had performed in some way unexpectedly; dispassionately, but with interest.

This was not the strange thing that happened, though. That was to do with the rabbits.

* * * * * * * * * * * * * * *

After we had eaten our sandwiches, and had seen many of the big animals and the very little ones – like elephants and ants - we found the 'Petting Zoo'. This was mainly for children, and you could pat and stroke these animals, without fear of losing a finger or even a limb.

When we went into the first enclosure, where the goats were, we looked down at the ground in disgust at all the muck and the straw. Helen turned to close the gate behind us, and at that point the goats started moving away from us. They did this in unison, and quite slowly, but they continued moving until they had reached the very back of the pen. They all stood, about ten of them, staring at us silently. They pressed their hinds up against the back of the bars – trying to maximise the distance between them and us – but they never once took their eyes from us. At least, then, I thought they were looking at Helen as well.

'They don't like us,' whispered Helen in a low voice, stating what was obvious.

'No,' I agreed.

'Let's find different animals,' she said.

So we did. We went to find the rabbits.

* * * * * * * * * * * * * * * *

We were both certain that there would be rabbits; all petting zoos have rabbits. After a couple of minutes we found a sign pointing to a small enclosure with rabbits and guinea pigs. We walked in and surveyed the scene.

I remember this clearly, although it seems so long ago. There were two children with their mum; they were stroking one of the rabbits. One of the children – a small boy – was trying to feed it a piece of hay. Two other rabbits, and a few guinea pigs, looked to be asleep on the other side on the enclosure. They were elevated off the ground about three feet, lying on a sort of wooden raised shelf. We walked over to them, and Helen bent over to look at one.

'They're not asleep – they're just dozing,' she said.

I bent over to stroke one, and as I did it pushed its ears flat against its head and shuffled backwards away from me. I removed my hand, surprised – and at that moment all the rabbits (there were five in total) seemed to react as one, as if a silent signal had been given.

They started to move about nervously, scratching at the straw beneath them and moving their heads about, quickly, from side to side. The rabbit being stroked by the children behaved the same way, and their mum pulled them away as it began to make strange breathy noises.

Then, they started to squeal – all of them. I had never heard a rabbit make a sound before, and I felt shocked by the noise they made. They squealed and bashed their feet on the straw, one of them bashed its head against a water bottle, which became dislodged and fell to the ground.

It was then, as the water bottle fell to the ground, that they started to fight. They lunged at each other, baring teeth, squealing, screaming, and tugging at fur and ears and necks. The mother and children had left by now, and Helen was leaving to find someone who could help – someone who worked at the zoo.

But I stood, in horror; transfixed. I literally saw fur flying and blood and skin beneath where the fur had once been, and I knew that this was because of me. I couldn't think why – what I had done – but I knew, with absolute certainty, that I was to blame. The moment it hit me – the feeling of blame – I ran from the enclosure, not looking back.

Helen returned with a zookeeper, a man of perhaps thirty-five. He looked over the carnage with a stony face. I stood in the doorway and watched, keeping a distance between myself and the rabbits. He walked over to one of them and looked at its wounds. He went to all five rabbits and examined them in a cursory fashion.

'They'll all be alright,' he said with a frown.

'Good. That's good,' Helen replied.

'What happened here?' he said, without any accusation in his voice.

'I really don't know,' said Helen, placing her hands on her cheeks. 'They just went mad...'

'Hmm...' said the zookeeper. But he seemed satisfied with this vague explanation. 'Sometimes, if something frightens them...not just rabbits, all animals. They just...' He waved his arm around the enclosure.

'Oh,' said Helen.

'Well – I'd better get them seen to...' He picked up his little radio attached to his belt. 'And thanks for the alert – we'll have to close this area for a couple of days, give them a chance to calm down properly.'

'That's OK,' we said, and we left him to sort it all out.

* * * * * * * * * * * * * * * *

Helen just laughed it off, on the way home. But the strangeness I remember is not just because of the rabbits – what happened to them and how they behaved – but how I knew; how I was so sure that they had reacted to me. I knew that it was me they were afraid of; me they hated.

Since that time, I have had many other occasions where animals have been scared by me. But I have never forgotten that time at the zoo - that baptism into what I had become.

Time One

Saturday 19th August 2006

It wasn't until around 9.30am that I woke up. I'd had a late night the night before; sitting on my own in my flat - on my settee - watching a film. It was about the Titanic disaster, and it had Kate Winslet in it. I hadn't heard of Kate Winslet back then, but of course I know who she is now. The film went on for ages, but it was very good. It made me cry at the end.

I lay in bed for a few minutes and finally got up around 9.45am. Everything seemed normal, and I don't remember having any extra special sensation of strangeness or foreboding. I made a cup of tea and sat at my little kitchen table staring into space. I can recall thinking about my up-and-coming course at the University, thinking that I was lucky to have gotten in, given the circumstances. However, I think that the circumstances, in reality, helped me in some way. I think everyone believed that it would be good for me – bring some structure and stability to my life. Perhaps it would have.

I decided to go out for a run. I went and had a shower and got my running clothes on. I knew I would need another shower when I got back, but I didn't mind, as I would probably have a bath instead. I like baths, and it would give me a chance to read the last fifty pages of 'The Mosquito Coast', my current book.

I remember looking at my watch as I left the flat for my run, it was 11.04am. I ran down the road – away from my flat and towards the park. The sky was a beautiful clear blue, and it was already very warm. I passed the row of Victorian houses that I always passed on each journey to the park. Each had black railings along the front, dividing the houses from the street, marking out territory for a hundred years.

Ahead of me, one of the doors opened and a man stepped out onto the pavement – he had a beard and sunglasses, and he stood and looked up at the sky. He was dressed in a bright blue tie-dye t-shirt, and as he stood, it was as if he was an extension of the sky itself - his shirt paying homage to the beautiful day. He was a hippy, and I had to run around him.

I stole a glance back at him just after I passed – he was walking away from me now, his head still tilted towards the sky. A moment or two later, I ran through the gates of Greenwich Park. I usually liked to time myself from this point, so I stopped for a second, and looked at my watch. It said 11.08am. I remember looking across the park at my route – the route I would always run. It was about three miles, and I liked to do it in less than thirty minutes. I set off, heading up towards the observatory.

As I ran, I quickly became aware that I didn't feel right. The 'bus-stop' sensation, the feeling of waiting, flooded over me in a matter of seconds. So much so, it made me gasp. I carried on running, and as I did, the park opened up to me. What I mean by that – and so much is so very hard to explain – is that everything was becoming clearer. It was as if I was putting a pair of really strong glasses on, and everything was coming into focus for the first time.

I could see the grass, the path, and the people – they were always there, of course – but now I could see them with incredible clarity. Each blade of grass seemed to stand out, independent – each with a meaning and distinction of its own. The path was curved, up the hill, and it was stretching on before me – further than was possible – towards the horizon and beyond. It was the road to success, to secrets and loves, to purpose and answers. And there were people; I could see them as they were – happy and sad, desperate, confused, abandoned and loved. I looked up, and the clouds seemed as if they were alive, each one with a shape and purpose created for it alone. These things were real to me, as real as anything I could name; but yet they were just images and ideas. I had no control over this - it was just the way things had become; clearer, sharper; more animated.

This was all flying around me, crowding my mind – but at the same time, everything was normal. I felt ordinary – a girl running in a park, enjoying the sun like everyone else.

The end came in an instant. I was not aware of the moment; it just happened. I was given no warning as it hit me like a hammer across the head. It was 11.12am, and I was taken for the first time - taken from the first Time.

And that is what it is like. It's not a gentle passing; a fading into grey and then black. Instead, it's just like being wrenched away by the strongest hands in the world. It is immediate and violent. And it is scary, really scary. That time, the first Time, was in many ways the worst - for although there was no dreaded anticipation, the shock was worse than anything I had ever known.

I suppose it happens in a moment, perhaps just a single second; but it seems longer. I have tried to measure it, and I can't - but if I had to give it a measurement of time, it's as if at least three seconds pass. The blackness comes first – blindness and deafness combined, and then no more air. This almost happens at the same time, and is the worst thing of all. It feels as if soil has been forced down my throat, and each time I try to take a single breath, but my lungs can no longer respond. I screw my eyes shut and wait for the blow. This comes just a moment later – a crashing blow to the back of the head. I cannot fall, cannot respond in any way – I can only feel. I now feel nothing but fear and pain. Then I am gone – still standing, sitting, laying - but gone. Just for a second. That second, I am empty. Lost in a universe that doesn't want me; that hates me. It has spat me out, destroyed me, brushed me away and wiped me from its memory forever. I know this is true; it is how the world wants it to be.

This is how it was the first Time; this is how it is every Time. I pass from one Time to the next in this way. I said that I feel nothing but fear and pain. But that is not the whole truth. I feel one more thing. I feel worthless.

Time Eighty-Two

I don't dislike football; I've just never been interested in it. I'm aware that other people are interested, that it's on television a lot, and that it's played all over the world. However, I've just never been interested myself.

But, as it turns out – and always turns out – my five months and one day coincide with the 2006 World Cup. Each Time, this is played in Germany. And each Time, England loses on penalties to Portugal in the quarter-finals, and Italy wins the final in the same way.

During Time Eighty-Two, I went to Germany for the World Cup finals. This is what happened.

* * * * * * * * * * * * * * *

On May 3rd I met Adam. I was sitting outside a crowded café in Leadenhall Market. It was a Wednesday, and the lunchtime crowd was mainly made up of City workers; men in suits and ties, ladies dressed smartly. There was also the occasional tourist wandering past, and walking inside to buy sandwiches.

I was sitting at a silver table – waiting for my jacket potato with cheese to arrive. I remember that I was beginning to feel hungry. A bird flew down and settled beside my table. He cocked his head at me, looking for food. But, at that moment, I had none to give it. We were both waiting.

Adam stepped out of the café, and looked around outside for somewhere to sit. He was wearing a grey t-shirt and blue jeans, both covered in flecks of white paint. My table had the only seat available outside – he spotted the empty chair and wandered over.

'Can I sit here?' He asked. He pointed to the empty chair.
'Of course,' I replied. He sat down.
There then followed a short time of silence. He sat with his

cup of tea and spooned sugar into it. He stirred it vigorously and put the spoon down on the table. He looked up at me and smiled.

'Nice weather for May,' he said.

'It is,' I replied.

I wished that I had a book. Then I could have sat with my book – a silent friend to occupy my eyes. Instead I was stuck making smalltalk.

'Are you on holiday?' He said, making another attempt at conversation.

'No. I live here in London,' I replied.

'Oh? Where in London?'

'I live at Lancaster Gate.'

'Oh, it's nice round there - opposite the park and everything. Do you have a flat there?'

'No. I live in a hotel.'

'Oh. You live in a hotel. But you're not on holiday?'

'No. I live there.'

'Must be expensive - hotels round there. That's what I do for a living. Paint hotels.'

'Oh.'

'Big painting jobs...fairly long contracts.'

'Oh.'

My jacket potato arrived along with a knife and fork. I said 'thank you' to the waitress and picked up the cutlery.

'What do you do...for a living?' He asked.

This was a good question. What did I do? I thought for a second.

'Oh. Not much. I mean - I'm a designer - a fashion designer.'

'Oh – right,' he replied. He seemed disappointed in some way with my answer. He looked down at his t-shirt. 'I don't know much about fashion.'

I smiled back at him, and then started to eat my jacket potato. The conversation ended there.

When I got up to leave, we said a brief goodbye.
'Nice to meet you,' he said.
'Bye,' I replied.

* * * * * * * * * * * * * * *

The following day I saw him again. It was lunch time, and he was sitting in a pub on his own. It was one of those modern pubs in the centre of London - all glass and pale wood. I could see him through the window, and he looked sad; I thought he looked sad, anyway. Perhaps he was just thinking sad things. I don't know why – in fact, I have no idea why at all – but I opened the door to the pub and walked in.

Adam looked up and saw me, and his face just lit up. He beamed a smile at me, and I could not help but smile back. We quickly agreed that we remembered each other from yesterday, and he explained that he'd finished work early as he was meeting a friend later. He offered to buy me a drink, and I accepted.

Two hours later, we were still sitting there. He was laughing at some crappy joke I'd made about a cat or something. He was actually very funny, and his jokes were better than mine by far. He had told me about his friend, and why he was sad.

He was going, along with his friend, to Germany next month for the World Cup finals. But his friend had pulled out. Adam's friend (who's called Pete) had been vague on the phone, and asked to meet to discuss this bombshell in person. Because this is what it was to Adam, a personal bombshell - a disaster of epic proportions.

Pete eventually turned up – almost two hours late – and explained his predicament to Adam. I sat quietly while Pete explained about being offered a job in Newcastle and the money being so good that he couldn't turn it down. It was obvious that Adam couldn't care less about the job in

Newcastle, but it was also clear to me that Pete would never change his mind.

'What about the tickets?' Adam asked.

Adam and Pete had arranged plane travel and hotels through a travel company, but this did not include tickets to any of the England matches. However, it did include tickets to a match between Japan and Croatia in Nuremberg. England were playing in the same location three days earlier, so that was good, according to Adam. Adam was happy to watch the England match in a bar or on a big screen set up in the town square, along with thousands of other England fans who will have made the journey. However, thanks to Pete, this was now all in serious jeopardy.

I thought the time for me to leave had come when the conversation, which had been difficult already, took a decided turn for the worse when Pete announced that he would try to sell his travel tickets to the highest bidder.

'You *are* joking!' said Adam. 'We were sharing a room! I'm not sharing a room for four weeks with someone I don't even know!'

'What can I do?' complained Pete. 'I can't go – someone might as well have the tickets. Mate, I've got to get some money back on the tickets if I can...'

The conversation went backwards and forwards in the same vein, with Adam getting less and less happy. I stared up at the ceiling. An idea began to form in my head, but it was a radical one. I looked across at Adam – he was angry, but more than anything he was sad. I hardly knew him, but what was happening just seemed so unfair. At that moment, it just suddenly seemed unfair that he should be made so sad. I had the power to put an end to that sadness. I looked towards Pete.

'I'll buy the tickets,' I said.

The conversation stopped suddenly.

'What?' Pete asked.

'I'll buy the tickets,' I replied.

'Why?' Pete was starting to sound confused.

'Why? So I can go and see the World Cup, that's why.'
'Do you like football then?'
'Yes…why not?'
Adam stared at me. 'Sandy, I still want to go. I want to keep my tickets,' he said.
'Yes, I know,' I replied. 'I'll go with you.'

Adam looked at me, but was rather looking through me. His mind was trying to assimilate the various possibilities of this new arrangement. In a moment, his World Cup trip had changed, from his perspective, from a disaster to a possible miracle.
'You'll go with me?' he said.
'Yes. I'll go with you.'
'But...'
'If you want me to… If you'd rather go with a bloke, that's OK.'
'No, no. I don't mind. I mean, if you want to come...'
'Yes. I'd love to go. It'll be fun.'
Adam looked happy but perplexed. He smiled at me and then just laughed. Then he stared at me for a moment.
'Are you serious? Sandy, are you serious?'
'Yes,' I replied. I turned my attention to Pete. 'How much do you want for the tickets?'
'Man, I don't know. I have them on me, I actually have them on me – but I'd need to change them to your name. They want a hundred and fifty quid to change them.'
'Pete, how much do you want for the tickets?'
'Well – they cost about two grand. Plus a hundred and fifty quid to change them to your name...'
'So…two thousand one hundred and fifty pounds - is that OK?'
'Yeah, OK...'
'Deal?'
'Yeah, it's a deal! Sandy - whoever you are! It's a deal!'

I wrote Pete a cheque. I told him to change the tickets into my name, and then give them to Adam when the cheque had cleared - when he was happy that he had the money. I looked Pete in the eyes as I said this, and I could see that he trusted me.

'That's fine, I trust you,' he said.

'I know,' I replied.

* * * * * * * * * * * * * * * * *

Each Time - after being awake for four days - a man dressed in a suit and pink tie comes to visit me. He is friendly, but unnerved by my condition. He is a solicitor. He explains that my mother has died while I've been asleep (I've been told this already) and that the Will placed the estate in trust for me. My father died when I was two years old, and I have no brothers or sisters. Therefore, the estate is mine in its entirety.

The estate is the house, a few other items, and about one hundred and thirty thousand pounds in cash. This is what's left. About a hundred and fifty thousand pounds had been spent so far on my care. My mother's sister had been named as trustee, but now I am awake again, I can take over both legal and beneficiary rights to the trust. My mother's sister is now living in New Zealand. This is all explained to me, and I nod at the appropriate moments. I sign five forms and the trust is mine. The man explains that a chequebook and card will be ordered for me; for the account where the money is. I sign more forms, and he tells me that the chequebook and card will be delivered here to me at the hospital. I ask for a cash advance, as I explain I may be leaving soon. He tells me that there will be no problem with that, and promises to bring the money tomorrow.

The next day, he arrives with one thousand pounds. He wishes me the best for my future, and leaves. This happens the same way every Time, with a few small variations. Therefore, two thousand pounds to see the World Cup is within my economic grasp.

* * * * * * * * * * * * * * * *

Adam and I swapped e-mail addresses, standing outside the pub. Each Time, I set up a new free Hotmail account. It's always available. It's sandy444@hotmail.com. I promised Adam I'd e-mail him the next day, and we'd sort out details. This time, I looked Adam in the eyes as I said this, and – like Pete – he looked as if he trusted me at my word.

'You're really coming, aren't you?' he said. He smiled as he said this. I smiled back at him, and gave him a peck on the cheek.

'Yes,' I replied. I walked off, and turned to wave once. He watched me go, waving back at me, but standing still.

* * * * * * * * * * * * * * * *

I made a list for the trip to Germany, but – apart from the obvious – I could only think of two things to put on it:

1) Change tons of money into euros. This would enable us to buy tickets to the England games from touts, and maybe even the final.
2) Buy some England shirts.

I made a trip to a sports shop at Piccadilly Circus, and bought three red and three white football tops. I buy small, and they fit me perfectly. Each top has a tiny gold star on it, which means that England have won the World Cup once. One star for one win. I imagine I am that star.

* * * * * * * * * * * * * * * *

The following evening, I sent Adam the e-mail I'd promised:

To: adambaxter@ukonline.co.uk
From: sandy444@hotmail.com
Subject: World Cup
Sent: Friday 5th May 2006. 19.26

Hi Adam

How are you doing? I am really excited about going to the World Cup finals. Hope you are too! Hope you can put up with me for 4 weeks!!

Please can you let me know when you have the tickets in my name? Can you also let me know where we are meeting, and on what day we are going? Was it on 8th June? I think your friend mentioned that date, but I can't remember now.

Anyway, please be in touch, and I'll see you in June!

All the best

Sandy

* * * * * * * * * * * * * * * * *

I struggled with the idea of adding kisses to the bottom of the message. No kisses – too formal. Kisses – too forward! I decided formal is better than forward.

Twenty minutes later, I received a reply:

To: sandy444@hotmail.com
From: adambaxter@ukonline.co.uk
Subject: Re: World Cup
Sent: Friday 5th May 2006. 19.46

Hi Sandy

I'm very well. Been working all day – need to finish contract ASAP. Have about 3 weeks left, I reckon. I know that Pete has told the travel company about you – they said that it won't be a problem, but I think he wants to wait until your cheque has cleared. He paid it in today. I think I will have the new tickets in a couple of weeks at the most.
I am still looking forward to Germany – I reckon we will have a great time! We are meeting at Stanstead Airport on 8th June. The flight out is at 12.50pm. We need to meet about 2 hours before. I will get there about 10am. I will have all the tickets by then, but I'll let you know as soon as Pete sends them to me.

Look, Sandy, I don't really know you - but we had fun in the pub yesterday, so I reckon we'll have fun in Germany! If you want to do some sightseeing, as well as football, that's OK with me. Just let me know.

Anyway, bye for now. See you in June.

Cheers

Adam

* * * * * * * * * * * * * * * *

There was a week to go before I left for Germany. I had my England tops, I had my euros, and I had my passport. My passport had arrived the day before. I was fed up with ordering passports, but now you can do it on-line, it's a bit easier.

Adam had e-mailed me to say that he had the tickets in my name. He had sent me a copy of the itinerary and reconfirmed when and where we were going to meet. He had tried to get a frequent flow of e-mails going between us, but I was a bit neglectful, often answering his e-mails in simple short phrases. I don't know why.

Deep down, Adam thought I was not going. But I was.

* * * * * * * * * * * * * * * *

Adam is thirty years old. He has fair hair and blue eyes. He's been married once, and divorced. He married when he was just twenty years old, to a girl he'd known from school. She left him for, in his words (and hers, I think), someone better. Adam is intelligent and funny, but he has low self esteem. He talks too much, but he does say some interesting things. He is quite good looking, but he is not my type. That is Adam.

* * * * * * * * * * * * * * * *

On the 8th June, I arrived at the airport at 9.45am. It was already fairly busy with holidaymakers, and a fair amount of people in England tops. I was one of them - wearing a red top and blue jeans.

We had arranged to meet by the check-in desk for our flight, so I wandered in that direction. I had one of those suitcases on wheels, and it trundled along obediently behind me. I passed two policemen with guns. They smiled at me and I smiled back. I wondered, just for a second, what would happen if one of them was to shoot me dead? If I were to lay here dying? What would it be like? Would I just die? I knew that I wouldn't. I knew that I would be back at Tottenham Court Road again. I just knew. But I pushed the thought out of my mind. This was not the time. This was my holiday.

Adam was already waiting. He was standing facing the check-in desk, with his back to me. He was wearing a blue jacket - a casual jacket, and jeans. I came up behind him, lent across and kissed him on the cheek. He turned around, startled, and stared at me for a second. His face became a picture of astonishment, and he smiled at me with wide open eyes.

'Hi,' he said, and lent across and kissed me on the cheek in reply. 'How are you?'

'You thought I wouldn't come?' I said.

'I don't know. I'm glad you're here. I've got the tickets.' He patted his jacket.

'Good.'

'Well… we have a while before we check in, about half an hour, I think. Shall we get a drink - a cup of tea, or something?'

'OK.'

We walked across the concourse, both lost in our thoughts.

* * * * * * * * * * * * * * * *

Adam and I had sex every night for four weeks. I remember those four weeks now as a blur mostly, but one thing - one particular thing - I remember well. I remember the Japanese man.

Generally speaking, I enjoyed myself a lot. Adam, I think, had the time of his life. We were there as a couple; as soon as we landed in Germany - when we had left England behind us - we became a couple. It was just what happened. We were on holiday.

Adam found me attractive – I have no doubt about that. But, more than that, he thought of me as a mystery. He would often look at me quizzically, as if trying to tease something from me, as if asking me why I was really there. If he had asked me that question outright, I would have had no satisfactory answer to give him.

As well as being a mystery, I also had money - lots of it. In fact, I'd bought eighty thousand euros with me in cash. I had it in my pockets, and in a bum-bag I wore around my waist. It was mostly in large notes, so it was not as bulky as I had expected. I was not asked to declare it, and no-one seemed to care.

Adam could not believe how much money I had. When I explained we were going to use it to buy tickets to the England games, and this directly after we had had sex - fairly successfully - for the first time, I thought he was going to cry. I watched him fall asleep that night, his mind fixed on the four weeks ahead; his dreams full of excitement and wonder.

* * * * * * * * * * * * * * * *

We were in Frankfurt first of all, and I paid a fortune for two tickets to watch England beat Paraguay one-nil. It was fun, and standing with thousands of others singing the national anthem, I felt part of something. I so rarely feel part of anything that I started to cry. Adam noticed and put his arm around me and smiled. I noticed others around me shouting and waving flags and some were close to tears as well. It was the emotion, the excitement, and I know Adam thought that I was just being carried along the same way. But, for me, it was more than that.

* * * * * * * * * * * * * * * *

A few days later we were in Nuremburg, and we managed to get two more tickets to watch England. Adam was so excited I thought he was going to burst. England won again, this time beating Trinidad and Tobago two-nil, and we both had a great time - a wonderful time.

We hugged and kissed when England scored, and as we came apart I saw a look in Adam's eyes. I saw he was falling in love with me. I suddenly felt terrible, as if I was offering him something I could never give. But, I smiled back and gave him a kiss on the lips. The feeling of being a traitor passed. He was having fun, and this was my Time. This was my Time.

We also had tickets for the Japan versus Croatia match, so we stayed in Nuremburg to see that game. This was part of our deal with the travel company, so we felt almost obliged to go.

The morning of the match we left the hotel early to visit the main Market Square in the old town, the 'Hauptmarkt', which was a 15th Century market and a bit of a tourist attraction. This would be a long walk, as the hotel we were staying in was miles from anywhere. But, the match was not until 3pm, and we both fancied a good long walk. It was a nice day, and as Adam pointed out, the 'exercise will do us good'.

As we walked out of the hotel, down a small flight of stone steps, we noticed a Japanese supporter - a man in his forties - standing on the pavement. He was looking a bit concerned; he had a worried look on his face.

I watched him as he tried to stop someone, a local man. He tried to ask a question, but the German man just carried on walking, as if the Japanese man were invisible. The German was wearing a grey suit and sunglasses, and carrying a small briefcase. He was too busy, too important to stop. The Japanese man turned to me and Adam. He looked at us and smiled.

'Ah, hello! England! Very good! I lost,' he said. His accent and use of English was almost a caricature of a Japanese tourist. I tried not to laugh, but at the same time tried to smile.

'Where are you trying to get to mate?' said Adam.

'Yes, to football! See Japan. Play today – no stadium. No find. Please - this map no good. Very rubbish! You England, yes? I see!' He pointed to my England top.

'Yeah, we're English,' Adam replied with a little laugh. The Japanese man was becoming quite funny.

'Yes! England! Very Good! David Beckham, Wayne Rooney – very good! Good ball control.' He smiled as he said this, obviously proud of the term 'ball control'.

Adam smiled back at him. 'The match is today, isn't it?'

We all knew this already - we were going to the same match - but Adam was thinking out loud.

'Yes! Match is today! But, I lost!'

'OK, mate. You're a bit early. Kick-off at three…' Adam pointed to his watch. The Japanese man did not seem to understand.

'We've been to the stadium already, mate,' Adam continued. 'Its miles from here... Listen - let me ask in the hotel. They have a good map on the desk, and they have copies. You need a better map. It's a long way from here. I'll get you a copy, and we'll trace the route. But, there must be loads of other, eh, Japanese going to the match, later on, all over the city. You should ask one of them. You could ask in Japanese.'

The man just smiled. 'Yes. Map – good map…'

'Right,' said Adam. 'I'll just pop back in here…'

Adam slapped me on the bum, and disappeared into the lobby of our hotel, leaving me to do my best. The man smiled at me and gave a little bow. I smiled back and nodded.

'I lost,' he said.

'Yes,' I replied.

'You lost too,' he said with a broad grin.

'No,' I laughed. 'I'm staying here – in this hotel.' I pointed with my right hand to the hotel beside us.

'No. I lost – football. You lost – all time.'

'I don't understand...'

'Yes. You understand. I lost – football. You lost – all time!'

He moved closer to me. His eyes stared into mine. He was still smiling.

'You no belong here.'

I felt myself going cold. I stared back at him.

'You no belong here,' he continued. 'I see you. I see. Five months, one day. No good. No very long. You no belong.'

I felt tears welling in my eyes. This man was terrifying me (I remember that I really did feel terrified), but I couldn't move. I thought: how did he know? How could he know anything about me?

'You no belong here. You go.'

'Go? Go where?' I asked. Tears were beginning to form and

roll down my cheeks.

'You go. You no belong. You leave. Five months, bad - too bad! You leave. You go Venice.'

'Venice?'

'Yes. You go Venice. You take boyfriend! Very nice! Much love! Nice bridge, many bridge – you go on canal. Go on boat. You go. You take boyfriend! You leave.'

At that moment, the fear dropped off of me like a coat falling from my shoulders and onto the ground. He knew something! He knew something about me, about my condition. He was trying to tell me something. I leant forward and grabbed his arm. He shook me off and stepped back. Just then, Adam returned with the map in his hand – he'd obviously had some success. He took a second to survey the scene, then realised something was wrong.

'Sandy, what's the matter? What's happening?' He said.

I couldn't take my eyes from the Japanese man. He continued to stare at me. I wanted to grab him again, so I stepped forward. I wanted to ask Adam to grab him, but I couldn't get the words out of my mouth. The man stepped back again. He turned to Adam, and pointed at the map.

'No need. I find.'

'What did you say to her?' Adam said in reply. He was confused and was sounding angry.

The man bowed quickly and, turning around, he began to walk off. After a few paces he turned again to face me.

'You no belong here! You go. You go Venice. You take boyfriend!'

He pointed at Adam and walked away a bit further. Then he turned once more. He looked at me, and said again 'You take boyfriend!' He was imploring me with his voice.

Adam put his arm around me but I shrugged it off. I screamed after him. 'How can I leave? How can I leave?'

I started to sob, and this time I let Adam hold me. The man did not turn again, but just carried on walking.

* * * * * * * * * * * * * * *

We were in Gelsenkirchen for the quarter-final match against Portugal. The whole city was crowded with England fans. It was the 1st of July, the day of the match, and we were both excited. Adam had asked me about the Japanese fan a couple of times over the past few days, and he assumed he'd made suggestions to me. But what could I say? I told him to forget about it, and he did. But I thought about it all the time.

I had already spent over three weeks with Adam. On the surface, we were still having as good a time as ever. But although Adam was happy with things, I was beginning to feel guilty. Why had I come? Why was I behaving the way I was?

I knew that I was playing a game, and that Adam was part of that game. I was being the perfect girl, trying to second guess Adam's wishes. I was trying to be a fantasy. And I think I had succeeded. Adam acted as though he had struck gold – he praised me all the time, told me I was beautiful. He held my hand and was proud to be with me. And I was proud of him – he was really nice. But he was not my type, and I was not the girl he thought I was.

I was starting to feel as if the game was coming to an end. I felt there was no way I could continue this relationship beyond this trip to Germany. But I was sure that Adam felt this was just the beginning.

* * * * * * * * * * * * * * * *

The match was not a good one, but the atmosphere was charged with emotion. I screamed and cheered. I booed when Wayne Rooney was sent off for squashing someone's testicles. And even though I was sure I knew the result, the emotion made me feel that this time could be different. But, when it reached penalties, I knew that we would lose. I looked at Adam, and his face showed that he knew it too. The tension around us was incredible.

'We are going to lose,' I said.

'Darling, no! We can still win! We can win! Portugal are rubbish at taking penalties too!' Adam replied. He stared at me, defying me to say otherwise.

I shrugged my shoulders. 'We are going to lose. Let's just watch.'

I hated watching the penalties. I knew what would happen – and it did. We lost. It was a disaster.

* * * * * * * * * * * * * * * *

Outside the ground, we shared drinks with the Portuguese supporters. We wished them well for the semi-finals, but Adam was devastated. It was as though he'd been kicked to the ground.

And I was upset too. I had felt a part of something, and now it had ended. It was stupid really, but – stupid or not – it had ended. And, it was important, important to so many people. It was important to me. During my stay in Germany, it had become important to me. And it was over now, and that, in itself, made me feel sad.

* * * * * * * * * * * * * * * *

We still went to the final. I paid over five thousand euros for two tickets to sit among the Italian supporters. We still wore our England tops, but we were given an Italian flag by an enthusiastic, overweight supporter, and we waved it and cheered for Italy.

The man who gave us the flag was called Mario. He lived in San Vito, in the south of Italy. He loved his sister (who was marrying a pig, he reliably informed us) and he cried like a baby when Italy lifted the tiny trophy for the fourth time. Four stars.

* * * * * * * * * * * * * * * *

We returned to England the following day. I had spent a

fortune, but I only had a month or so left in this Time, so that was fine. Apart from England's failings, the trip had been a great success. Adam kept saying that he would pay me back some of the money, but we both knew that would never happen. On the short flight back, Adam seemed nervous. Adam now loved me, but I did not love him.

As wonderful as the trip had been, the scene at the airport after we landed was terrible. Adam told me that he loved me, that he wanted us to continue, as boyfriend and girlfriend, here in England. He said he would do anything for me.

I had felt like a traitor during the trip, and now I knew the extent of my treachery. I had used him to make me feel happy, to live out a fantasy – a girl in shining armour. I had done everything for him, and now he was addicted to me. Not to me, but to what I had become – what I had pretended to be.

I had lived out that fantasy, but the fantasy was not mine alone. It was our fantasy. Not just mine, it was our fantasy.

* * * * * * * * * * * * * * * *

The last month of this Time was awful. I felt as guilty as hell. Adam tried to contact me about a hundred times. I did answer his e-mails, but I threw away my mobile phone. I'd only bought it for the trip.

Now the trip was over.

* * * * * * * * * * * * * * * *

Back home in Italy, Mario felt like a new man. He had been as drunk as it was possible to be when he arrived at the family celebration in his parents' house in San Vito. Everyone was waiting for him to return – he was the only family member to have attended the finals, and, unbelievably, the final itself.

Everyone wanted to know what he had done, what he had seen, what he had felt when Cannavaro lifted the trophy into the air. Only he had the answer to these questions. He was a hero.

His sister was there with her fiancé Paulo. Mario cried as he held him and told him that he loved him. Paulo loved his sister, and so Mario loved him. Paulo swore on his life and the Blessed Virgin Mary that he would never do anything to harm his sister – that he would always care for her as Mario himself would wish. And, furthermore, that he was unworthy to have such a brother-in-law as Mario, who himself, with his own eyes, had seen Italy's victory. Mario cried again when Paulo said this.

Mario saw a girl at the party, a girl he knew. A girl he loved. He spoke to her – really spoke to her – for the first time that evening. He told her that he had been a fool, that he should have told her of his feelings long ago – but who was he, the son of a mechanic, to profess such things to such a beautiful girl? She held his hand and told him that she would see him, that he could take her to the cinema, if he wanted to…

Hours later, Mario fell asleep in his old bedroom at his parents' house – the house of his childhood. He dreamt not of the football or of his sister or the girl at the party, but instead of the girl with the England shirt and the Italian flag. He saw her beautiful smile in his dreams – a smile of the mouth, but not of the eyes.

This is another dream.

I'm shopping in a big department store; there are women's clothes all around me. Some are hanging on rails, but some are just in piles on the floor. These have been discarded, and I know I'm responsible for leaving some of them there. I know I should have hung them back up – that would have made more sense. But I didn't - I just left them there, and I feel guilty.

I'm standing in a queue, waiting to buy a pair of jeans. They are faded blue with a little American flag on them. My right hand is resting on a pushchair - a tiny baby is asleep. It's Jack, and he's six weeks old. He's covered in a little blue blanket, and there's a white teddy bear in with him as well. It's looking up at me, eyes wide open; but Jack's eyes are closed.

Two girls are shopping behind me. One of them leans forward and looks in at Jack. She smiles and says something to me – something kind about my baby. I smile back but I can't understand her. I don't know why, but I just can't. They both lean across and start talking to Jack, and I'm afraid that they might wake him up.

But I would like to wake him up, to hold him in my arms and cuddle and kiss him. I want to hold him close to me and rest my head on him. But I don't want to disturb him - I just want him to be asleep, to be happy and content. It's enough for me that he's happy – happy and alive.

I wake up – tears are streaming down my face. And I'm smiling. These are tears of happiness, not the other kind.

Time Ninety-Six

Saturday 6th May 2006
1.45pm

It's a Saturday, and I'm feeling a bit ill. I'm sitting on a bench overlooking the River Thames. It's a lovely day – sunny and warm. I'm wearing a red t-shirt, with the word 'blaze' on it. I bought it yesterday at Covent Garden.

I am surrounded by pigeons. This is because I am feeding them little bits of bread from my egg and cress sandwich. One of them only has one leg, and I try to give him more bread. I'm sure he is grateful, but it's hard to tell with a pigeon.

I am ill because of ABBA. Actually, because of people pretending to be ABBA. I went to an ABBA tribute night in Hammersmith last night. It was very good. I went alone, and left alone, which is sometimes as it should be; uncomplicated. It didn't finish until 3am, and I stayed to the end. Most people did. I got back to my hotel at about 3.30am, and had a bath. I went to bed with a headache at 4.30 this morning, and woke up with a headache at 10 o'clock. I still have a headache, and I just feel a bit under the weather.

* * * * * * * * * * * * * * *

A man carrying a saxophone enters my view from the right, and stops in front of me, about ten yards away. He props up his saxophone next to the river wall, and puts a cap down on the ground. He looks up at me and my pigeons, and then walks over to me. He has a beard.

'Hi…listen, I always play over there,' he points to where his saxophone is waiting. 'And, well, hopefully I won't annoy you too much. I don't want to ruin your lunch.'

He glances down at the remains of my sandwich, most of

which is inside a bird with one leg.

'That's fine,' I reply. 'I like music.'

'Ah – that's good. I do as well…'

He has an Irish accent and, beneath the beard, is probably about twenty-one. I smile at him.

'Well then,' he says. 'I'll go and play…'

He looks as if he might be homeless, but I'm not sure. Perhaps this is just his living. He starts to play, and he is brilliant. People actually stop to listen, at one point he has quite a crowd. The pigeons are not as keen, and retreat to wherever pigeons go.

I sit and listen for about an hour. My headache disappears. He smiles at me between songs, and I smile back. A few minutes later, I'm ready to go. I realise how stiff I am from sitting on the bench. I stand up and give a little stretch. There is no one watching now, only me. I walk over to where he is playing and I wave goodbye. He carries on playing, but his eyes say goodbye instead of his voice. I pull the purse out of my bag and look inside.

'Why not?' I think to myself, and put fifty pounds into his cap. I say 'bye' and walk off with a smile. Behind me, he stops playing.

'Babe, you're an angel!' He says.

I laugh back at him. 'It's OK. Bye!'

'You're an angel! Listen, babe, just wait a minute! I've got a song for you - a special song...'

I smile back again. 'OK,' I reply 'but I have to go in a minute.'

'OK, babe,' he says. But suddenly he looks worried. He stands for a few seconds – seems unsure what to do next. The smile has left his face. I think he is not going to play, and then he puts the reed into his mouth. He plays the song I hear each time I awake.

* * * * * * * * * * * * * * *

I walk back to him and stare. I feel tears starting, and I fight them back. He plays for a few seconds more and then stops. He looks at the ground. Then he looks at me - a look just like a guilty child.

I can't think of what to say. There are a thousand questions in my head.

'What was that song? How do you know that song?' I finally say.

'Man...' He looks up at the sky.

'What was that song?' I know, any moment, I'm going to start to cry.

'Babe...' He's starting to sound upset. 'Oh, babe...you're a dream! You're an angel! What could I do? Fifty pounds...' He looks down at the ground, speaking to himself. 'What could I do?'

I am crying now, and he looks as if he will cry any minute.

'Oh, man. I'm so busted!' he says.

'Listen, what was that song?' I say, trying to hold my voice together.

'No more.'

'Please...'

'No. No more.'

He reaches into his pocket and pulls out a piece of card. He takes a pencil from his back pocket and writes for a few seconds. He presses the card into my hand. 'You're beautiful,' he says. 'Now, no more...'

He picks up his cap and folds it in two, protecting the money inside. He looks at me quickly, and, although he's still looking upset, he smiles. 'Babe,' he says. 'You may be beautiful, but I am so busted!'

I cannot think of a thing to say to him. His last word to me, to himself, is 'Shit!' as he walks off towards Waterloo Bridge.

* * * * * * * * * * * * * * * *

Everything is spinning around me. I try to concentrate on

what has just happened, but my mind is moving in all directions. I open my hand, and look at the piece of card. He has written on it in grey pencil, but the markings are very light, as if he had hoped they would just fade. But they haven't. It reads:

> *Andy's - Cattleborn Street, Donnybrook.*
> *...with your love.*

That's it. Not 'with my love', but 'with your love'. And there's an address. That's all. I need to think. I need a bath.

I go back to my hotel, and have a bath.

* * * * * * * * * * * * * * * *

The bathroom at my hotel is very nice. I stay at this hotel (The Lancaster Hotel) every Time, mainly because the bathrooms are so big. The baths are plastic and blue, but big and deep. I have a big bottle of 'rejuvenating' bubble bath from The Body Shop. It smells a bit like peppermint, and it has never rejuvenated me – not in any sense that I am aware of, but it is very bubbly. I have tried many bubble baths, over many Times, but this is the bubbliest of them all. I like bubble bath, and I particularly like this bubble bath.

I lay there, staring up at the ceiling. I close my eyes. The bubbles pop and crackle around me, in a quiet, unobtrusive way. I try to consider my choices – what have I learnt? What I can do? I think for a long time.

These are the things I have learnt:

1) I am not alone. Other people are in this with me – the Japanese man in Germany, and now the Irish man with the saxophone. They know things about me, about what is going on. But, I don't know who they are.

2) These people are giving me clues. I now have a piece of paper, given to me by the saxophone man. This is a big clue.
3) The saxophone man wanted to help me, but now he's in some kind of trouble. I don't know what this means.
4) The piece of paper, I am certain, is connected to the song - the song I always hear.

These are the things I can do:

1) Find the saxophone man again. This would be very difficult - and there's not much point. He told me he would say no more.
2) Find out what the card means, and then act upon this information.

Number two is the best option here.

* * * * * * * * * * * * * * *

I sit up in the bath, and lean across to put in more hot water. The bath is getting cold. I have thought for over an hour, and narrowed it all down to six points. It has been hard to concentrate, because I keep thinking about Chris. I imagine that Chris is here with me. I know he would have no clue what to do, but it would still be nice if he were here - if I had his support.

I think about going to see him tomorrow - get things started again. But things are different this Time. I have information. I have clues.

* * * * * * * * * * * * * * *

I've met up with Chris during thirty-eight separate Times now – I always do the same thing. I dress to look my absolute best, walk into the bookshop and up to the counter when a) there are no other customers and b) Chris is there alone. I chat about John Grisham books and all that stuff, and then I faint. The first time I fainted, during Time Fifteen, I actually did faint. Chris came around the counter to catch me, and sat me gently in a chair. That's when he first asked me out.

Now, I don't really faint – I just pretend. I probably should just chat to him, smile and say nice things, but fainting has worked nearly forty Times now. I'm on a winning streak. Every Time, we have ended up going out.

However, Chris does not always make it in time to catch me, and once, in Time Thirty-Four, he just stood there and watched me fall. On that occasion, I jarred my kneecap, and it hurt so much that I really did pass out. The medical staff at Bluewater came to my aid, and I walked around, feeling both stupid and sorry for myself, with a serious limp for over two weeks. But, even then, Chris still asked me out for lunch.

Chris is lovely. He is twenty-eight years old, so he's a bit younger than me when I'm thirty-one - which, of course, I always am when we meet. He is studying for a degree in English Literature. He likes books, and he wants to teach. He doesn't have a great deal of money, so he works in the book shop at Bluewater three days a week. He always works Saturdays, which is a good thing, because that's when we first met.

He's not really good looking, but I think he's lovely. He has dark hair and brown eyes. He is the kindest man I've ever met. Every Time, he loves me. Every Time, he falls in love with me. He does this every single Time. I love him so much that I can hardly believe myself. Sometimes I think about him and it makes me cry. It makes me cry because we have no future. And because, if we did have a future, I think it would work.

I would like, more than almost anything, to have a wedding day. But I can't work out how to squeeze 'meeting to marriage' into five months. If I were Britney Spears – it would be easy. But I'm not. It's an idle dream, because, apart from the logistics, I think it would upset me in the long run. What's the point in marrying, when you're like me?

Mostly - almost every Time really - we make love. I don't mean every time we meet - not every day. What I mean is that our relationship, each Time, progresses to sex quite quickly. The last few Times, it's been sooner rather than later. This is because I am now easier to get into bed. At least, this is true as far is Chris is concerned. This does not apply to everybody.

I now have only one real rule with Chris – contraception. This is compulsory. I have been on the pill, but, most times, we use condoms. Chris is happy to use condoms, so I merrily go along. This rule exists because of Time Sixteen, my worst Time and my best Time.

Time Sixteen has changed me forever, invaded my dreams, made me more happy than I could ever believe, and sadder than I've ever been.

I hate Time Sixteen, and I love it. This is what happened.

Time Sixteen

Saturday 8th April 2006

It was only three weeks after waking from my coma that I walked into the same bookshop to see Chris again – ready to fulfil the promise I'd made the Time before; in Time Fifteen. He had asked me out with less than an hour left – just an hour before that Time ended, but I had agreed to come back and see him.

My recoveries were getting faster now; I'd discharged myself after only a week, and then spent two weeks resting and generally getting stronger. I was still looking a bit pale, and feeling a little tired - but I was well enough to faint.

After all, I basically only had to make it to the bookshop, smile a lot, have a chat and then faint away – hopefully into the arms of Chris. That was my plan, to reproduce the Time before, except this Time there would be over four months left. That would give us plenty of time to get to know each other.

* * * * * * * * * * * * * * * *

Everything worked out as planned; I fainted and Chris caught me. As I rested in the chair, watched by the odd interested person passing by, my eyes were firmly fixed on Chris. I was looking carefully at his face, trying to read his eyes. I remembered seeing the concern and the kindness last Time, and I was looking for the same again. I was trying to reassure myself that I was not mistaken in any way. After all, last Time, I had really fainted, and perhaps my vision and my emotions were a bit blurred. But, as I watched, he seemed to have the kindest eyes I had ever seen. I had not imagined it – if anything, it seemed magnified this Time around.

I felt happy that I'd been right, and I was about to speak – to say a 'thank you for catching me' – when I saw something else. Just for a second, as his eyes looked down into mine, I saw recognition. It was unmistakable; and although it seemed impossible, I was certain that he recognised me. Then the look left his eyes – like a cloud passing quickly across the sun. I stared at him for a moment, astonished – and afraid that he would see my surprise, I looked away.

I can't explain how amazed I really was by this; how wonderful it made me feel.

As I pretended to feel better, and declared I was ready to get up and go, I waited for Chris to make his move. For a few horrible seconds, spent in awkward silence, I thought he was going to simply say goodbye.

But, finally, he plucked up the courage to ask me to share his lunch break, and I readily agreed. I told him I'd be back at one o'clock to meet him, and I could tell that he wasn't sure if I'd really come back. But this Time I certainly would.

* * * * * * * * * * * * * * *

At exactly one o'clock, I walked back into the bookshop, ready to meet Chris. He was still at the till, serving a man in a brown leather jacket. The man was also wearing leather trousers, which made him look gay. I sidled up to him and smiled at Chris. He smiled back but maintained his professionalism as he completed the transaction.

The man was buying four books – three of them were about cookery (which confirmed my suspicions) and the other was about travel in Peru. The cover of the travel book showed a small coach moving along a barren road, with a beautiful landscape, at sunset.

The man saw me looking at the book – his book now – and caught my eye. I smiled, slightly embarrassed, and all of a sudden I had a powerful mental image of this man and a load of his friends on some kind of bizarre gay coach holiday in Peru. I could see them, driving along the barren road in the little coach – staring out the windows at sheep and rocks, wearing nothing but leather trousers and mirror sunglasses. This stupid image made me smile more, which I think the man took as a cue to start a conversation.

'Have you ever been to Peru?' He asked.

'No, never,' I replied.

'Ah – you should go! It's a wonderful place!'

I wanted to ask why it was wonderful – I was genuinely interested – but I could sense precious minutes of Chris's lunch break slipping away. I turned to Chris.

'Ready?' I asked.

'Yep,' he said, smiling, and signed-off the till by pushing a few buttons. When the till gave a long beep, seemingly satisfied, Chris came round to the customer side.

'Let's go,' he said.

I looked up at him. 'That man's gay,' I whispered.

'Which man?' He whispered back.

'The man buying the book – the book about Peru...'

'Oh? Was he? Is he?'

'Yes. He was wearing leather trousers...'

'Oh. Well – I suppose he must be then...'

I smiled up at him, laughing at the silly but easy start to our conversation. Chris had whispered when I whispered, as co-conspirator, and it sounds strange now but I was impressed by that. He was willing to go along with me – to join in. As I walked alongside him, I felt myself growing to like him more already.

* * * * * * * * * * * * * * *

The lunch date was a success, and we arranged to meet that evening and go to dinner. Chris tried to be a bit nonchalant, but still came across as totally eager. I toyed with the idea a bit, for good face, then agreed to meet him again. We arranged to have dinner at a tapas restaurant called 'La Tasca'. This was also located at Bluewater, so I would have five hours to kill if I was going to wait for him. It was not worth travelling back to Lancaster Gate, as that would take far too long.

I was considering my options, when I remembered that they had a spa there, right there at Bluewater. I checked at the Concierge, and discovered I was right. I found it a few minutes later, and booked myself in for a half-day session, with two treatments. I then rushed off to buy a swimming costume.

The trip to the spa turned out to be an excellent idea. I stayed until twenty minutes before we'd arranged to meet (including 'getting ready' time), which meant I spent over five hours there. I had a back massage and a facial – the back massage was best. I read the remainder of my book (The Beach by Alex Garland) with my feet dangling in a little spa pool, and I spent quite a while in the hot tub, basically just getting hot.

While I was sitting in the tub, I found myself drifting off. I wasn't dreaming, but just deeply in thought. I was thinking about Chris, and what on earth I was doing. Part of me was wondering what the point was to all this, seeing as it would all end, whatever happened, so soon. But, another part of me was more positive – after all, I had over another four months left in this Time. I could have fun for four months – spend some time in the company of someone I enjoyed being with. What was wrong with that?

Chris was shy, and I liked that about him. I thought he probably had hidden depths, whatever that really means. At least, I thought he was worth exploring. I felt like he was like a town that I had just stepped into; one that was worth having a look around.

As I dried off, I found that I was almost excited about having dinner with Chris. I couldn't really think why, but my instinct told me that it was good idea – that something special would happen as a result. I was at a loss to understand these feelings, but they seemed very strong and somehow pleasant.

When I had dressed, I looked at myself in the mirror. Was this someone that Chris would like? I was disturbed by myself, thinking this way – my opinion of myself was dropping; I was starting to feel emptier, less worthwhile each Time. I looked at myself again – would Chris see any worth in me? Would he be able to see inside me – see beyond what I had become, what I was becoming? Would he be able to see who I really am?

I suddenly felt positive – I believed that he would. The thought made me smile, and I looked at myself again; this time just to check my hair and lipstick.

* * * * * * * * * * * * * * * *

La Tasca is a pleasant tapas bar – there are tables that look out onto a central inside area, with doors out to a big fountain. Chris and I sat at one of those tables, watching the people as they wandered about, but mostly watching each other. It transpired that Chris had reserved this table for us during the afternoon, and it was a good job that he had, because it was very crowded.

We spent the evening getting to know one another. He told me about his childhood in Gravesend, his move to London, and then back to Gravesend. He also told me all about his university course; his friends and his enemies.

Chris sat open-mouthed as I explained about my coma – I had considered not mentioning it at all, but decided that honesty would be the best policy. My coma was not something I could easily hide away. It was on my mind a lot of the time, and it was nice to share it with someone. Chris sat in silence as I explained it all – leaving out the crazy stuff at Tottenham Court Road, which although it happens each Time, I am no closer to understanding myself. He seemed shocked, unsure how to reply.

'Do you believe me?' I asked

'Yes,' he replied, looking me in the eyes. I stared back at him.

'I believe you – that you believe me,' I said.

'But, it must be mad, being asleep for thirteen years – all that time…'

'It's not sleep…not like being asleep. There are no dreams – nothing to remember. And it's not refreshing - it drains you.'

'Was it scary?'

'What do you mean?'

'I mean, the coma…waking up after all those years. Was it scary?'

'No. It's not. It's just nothing.'

We sat for a few moments. He picked at the potatoes on his little plate. I looked at him across the table. My mind began to think worrying thoughts: 'he thinks I'm a freak,' 'he's trying to think of a way to leave'. But when he looked up at me, I knew that was not the case.

'It must have been terrible,' he said.

I reached out and put my hands on his right hand.

'It's fine,' I said. 'Look at me. I'm fine. Let's talk about something else.'

'I'm sorry. I didn't mean to go on…'

'Listen…' I smiled. 'Chris, you're not going on. Tell me about you. I want to hear about you.'

And, as I sat and listened, I realised that I did.

Time Sixteen

Thursday 20th April 2006

I often think of each Time as being like a little life. A tiny life that's self-contained. I am born each March, and leave each August, and the fact that I live for such a short time, and then just begin again, has resulted – in many ways - in a hardening of attitudes about the consequences of my actions.

For example, if I were to kill someone – not that I ever would, of course, but if I were to – then I am certain that the Time following their death, I could simply find them again, and they would be as right as rain. I could just walk right up to them and say 'hello', and they would reply in kind, very much alive. More than that, they would be going about their business oblivious to the fact they were dead in one Time, and alive in the next.

I don't really understand time at all any more, and to be honest, I try not to think about it. But, of course, I think about it a lot.

I say all of this to explain how I came to get pregnant. Firstly, I had grown to like Chris very much, and it soon became clear that he wanted a relationship with me. I was more than happy with the idea - it excited me - but always I felt aware that time was pressing on me like a flat stone, crushing me downwards towards August. I see it this way; as if March is above me and August below me, and I am being pushed down with an ever-increasing force.

I am often aware of this pressure, and it makes me feel like I have to do things quickly. A better way is to say that I live life in fast-forward, trying to cram as much as possible into the days I have left. I try to fight this urge, to relax, to savor whatever happens – but I always find it very difficult to do. Sometimes, it's as if I am propelled forward without control, like I'm running down a steep hill, unable to slow down.

The consequence of this feeling of pressure, of wanting to live in fast-forward mode, made me behave stupidly.

* * * * * * * * * * * * * * * *

I had no intention of sleeping with Chris - and I'm certain he had no idea he would be sleeping with me - when we ran from the car to his flat in Gravesend during a torrential rainstorm. He had to park about fifty yards from his door, and we dashed along the road giggling and getting drenched.

Chris fumbled with the key in the door – with me shouting 'Come on! Come on!' not really helping - and we tumbled inside as one person, closing the door on the rain behind us. We laughed at each other as we stood dripping all over the carpet in the tiny hall. Chris guided me upstairs to his living room (only the hall was downstairs) and switched on the light. It was my first visit.

He went to the bathroom to get towels, and I looked around – reading the spines of books in his bookcase, and CDs in a pile on the table. He had tidied up.

He gave me a towel and went into the kitchen to make tea. We had seen each other almost every evening since our meal just twelve days ago, and also had a day trip to Whitstable, which had been fun. It fact, it had all been fun, and I was sure Chris felt the same. He was very keen on me, I could tell that, and he really made no secret of it. For myself, I felt the days slipping from me – April would soon be May – and as I stepped-up the pace of the relationship, Chris was happy to run to keep up.

We slept together that evening because of the rain (I had to undress to get out of the wet clothes that were by then sticking to my skin) and for a hundred other silly reasons. But mostly it was because I wanted things to move on, wanted to fast-forward our relationship.

It sounds funny, but it was a selfish move on my part, and I'm not sure Chris fully approved; not at the time anyway. He was completely unprepared, even though he knew I was staying over. He had already set up a camp-bed for me in the small alcove between the kitchen and the bathroom, and in his mind that is certainly where I would have been sleeping.

However, it didn't turn out that way. I remember thinking that Chris may have been naive to believe there was no possibility of sex that evening - or that he really did think it was possible, but pretended not to.

But, on reflection, I'm certain that he didn't believe for a second that anything was likely to happen. And I know that I never gave him any indication before that night that I was ready for anything more than a cuddle.

Because he was unprepared, he didn't have any protection. He explained this to me with some embarrassment, but I said that it didn't matter. For a second he seemed taken aback, and he was unsure how to proceed. Even then I knew why. He was wondering why I would be willing to take the risk, and whether he should take the risk as well.

In his mind, two possibilities came to the fore. Firstly, that I was unlikely to get pregnant because of the time of the month, or because I couldn't. Secondly, and more likely, was that I was on the pill. And if so, this raised other issues that he didn't have time to resolve at that moment.

I had put him in a difficult position. He had made it obvious that he liked me, and I knew that he was scared of losing me. If he rejected me now, he ran that risk, and I didn't think he would be willing for that to happen.

As well as that, I was sure he really wanted to make love to me, and I thought that might tip him over the edge. It did.

* * * * * * * * * * * * * * * *

I really, truly had not intended the evening to end with us together in bed; not when we were crunching popcorn at the

Bluewater Cinema complex two hours before. But the wet clothes combined with being together in his flat just presented the opportunity, and I decided to make Chris the offer he chose not to refuse.

While Chris was making the tea, and the ideas were forming in my head – before anything had happened that evening - I was aware that I was almost certainly ovulating. Each Time before, I had ovulated around this day, April 20th; this had been the case the last Time and the Time before that and all the Times before that as well. But I wasn't certain – I hadn't kept a record or anything. However, I thought it was likely that I was.

This didn't make me not want to make love; I just didn't mind. I really didn't care. I remember clearly thinking that it didn't matter at all. My head was full of reasons why.

These are the reasons why I didn't mind:

1) If I was to get pregnant, then it was just a detail, because come August, everything would simply start again. No back pains, no giving birth.
2) If Chris had some terrible infectious disease that he was willing to pass on to me, then point one applied in the same way. In August, all my viruses would be wiped away.
3) I didn't believe that Chris was carrying any kind of infectious disease – I think he would have told me if that were the case.
4) Chances were that I wouldn't get pregnant anyway, and everything would be fine.

Everything was fine that evening, and we felt no regrets in the morning. We were the same to each other as we had been, still having fun, falling in love. But I did get pregnant.

Time Sixteen

Saturday 6th May 2006

I was two days late; and I was always very regular. As I walked down to the chemist at Queensway, to buy a pregnancy test, I felt certain that it would tell me that I was just late. I couldn't believe that one night of unprotected sex would leave me pregnant. I had known women, when I was eighteen, who had tried for months, for years, to get pregnant. Surely, in my case, it couldn't be that easy.

But – easy it had been, and as I stared down at the little blue line, I knew without a doubt that I was as pregnant as it was possible to be - completely pregnant. There was no grey area with these tests – you either were or you were not. And I was.

* * * * * * * * * * * * * * * *

According to the 'Pregnancy Dates Calendar' (which I found using Google) I was already four weeks and two days pregnant. I couldn't believe it, as I'd only just found out! (And I'd only first had sex with Chris less than three weeks ago!). It also told me that on June 29th I would be twelve weeks pregnant, which would be the end of my first trimester.

I quickly worked out that I would be nineteen weeks and two days pregnant on August 19th. I sat and stared at the screen for ages, and finally noted the dates down on a piece of paper. A bundle of things floated around my head. One of these was whether I should tell Chris. I decided almost immediately that I should, but I wasn't sure how best to tell him.

I put that to one side, and thought about all the other, even more scary things. There were so many thoughts, flooding my head, that I compressed them into one undeniable fact - I was pregnant. I had never been pregnant before, and, above all, I couldn't help feeling happy. But – happiness was one thing I could not afford to feel, given the circumstances.

* * * * * * * * * * * * * * * *

I told Chris I was pregnant that same evening. He looked at me in a bewildered fashion, and I thought for a second he was going to get up and run off. But he didn't – and we spent the next two hours discussing what to do now. The knowledge I had – that this Time would end for me in a few months - made the conversation difficult to say the least. But it needed to happen, especially for Chris.

Of course, regardless of all that, I also needed to talk about it all with someone; and who better – who more involved – than Chris himself. We were falling, perhaps fallen in love with each other, that was for certain - and that fact made the whole thing easier.

Chris wanted us to stay together; to bring up the child as a couple. There was never any talk about ending the pregnancy, not from either of us. He never asked me if I wanted anything other than to have the baby – perhaps he could just tell; perhaps, even then, he knew better than me.

I was amazed how much impact being pregnant had on me. I became a different person – alive in a different way. When I think back now, it made me extremely happy. That was the main emotion I felt. I also felt confusion and some panic – but happiness is what I remember best. This was in the first few weeks, of course - before it made me lose my mind.

* * * * * * * * * * * * * * * *

My relationship with Chris continued to flourish. Lancaster Gate is such a long way from Gravesend that I amazed Chris by renting a flat about a mile from where he was living. And whereas Chris was living in a small, one-bedroomed flat with a view of a disused bakers shop, I was renting a two-bedroomed modern apartment overlooking the river. Two weeks after renting the place, Chris moved in with me.

The weeks that followed are now something of a blur in my mind. It seems, and it was, such a long time ago; but – although much of the Time is little more to me now than a vague impression - there are still many things that do stand out in my memory. Painful things.

I can't be totally sure of my feelings, although I am certain about how I felt towards the end. In reality, it was the end, those last few weeks – perhaps even the last few days – that left such a profound mark on me; a scar that I can still feel today.

* * * * * * * * * * * * * * * *

I was ten weeks pregnant when Chris moved in. He didn't have a lot to bring – just a load of books and CDs, and a few clothes. It was then, for the first time, I realised how few clothes men actually have. I remember standing in the main bedroom of my flat, amazed as he spent about four minutes unpacking the two bin liners that constituted his entire wardrobe.

'Is that really it?' I asked.

'Really what?' he replied.

'Your clothes - is that all the clothes you have?'

Chris looked down at the two empty bags, and across at the drawers and wardrobe where they now were safely resting.

'Well…' he said. 'Yes. I don't need any more clothes.'

'Yes you do. You do need more clothes. Everyone needs more clothes.'

'Why?' He looked at me with a slight smile, ready to stand his ground.

'Because…' I thought for a second. 'Because, sometimes it's cold, and sometimes it's hot. And it's good to have a choice. You don't know what mood you'll be in when you wake up.'

'If it's hot, I'll just put less on. And I don't need a choice. I always feel the same.'

'No you don't.'

'I do when I wake up. I feel tired and grumpy.'

'Then you need more tired and grumpy clothes...'

We had a number of conversations in that vein, and we have had hundreds of similar conversations in the Times that followed. But I remember this particular day because I was suddenly aware of the ordinariness of it all. We were having an ordinary conversation about clothes. We were an ordinary boy and an ordinary girl doing ordinary things. It struck me at that moment that it was all I really wanted. I wanted to be an ordinary girl.

* * * * * * * * * * * * * * * *

As the pregnancy progressed, I became more and more focused upon it – upon it as part of myself. I read books about pregnancy, in order to gather information about what was going on inside me. And the more I read, the more I felt the enormity of what was happening to me.

Chris was very supportive, and came home from work with discounted books which I devoured in the bath and lying in bed at night. I could feel sensations in my tummy, and every book, every conversation, every sensation I felt made it seem more and more permanent.

Before I was pregnant, I knew the limits, and this seemed a good thing. It was uncomplicated. Five months was not long enough to grow a baby.

But now it consumed me like a fire – it burned away at me and filled my thoughts and my dreams. I wasn't just pregnant; I was going to have a baby! That's what everyone said – that's what all the books said.

And that's what Chris said. 'We're going to have a baby.'

That's what he told me. He didn't just say 'Sandy, you're pregnant.' He said 'We're going to have a baby!'

Everybody told me this. People, books, Chris - they all said the same thing. And slowly, slowly; in small degrees and stages – creeping up through dreams and daydreams, conversations and discussions – this is what I came to tell myself.

I was going to have a baby.

Time Sixteen

Sunday 30th July 2006

So much happened between May and the end of July, but I can remember so little of it now. My tummy was getting bigger each day – I had a tape measure and Chris would help me measure my bump each morning. I remember feeling frightened and sad in June, still ruing the fact that in August my Time would end. I also remember the morning sickness – the time spent with my head in the sink or down the toilet bowl.

But by the end of July I was gloriously happy. I was truly in love with Chris – he was so nice I would often hug him for so long that my shoulders would begin to hurt. Then, of course, I'd let him go. But, my happiness was inextricably tied up with my baby. I was utterly convinced by the end of July that my pregnancy would last for nine full months, and I would have a baby; a normal baby, an ordinary baby.

There was some method to these beliefs, some reasoning behind them. I thought - I wanted to believe - that I had found the key. This Time things were different - this Time I was carrying another life that was in some way distinct from me. Although dependent on me, it was not me. The baby had a life of its own, and it was alive in a way that I was not.

What I mean is that it surely did not have to return in August, to begin a new Time. In fact, it couldn't do that, because it would cease to exist. Therefore, because it was a person in its own right, and dependent on me for its survival, I saw a door open up that I hadn't realised existed. I came to believe that this Time, Time Sixteen, would be my last. I was certain of it, and began to deny any other possibility.

The baby would keep me here – I would continue on to grow it, through August to September and beyond. All the other clues melted away – this was all that mattered. I believed that I was here to stay, that we were all here to stay; me, Chris and the baby, living together in Gravesend. Sharing the birth, celebrating Christmas, feeling winter weather again – perhaps even snow - and wearing a coat. I would by a big thick winter coat. Two coats, one for me, and one for the baby.

I was certain of these things, back then. I was so sure. I became obsessed with the idea of remaining beyond August 19th. I thought about it all the time, and believed that it would happen. I made myself believe this, and created a fantasy about the future. I began to live in this fantasy, and as a result the present slipped away. Reality lost its grip on my life, and the other, more pleasant, fantasy took over.

I couldn't bear the thought of losing all that I had gained – my new life in Gravesend with Chris, the baby I now carried around with me, and all that these things meant. They meant more than anything; this was my life now, and I loved it. This was my life.
 These things made the fantasy grow stronger, and I was happy to let it grow. I nurtured and fed it, and it took me over.

I discussed the future with Chris, and he engaged in the conversations as though it were totally normal. He did not flinch when I talked about what we would do in September, in October – for him this was nothing unusual. But for me it was amazing. This wonderful, precious baby had offered me a way out of my nightmare. And I was willing to grasp it with both hands.

Time Sixteen

Saturday 19th August 2006

Of course, it was just a fantasy. Having a baby, making a life with Chris, living beyond this prison of five months and a day – it was just a fantasy.

I knew this as I awoke on Saturday morning, August 19th - the morning I always leave. The morning I am taken. It hit me with a sickening thud. My awareness of the sounds in the room, the colours seeming so vibrant, made me realise that the end of this Time was fast approaching.

Since the first Time, I have become increasingly 'tuned in' to my environment during the last few hours. Everything becomes more vivid, more brilliant. Details that were blurred become sharp - colours are brighter, sounds more defined.

I lay in bed, staring up at the ceiling, listening to Chris stirring next to me. I felt sick to think it would all be taken away, so sick that my stomach began to convulse. I felt a wave of nausea crash over me – I ran to the bathroom and threw up into the toilet. I was sick for about five minutes, retching and then waiting for the next wave. Finally I sat down against the sink, and looked up to see Chris standing in the doorway.

'Are you alright?' he asked.

I just looked at him, unable to speak. Tears were starting to well up in my eyes.

'Is it morning sickness?' he asked, now sitting down beside me. I shook my head.

'Come back to bed,' he said. 'You'll feel better in a little while. I'll make you a cup of tea.'

He helped me up and walked me back to bed, and I lay there while he made the tea. Thoughts flew around my head like little birds, like swallows, darting from side to side. I looked across at the digital alarm clock – it said the time was 08:06.

I closed my eyes. I tried to imagine what my baby would be like when it was born, and when it was older – on its first birthday, when it was three years old, five, seven... I didn't know the sex; my scan was booked for August 27th, but I was sure it was a boy. I knew he would be clever, handsome, loving – always share his toys, never pinch other children. I had called him Jack, and he was my son. He belonged to me; I loved him. He was my son.

I couldn't imagine that he would not be born. My mind raged against what I was coming to believe – that I had just three hours left! Just three hours left with him. It seemed impossible! Surely this can't be the end! I rested my hands on my tummy, felt small movements inside. This baby was mine; it was part of me.

My fantasy had changed to a wish. I said it over and over in my head. I thought it with all my strength, with all my will; over and over, over and over.

'Please let me take him with me...'

Time Seventeen

Saturday 12th March 2006

But he didn't come with me. I left him behind – somewhere. When I awoke from my coma, I felt the emptiness - not just inside me, but all over me. I didn't need to feel my flat, emaciated stomach to know he wasn't there. His absence was evident from the first moment; the lack of him was all around me.

I felt sadness far worse than I had ever known. I was like a boxer, covered in blood and bruises, punched and punched until there was no hope of getting up. That's how I felt. That is how it was.

I have never, ever, recovered from the Time I was pregnant. It has scarred me, left me shell-shocked and with feelings so vast I cannot even begin to understand them. But, no matter how large they seem, they cannot fill the gap that has been left.

I still feel that way now – the emotions are often still as raw. And they can cause me as much pain. Not always, of course, but often. And yet, I am still a servant to these emotions - these immense, enormous feelings that I cannot control; that sometimes, even now, threaten to swallow me whole.

Time Ninety-Six

Saturday 6th May 2006

I lay for over two hours in the bath, the events of the day buzzing in my head. Bizarrely, the meeting with the mystery saxophone man competes for space in my brain with snatches of Abba songs remembered from last night. But the bath does help me to hone my thoughts, and a plan of action begins to form in my mind.

As I get out and dry myself, I have an idea of what I should do next. I stand in the bathroom, rubbing my hair with a towel, and humming 'Dancing Queen'.

I get dressed and walk down to the hotel lobby. The lobby is bright but small, with pastel blue walls. I imagine that once it was grand – it has a winding staircase leading up to the first floor. But the lobby, like the whole hotel, has fallen on hard times.

At least, it does its best to give that appearance. Damp patches are starting to appear here and there, little frayed pieces of carpet go unrepaired, small stains are left to fester. However, it's a nice hotel, friendly and familiar, and it suits me fine.

I ask Lena if I can use the Internet. Lena is Russian and she is in charge of reception. At least, she is when the manager is not there; which is often. Lena is twenty-nine, and she has a degree in business studies. She has a boyfriend called Toby, who is a courier. Toby always, always tries to chat me up every time we meet – whenever the three of us are standing at reception at the same time.

Lena thinks he is funny, very funny, but I don't agree. I don't like Toby – there is something odd about him. But Lena likes him, and - let's be honest – there's plenty that's odd about me.

Lena collects the password to the Internet computer from a locked wooden drawer. She fumbles with the lock and mumbles things in Russian. While I wait, I try to work out how many Tobys would equal one Chris. I eventually decide on thirty-five thousand - thirty-five thousand Tobys to one Chris. But I would rather have one Chris than have a million Tobys. I would be happy with one Chris. I would be happy.

Lena eventually prises the password from the drawer and we walk over to the computer, tucked away in an alcove. Lena types in the password and then I sit down. I avert my eyes while she types it in. Lena trusts me, I know, but this - I have learnt - is what you do when someone is typing a password. You look away.

At the hotel, you get fifteen minutes of Internet connectivity for one pound. This is four pounds an hour, which to me seems a bit expensive. However, as I'm never going to pay it, it doesn't really matter. My slate is wiped clean, so to speak, each Time.

I type 'Donnybrook' into Google, and Wikipedia tells me there are a number of places in the world called Donnybrook - six, in fact. There is one in Ireland, one in South Africa, one in America, and three in Australia.

Next I try typing 'Donnybrook' with 'Cattleborn Street'. I get results back for 'Donnybrook' and 'Cattle', but to my dismay – after searching on-line maps for forty-five minutes – I realise there is no Cattleborn Street listed in any of the six towns.

I refuse to give up, and spend two further hours hunting down maps from all over the Internet. Eventually, I have found detailed maps of all six towns. There is no Cattleborn Street. I have spent twelve pounds.

I go back to my room and lay on my bed. What should I do? Will I have to visit each town – go to Australia and South Africa? I can imagine myself walking from town to town. In my head there is a desert stretching out before me – each town is visible on the horizon. They all look too far away.

I consider what I should do. I decide that I will phone all the tourist offices tomorrow. I will get the password for the Internet again and find out all six numbers, then call each of them. If no one knows anything, I will go to Dublin – it is nearest.

Suddenly, I remember something – a clue. The saxophone man – he was Irish! He was from Ireland! Donnybrook is in Ireland.

The decision is made. I will go to Dublin.

* * * * * * * * * * * * * * * *

I discover that, although you don't need a passport to visit Dublin, you do need some form of photo ID for the flight – like a driving license or, indeed, a passport. I have neither of these this Time, so I will have to apply for a passport and wait. I do this from the hotel Internet computer, knowing I would have a two week wait at least.

I resign myself to the wait, and decide to make some plans. I need to think ahead. I decide to make a list of assumptions.

This is my list of assumptions:

1) That the saxophone man was being truthful. Obviously he knew about the song, but my first assumption is that he is not leading me on a wild goose chase; but instead that the address he gave me would help me find out about the song.
2) That the address relates to Donnybrook in Ireland, and not Australia or somewhere else.
3) That, although the address didn't seem to exist, I will be able to find it somehow when I am there.

I am one of those people that would rather be looking for

something than just thinking about where I put it. I am also an optimist, at least in that respect. I always believe, when I am looking for something, that I will find it.

So, although there seems to be no clue about Cattleborn Street on the Internet, I am convinced that I will find it when I arrive in Dublin.

I have a mental image of Cattleborn Street in my head, an image I have built up while waiting for my passport to arrive. I imagine it to be like 'Diagon Alley' in the Harry Potter books. I think it will be a dark, long street, accessed only by using the magic words from the back of a pub, or maybe a library or launderette or somewhere like that; somewhere communal.

I have the magic words, courtesy of my saxophone playing friend. They are 'with your love'. Those are obviously the words that will whisk me into the dimension of Cattleborn Street, with all its magic and wonderful secrets.

Of course, I don't believe any of this. I think, in reality, that it will probably be a normal street with a few shops in it – one of them called 'Andy's'. But I still assume it may prove difficult to find. That is my instinct.

I have read all six of the Harry Potter books, and I think they are really good. But I have grown to dislike them. This is because I will never get to read the seventh and last one. I will never know what happens. I have my own theories, of course, but - unless I can persuade someone to tell me (either the author or someone on the editorial staff of the final book) - I may never know for sure.

I have considered holding the editor or someone closely connected with the books hostage, and then forcing them to tell me the plot and ending of the seventh book. But that seems a bit extreme, and I'm not sure I care to that degree.

However, I have at times given this idea serious consideration; but mainly when I am pretty bored.

* * * * * * * * * * * * * *

The two weeks passed slowly as I waited for my passport to arrive. In the end, my grand plan was really that I didn't have a plan – just to go across to Dublin and have a look around. For the first Time ever I had been given information – possibly good information, and I was anxious to put what I had learnt into practice; anxious to get going.

I bought a good map of Dublin, and a not so good map which included the suburb of Donnybrook. It looked to be about an hour or so from the centre of the city, if you were on foot. I decided to find a hotel nearer to Donnybrook than the centre, as my investigation would be focused there. However, I decided that I might as well take a look around the city while I was visiting.

* * * * * * * * * * * * * * * *

A few days before my passport turned up and I sprang into action, a strange thing happened. I was sitting in the lounge of my hotel, watching something about the Iraq war on Sky News, when I suddenly felt as if someone were watching me. It was an overwhelming feeling - not like when you just have an 'idea' that someone might be watching. Instead, I felt certain that someone was looking at me; closely spying on what I was doing.

I looked all around me, my eyes darting all over the lounge. The room was empty except for one elderly man reading a book. He was engrossed in a copy of 'Omerta' by Mario Puzo. I had read this book myself, and it was very good. He seemed to be enjoying it, and it didn't seem as if he was interested in me at all. I looked over at the windows – there were two large ones facing out to the street. There was no-one looking in. There appeared to be no-one watching me at all.

But I felt...how did I feel? I felt naked – as though I were exposed, uncovered to somebody. I felt that they were staring at me with intent, their eyes boring into me - searching every part of my body, and even my mind.

I stood up and walked out of the lounge. The feeling followed me past reception and out into the street. I looked all around outside – stood stupidly staring at people as they passed and, in equal measure, staring into space. Then, as quickly as it came, the feeling left me. Only its echo remained. I was alone again.

I sat down on the small steps of the hotel and thought about the feeling and what it was like. It had been only a few moments ago. It had been so strong, but already it was fading into nothing.

How had it felt? Powerful? Uncomfortable? Yes, but more than that – something else instead. I searched my mind. It had felt… what were the words? Restricting? Invasive? Yes – but again it was more than that.

It felt… good - almost erotic, but yet as though I had no control. It was pleasant, but scary at the same time. As I searched and searched, trying to capture those moments before, it faded away and was gone.

I went back inside the hotel. Everything still looked the same. I don't know why, but I felt as though something may have changed. I went to the bar and ordered a Diet Coke, and charged it to my room. I went upstairs and lay on the bed. I drank the coke and wondered what the feeling meant, or if it had any meaning at all.

As I lay on the bed, I felt myself drifting off to sleep. It was only three o'clock in the afternoon, but I was starting to feel tired, as if I had run a mile, maybe even two. I sank into a deep sleep, and when I woke up it was nearly midnight. The feeling, whatever it was, had worn me out. But, other than that, it left no other mark or memory, either physical or otherwise.

But this feeling had been a warning. And when the time came, I would choose to ignore it.

Time Eighty-Four

I spent all of Time Eighty-Three racked with guilt. This was because of Adam. I don't know why I dumped him at the airport like I did - I would never have behaved like that with Chris, and I certainly wouldn't want anyone to behave like that with me.

It was true; we had a great time in Germany. Adam had a fantastic time. But I pushed it too far. I gave him way too much. I was playing a game, and when the game ended I just discarded him. I did feel guilty at the time, but not enough to act in a way that would not hurt his feelings.

I think back now and wonder what made me just leave him like that at the airport, after behaving like he was the love of my life for four whole weeks. Was it because I wanted to punish him in some way; but why? Was it because of my life – or lack of it? Was it because he is not Chris? Because of me – because of who I am; what I've become?

And what have I become? A ghost. That's exactly what I am - a ghost. I don't belong here. I don't belong anywhere. But where can I go?

I decided to put things right, at least, as far as my guilt towards Adam was concerned. This is what I did.

* * * * * * * * * * * * * * * *

I didn't even know if this would put anything right, at least not in Time Eighty-Two. But, given my circumstances, this was the best I could manage.

I sent off for my passport straight away, and then - on the same day and at the same time I had previously sat at the table in Leadenhall Market eating my jacket potato - I went and sat in the same place.

There was always a chance Adam would not appear this

Time – these little things change sometimes. But never the big things – they always stay the same.

But, as I expected, Adam did appear. He sat with me, and tried to make conversation, just as he had before. This Time I was a little more forthcoming. I told him a bit about myself, perhaps even flirted a little. But, in the end, as before, we went our separate ways.

Part two of my plan was put into practice the next day. I hung around outside the pub where I knew, or at least hoped, Adam would be sitting looking sad because of Pete. I snuck a look in through the windows at the front a couple of minutes before we met last Time, and there he was. Same table, same sad face. I walked in and said hello.

We sat for ages; as we had previously. We, if anything, were even friendlier than before, more relaxed with each other. It was almost as if I had left an imprint of myself on him; as if he knew me in some unconscious way.

What kind of imprint did I leave on Chris? This made me think, and my mind kept wandering. However, I smiled at the right places and was as nice as could be.

Pete arrived, and - after much discussion between the two of them - I offered to buy the tickets. The deal was closed, I gave my e-mail address to Adam, and we left pretty much as before. So far, everything was going well.

* * * * * * * * * * * * * * * *

A couple of weeks later Adam e-mailed me to say that he'd received the tickets from Pete. They were now in my name. That evening, I lay in the bath at my hotel, trying to decide how to behave.

My instinct told me to go along as before, play the part of a fantasy girlfriend, but this time continue after we got back from Germany until the Time ended. But, I knew I had two other options…

Firstly, I could refuse his advances. Be pleasant – pay for the tickets to the matches – but just go along as a friend. Maybe have the odd kiss, but leave it at that. After all, I'm sure he wasn't expecting what happened during Time Eighty-Two. He may have hoped – but he wasn't expecting; I'm absolutely certain of that.

This way, his disappointment would not be so acute when we went our separate ways. This was one option.

Then, there was another option. I could go further this Time. I lay in the bath remembering what happened in Germany, and struggled to imagine how much further I could go. I could be even more loving towards him, be even flirtier, and make even more advances – more suggestions.

I could show more interest in him – make him feel really special, loved, interesting. This was a reasonable option – considering the purpose of all this was to make up for before. But, well, there is a line to be drawn – and I thought the sheer effort of being so nice for so long might be too much for me to cope with.

Eventually, I decided to go along with my instinct; simply to do as before. Only this Time, I would carry on after the trip had ended. This Time, I would not dump him at the airport, but I would be his girlfriend for as long as it was possible for me to do so.

* * * * * * * * * * * * * * * *

Everything went smoothly in the run up to the trip until I broke my arm. Actually, it was a hairline fracture of the wrist, but it hurt like mad.

I fell over right outside the hotel. Someone had left a large flat stone on the pavement. It was the base of a sign or something, and I tripped over it and fell awkwardly on my wrist. My wrist came between my face and the pavement, so I was thankful for that.

Lena, the receptionist at the hotel, was overflowing with sympathy. She placed a cold compress on my arm, to reduce the swelling, and went off in search of the builders who had committed this atrocity. She knew they were in the hotel somewhere – rewiring something or other – and the sign-to-be, with the base already in place, was intended for later use. It was to warn people of an open cover in the pavement, which they were going to be peering down during the afternoon.

She returned a few minutes later with two sheepish looking workmen in blue overalls. One of them was Polish, and he made the disastrous mistake of telling Lena that he could speak Russian. This led, not to empathy, but to a five minute lecture - in Russian - on the dangers of leaving the bases of signs unattended.

In reality, the Polish man spoke Russian quite badly and therefore understood very little of the telling-off he was getting. But he did understand the gist of it.

They were both made to apologise to me. I smiled, feeling stupid, and wishing I could see a doctor. Lena arranged for me to take a trip to the Out Patients department at the nearest hospital. More than arranged; she took me herself in her blue Ford Fiesta.

My arm was now in a cast, and the nice Chinese doctor at the hospital had advised me that I would need to keep it on for at least a month. It felt much better, now it had been patched up.

Lena had been so helpful when I fell that I decided to buy her a present. The following day, I walked to a sweetshop near Queensway and bought her a big box of chocolates. It had a picture of a kitten on the front and a purple ribbon, but the selection was limited.

However, I need not have worried about the kitten. Lena was overjoyed when I presented her with the chocolates, and she lent across the counter to kiss my cheek. After a brief chat, she asked if I would like to join her for a drink that evening. With the absence of any real reason not to, I said that I would. We arranged to meet in the hotel bar at eight o'clock.

* * * * * * * * * * * * * * * *

Lena had dressed up for our evening – I had not. She looked as though she had spent many hours preparing for our grand night in the hotel bar – I looked as if I hadn't really bothered.

After all, we weren't even going outside the hotel! But, as she sat down opposite me with a big smile, I couldn't help thinking that I had slighted her in some way by not making an effort to dress up. I had thought it was likely to be a casual affair. I was wrong.

Lena had lived in Moscow with her parents before coming to England two years ago. This much, and a lot more, I learnt in the first fifteen minutes of the evening. She wanted to talk – to tell me about her life and what she hoped would happen to her now she was in London. She liked Moscow but loved London.

Eventually, she talked about boyfriends. She told me she felt 'only lukewarm' about Toby, and asked me if I had a boyfriend. I had to think. Did I? During this Time, Time Eighty-Four, the answer was no – but I had spent years with Chris. We had shared a lifetime together. If not a lifetime – that wasn't possible for me – we had certainly spent a long time as a couple.

'Yes,' I said.
'Oh! I knew that! I knew that!'
'Oh? How?'
'How did I know?'
'Yes. How did you know?'
'Hmmm...' (she drew out the 'm's). 'Because, you are a pretty girl...also because you look like you are in love.'
'Yes. Well, yes I am, I suppose...'
'Ha! See! You are in love!' she laughed.

I laughed back, unsure why I was laughing.
'You see,' she continued. 'You see?'
I did not see.
'See what?' I said.
'You see? You are free to love! Love makes you happy! You are happy, because you have a handsome man! You will love him, you will get married. You will have...many children!'

But my love did not make me happy – it made me sad. Chris was not handsome, not in any traditional sense. I do love him – madly. But we will not get married. We will not have children. All of these things are beyond me.

I smiled back at Lena, and, although I thought it impossible, she failed to see the sadness in my face.

'One day,' she said, pointing at me. 'I will be happy like you!'

* * * * * * * * * * * * * * * *

We agreed by mutual consent, but at Lena's suggestion, to meet up the following evening for another drink. I had to admit to myself that I had nothing special to do, so it seemed like an adequate diversion while I waited for the World Cup Finals to begin.

When we met up in the bar the next evening, Lena was in a more somber mood. She had received a letter from a University in Moscow, offering a free extension to her course in Business Studies.

'This is not an offer,' Lena told me, waving the letter about in front of me. 'They want me to return to Moscow to live. I know now one thing - if I go home to see my parents, I will not be able to come back here.'

'Are you sure?' I asked

'Yes, I am sure. I am Russian. I am very sure.'

Lena went on to tell me that she had no intention of returning to live in Moscow. She felt that Russia was a nation where power was everything, and now that power could be bought and sold so easily, she said that the worst people had all the authority. I said that I thought perhaps it was the same here in England, but she dismissed this.

'Maybe,' she said. 'But not in the same way.'

As part of her explanation to me of why she was desperate to stay in London, she told me a story about her childhood. She intended it to explain something about Russian society - some of it she remembered herself, some had been told to her by her parents.

It was a good story, and it helped me to understand something about myself; about my situation. In fact, it was eventually to prove invaluable to me. One day, it would help me make a very good decision. The best stories we tell are about ourselves. This was the story she told.

* * * * * * * * * * * * * * * *

Elena Alexandrovna Babanov, known to all as Lena, went missing when she was just six years old. It was April, 1983, and it was a Monday. She had been on a school trip to visit a circus about twenty miles from her school, which was only five hundred yards or so from her home, located fairly near the centre of Moscow.

Two coaches had set out to the circus that Monday morning; Lena had been on one and her best friend Svetlana had been on the other. After the circus had run its course, the children were allowed half an hour to look around at the animals. During this time, Lena and Svetlana arranged to travel home on the same coach - so they could sit together and talk. They asked the teachers traveling on Lena's coach, and they said this would be OK.

But, when the time came to leave, Lena had been distracted

by two clowns who were getting changed. They were a husband and wife team, and they chatted with Lena about living at a circus, and even gave her a red nose to keep. It was made of foam.

Lena's coach left because they thought she was going back on the same coach as her friend. Svetlana's coach left, after waiting for a few minutes, because they assumed Lena had simply decided to go back on the same coach she had traveled there on.

Svetlana was bemused that her friend had not joined her on the way back, but submitted to the greater wisdom of her teachers - after all, these were the educators of Soviet society. How could they be wrong about such a simple thing?

When Lena realised - about ten minutes later - that both coaches had left, she should have just gone back to the clowns, and waited for someone to come back for her. But, because she was afraid of being punished for missing the coach, and because she was six, she decided to walk home.

The circus was being performed on a large wasteland on the vast outskirts of Moscow which trail off to the east. Lena had noticed which way they had driven towards the site, so she simply reversed her course and walked back the way they had come. In her childish mind, she even had thoughts of perhaps beating the coaches back to the school - if perhaps she ran...

* * * * * * * * * * * * * * *

Five hours later, she was sitting crying on the side of a small road. She had been heading in the right direction, but had made little progress. A few cars passed by without either seeing her or stopping, but then a large black car slowed and pulled over beside her. A man leant out of the window.

'Little girl,' he said, with a quiet voice - a voice like her teacher's. 'Are you alright?'

'No - I missed my coach,' Lena replied through her tears.
'Where are your mummy and daddy?' the man asked.
'At home...'
'Would you like me to take you home?'
Lena nodded.
'Come and get in, then.'

The man stepped out of the car and took her hand. He was dressed in a smart suit with a grey tie. He was not dressed like one of her teachers. He led her round to the other side of the car and strapped her into the passenger seat. She had never seen a seat belt before. Then, together, they set off towards the centre of Moscow.

'Where do you live?' asked the man, his voice still soft, almost a whisper.

'In a flat - there are three blocks of flats; I live in the middle one.'

The man smiled. 'Yes, but in which part of Moscow do you live? Do you live in Moscow?'

'Yes, but I can't remember which part.'

'Oh, perhaps you'd better come to my office. We can help to find your mummy and daddy from there.'

Lena thought for a second, and then remembered something. 'Oh, I live near a metro.'

'Ah! A metro station! Do you remember what it's called?'

'Yes - it's near my school. It's called...Baumanskaja.'

'Ah! You live near Baumanskaja! I know where you mean. Let's go there now, and find your flats. We will find your mummy and daddy.'

Twenty minutes later, they had arrived in Baumanskaja, a suburb of Moscow just outside the ring road. Lena started to recognise places and shops, and knew that this man was taking her home. She had never doubted it.

It took a further ten minutes for Lena to pinpoint her three blocks of flats, but she did so by the broken fences torn up and used for goalposts by the local boys. A couple of minutes later, they pulled up outside the entrance to the block of flats that contained her home.

* * * * * * * * * * * * * * * *

On the fifth floor, her parents were sick with worry. A teacher had called over three hours ago, visited to tell them that Lena had been lost. They had returned to the circus when they realised their mistake, but by then Lena had started the long walk home.

The police had visited an hour ago - a sickly looking man who coughed into a dirty handkerchief while assuring them that they were doing their best to find her.
'But, of course,' he wheezed. 'Moscow is so huge…'

* * * * * * * * * * * * * * * *

Lena walked up the stairs, five floors, to the door of her flat, and the man followed. By now, Lena had learned the man was called Alexei.
She knocked on the door, and heard footsteps from inside running to open it. When it was opened, and Lena's mother saw her daughter looking up at her, alive, she collapsed on her knees and hugged her.
'Lena, Lena, we've been so worried.' This was all she could say.
Alexei bent down, and addressed Lena.
'You're home now,' he said.
Lena's mother ignored him and continued to hug her daughter, savoring this unfamiliar happy ending. Lena's father, noticing Alexei for the first time, stepped forward to shake his hand and thanked him for bringing his daughter home. Alexei agreed to stay for a few moments, for some tea, but said he did not want to intrude.

Alexandra Vadimovich Babanov, Lena's father, was angry. He was angry with the school, for leaving his daughter on a piece of wasteland, and especially angry with the police, who had appeared to be next to useless. Father and Alexei discussed these things while Mother prepared Lena for bed. Marina Ivanovich Babanov, Lena's mother, combed her daughter's hair and washed her face, taking time to enjoy the simple pleasures that she so nearly had lost.

'Ah, Alexei - the police are useless! They are corrupt! All the authorities - they don't care about us!' Father waved his arm around him. He leant forward, and whispered. 'My daughter, God forbid, could be... you know... and would they care? Hah!'

He had already drunk six vodkas - for his nerves, before Lena arrived, and he was now in double figures.

'Look at my flat!' he continued, beginning to sound as drunk as he was. 'That pig of a caretaker - that fat bastard! He robs us blind! Already, he robs us! Now, he wants more than that! Twenty-five percent more! For utilities! Hah! What utilities? The lift never works! The stairs are never swept! There is damp in the kitchen - damp everywhere! He is worse than the authorities! They are all bastards! They are all thieves!'

Marina returned from putting her daughter to bed. She stood behind her husband, and rubbed his shoulders.

'Don't bother our friend with these things,' she said, smiling across the table.

Alexei cleared his throat. He felt he had to speak. He looked at them, almost apologetically.

'My name is Alexei Labinov. I am sub-director of the Moscow KGB.'

In the next few seconds, a number of things almost simultaneously happened to Alexandra. Firstly, he became aware of where he had seen the face of his new friend before -

it was in the newspapers. He also sobered up in an instant, and his sense of clarity became tuned to a feeling of total despair.

He looked across the table at the second most powerful man in Moscow (everyone knew the real power lay with the KGB) and wished he hadn't said a thousand things that he had in fact said during the last twenty minutes; things that could not be unsaid.

Finally, a new thought hit him; would he have lost his daughter in exchange for never meeting this man - if he had never bought her home? To his pride, he concluded to himself that things were best as they now were.

Marina had become as white as a ghost. She had been that way when she was first told about her daughter being missing, and now she had suffered her second shock of the day. Even as pale as she now appeared, Marina was a beautiful lady, and her dainty hands gripped her husband's shoulders with fervour.

This time, it was Alexandra's turn to clear his throat. He stood up.

'Sir...' he began.

Alexei raised his hand with a smile, at which Alexandra stopped speaking. He put his hand down and looked at them both.

'Comrades,' he said. 'Tonight is a happy night for you. I was lucky enough to bring your daughter home - lucky enough to share your tea and eat at your table.'

Lena's parents stared at him. Marina smiled, but her face was still a mask of fear.

Alexei sighed. 'Comrades, your opinions are your own affair. Why should I bring bad fortune upon such gracious people?'

Marina swallowed and spoke, but her voice seemed weak and reedy.

'Comrade, whatever happens because of this night, I thank you as a mother that you brought our daughter safely home to us.'

Alexandra nodded in agreement to this, but added nothing further.

Alexei looked again at them both. They did not believe him - they thought there would be reprisals. He sighed. He felt suddenly very tired.

'Please, sit,' he said. 'I want to tell you a story…'

Lena's parents sat down at the table, and Alexei began his story.

'When I was a young man I lived and worked in Orekhovo, about fifty miles to the east of Moscow. I was in charge of the Workers Soviet at the factory - but I was not an important person. One day, while I was at work, my wife came to see me and tell me that my daughter was sick. But I stayed to the end of my shift, like a good Communist, and when I finished I went home. When I saw how sick she was - a terrible fever - I rushed her to the hospital. But the doctor - there was only one that day - was nowhere to be found. The administrator came back and told us that he was sleeping - that he had just finished a twenty hour shift and was exhausted. She advised us to come back in the morning, and gave us some medicine for the fever.

'My wife was terrified, looking at my daughter, but I remember thinking how proud I was of my country - the doctor, working for twenty hours for the Soviet people. This, I thought, is how people should work - for the good of each other.

'But in the night my daughter died. She was only six years old - just like your daughter is now. And the doctor, I later discovered, was not resting, but drunk. He was drunk on duty, and the administrator had covered for him.

'From that day on, I threw myself into my work, became more involved in politics, my Workers Soviet became more influential. I saw that power was the key to life. If I had had the power, the hospital would have done everything to help my daughter. But I was not powerful enough, and so she died.

'Five years later, after three purges by Stalin - all of which I survived - I became commander of the entire district. The doctor was still working at the same hospital, and there were now many complaints about his drunkenness.

'Just two weeks after taking charge of the district, I had the doctor arrested on a ridiculous charge - 'Praise of Western Technology', or some such thing. I just wanted to talk to him, to tell him what he'd done; to me and my daughter, and to my beautiful wife, who had killed herself just weeks after our daughter's death.

'But when I spoke to him, in the cells, I was filled with rage. I literally dragged him to my car and drove him to the cemetery. I made him stand over the graves of my wife and daughter and say sorry for what he had done. He cried like a baby and he said sorry a thousand times. But he would have said anything, and it was not enough.

'I put him back in the cells, with the idea of having him released in the morning. But I couldn't go home, and I couldn't sleep at my desk. I just kept picturing my daughter dying, and finding my wife's body in the bath at our home - all that blood from just one person. My anger grew and grew, and so - in the middle of the night - I went down to his cell and beat him to death with my bare hands. It took so long - I was exhausted afterwards. I went home and I slept for hours. I was so tired.

'I had never killed anyone before. Some people enjoy it. But I hated it. And I hated myself for doing it. But, I did it, and that is that.'

Lena's parents listened to the story in silence. Marina stared at Alexei's face - he was an old man, really. He looked sad and tired.

'Comrade,' she said. 'I am sorry about your daughter…'

'Yes, I know,' Alexei replied, with a slight move of the hand. 'You understand. You can imagine what it is like…just for a few hours this evening, you could imagine…'

Marina nodded.

'So,' Alexei said, standing up. 'I have brought your daughter home to you. I could not save my own, but I have brought yours home. We have shared something. Do you understand? I will leave you now, and I wish you only good health, and that your daughter grows to be a beautiful woman.'

They said awkward goodbyes, and Alexei started to walk down the stairwell. Just before they closed the door, he turned back once more.

'Your daughter,' he said, 'is very lucky to have such good, kind parents. Goodnight, comrades.'

And with that he was gone. And Lena slept soundly in her bed, dreaming of the clowns, and the red nose, still safely in the pocket of her coat.

* * * * * * * * * * * * * * * *

Three days later, Sergei Ivanovich Kabalin - the caretaker of the block - knocked quietly on the door of Lena's flat. He spoke to her father and mother, and told them not to worry about the increase in rent for utilities, and that he would, in fact, be halving their rent as from the next month. He looked as if he would drop down dead any moment, or as if his dead mother had just popped in for a chat. Marina thanked him for this unexpected kindness, but he just nodded and left quickly before he collapsed.

A day later, engineers arrived to fix the lifts. They worked again for the first time in two years.

* * * * * * * * * * * * * * * *

Later that same evening, lying in bed, I thought about what Lena had said. She was scared of the power that people could potentially hold over her. She described it as a power that could buy anything, do anything; where someone could escape from any crime, any prison.

The more I thought about it, the more I considered the possibility that she had a good point. Perhaps that was what I was missing. I had no power to change my situation, to escape from my prison. Perhaps there was a way of getting the necessary power to change the way things were.

Lena was right. But in my case, knowledge would be the power. Understanding what was happening to me would be a step towards getting the power to change things. Suddenly I felt as if I had the kernel of a plan. I would seek out that power, and each Time I would grow stronger and more able. Then, one day, perhaps I would have enough power to escape.

But not this Time; this Time I was going to watch football.

As I drifted off to sleep, a final thought struck me. Lena wants to leave Russia behind, to escape from the power, but conversely, I want the power to escape.

* * * * * * * * * * * * * * * *

I fractured my wrist just two weeks or so before the trip. I spent the rest of the time relaxing, reading books – I read about four different books while lying in the bath. I tried to prepare myself for the time ahead: Operation Adam.

I felt confident I could make a success of the trip – that, come August 19th, I would have put things right. That, next Time, my guilt would be gone. Or at the very least, I would have done my best.

I was ready to go.

* * * * * * * * * * * * * * * *

The upshot of all this was that when I turned up at the airport to meet Adam, my arm was in a cast and a sling. This Time I had a bigger suitcase; still on wheels. I had not taken enough clothes last Time, and this Time I made up for my previous errors. In fact, I had ten England tops with me – including the red one I was wearing.

Adam was again overjoyed to see me, but looked dismayed when he saw my arm.
'What happened?' he asked, after we had said hello.
'I fell over,' I replied. 'I broke my arm.'
'Oh – are you OK? Does it hurt?'
'A bit - but I'm alright.'
Adam seemed unsure how to react. He was obviously sympathetic about my arm, but he was also very happy to see me. He was trying to smile and look concerned at the same time. He gave in and just smiled at me. I smiled back.
'I'm really glad you made it,' he said. 'Shall we get a drink before we check in? I'll carry your case.'
'It's got wheels…'
'I'll wheel it for you, then.'
'OK.'
We both walked off in the direction of the café. I put my good arm through his.

* * * * * * * * * * * * * * * *

In Germany, everything went to plan. My arm began to heal nicely, and Adam fell in love with me – the fantasy girl – all over again. On the morning of the Japan versus Croatia match I stayed in the room of our hotel, pretending I was ill. I did not want to meet the Japanese man again. I was sacred of him.

Adam was full of sympathy, and he said he would forget going to the match and stay and look after me. I was genuinely touched, and lay on the bed with him – my head on his chest.

However, about lunchtime, I pretended to feel better – much better, and we decided to go to the match after all. Adam said that we should get a cab, but I said that the walk would be nice.

It was a beautiful sunny day, and we set off to walk the four miles or so to the stadium. It was only about one o'clock, so we had time. The match was at three o'clock, and missing kick off would not have been the end of the world. I'd seen it before, anyway.

We passed shops and warehouses and busy streets full of people. I found myself constantly looking out for the Japanese man, and kept feeling a bit scared every time I spotted someone wearing the blue Japan top – which was, of course, often. I tried to put it out of my head, and enjoy the sunshine and the walk. It was difficult though, and I felt preoccupied, distant.

About thirty minutes into our journey, I started to feel a bit lightheaded. I realised that I'd had nothing to eat all day. This was part of my 'feeling ill' - I pretended to have lost my appetite.

I told Adam I felt a bit odd, and at his suggestion we looked for a café to stop and have something to eat. We still had a way to go, and Adam was worried about me. He told me I'd probably feel alright soon, and that I shouldn't get tired out. We walked along looking for a café, hand in hand.

We found a little café with wooden tables and chairs and green umbrellas outside on the pavement. It was on a main street, but only one or two of the outside tables were occupied. We sat and ate sandwiches and I drank lemonade. I still felt lightheaded; in fact, I was starting to feel a bit sick.

While we ate, I looked across the table at Adam. He looked back at me with love, happiness, concern. I smiled at him – reached across and took his hand. I felt a sudden burst of emotion, a lump formed in my throat and tears started to well up in my eyes.

Here was a man who loved me. I had made him love me. But Chris, he loved me for what I really was. I was no fantasy to Chris – I was just me. Tears started to roll down my face. I was betraying Chris. I felt guilty. And not just guilty – I felt ashamed.

But what could I do? I was trying to do what was kind, what was good; surely I was? I was trying to put things right – this Time.

And this is all I have. I have no future - just this.

Suddenly I was feeling dizzy; more lightheaded than before. I tried to clear my thoughts, but Chris filled every part of my mind. He took over my thoughts completely. But not only was he in my head, he was also there alongside me. It was as if he was really there, standing right beside me at the table.

As I held on to Adam's hand, Chris was there with me, stroking my face and hair. He kissed my cheek and whispered in my ear 'It's alright, darling. It's OK...'

And in my mind Chris was also there. He stood beside me, at the café, and he stood in front of me, smiling, in my head. I could not separate the two visions - the Chris beside me and the Chris in my mind. They mingled and blurred into one; they danced before me as if drunk.

The Chris in my mind held the hand of a little boy - a beautiful little boy. It was Jack. Chris bent down beside Jack and spoke to him.

'Look, it's Mummy,' he said. Jack smiled across at me.

I looked at him, my little boy, my son! 'Oh, darling...' I said - my voice only a whisper.

I could not contain my emotions. I was sobbing now, shaking. My face was wet with tears. I looked up and saw Chris. He was smiling at me.

'I love you,' I said, this time the sound of my voice was only a sigh. But Adam heard me, and leant across - his hand holding mine tightly, his other hand stroking my arm.

'I love you too,' Adam replied, squeezing my hand; touching my face. I looked across at him – across the table, shocked to see his face; to see Adam there, and not Chris. But although still shaking, I smiled, and leant across and kissed his cheek. But I had not been talking to him – I had been talking to Chris.

* * * * * * * * * * * * * * *

I thought I was going mad. I made it through the trip to the final day, but my thoughts became jumbled and confused. I couldn't focus on anything, and I felt like a jigsaw in a box.

Adam was as happy as could be, so the plan had gone fine. But I kept crying, and I had to cry in places where Adam wouldn't see me, which was difficult. I cried in bathrooms. I cried into my pillow at night while he was asleep.

This was my eighty-fourth Time. I felt I was losing my mind - I was worried sick that I was going mad. And the worrying made me feel even madder.

But, in a bizarre way, the fact that I was going mad seemed perfectly sane. Surely, anybody in my situation would go mad? Maybe not at first, but after eighty-four Times? And what about after one hundred Times, two hundred Times, a thousand? How could anyone's sanity survive?

I began, ironically, to worry about the future. For someone with no future at all, I worried about how my mind would cope in the Times ahead. How long would this go on? I thought about this a lot, and reached the conclusion that was unavoidable; forever.

* * * * * * * * * * * * * * *

On the flight back to England, I resolved to put my worries to one side. There was nothing – absolutely nothing - I could do. Not that I knew of, anyway. The Japanese man had mentioned Venice, and perhaps I would go to Venice again next Time – but why I had no idea.

But, for now, I was here for Adam. For another seven weeks, I existed for Adam.

* * * * * * * * * * * * * * *

Adam sat beside me on the flight home. He kept looking across at me, smiling but worried. I knew he thought I might want to leave, and he wanted me to stay.

I took his hand and smiled, then closed my eyes and rested my head on his shoulder. I placed my other arm around his waist and stroked his side. And there I stayed. I felt his whole body sigh with relief, but his relief did not pass through me. It just bounced off.

* * * * * * * * * * * * * * * *

Once we had landed, we waited for our cases beside a revolving belt. The belt was surrounded by people returning from Germany, but not a single case appeared. Adam had his arm around me, gently stroking my 'bad' arm. I had had the cast taken off ten days ago in Germany, and it felt as good as new.

As I waited - steeled myself - to profess my love to Adam, I found myself thinking about my arm; about how it felt now. It didn't hurt at all. I wondered if this was a clue. This made me feel a bit better. I thought 'I must start looking for more clues. Next Time, I will hunt for more clues.' I was filled with the notion that if I discovered the right clues, perhaps one big clue, I could escape. For a few moments, I was sure of it.

Adam was not a clue, but he was the reason I was - once again - standing at Stanstead Airport waiting for my bag. This Time there would be no scene, no tears – just hugs and smiles.

'Adam,' I said, as I looked up at him.

'Yes?' he said in reply. He seemed a bit shaken – I think he realised I was going to say something important. I could see in his eyes that he didn't want to lose me.

'Adam. What do you want to happen?'

'Happen?'

'Yes. Adam – what do you want to happen now?'

'What – now we're home?'

'Yes – what happens now?'

Adam looked at my face. He was searching, like me, for clues. But he was looking for different clues. He smiled - a nervous smile; a childish smile.

'Sandy – you know what I want.'

'Me?'

'You - I want you.'

'Your wish is granted.'

It was that simple. I smiled and kissed him. I held him and hugged him. He ran his hands up and down my back and squeezed me tight. He was happy. My plan had succeeded. It was so easy. I was redeemed.

* * * * * * * * * * * * * * * *

For the next seven weeks, Adam and I stuck together. He visited me at the hotel several times, and Lena assumed that he was the boyfriend of our conversation. But he was not. That made me cross, that she couldn't realise I loved Chris. But how could she know? I was cross at myself for being cross.

And I hid all this from Adam. I was still in character.

* * * * * * * * * * * * * * * *

On the last day, August 19th, Adam and I had gone out for the day. Adam was working in Birmingham, and I had spent the last week there with him. We had decided to walk along the canals during the morning, and have lunch in a French restaurant in the centre. I don't like French food, but I didn't mind as I knew I wouldn't make it to the restaurant anyway.

We walked for ages along the canals, hand in hand. I kept looking at my watch, aware that 11.12am was looming.

'Are you late for something?' Adam smiled.

'Sorry?'

'You keep looking at your watch.'

'Oh, do I? Sorry...' I smiled. He smiled back.

It was 11.05am. We had had fun – lots of fun. There was no denying that. I had felt like my mind was unraveling, but I'd managed to keep it in one piece. Or at least keep the jigsaw in the box. In fact, I felt a bit better, and had been less stressed the last few weeks.

However, at the moment, with just seven minutes to go, I felt as nervous as usual. I knew what was coming, and I hated it. I hated it. I was breaking my golden rule, spending the last few minutes with someone else – not alone. I toyed with the idea of sneaking off somewhere under the pretence of trying to find a toilet.

But I had come this far. I had made it to the last few minutes. Adam was still happy. There was nothing more I could do now. I had no idea what would happen, for Adam, this lunchtime. Would I still go to lunch at the French restaurant? Would I just fade away – would he forget me? Or would some ghost of me, some part of me, live on in this Time? Be with Adam and hold his hand? I had no idea at all.

We came across a bench, and I sat down. He came and sat beside me. A man cycled past on a bike, wearing a yellow cycling shirt and sunglasses. I glanced at my watch. Four minutes left.

'Adam,' I said, looking not at him, but out at the canal. 'Are you happy?'

Adam looked across at me.

'What, with you, or with life?' he replied.

'Both.'

'Yeah - I'm happy with both.'

I turned to face him.

'What kind of person am I, Adam? If you had to describe me to someone, what would you say?'

'Can I be rude? Who am I describing you to?'

'To a nun - someone like that. Don't be rude. I'm serious.' I gave him a smile. 'I'd just like to know…what you really think of me.'

'I love you.'

'I love you too…but what else? What kind of person am I?'

Adam thought for a moment. He looked out across the water. A canal boat slowly made its way past. It was red and bottle green and the sun shimmered off the surface of the roof. It was a beautiful scene; beautiful colours - so alive, so vibrant.

I flicked my wrist so that my watch came into view. Less than two minutes.

I was beginning to feel sick. The sickness that comes from knowing what will happen soon. It was the same sickness I have every Time.

'If I had to describe you to someone,' he said, 'I would say you were beautiful. And that you were funny. I'd say that you were lovely… lovable… and kind… and sexy…'

He leant across and placed his hand on my thigh. I touched his hand with mine. I looked across at him and stared into his eyes.

'But, have I been…' I couldn't think how to say it. 'Have I been the kind of girlfriend you would have wanted? Am I the kind of girl you would have liked?'

Adam smiled at me, and touched my face with his hand. 'You've been a perfect girlfriend,' he said. 'You're a perfect girl.'

I leant across and kissed him on the cheek. We sat together in silence for a few moments.

Adam turned away and looked down the towpath. In the distance, a little girl was pulling a wooden duck along the path ahead. It kept bumping over stones and falling over. To her, this was funny, and she laughed. I stole a glance at my watch - fifty five seconds left.

My time with Adam was over.

I looked straight ahead of me, at the far side of the bank. I closed my eyes.

He was proud to be with me. He enjoyed my company. He

enjoyed me. Our Time together – this Time - had been a success.

And he loved me. And I liked him. He was funny and he was kind. But he was not Chris. I loved Chris. These were my final thoughts during those last moments.

I opened my eyes, and stared out across the canal as the final seconds passed. I placed my hands in my lap, so that my watch was in view. Eighteen seconds left. I felt the fear start to grip me – take hold of me.

Adam turned towards me. I was afraid. I was afraid of everything. The fear was all I had left. I kept my head down – looking downwards, so that he wouldn't see the terror on my face. He spoke to me – his voice was light, carefree. He was happy.

'I'm feeling really hungry now. Shall we go and get something to

Time Ninety-Six

Tuesday 23rd May 2006

The day after my passport arrives, I leave for Dublin. Aboard the short, one hour flight, I have another strange sensation. I feel as though I am shifting backwards and forwards between the present and the past, between the two tenses. I am and I was; I go and I went.

I sit back in my seat and close my eyes. I feel confused, dizzy. The sensation drifts away, and I am left in the present. At least, the present as it is for me – my eternal present.

I am starting to feel more concerned – concerned about myself. Although physically, and in many other ways I feel fine, I am beginning to feel as if my mind is unravelling. I haven't been to see Chris for two Times now, and this is strange for me.

Perhaps I am missing him – he is a stable influence in my life; that is certain. He loves me, and I need to be loved. But in this Time, he doesn't love me, because he doesn't know me. That makes me feel sad, but I have begun to wonder if he is part of my problem. I decide that the lack of Chris is part of the problem, not Chris himself.

I also decide that the feelings of confusion are probably natural - for someone like me. After all, I *am* confused, and anyone moving back and forth, from March to August, Time and Time again, would be confused as well.

I have a bag of nuts on my lap. I have been eating them carefully, as nuts give me a tummy ache; but not if I eat them slowly. I run through my plan, or lack of it, in my mind. A fat man sitting next to me is reading a magazine about aircraft. Very apt, I think to myself. He has eaten his nuts already.

We land in Dublin. It is 7.30pm, and it's getting a bit chilly. I am under-dressed, but I have a jacket, so I put it on. I pass through the terminal and out of the building in no time at all. My bag is the first off the conveyor belt. 'What chance of that?' I think to myself. I also think, 'someone needs to be first,' and today that is me.

I catch the airport bus to my hotel, a large hotel between Donnybrook and a place called Ballsbridge. The drive into Dublin is interesting; I have never been to Dublin before, so I look out the window the whole way. I cannot stop myself looking for Cattleborn Street, as well as expecting to see the saxophone man on every corner. I see neither.

The hotel is grand, and the room is spacious and nice. I order Irish stew to eat in my room, and then have a bath. The stew is lovely, and so is my bath. I finish my copy of 'The Troublesome Offspring of Cardinal Guzman' by Louis De Bernier, which was a bit gruesome for me.

I lay in the bath and contemplate my situation. What do I expect to find? I expect to find something - some information; some information about the song. I am following a trail, that's what I tell myself - a trail that has led me to Dublin so far. I close my eyes, because I have no real answers. Thoughts, feelings, ideas - they flow around my head. They bob up and down like the little yellow duck in my bath. I feel my breath shorten, and I begin to feel anxious. I open my eyes and breathe deeply, slowly. I feel better each time I breathe. In a few moments, my breathing returns to normal.

Tomorrow I will find what I am looking for. I feel that I must.

Time Ninety-Six

Wednesday 24th May 2006

After breakfast, I head out to discover Donnybrook. I have the note with me, although, of course, it is committed to memory. Cattleborn Street is my destination, and I spend all morning wandering the pleasant streets of Donnybrook to no avail. Trees line the avenues like soldiers, and mothers hurry their children off to school. The houses are grand, tall, and full of history. There is no sign of Andy's, and no sign of the street.

I ask a number of different people about Cattleborn Street and its whereabouts, but no-one knows a thing about it. No-one has heard of it. Soon I start to worry – perhaps it doesn't exist at all. Perhaps it's in Donnybrook in North Dakota, or South Africa or Australia. After only two hours searching, I am already losing heart.

I want Chris to be here with me. We could walk hand in hand along Donnybrook Road, share lunch together, have fun. I stop walking. It hits me like a bolt of lightning - I feel depressed. I feel depressed; that's what it is! I am not going mad – not totally anyway. I am feeling depressed.

Perhaps I have depression. I don't know. But putting a name to my feeling has an effect. Realising that I feel depressed makes me feel a bit better. Gives me some control, or at least the semblance of control. Perhaps I need therapy – but what would I say? How could I explain? I don't know, but I also feel hungry. I start walking again, off in search of food. I am in Dublin, a depressed girl in search of food. I feel, at the moment, as though I know who I am.

* * * * * * * * * * * * * *

I have lunch in an Italian restaurant - it is amazingly

expensive and not that nice. The pasta is a bit cold and I have to send it back. The waitress, who is obviously not Italian, but perhaps Bulgarian, almost sneers at me as she returns with my plate. It has been microwaved; the plate has that 'microwaved feel' to it (the plate is hotter than the pasta).

The food makes me feel less hungry, however, and the idea that I might be suffering from depression has put my thoughts into some kind of perspective. All in all, I feel a bit happier. I do not tip the waitress and she, in consequence, stands by the door to the street and does not open it for me. She makes a show of not opening it for me – which is stupid because there is no-one else in the restaurant at that point.

She looks me up and down. 'Did you enjoy your meal?' She says this almost as a challenge.

Years of English politeness bubble to the surface. I cannot suppress them, so I reply 'Yes, thank you. It was very nice.'

She stares at me, incredulous but satisfied at my reply, and turns around. I stand for a second. Suddenly I feel this is a test of confidence – my confidence. It is a test of my ability to deal with difficult situations. I decide, in a moment, to face up to my fear. She had issued a challenge – I would not disappoint her.

'Excuse me,' I say. 'I've changed my mind.'

She turns to face me, and then walks slowly back. 'What you mean - changed your mind?'

'Not "what you mean". It's "what do you mean".' I reply.

She looks confused, but unmoving. Her face is stony, contemptuous.

'I not understand...'

'It's not "I not understand". It's "I don't understand".'

Her face flickers for a second. 'Ah! You correct my English! I understand now!'

I look at her, unable to think of a suitable reply.

'Why you do that? You understand me, yes?' She says.

I shrug my shoulders.

'You don't speak Hungary! You try say in Hungary!' She is

getting cross.

'I don't want to.' I reply.

'Ah! You funny! You funny girl!' She is getting crosser. 'You laugh at me! You go away!'

'The food was crap.'

'No – you crap! You go now! You crap! You crappy crap person!'

I couldn't help but smile at the expression.

'Listen,' I say. 'I have nothing against you or against Hungary, but you are too rude to be a waitress, and the food here is rubbish.'

By this time the owner has appeared from the back of the restaurant, but he strangely hovers in the background, seemingly either afraid of me or perhaps of his demon waitress. She raises her voice a decibel further as she shouts back at me. By this time I am walking off.

'No! You rubbish! You are rubbish person!'

'You are *a* rubbish person,' I correct, shouting back.

She did not, I think, understand this as a correction, but instead as an insult. At this point her English deserts her, and she launches into a tirade of Hungarian abuse, all of which, the meaning if not the emphasis, is lost on me.

I smile to myself as I quicken my pace. I feel a bit better. I will continue my search in a more positive frame of mind.

* * * * * * * * * * * * * * * *

Gradually, I slow down and walk towards the bus station. I have no intention of getting a bus, of course. I don't even know where all the buses go – or even if I did know the names of the places the buses go, I wouldn't know where the places were, or where I was when I got there.

Instead, I intend to talk to the bus drivers and any other bus-related people I can find. They, I think, are the sort of people who might know lots about the roads in town.

There is a large bus depot – opposite an even larger church – at one end of Donnybrook Street. It is grey and orange and blue, and it is utilitarian. It looks like nothing other than what it is – a bus station.

Overhead a flock of birds circle around - they seem to be looking for something too. I watch them for a minute, wondering what is going through their minds. I think, for a second, how frightening it would be to see inside the mind of a bird; how shallow and empty it must be. I suddenly remember a Time before when I felt that way - like a bird - not so long ago. I can't remember when it was, and then the memory passes.

However, thinking of birds - trying to recapture a memory - makes me suddenly remember something else. I remember the pigeon with one leg on the South Bank, which in turn means I remember the saxophone man. This memory makes me stop watching the circling birds, and head into the station.

* * * * * * * * * * * * * * * *

I look around for a moment. There are a few passengers milling about – including one man in a blue coat with an enormous parcel, about the size of two televisions – one on top of the other. Perhaps that's what it is; but I can't tell as it's wrapped in brown paper.

However, I can see no sign of any drivers or staff, not even in the cabs of the buses. I skirt around the sides of the bus lanes and see a door on my left. It is wooden and painted bottle green, and has a sign attached with the word 'Canteen'. I look around again. There is no one about - no one wearing a uniform, anyway.

I push open the door and walk inside. The canteen is incredibly small – just two wooden tables painted in the same green as the door, and eight chairs – four to each table. There is a shelf along one wall, with a kettle and tea, milk and sugar.

On the wall are two posters – one is of the Irish football team, and the other is of Britney Spears, pouting for the camera. One table is empty, but the other is full of people. That's to say, four people, sitting around - playing cards. They all look up, as one man, the second I walk in - walking into the canteen puts me almost right beside them, as they are sitting only eight feet from the door.

'Can I help you, miss?' says the man sitting directly across from me.

I explain that I am looking for Cattleborn Street, and I am met with the usual blank looks. They all shake their heads and say they have never heard of it. I thank them and turn round to leave.

'Sorry to interrupt your game,' I smile as I open the door.

'It's OK,' says the same man who had spoken first. 'If you had to sit every day with this lot, you'd be glad to be interrupted!'

I smile at him, and then turn to pass through the door.

'Where are you from?' He asks.

'London,' I reply.

'Stay and play cards.'

I thought for a second. I had days to search – weeks. I could stay for a few minutes. I could even have a cup of tea.

'OK,' I say. I shut the door and pull a chair up to the table. The man who asked me seems surprised. I like surprising people, so I'm pleased that he is, or at least seems to be. The other three simply shuffle up to make room for me. A small electric bar fire is on the wall behind us – it is on number '3' and the room is warm. It makes the atmosphere cosy.

'Would you like a tea?' says one of the other men.

'Yes, please,' I reply with a smile. 'Milk and two sugars, please...'

'Ah, lovely! My kind of girl!' He smiles back, but in a friendly way.

The four men look of a similar age, probably in their late

fifties. One has a large scar on his face – like a burn of some kind. He avoids eye contact with me, and I wonder if he is self-conscious.

'We're playing Rummy,' says the fourth man.

I think of him as the fourth man. The first man is the one who spoke first. The second is the man making me tea. The third is the man with the scar, so the fourth man is the one that's left – he is the one holding the cards.

'Oh – OK, that's fine,' I say.

'You can play Rummy, then?' He says. He sounds as if he doubts my word.

'Of course,' I reply.

'Of course she can play!' says man number one. 'Do you think they don't play Rummy in England, Dugan? Do you think it's only us that play it here in Dublin?'

The fourth man, Dugan, goes red in the face. He looks down at the cards. 'I was just asking her,' he mumbles.

The second man brings back my tea. We all sit down and start to play. Dugan deals the cards.

'OK,' he says. 'Fours and threes are good, along with a straight run or runs of four and three. Aces are low. OK?'

I nod and smile. I know how to play Rummy.

I convince Dugan and the others by winning the first two games. We talk while we play. They tell me all their names, and I tell them my name and about my coma. They are fascinated by the coma and ask me all kinds of questions. All except the third man – he doesn't speak but smiles and nods at the appropriate times. He is also interested in my stories.

They ask about my recovery, whether I saw God, if I was sad to lose all that time - all those years. I answer them honestly. I feel, somehow, that they could ask me anything, and I would answer it. I would answer anything at all.

After the third game, which is won by Dugan, the first man stands up. 'That's it, I suppose…' he says. The first man is called Liam.

Dugan picks up the cards and puts them on the shelf. I have the impression that they have rested there for many years. He looks at me. 'We have to go – back to work…'

'Oh? OK. Well, thanks for the tea - and the game of cards,' I say with a smile.

'You are most welcome,' says the second man, Martin, and he gives a little bow.

'Nice to meet you,' I say.

'Bye, now,' says Liam, and they both walk out the door.

'Yes - nice to meet you,' says Dugan, and he follows them out.

The third man, Ryan, is still putting on his jacket. He, like the others, is a bus driver. He has not spoken a word, and I wonder for a moment if he can speak. But as he leaves, he stops as he passes me. He gives me a shy smile, and offers his hand for me to shake. I take his hand and shake it. He lets it go, dropping his hand by his side.

'Sandy,' he says. 'That's a beautiful name, so it is.'

He turns and runs to catch up his friends.

* * * * * * * * * * * * * * * *

I am left alone in the canteen, and I almost immediately feel out of place – an intruder into another world. I stand for a moment, trying to commit the surroundings to memory. I would like to remember this, so I try hard to build a mental picture. I am just about to leave when the door swings open, and man dressed in black with a shiny badge - an inspector - appears before me. He stops, surprised, as he sees me in front of him. He stares at me for a moment.

'Can I help you now?' he says.

'Yes… I was just…'

'This is a staff canteen, you know…'

'Yes, I was only…'

'Now…' His eyes narrow slightly. 'Were you looking for

anyone special? Anyone here you know?'

I am about to tell him about the invitation, the game of cards, the tea - when suddenly I feel I should tell him nothing. That if I tell him, I will get the others into trouble. He is looking for a reason to cause trouble for the others. I just know this.

'No. I'm fine,' I say. I walk past him and out into the station. I carry on walking.

'Miss!' he shouts, but I don't turn around. There is a moment's silence. He is thinking. 'This is for staff only!'

I just keep walking, and then I quickly glance around. He is standing at the doorway to the canteen, and I am walking away.

But he is not welcome there, and I am.

* * * * * * * * * * * * * * * *

I spend the next two hours wandering around the parts of Donnybrook I have not yet seen, and popping in and out of shops asking if anyone had ever heard of this elusive Cattleborn Street. I start to think that perhaps there is no such place as Andy's, no such street as Cattleborn – or, even worse, the only person who knows where they are is the Hungarian waitress, who would certainly be reluctant to give me any useful information.

Around three o'clock I stop for a rest. I sit down on a low wall on the high street – Donnybrook Road – and slowly it starts to rain. Donnybrook is a nice place, but nowhere looks nice in the rain.

I look across the road and notice a small estate agents tucked between two much larger shops. It has a single street-facing window, splattered with cards detailing various properties. I cross over and take a look. Properties are shown in all sizes – from small student flats to large detached houses. The sign above the shiny black door reads:

Swan and Bolton
Estate Agents

It is a modern building, with an old fashioned door. I push on the door and it swings inwards. They may know nothing about Cattleborn Street, but I will, at least, be out of the rain.

Inside a girl is sitting at a desk. She is surrounded by sheets of papers and folders, all strewn about in a hap-hazard fashion. It appears as though she is in the process of sorting them out. She looks up at me and smiles.

'How are you doing?' she says 'Did you see something you like?' She nods towards the window.

'No – not really,' I reply. 'I wonder if you'd know – I'm looking for a street here in Donnybrook - Cattleborn Street. Would you know where it is?'

The girl stares for a moment – thinking. She has a pretty face - probably about twenty-one, I think. She speaks with an English accent, but with a hint of Irish about it. She taps the table twice with her index finger.

'No. I don't think I do. Is it definitely here in Donnybrook?' she asks.

'Yes, I think so...'

'Well, I know most of the streets and roads around here, being an estate agent...' She smiles. 'Also, I've lived here for two years... Sorry I can't help...'

'That's OK.'

'I've got some quite detailed maps over there. If you want to have a look, you're welcome...' She points across to a pile of folded papers resting on top of a black filing cabinet.

'That'd be great,' I say 'I'll just have a quick look...'

I spend a few moments looking listlessly and hopelessly through the maps. The road names are very small, and I have to stare hard to read them. The girl goes back to her sorting out. After a moment she looks up.

'I'm Emma,' she smiles.

'And I'm Sandy,' I smile back. 'Pleased to meet you.'

Emma nods, and returns her attention to the folders.

I look back at the maps. I know there is no chance I will find anything here. I start to think. What shall I do? Where do I go from here? At that moment, I am at a loss. I start to slowly tidy the maps away.

Suddenly there is a noise above me – from a room above my head. Someone shouts out – a woman with a loud voice – deep and loud; Irish.

'Emma! Em! Have you got that print of that property over in Clonskeagh? The shitty cottage with the leak at the front and the dead woman at the back! Have you got it, Emma? The one with the dead woman!' She shouts the last sentence at the top of her voice.

'We've got a customer!' Emma shouts back.

'I can't hear you!! Have you got it or not! It was up here yesterday! You've moved it, haven't you? Why did you move it?'

'I didn't move it!' Emma shouts back. She winks at me. 'You moved it because you're senile, and now you've forgotten!'

'Ah! Don't blame me for your shortcomings! You moved it and wouldn't know because your head's full of sex and boys and girls or whatever it is you fancy! I can't remember what day it is – whether it's boys or girls today!'

'It's always boys!'

'Ah! Liar! It's illegal here, all that, you know!'

The voice becomes much louder and there are footsteps on the stairs above me. Someone runs down the stairs and into the shop. She stops dead.

'Ah, Emma...' she sighs. 'You didn't tell me we had a customer!'

She smiles at me, looking a bit flushed. She is a short woman, perhaps in her early fifties. 'It's this assistant of mine,' she explains. 'She drives me mad! Hopeless, she is!'

Emma smiles at her, a comfortable smile. 'Without me,' she

says, 'you'd sell nothing. You'd be out on the pavement, sitting there begging.' She points to a doorway across the road. 'Anyway,' she continues, 'Sandy was looking for a street here in Donnybrook. Do you know it? Cattleborn Street. I've not heard of it.'

'Cattleborn Street?' repeats the lady. 'Cattleborn, is it?'

I join the conversation. 'Yes. Cattleborn Street.'

'Well...I do know it. Yes. It hasn't been called that for a while, but it used to be called that. Cattleborn Street, it was.'

I can hardly believe it.

'You know it?' I say, looking her in the eyes.

'Yes, they renamed it about twenty years ago, after that poet who was a poof. Ah, but they're all that way, aren't they? Emma – what's that road called now, the one named after the poet? Ah, what's it called?'

Emma and I look at each other. We don't know.

'Let me think now,' she continues, rubbing her chin. 'He's a poet, and he's a poof. He lived ages ago... Ah, I know! Byron! That's it! Byron Street!'

'Byron Street used to be Cattleborn Street?' said Emma. 'I never knew that!'

'Ha! Senile, am I?' she said, prodding Emma in the chest. She turned to me.

'Now then, young lady - Sandy, is it?'

I nod in response.

'Well then Sandy, Byron Street is about ten minutes walking from here. I'll show you on this map...'

* * * * * * * * * * * * * * * *

Rather than walk straight there, I go into a small café to have a think. I order a cup of tea and a piece of apple pie from the counter, and sit at one of the empty tables. The tables have red and white tablecloths, each with a little vase of daffodils.

I sit and stare. I have found Cattleborn Street. Presumably, when I get there, I will find the shop, if it is a shop. I am looking for a song, so I'm pretty sure it's a music shop of some kind. Or perhaps a second-hand shop – like a charity shop.

I sit and pick at my apple pie. Soon I will probably have what I came here to Dublin for – surely someone in the shop will be able to help me. But I have a bad feeling about it all. My instinct is not happy. I wonder if perhaps I am just nervous, but it seems more than that.

I am a girl. I'm thirty-one, but I'm only eighteen really. And, in so many ways, I'm much older again. I've lived for so much longer, seen so many things. But, through all of this, I feel unable to cope. I stare at my tea. Is this an answer – this song? Or is it just a dead end? Or even just another question? What will I do if it's a dead end – if it offers no clues? What will I do if I have to carry on as always, walking from Time to Time? How would I cope? In the future - in the Times to come - how will I cope?

I feel like I'm coming apart at the seams. I wish Chris could help me. I know he would if he could – if he understood. I know that he would.

But he can't help me, not this Time. I miss him. I could have spent time with him, instead of walking the streets here in Donnybrook. I need him. I need what he promises; stability, normality. Not this. Not this.

I wipe away my tears. The girl behind the counter is watching me – torn between offering me a tissue and pretending she hasn't noticed me cry. I have to get out. I stand up and walk out into the street. I quickly get my bearings, and without thinking any further, I head off down the road, following the directions I've been given. I walk now with certainty. I quicken my pace – on a mission.

* * * * * * * * * * * * * * * *

Byron Street is tiny. There are about eight houses either side of a road barely wide enough for one car to drive down. I look down to the end, and on the left, sticking out from a wall, is a sign. My heart leaps in my chest.

It is a rectangle, white – made of frosted plastic with a dim light inside. It reads 'Andy's'. It has a picture of a black disk below the word, and a black guitar.

I walk up the street, past wooden doors opening out on to the pavement. A cat watches me pass, staring up at me with green eyes. Reacting as animals do when I appear, it suddenly dashes past me and off into the distance.

I arrive at the door beneath the sign. The door does not look like the entrance of a shop – more like that of a house. There is a tiny window out to the street. Net curtains prevent anyone seeing in.

Above the door is a painted sign – hand painted and stencilled. The sign is dark green, with black lettering. It is difficult to read, as the black is fading. It reads:

Andy's Record Emporium
Rare, Used and New Records
For Anarchists Only

I look up at the sign for a few moments, and then down at the door. I turn the handle and it opens inwards. I step into the shop.

It is quite dark inside, lit from the ceiling by two small fluorescent light strips; but it is indeed a record shop. There are three long racks of records, stretching from the door up to a small counter at the far end. Behind the counter is a little girl, about ten years old. She is sticking labels into a book. She is concentrating hard on her task – her eyes screwed up with the effort. She looks up at me, her head barely above the high counter.

'Good afternoon,' she says.

'Hi,' I reply.

'Have a look…' She gesticulates towards the records on the

far wall.

'OK. Thanks...'

I walk over to the wall, and look at the hundreds of records in the racks in front of me. They are all in brown sleeves. They have numbers written in the corner of each sleeve, but no words. I pick up one of the sleeves and peek at the record inside. It is in three pieces.

I'm not sure why, but this alarms me terribly. I put it back gently and turn to the little girl. She is staring across at me, as if she has been watching me all the time.

'Are you looking for anything special?' she asks.

'Well, yes...' I begin, but the little girl puts a finger to her lips. I stop talking and just look at her.

'I'd better go get my dad,' she says. She walks out through an open door behind the counter.

As I wait I hear voices from the back of the shop - a man and a girl. They are sounding cross, concerned. I am starting to feel a bit panicky, so I try to breathe slowly – calm myself down. I walk to the front of the shop and look down at the counter. The girl's book is open – she is making a flower from different coloured square stickers. She has finished the pot and the stem, but not the flower itself. There are no petals.

I turn the pages, suppressing a feeling of guilt for even touching her book. Each page has a picture of a flower or tree, but each without petals or leaves - and then the first page, a rabbit: headless. But the rabbit is not headless, not exactly; it is unfinished - as if the head is yet to be added. I fold the book back to the page it was previously on, withdrawing my hand. My hand feels cold. I am afraid.

A man walks out from the door behind the counter. He has a yellow tea towel in his right hand, and his shirt sleeves are rolled up. He has been washing up.

'Good afternoon, miss,' he says with a slight smile. 'Are you wanting anything special? Are you looking for anything at all?'

'Yes. A friend of mine sent me. He gave me this address. I thought you might me able to help me,' I reply, trying to speak with some confidence.

'Oh?'

'Yes. He... I was looking for a song - a record.'

'We have lots.'

'Yes, but I'm not sure what it's called. It has some words in it. 'Please paint my heart...' Those are the words...'

'Right...'

'Do you know it?'

The little girl returns and stands beside her dad. He looks at me, and then leans across the counter towards me.

'And what would it be worth to me, if I did?' he asks - suggestion ripe in his voice.

My eyes open wide, and I stare back at him. Surely he can't mean... I gather my thoughts as he continues to look at me. There is something bizarre about the way he asks; something perverse. Surely he can't mean sex? Or money? Perhaps he just means money, that's all. After all, I would expect to pay. I glance at the little girl beside him – she is staring at me, impassive. I open my mouth to reply, but he continues:

'I'll tell you what it's worth to me - more of this...' His arm makes a sweep of the shop. 'More trouble, that's what it's worth to me – for me and my little girl. More trouble...'

He looks around him, and for a moment he seems almost bewildered, as if this is not his shop - as if he has found himself, suddenly, someplace else. Then he leans closer to me and whispers, his face now just inches from mine.

'Do you know where you are now?'

I feel confused, afraid - and I don't want to stay here any longer. 'Listen...' I start to say.

'No. You listen,' he says. 'I've got your record.'

He leans under the counter and pulls out a white paper bag. He passes it across to me. As I take it he holds my other hand, gently but firmly.

'It's yours,' he says. 'Please paint my heart with your love.

That's what it's called.'

'Thanks,' I say, almost involuntarily.

'You are most welcome,' he says. He points to the door. 'Goodbye, now.'

I am being asked to leave. The girl remains silent beside him, still staring; but now with tears in her eyes. I see them glistening with the reflection of the lights above, but these lights seem duller now, and I sense the dimness around me, the lights slowly, but mechanically, going out in the shop.

I say goodbye, quietly, and resisting the urge to run, I walk out of the shop without looking back. The air is warmer in the street than inside, and it is sweeter, fresher; more pleasant. And I am glad to leave – pleased to be out of that terrible place.

For that's what it is – a terrible place, truly dreadful.

But I have what I came for. I have the song.

* * * * * * * * * * * * * * * *

When I get back to the hotel, I feel shaken. I feel as though I've run a long way. Exhausted, I carefully place the record on the bedside cabinet, and lay down on the bed. For some reason, I am close to tears.

It has been a strange day, even by my standards. But the record shop wasn't just strange – it was frightening. I try to work out why – why it made me feel so uncomfortable. I was only there for a few minutes - probably ten minutes at the most. But even now, just thinking about it makes me feel cold.

I realise I do feel cold. I am shivering. I decide to have a bath.

* * * * * * * * * * * * * * * *

While I run the bath, I carefully take the record out of the white paper bag. The bag is screwed up – it has been used before. This record is in one piece, but it looks old and scratched. In the centre is a dark blue label, with gold printing. It says:

> *Please Paint My Heart with Your Love*
> *The Blue Lounge Summer Jazz Quartet*
> *Produced by Richard Sturrock*
> *Lyrics by Richard Sturrock*

I flip the record over. The same label is on the other side. I assume this means that there is only one song on the disc; my song. I will have to play it to check. I look at my watch. It's 5.15pm. I was considering going into the city centre this evening – look around for record shops, have something to eat. But that is out of the question now. I am totally wiped out. I put the record in the drawer of the bedside cabinet, and go into the bathroom.

* * * * * * * * * * * * * * * *

As I lay in the bath, I start to feel better. The hotel has supplied me with a small bottle of 'Alpine Forest' bubble bath. It smells a bit like aniseed, which is a smell I like. It is, in addition, very bubbly, which is also good. I try to read my book – 'The Five People you Meet in Heaven' by Mitch Albom – but I can't concentrate. I drop the book over the side of the bath and close my eyes.

Thoughts swirl around in my head: the men at the bus station; the estate agents; the waitress at the restaurant; the little girl in the shop. They pass before my eyes, almost in synchronisation. It is as if they are riding a merry-go-round, and I am standing at the side watching.

I begin to drift off to sleep. As I do, the procession picks up speed. The people start to move faster, to blur into one. As they move, round and round, faster and faster now, I can no longer tell where one person ends, and another begins.

* * * * * * * * * * * * * * * *

From the bus station, Ryan walked the five minutes to his home in Clonskeagh. He lived in a cottage, one of a group of twenty terraced cottages strung out along Beaver Row. Working class cottages, but slowly becoming chic.

He arrived home, and he was alone. He put the television on in the kitchen and switched on the kettle. He put out three mugs. He always enjoyed the sound they made as he put them down on the table, china on wood - clunk, clunk, clunk. It was a satisfying sound - the sound of routine.

While the kettle boiled, he looked out of the window onto the road. There was so much traffic now – bicycles fighting for room. Literally fighting - snarling at the greedy cars, like the bicycles in 'The Third Policeman' by Flann O'Brien. They were alive in that book - full of passion; Irish.

It was never like this – not in the past. It was quieter here. The roads were calmer. Not so many languages on the buses - just Gaelic and English. If Ryan had his way, it would be just Gaelic.

But he'd liked the girl at the bus station, who taken the time to play cards. She'd taken the time out of her day to spend twenty minutes playing cards with them. She was English, but he'd thought she was nice. She had a kind face, she was pretty. But now, everybody likes the English anyway. Now they're our friends, he thought – we're part of Europe now. Not Irish; European.

He remembered his father, drunken, shouting at him. 'Ireland is for the Irish, Ryan! It's the home of the Irish!' There was no place anymore for his father here, a republican until he died. No place for him now.

The English were buying the cottages, turning them into 'modern homes'; and waiting for the Irish in them to die. Next door, a 'For Sale' sign stood almost beside his front window – so close were the windows at the front to each other.

Last week, Mrs O'Neill had died - fallen off a chair changing a light bulb at the back of the house and broken her neck. She was seventy-three. Just days later, estate agents were crawling all over the house. Measuring, taking photos, writing things down. Now it's for sale, to be sold to people with no history here. No reason to be here.

There was a key in the door. It was not his wife, it was his lodger. She was foreign, but friendly. She was no trouble, and they needed the money. She smiled hello, but she looked sad. Ryan smiled back, and pointed to the kettle.

'Thank you, Ryan,' she said. 'Did you have good day?'

'Yes. I did. Did you – have a good day?'

'No – I did not today.'

Bianka explained that she had been turned down for the job she wanted, a job she had set her heart on. In Hungary, she had qualified from University as a technical engineer, but now she couldn't find a job. Not in Dublin. Instead, she was working in a restaurant, and she hated it.

'I do bad in interview,' she said. 'That is why. My English no good.'

'Your English is fine,' said Ryan.

'No – no good. Girl today, she tells me. She tells me – your English no good.'

'She was wrong. Your English is fine.'

Bianka knew he was wrong, and the girl was right. But she smiled back at him.

'You are kind. You are kind man. But my English improve. You will see. Then, I will be Technical Engineer.'

Ryan smiled back. He didn't really even know what a technical engineer was. She had explained it to him, but he had forgotten, or just wasn't listening. He felt sorry for her – alone here in this country. Ireland was a strange country – strange now even to him.

His wife would be home soon - married now for thirty years. Even with the scar, she didn't seem to mind. He'd had it for twenty years - most of his marriage. He had been drunk, came home from the pub and decided to light a fire. It was past midnight, and he was poking it to get it going. A black poker, with a diamond shaped tip. The room was getting hotter and hotter, but he kept on poking and putting on coal.

The heat had become overpowering; he felt sick, sleepy. His eyes were closing. He saw his friends, back at the pub. They were singing, and standing around him. Surrounded by smoke, they were drinking his health.

'You're a fine man, Ryan!' they said. They raised their glasses. 'You're a fine man!'

And then his wife was there, screaming at him, pulling him. He felt pain in his face, smelt burning in his nose. He was sick; then his wife – pouring water on his face. It was cold, and then hot again - and then nothing.

He was in hospital for two weeks. He had fallen asleep on the grate, and the poker had rested across his face. He was burnt, badly burnt, and it was his fault.

He felt sick again as he thought about it – looked at the same fireplace, the same grate. His wife had thrown out the poker.

His wife turned her key in the door and arrived home. She said 'hello' to Bianka and kissed her husband. He smiled at her and she patted his hand. She loved him, and he knew this. He loved her too, but he still felt he had brought shame on them. He couldn't give her children, this had just not happened, and he had scarred himself because he was drunk. People talked, behind their backs, even to her face. But it was so long ago now.

She remembered, every day, pulling his heavy, drunken body away from the fire. She remembered the effort and the heat. She had saved his life, and she was glad. Not just glad he had lived, but glad it had happened. This, she could never tell him. What kind of wife would tell her husband that?

But before, he was a drunkard. He spent his evenings in the pub, leaving her alone at home. They had so little money then – so much spent on drink. But afterwards, everything was different. He never drank again, he was always sober. He stayed at home with her, and they watched films and talked. She fell in love with him again, and she knew – she saw – that he did with her. What had happened was a wonderful thing, even if it seemed so terrible. So terrible, Ryan would not speak of it, even with her.

As they sat down to drink tea, Ryan remembered again the girl at the bus station. She had not looked at his scar. She had pretended not to notice. She was kind, and Ireland was full of so many kind people. The girl, his wife, their lodger - they were all kind. Mrs O'Neill next door, she was kind, before she died. Perhaps she is still kind now, he thought. But he did not know for sure.

He drank his tea in silence – he was happy in his home. He loved his wife – he was content. Suddenly, he felt sad for the girl, for Sandy – he remembered how she had talked about her coma. She had lost thirteen years of her life. That must be terrible. She was such a young girl as well, to be robbed of so much.

Then he remembered her face, why he couldn't bring himself to speak to her at first. He knew she would think it was because of his scar – but it wasn't. He remembered now why. It was because her face seemed so empty, as if her life had been drained away. He was good at reading faces, people always told him that; but hers was a face he couldn't read.

She had a pretty face, and she smiled a kind smile; but behind that, there was little to see. He took a sip of his tea. 'To be sure,' he thought. 'A coma is a terrible thing.'

Ryan thought he knew very little about the world; about people. But he knew a great deal.

Time Fifty-One

Saturday 1st July 2006

I have traveled all over the world; seen all kinds of places and met lots of strange people, but I hardly ever go on holiday.

By that, I mean that I rarely go away with someone I like - just to relax and spend some time together on a beach or something. But that's exactly what I did during Time Fifty-One. And the 'someone' that I went with was Chris.

I had got together with Chris this Time in the usual way (by pretending to faint) and, although I was still living at the hotel in Lancaster Gate, we were seeing more of each other than normal. By now, I felt completely comfortable with him, and this Time he seemed to respond by becoming relaxed with me very quickly.

Of course, I now knew all about him - the things that he liked and the things he hated. For example, I knew that he liked me to hold hands with him, especially when we were out together. I think this was simply because he felt close to me, and also because he was proud of me. So I held hands with him.

We held hands almost from the onset of our relationship, as I was already aware how much he liked it.

Because we were, this Time, very happy as a couple, I broached the idea of going on holiday with him over a cup of tea at the food hall in Bluewater.

'Oh? Where could we go?' he asked me, trying to be nonchalant, but his eyes betraying a trace of excitement at the prospect.

'I don't know. Where do you think?'

'Well... I'm not sure, really. I want to go, but I'm not sure how much I can afford to go anywhere. Studies have just finished, and I need to work...'

'I can pay...'

'Sandy, I don't want you...'

'Chris, I can pay. Just name somewhere.'

'Well...what about Scotland? Edinburgh? That's nice...'

'What about Hawaii?'

'Hawaii? That's not in Scotland!'

'Come on! What about Hawaii? It'll be fun!'

'Sandy, I can't afford to go to Hawaii! I can't afford the time off, I just can't afford to do it...'

I could tell in an instant that Chris was not making excuses or pretending he didn't want to go to save face. He was genuinely concerned about me spending all that money, and he was also concerned about his job. I leant across the table and kissed him on the lips, then I held his neck and kissed him again, stroking the side of his face with my left hand, a face I knew so well.

'Chris,' I whispered. 'I'll pay. Please come with me. Please let's go. We don't have to go to Hawaii, but let's go somewhere, together...'

I felt his face relax, and knew he had given in already.

'OK. Let's go together,' he said. 'But let's go somewhere less expensive. I need to have a say as well, about where we go.'

I smiled and nodded, still holding the back of his neck. Two weeks later, we left for Hawaii.

Time Fifty-One

Saturday 15th July 2006

Persuading Chris to go to Hawaii was, in itself, not that easy; but persuading him to go for a month was much harder. To Chris, who is actually quite conservative by nature, a holiday lasted for two weeks at the most.

He would often tell me about the holidays he had spent with his family at the seaside when he was a little boy - about how he would look forward to them for weeks, and about how he and his brother would play together on the beach for hours. He still had his bucket and spade from those times, safely on top of the wardrobe in his flat.

Chris took a few days to come around to the idea, and I had to make a few concessions and promises in order to ensure his agreement.

These are the concessions and promises I made:

1) That he could take his bucket and spade with him, so he could make sandcastles on Waikiki Beach.
2) That we could stop over in Los Angeles, allowing Chris to see Hollywood - something he had always wanted to do.
3) I made promises regarding all kinds of romantic activity, some of which were quite inventive; but most of which I assured him would not happen until we had reached Hawaii.
4) I promised to play 'Travel Scrabble' with him on the flight, a game he enjoys very much.

Bizarrely, it was the first point that created the most discussion. I couldn't understand why anyone over the age of ten would insist on taking a yellow plastic bucket and spade on a beach holiday, let alone on a trip to Hawaii.

For me, Waikiki Beach conjured up images of sunbathing, sitting on white sand drinking lemonade, and swimming effortlessly in a beautiful, crystal clear sea.

What it did not bring to mind was making rows of sandcastles in the shape of a medieval tower from a plastic mould with a handle on it. However - and this was my real issue - I could seriously imagine Chris doing that very thing. I could picture him surrounded by dozens of white sandcastles, standing proudly with his spade in his hand.

When I shared this image with him, and asked him if he was really serious, he replied that he was, and said that each sandcastle built would be a testament to the happiness of his childhood.

I had no answer to this.

Chris was also intrigued and seemed quite excited by the promises made in point three, although we both agreed that one of the things promised may not be physically possible. However, he seemed equally excited about the possibility of endless games of Travel Scrabble during the flight.

Sexual activity with Chris was never an effort; it was always enjoyable for us both. I made no real demands upon him, and he made very few upon me. But the thought of playing Travel Scrabble for hours seemed as if it would take more effort than I was physically, and mentally, able to give.

I could imagine myself staring at seven tiny squares, struggling to make any kind of word at all, while my English Literature student boyfriend would nonchalantly arrange his tiles into words worth more than forty points at a time. I would be bored and humiliated simultaneously.

When I broached the possibility of leaving the Scrabble in England, he just looked me in the eyes and said, 'you promised.'

It really was to avoid the Scrabble that I decided to travel first class. I knew that Chris would never agree to it (because of the expense), so I had to book the tickets electronically, and ensure that he would have no clue until we reached Heathrow Airport.

This was important, because Chris was reluctant for me to spend too much money on him. He felt guilty that he was unable to contribute financially to the holiday, and would have been upset if he felt I was going overboard with the spending. And going overboard I was, as the two return flights, first class, cost an incredible £18,541.80!

When I booked this on-line, at my hotel, I stared at the screen in disbelief for at least a full minute. My hand actually trembled as I confirmed the flights by clicking on the red button marked 'confirm', even though I knew, so to speak, I'd get the money back next Time.

However, first class travel, on American Airlines, meant having a seat that turned into a bed. In fact, it was a seat that reclined flat, but with a pillow and a blanket - it was as good as a bed. Therefore, it was possible to fly from London to Los Angeles (eleven hours overnight) and just sleep the whole way. This seemed like that perfect solution to the Travel Scrabble problem - eighteen-thousand pounds to avoid a game of Travel Scrabble. It was a small price to pay.

* * * * * * * * * * * * * * * *

We arrived at the airport at tea time; but our flight was not until 9pm that evening. We went and had tea in one of the many cafés before making our way to the check-in desk. Chris dropped a piece of toast while we were eating, and it landed butter side up. He took this as a good omen for our holiday.

We arrived at check-in about 6.15pm, and it was already very crowded, dealing with three separate flights - one of which was ours - and another a flight to Chicago which was leaving in just over an hour.

A few of the staff were trying, seemingly in vain, to separate the Chicago passengers from the rest. Actually, they were doing this successfully - but chaotically. Chris was wheeling the trolley forward, ready to join the mêlée, when I took hold of his elbow.

'This way,' I said with a little smile. 'We're first class.'

The first class check-in desk stood alone at one end of a large row. Beside it a small queue of people waited to check-in as business class passengers, but the desk for which we were now aiming had no queue at all.

A smartly dressed, uniformed girl sat behind the desk, staring into space. As we approached, her face sprang to life and broke into a welcoming smile. The way this happened unnerved me a little, and made her seem a bit like a robot.

'Hi! How are you all doing? Which flight are you on today?' She said, with a broad American accent. She spoke in both a friendly and professional tone.

'We're fine,' I said, smiling back. 'We're on the flight to LA.'

I passed across the printed e-mail confirmation and my passport, as Chris dug out his passport from his bag. She ignored the confirmation and typed my name into the screen in front of her.

'Excellent. Thank you, Ms Glover. And can I see your passport please, Mr. Carrey?'

Chris dutifully handed over his passport, and she tapped a couple more keys on the screen. There was no keyboard.

'Thank you, sir. You don't have pre-reserved seats, I notice; but there are only two other people in first class this evening. There are twelve seats in total; would you like to choose now?'

She swiveled the screen around so we could view a seat plan of first class. Two seats at the front were marked in red - reserved - but the rest were blue. I looked across at Chris, nodding to him to make the decision. He chose the two seats in the opposite row at the back.

The girl smiled and handed us our tickets. 'That's a good choice, Mr. Carrey. You will have some privacy...'

As we walked away from the check-in desk, freed from our luggage, I braced myself for reaction.

'First class?' said Chris, turning to face me.

'Why not?' I replied. 'We have beds. It'll be more comfy. We can sleep...'

'Yes, but, how much...'

'Chris,' I began, holding his hands. 'I have money. I have quite a bit of money - you know that, don't you?'

'Yeah, I suppose...'

'I can afford this...We can afford this. It'll be nice to be able to sleep through the flight. If I can lie flat, then I know I'll be able to sleep. Then we can make the most of tomorrow...'

'Yeah - it'll be fun going first class, but...'

I leant across and gave him a kiss.

'Come on,' I said 'Let's go to the first class lounge. We can get free food.'

* * * * * * * * * * * * * * * *

The flight took off twenty minutes late at 9.20pm. We were served dinner just fifteen minutes later, with china plates and silver cutlery. It was the best airline food I've ever tasted. We had two cabin staff serving in first class, and there were only four of us passengers in total.

The other couple were Matt and Sheila; Matt ran a business in California making and selling microchips. His wife, Sheila, was his business partner. They were both a bit perplexed when we said we were students, but they let it pass.

We chatted only briefly; they had walked back after dinner to say hello, and to say that they would be reading for an hour or so, and then 'turning in'. They hoped that we wouldn't mind if they kept their lights on for a while. We told them that we didn't mind at all, and that we would probably go to sleep when they did.

They thanked us for our flexibility - we were new to the first class game.

Chris played about with the in-flight entertainment for a short while, and then we talked about our plans for the holiday. We were going to Los Angeles for two days - enough time to see Hollywood and Venice Beach - and then heading off to Hawaii. Our return flight was booked for 19th August, at 1.30pm. This was deliberate, because I would pass out of this Time at 1.12am Hawaiian local time (11.12am Greenwich Mean Time) on 19th August, meaning I would not have to make the flight home.

Therefore, our holiday was actually thirty-six days in length. I again had to talk Chris into the extra few days, but as we were going for a month anyway, a few more days seemed neither here nor there. But, for me, it was a really nice way to end a Time, and I only had to fly one way.

I had no trouble sleeping on the flight at all. I was vaguely aware that Chris was awake sometimes, next to me, but his fidgeting just played around at the edges of my dreams.

I dreamt that I was riding on the back of a big whale; the whale was cross with me because I hadn't paid for my ride.

'I'm not a charity, you know…' It said, and blew water out of its spout by way of reproach.

I think the turbulence of the flight contributed to the dream, and eventually woke me up. Chris was sound asleep beside me, his foot hanging off the end of the reclining seat. I lifted his foot gently back on to the seat and looked at my watch. Still on British time, it told me the time was 6.55am. We were almost there, and I'd slept for nearly eight hours. Not only that, but Travel Scrabble had not even been mentioned, let alone played.

* * * * * * * * * * * * * * * * *

Chris woke shortly after me; he had lain awake for some of the night, but had slept - by his estimation - for about six hours. We were served a delicious breakfast, and we both felt completely wide awake when we landed in LA, 12.20am local time.

This had been a miscalculation on my part.

However, by the time we had cleared customs, collected our bags, hired our car and driven out to Santa Monica where our hotel was - after getting lost no fewer than three times, once totally - it was almost 4am.

We unpacked enough stuff for two days, lay and rested on the bed for a couple of hours, and then set off to have breakfast - the second in eight hours - in the hotel restaurant.

The hotel restaurant was actually adjacent to the hotel - leaning against the left side - and served traffic both from the street and the hotel itself. We were one of few tables occupied at 6.44am, and we had a breakfast of tea, toast and pancakes, planning the two days of our stopover together; boyfriend and girlfriend, in Los Angeles, on holiday.

* * * * * * * * * * * * * * * * *

We drove out to Hollywood that same morning, with a view to returning to Santa Monica for 'a go on the rollercoaster' on the pier that evening. We parked the car on a meter on Sunset Boulevard - the street of dreams that featured in so many songs and films.

It actually was a bit rough - in fact, it was very rough, and I felt slightly nervous about leaving the car parked there. Chris, however, was in awe of it all, and he strode along taking photos of anything and everything; including a Chinese drycleaners.

As we walked further along the street, things became slowly more 'touristy', and we soon found ourselves amongst an array of little shops selling various souvenirs. We bought a 'Map of the Stars' Homes' for three dollars, which also included a plan of our current location. Using this as our guide, we walked for a further two minutes, turned right up Highland Avenue, and then, turning left onto Hollywood Boulevard, we came to The Chinese Theatre.

This is where all the hand and footprints are, pressed into the cement on the pavement by countless celebrities. This was the main attraction, as far as Chris was concerned, as he had read a book once which had described it all in detail. The description, told through the eyes of a child during a time of depression, inspired Chris to want to see it for himself.

We wandered amongst the footprints for some time - I tried in vain to recognise most of the names; scrawled in the wet cement with celebrity fingers from the past. After a while, I sat down on a low wall while Chris continued his inspection. I drank from a small bottle of water and just watched; people studied the grey flat stones, set in the pavement, almost as if they were graves.

There was a sense of reverence. People pointed and chatted about the various celebrities - their names and dates staring back at them. Some dated back over fifty, sixty, even seventy years; so in some cases these truly were a memorial to those that had since died.

I took a sip of my water. I was alive; but this - these tiny monuments - was all that remained of so many people. These stones held more of them than was actually left; the fingers that wrote, the hands and feet that pressed with pride into the cement - all wasted to nothing. The skin and muscle and blood just liquid in the soil; they had dissolved into time and space and emptiness.

I felt I was sitting in a garden of remembrance, these names crying out to be spoken again; to not be forgotten forever. But it seemed, as I sat alone for a few minutes, that this was the destiny for all people. To leave behind inadequate reminders of what they had once been, of what they had achieved, of what they had meant to others. It seemed a terrible, empty destiny; full of waste and grey and futility.

But I was alive. I was alive. I could outlive all of these stones. They would turn to dust and be forever gone, but I would not. In my own way, a way forced upon me, I would be alive for all time. Perhaps not in the normal sense, the expected passage of time passing me by, but I would be conscious, able to feel, able to drink bottled water. I would not become just stone; not just an inadequate reminder.

Even Chris, he would always be here with me, always twenty-nine years old, always in love with me. I looked up to the sky - it was a cloudless day - and tried to understand the vastness of it all. It stretched out above me as if forever, but yet it was finite - it went round the earth once, and then began again.

I was like the sky, I thought - vast and astonishing, always able to feel and to love; to be loved. I was unique; amazing. I was not a freak, a mistake. I was something special; something to be treasured. They should take my handprints, I thought. They should ask me to press my hands into this cement. I am a celebrity. I should be in a museum; preserved for ever, because I am so important.

And then I understood. I am preserved, and perhaps that is because I am significant. I so often feel worthless, but maybe that is not real. Perhaps my importance is what is real. Perhaps I just needed to understand that; to accept it, and everything would be fine.

Chris was suddenly beside me. He was sitting, touching my hand, asking if I was ready to go.

'Ready to go where?' I asked. I was puzzled, as if his question could have no answer.

'Let's go and get the car, and drive to Beverly Hills,' he

replied.

We both stood up together, and I instinctively took his hand. Beverly Hills seemed as good a place as any to go, and we started back the way we had come. The sky above Chris was the same as above me; we walked beneath it together. It belonged not to one of us, but to us both.

* * * * * * * * * * * * * * * * *

That evening, we rode the rollercoaster on Santa Monica Pier. I closed my eyes and felt my body rattle round the track. It was as though I was attached in some way - held on by a force stronger than I could ever be. Chris was sitting right next to me; being pushed against me by the swing and sway of the car as it moved along.

I opened my eyes and smiled at him - shuffled closer to him so our bodies were pressed together. We held hands and continued around the track, faster, then slower; but always round and round.

I remember thinking; perhaps this is how things should be. I squeezed Chris's hand tightly. Perhaps this was, after all, an acceptable way to live.

* * * * * * * * * * * * * * * * *

But that night, lying in bed, I found that I couldn't sleep. Chris was lying beside me - snoring gently into his pillow. I reached across and touched his hair, pulling at a few strands and holding them between my fingers. He let out a strange mumbling noise, so I let go, afraid I would wake him up.

We had had a great day, and we were exhausted. However, tired as I was, I couldn't get to that point where I would drift off to sleep. I was bothered by something, and I couldn't focus on what it was. I slipped quietly out of bed and walked to the window of our room. We were in a hotel facing the beach, and when I strained my eyes I could make out the outline of the rollercoaster on the pier; it was almost swallowed in darkness.

The rollercoaster had been fun, going round and round with Chris at my side. I was safe in the car, held in by the force of nature. It was like with my life - I am attached to the things around me by a certainty that goes beyond the simplicity of life and death.

These thoughts made me feel happy, but one thing I didn't like; not at all. I realised this while staring out at the shadow of the rollercoaster, and knew that this was the reason that I couldn't sleep.

I had enjoyed the ride that evening very much, but it was essential that I was able to get off. To go round for ever means it is no longer a ride; it is something else. What that something else was I couldn't think, but it was not just a ride, not just an attraction for me to enjoy and be a bit scared.

As I continued to stare out at the pier, the rollercoaster became a symbol of my life. Its darkness appeared hollow; monstrous. It was an absence of something - a dark space into which I was falling. It made me shiver all over; I was naked, and I felt suddenly cold.

I climbed back into bed, pulling the quilt over me. I still felt cold, and the quilt and the heat of the night did not help.

* * * * * * * * * * * * * * * *

That night was the first time I truly realised that my life was a prison. I had thought about it in many different ways before, and throughout most of that day I had felt very positive about everything. But it was as if, that night, I was overwhelmed with the reality of my situation.

I was falling; falling forever into nothing. I loved Chris now, but one day he would be nothing to me. He could die, and I would feel nothing. I could kill him, and I would feel the same.

Time would chip away at everything; at meaning itself, and finally at my sanity. I would search Time after Time for things with meaning, things that would stimulate me, create interest or raise emotions in me. And eventually, one Time, I would fail. I would be left with nothing. But onward I would fall, relentlessly and blindly tumbling into a darkness that would swallow everything about me, leaving me totally empty.

I would be completely lost; helpless, and without any hope. I saw that clearly for the first time. That was my future.

Over the next few nights, like that first night in Santa Monica, this realisation did not help me sleep any better.

Time Fifty-One

Tuesday 18th July 2006

Our first day in Hawaii was wonderful. We walked down to Waikiki Beach early in the morning, around 8.30am, and lay our towels down on the fine white sand. Chris helped me cover my pale skin in factor 35 sun block, as suggested to me by the local lady who had served us breakfast at the hotel. She had looked at my auburn hair and slightly freckled skin almost in dismay, and raised her index finger to me by way of emphasis.

'Oh! You must be careful! Careful you no burn! You very pale, and you one Malihini! You must buy plenty of lotion. Rub, rub, and rub!'

She rubbed her own face and arms to further explain her meaning.

'Sun here is very hot,' she continued. 'Where you come from?'

'England,' replied Chris.

'Ah! Dis no England,' she said. 'Dis Whyee.'

With that she turned and left, everything explained to her satisfaction.

* * * * * * * * * * * * * * * *

Waikiki Beach was absolutely beautiful. It was, admittedly, very commercial - but if the hotels and parasols were to disappear, it would be truly picturesque. The sand was white and the sea was absolutely clear - exactly, I felt, how a beach should be.

Chris had, I discovered, failed to pack his bucket and spade after all. When I teased him about it, he threatened to go and buy another in one of the many 'seaside' shops nearby. But he didn't, explaining that the sand was too fine for a good quality sandcastle.

Instead, we sat on the beach reading and talking. I was reading 'Birdsong', a book that engrossed me, and as I sat reading I was aware of the incongruity of the descriptions of World War One trenches and the scene I met each time I looked up. Between chapters, Chris rubbed lotion into my back and kissed my neck. We paddled in the warm sea and, during the afternoon, floated out a little way on pink and blue inflatable rafts that we had bought after lunch.

We had dinner in a pizza restaurant, and there we made plans to hire a car and visit the many places that interested us that were dotted around the island. We had a month together in Hawaii, and we both wanted to make the best of the days and weeks ahead. It seemed, even to me, like a really long time, and I was committed to making it a holiday we would both enjoy. I was determined, at least, to have some good memories to take with me to the next Time.

So far (although we had only been here a day), Chris had failed to mention the possibility of him 'cashing in' on some of the more sexually interesting promises I had made before leaving England; made in order to entice him half the way around the world.

When I leant across the table and, in a low whisper, reminded him of one or two of the promises made, his face became serious for a few seconds. I thought he was teasing me, so I smiled at him and raised my eyebrows in a suggestive manor.

But he reached over to me and held my hands; then began stroking my knuckles with the tips of his fingers.

'Sandy,' he said, fixing me in a gaze. 'I just want you. I don't need you to be anything else; to be a kind of fantasy. You already are. I just want you exactly as you are now.'

I felt a lump in my throat, and tears forming in my eyes. I was not embarrassed for him to see me cry; or for him to see the effect his words could have upon me. I placed the palm of his right hand on my face and let him feel the tears as they ran down my cheek.

As we walked back to our hotel that evening, I held Chris to me as if he was an attachment I needed to survive - like an oxygen tank. We cuddled our way along the seafront, in the company of hundreds of other couples wandering in both directions. Some were on honeymoons, some married for years. Others had perhaps only met here, maybe just a few days ago.

I didn't know anything about them, and I didn't care. I only cared about Chris. I still held on to him, pressing my face against his shoulder and chest, trying to store this closeness up for the Times to come. I was trying to vaccinate myself now - protect myself against an empty, hopeless future; a future where I may no longer care.

Back in our room, we made love for the first time since reaching Hawaii. The promises I had made were put to one side that evening, and I just lay on my back, whispering my love in his ear, and stroking his shoulders and arms with my fingers.

* * * * * * * * * * * * * * * *

We hired our car the following morning from a rental company just a short walk from the hotel. They stored all their cars in an underground car park, and the friendly staff gave us the choice of four different cars, as we were hiring for three weeks.

In the end we chose the smallest one, as there were only two of us. It looked almost new, and had only two thousand miles on the clock. I liked it because it was red, and Chris liked it because it had a compass stuck to the dashboard.

'Could be useful,' he said, both to me and the girl who was showing us around. Neither of us could think why.

Chris was keen to see Pearl Harbour, so we decided to drive out there straight away. It was only 10am, and the journey, we guessed from the map, would be less than an hour. This gave us time to have a look around before having a late lunch somewhere nearby.

Chris, who had been reluctant at first and a bit hesitant right up to the day we left, had thrown himself wholeheartedly into the holiday. He was like a child with a new bike - everything was fantastic and he was just excited to be here. This enthusiasm quickly rubbed off on me, and the month that stretched ahead of us seemed like a very long time indeed. Like him, I had become determined to make the most of it.

* * * * * * * * * * * * * * * *

I can't drive. This is because I would have to apply for, and then spend about three out of every five months waiting for a date for my driving test, only to see my license vanish at the end of each Time. Therefore, I always explain to Chris that I am unable to drive; and he is always ready and willing to ferry me about in his Vauxhall Corsa.

Hawaii was no exception (minus the Corsa), and we set off for Pearl Harbour with me firmly planted in the passenger seat of our hire car, and Chris at the wheel.

Chris is a very good driver, and he is considerate to other road users. At least, he is when I am in the car. However, driving on the 'wrong side' of the road seemed to throw his driving skills a little awry, especially when approaching a junction. He tended to wobble about a bit when turning left, which made me feel nervous at first.

However, he improved throughout the length of our journey, and by the time we reached Pearl Harbour, he seemed to have got the hang of it.

We parked in a large car park directly in front of the entrance - there were already two coaches parked; one of them disgorging tourists with cameras at the ready. We slipped in front of them while they were still milling about, and entered by the visitors' centre.

We were given a ticket each (which were free), that entitled us to a short film about the attack, and a trip out to see the sunken wreckage of the USS Arizona - the ship which saw the greatest loss of life. In fact, the first thing we learnt was that Pearl Harbour was actually called the 'USS Arizona National Memorial' - and it had been designated a national park.

The film was very interesting. The miniature cinema was quite cold, and I had to snuggle up to Chris to keep warm. I was wearing green shorts and a navy blue top, ideally suited for Hawaii in July, but not for Hawaii's over-zealous air conditioning.

The film told the story of the Japanese attack on Pearl Harbour, and how the assault was considered by the US Navy to be a cowardly act. The day of the attack, December 7th, 1941, became known as 'The Day of Infamy'. All this we learnt from the film.

After we left the cinema, we waited to join a group of people who would be boarding a small launch, which would take us out to the site where the USS Arizona sank. As we waited, Chris and I chatted and ate sweets that we had bought in the shop. We leant on the rail looking out across the harbour; the sun was shimmering like gold on the surface of the water, and it was hard to imagine scenes like we had seen on the film ever happening here.

It was easy to see the large memorial floating as we looked out across the water, and knowing it was a memorial made it clear that something important was beneath it. The breeze was blowing off the harbour in short bursts, each one cooling my skin for a few seconds, before the sun regained its grip. I wondered how cold it must be down at the bottom of the water.

For a moment, I imagined myself there, beneath the clear water looking up at the sun. The sun would be shining so brightly, but never reaching me with its warmth. Only its light would ever penetrate - and while those who moved about above me, on the surface, were able to feel its fullness, I would always be cold. I would be forever cold in a place that is always warm.

Just as the launch arrived, I noticed a Japanese man standing a little way along from me, holding a video camera in one hand. He was facing away from the harbour, towards the visitors' centre. Maybe it was because I was now part of a group, waiting for the launch, that made him seem separated - but he seemed isolated; lost.

As we started to board the launch, he looked across in our direction, and then placed a hand over his eyes to shield them from the sun. He had no sunglasses, but instead he was wearing a blue baseball cap with a red letter C on the front. He was, at first, leaning on the rail, his right hand blocking out the sun from his face. But then he suddenly stood up straight, as if to attention, and when he took his hand away, it seemed as though he was looking right at me.

The way he stood upright, almost in military fashion, made me think that perhaps the setting had some special meaning for him. He looked about fifty years old, and I wondered if maybe his father or a relative had fought here during the war.

All of this I thought as he continued to stare at me. He was only about sixty feet away, and as I boarded the launch holding Chris's hand, he opened his mouth as if to say something. I fully expected him to call out to me - to make some comment in my direction, but instead his mouth remained open in the shape of an 'O'. His face contorted into a sudden but unmistakable look of surprise, and he brought up his right hand to cover his mouth.

As the launch headed out to the Arizona, he remained rooted to the spot, speechless - his hand over his open mouth, his eyes following me as I moved further and further from his view.

* * * * * * * * * * * * * * * *

As we stared down though the Perspex on the floor of the memorial - down to the wreck of the ship below - I wondered if I should mention the Japanese man to Chris. Looking back to shore, I could no longer tell if he was still there, and I began to think that maybe I had imagined it - his look; or if perhaps he was looking at someone else.

After all, it seemed impossible that he should recognise me. And if he had, or thought that he had, it must surely be a case of mistaken identity.

Suddenly I had my answer. That was it - he had thought I was someone else; someone he least expected to see here in Hawaii. Perhaps I looked like a lover from the past, or maybe just a friend from Japan.

I decided not to mention him to Chris. I told myself that this was because it was a pointless story. It was like saying 'I saw a man who I don't know looking at me because he thought I was someone else'. I said this to myself, in my mind, and it sounded a bit silly.

So instead I used the thirty minutes we spent on the floating monument reading the information they had provided and looking down beneath the gentle waves. The water was mixed with oil, still seeping from the wreckage. It clung to the surface and the sun shone brightly upon it; making the colours light up and dance as if in celebration.

* * * * * * * * * * * * * * * *

The month we spent together in Hawaii is amongst some of my fondest memories. It would take too long to list all the things we did, and in truth I can remember only a small amount of them.

As with every Time, memories escape me and become more confused as each Time becomes more distant from the most recent. I have developed a system; I suppose it's a discipline, which enables me to remember as much as I can for the future, whatever that may be.

I spend many hours during each Time writing down notes about the Times I have spent previously. I, of course, know that these notes will be lost to me on each 19th August - but the very act of writing them helps to consolidate what I remember in my mind. In this way, I have remembered many things that I'm sure I would have forgotten.

Some Times are an exception to this and, no matter how hard I try, I cannot bring back what happened. It's as if my memory has a blank space in it, and it makes me sad to think of all that I've forgotten.

Time Nine is one such Time, as is Time Twenty-Four. I can remember virtually nothing that happened in either of those Times - I only have the vaguest memories of what I did, but there is no detail at all.

I only remember one thing that happened in Time Thirty-Two, and that was getting my finger caught in a revolving door at a department store in South London. I think it is the pain (and it really did hurt) that helps me remember, but there is nothing else from that whole Time that I can recall. It is just a blur; a vague impression.

Many of the days I spent in Hawaii are like this; blurred and out of focus. But I remember how I felt; the closeness I felt to Chris, the happiness for just being there.

I can remember the lovely weather, the beautiful beaches and the high waves. Once, we swam out to a rock near a beach at a place called Chinaman's Hat, and sat for ages watching small fish swim around beneath us. They had little yellow tails, and it was as if there were thousands of them. Perhaps there were.

We visited a Japanese garden, where we spent a peaceful

afternoon; and I fell asleep under a tree while Chris was trying to take photos of a large white butterfly.

I have many other memories as well, which have merged into one. Memories of times spent lying on beaches, swimming in warm seas, eating fruit for breakfast and making love in our hotel room.

We had a small balcony, which looked across to Waikiki Beach. Some evenings we would sit together there, reading or talking about nothing. In all the Times I have spent with Chris, and there have been many, I have never known him so happy, so content.

But Chris is usually happy, and I think he is happy, in part, because of me. We are meant to be together, and this holiday made me certain of it. Chris makes me happy, and I do the same for him.

But happiness is not enough, not in itself. We have no time, no future. And I resolved to myself, during the last week on Hawaii, that I would try to put that right; that I would do everything I could to escape.

* * * * * * * * * * * * * * * * *

For the first time I became absolutely certain that I wanted it all to end; to just grow old and die with Chris. My days in Los Angeles, with the rollercoaster, had given me a glimpse of the darkness, the madness that awaited me in the future. This terrified me, and spending this happy month with Chris made me realise that he meant more to me than I ever knew before. Those two things made me sure that I could not continue living as I did; that someone must know how to help me, how to give me back my life. That somewhere on this planet there had to be a way out.

And Hawaii seemed so far away, so far from anywhere else, that perhaps this was the place. Surrounded by so much sea, so isolated, it would be easy to be forgotten. Maybe, this Time, they would just forget me. Whoever they are, maybe they would just forget me.

* * * * * * * * * * * * * * * *

But of course they didn't. And the night before I left I had the cruelest dream. I dreamt that Chris and I had discovered an island - a tiny island off the coast of Oahu, not far from our hotel. And if I lived on this island, I would be free.

In my dream, I explained to Chris all that had happened, and why I needed to live on this island. I pointed to it from the balcony of our hotel. Chris told me that he would live there with me; that he knew all about what I'd been through, and that he believed and loved me.

We stood on the balcony looking at our future home. It was beautiful and had everything we needed to live a wonderful life. We would get married, have babies together; a family. Our children would play with the other children on the island - they would paddle in the sea and chase each other along the beach. We would teach them to make sandcastles, and sing to them and play games.

Perhaps Jack would be there, I thought. I asked Chris, and he told me that Jack had been there all along, just waiting for us to arrive and live with him. He was happy there; had always been happy, and he just wanted his mummy to come and make everything complete.

It all made sense; everything had happened for a reason. Everything had led me to this place, to Chris, to the island, to Jack.

The dream was a culmination of all that had happened that month - the happiness I had felt had imprinted itself upon me in some way that is more than a mere memory.

I lay there, smiling to myself, and tears rolled down my face as I slept.

I woke during the dream - standing on the balcony, holding Chris - and it took me almost a minute to realise that I was in bed; it had seemed so real. I sat up and wiped my eyes with the quilt, and looking around realised that I had just been dreaming.

I felt sick with disappointment, and I climbed out of bed and walked onto the balcony. The sun was already in the sky, and people were heading to the beach - towels and bags in hand. But there was no island.

And then I knew the date. It was August 18th - our last day.

* * * * * * * * * * * * * * * *

The dream had shaken me more than I realised, and I felt sick and faint all through breakfast. I didn't want our last day to end on a low, so I tried to act as normal as I could and think the sick feelings away.

In fact, although I felt preoccupied much of the time, we had a really nice last day. We visited an aquarium in the morning, where Chris succeeded in tickling a fish in an open tank - a task he had bet himself he couldn't do. The 'fish-tickling' incident was frowned upon by a stocky member of the aquarium staff, who had spotted Chris at the last moment with his hand in the tank. When challenged, Chris apologised profusely, but could offer no valid explanation for his actions. We both sidled off together looking remorseful, but spent the next half an hour laughing stupidly about it - always fearful of again meeting the same member of staff.

We had a lovely afternoon paddling in the sea and sitting on Waikiki Beach enjoying the sun, and that evening we went back to the hotel to pack. This I did half-heartedly, as I knew that this night I would be gone; I would never make the flight.

* * * * * * * * * * * * * * * *

I had never slept through being taken before, never slept through the moment of leaving, and I was determined to do so this Time. Chris switched off the light at midnight, just over an hour before the end of the Time. Hawaii is ten hours behind London, so 1.12am here would be 11.12am in England - the time of my departure.

I lay awake for what seemed like ages, and became convinced that I would be awake when it happened. I said goodbye to Chris in a whisper - so quiet that he could never hear. I was really sad that our Time together was over, and that it was ending like this - that it had to end at all.

But just when I thought I would never sleep, soon after checking my watch and discovering that it was 12.28am, I drifted off. I remember being vaguely aware of Chris moving in the bed, but I was too tired to move myself. Then I was asleep.

The next thing I knew, something, someone, was on top of me. I woke with a start; terrified. It was so dark that I couldn't see. I tried to cry out, but someone was holding something over my mouth. I could hear breathing beside me, above me - it was Chris's breathing - and he, they, were forcing something down my throat.

I was choking, pressed down into the bed; my eyes wide open, bulging. Then they hit me, with such force I felt I was knocked off the bed and onto the floor. I felt such pain; such fear, someone holding me down; Chris there, either helping or helpless, and then nothing.

Of course I was confused, and leaving the Time in the usual, terrible way, became mixed with the strangeness of sleep. But this was the first, and the last Time, that I have been taken while asleep. Needless to say, I have always stayed awake since.

Apart from when I was murdered, of course, but I don't remember anything about that. You don't remember things when you're dead.

This is another dream I have.

I'm on a train – it has slamming doors and large, armchair-like seats. I am sitting on one of the seats, and Jack is sitting beside me. We are drinking orange juice from a carton, each taking a turn. Jack gets up and stands on the seat next to me to look out of the window. He points and says 'Mummy, look at all the people'.

I look out beside him and see people standing in a row – they are spaced apart and are waving up at us – waving at the train; waving at me and at Jack. They are all standing in a field, full of corn stalks. Jack grins at me and waves back furiously.

I smile at him, encouraging him to go on waving. But as I look back out of the window, look at the people, I realise something is wrong. I stare hard at the faces – they are waving, but not smiling. And I see the clothes they are wearing, a kind of uniform; ragged, dirty, prison camp clothes. I look beyond them, and see people in the distance, further behind. There are just a few of them, and they have rifles, the barrels glinting in the sun.

Silently, one of the people in the long row falls, as if they had simply fainted, then another, and another. Jack has stopped waving, and is staring out at the scene. It is terrible, macabre. I take his hand.

'Jack, come away from the window!' My voice is full of fear.

Jack just continues to watch, so I reach across to pull him onto my lap. But he doesn't move – it's as if he is made of stone. He has become too heavy.

As I tug him towards me, I realise that they have seen him; the men with the guns, they have seen him looking out of the window, waving. I know they will come for him and take him away – that he will have to join the row of people.

In my panic, I pull with every fibre in my body, and he tumbles backwards into my lap, as if we had been playing a game. He looks up and me and smiles.

'Can I have more orange juice?' He says.

I can barely speak, I am so scared. I can hear them now, voices on the train, pushing their way along the corridor – towards us; towards Jack.

'Jack...' I start to say, but I cannot say any more.

'Never mind, Mummy,' he says, looking up at me. 'But it's your fault. You let me look out of the window.'

I have no reply; I just stare into his eyes, barely seeing through the tears. He smiles at me, and as the door to the carriage crashes open, he says, 'You didn't look after me properly'.

I don't have this dream very often. But this dream is the worst of all.

Time Ninety-Six

Thursday 25th May 2006

It's 5.15am, and I'm being sick in the bathroom. This is because I've just had the dream about the train, and that always makes me sick. I hate that dream more than any other, because in the dream Jack blames me for what happened. But it's not my fault.

* * * * * * * * * * * * * * * *

A few minutes later, I'm lying back on the bed, staring up at the ceiling. I feel better now, having been sick, and the dream is starting to fade. I have this dream about once every four or five months, which means that I have it about once every Time.
   As the dream fades, my thoughts are instead filled with my mission. I have found out who wrote the song - it was Richard Sturrock. Now I need to find him. I still feel tired, but I decide to get up.

I have become convinced, over the last few hours, that Richard Sturrock has information that can help me. He must have written and recorded the song, and somehow put it in my head as a message. That's what I think. I don't now how he did this, or even what it means, but I'm convinced that it means something. I just need to discover what that something is.
   I consider how I can best go about it, how I can find Richard Sturrock. I think about what I need to do.

These are the things I need to do:

   1) Play the record - perhaps the song itself holds a clue.

2) Find out where Richard Sturrock lives.
3) Go and see him, and ask him about the song.

I decide that this is a good sequence of events - and so this is the order I'll follow. Firstly, I'll play the record. In order to achieve this, I just need a record player. I think for a few more minutes, and decide upon a course of action. I decide to ask at the hotel where I can go to buy a record player, and then I'll simply go and buy one, and bring it back to my room. That way, I don't have to take the record around Dublin with me, and run the risk of it being broken or lost.

This course of action seems so simple, after so much that has seemed so difficult, that I start to feel more positive. While I am still certain that I'm depressed, I also feel as though I am getting somewhere. I am making some progress, and this feels good.

* * * * * * * * * * * * * * * *

The hotel receptionists are very helpful, and they go out of their way to help me locate a shop selling record players. If I'd wanted a CD player, or an mp3 player, that would have been easy. But record players are becoming a thing of the past, and therefore a bit of a niche market. I wonder, for a moment, what happened to my vast collection of singles?

After a few phone calls, we find a small shop quite nearby that sells all kinds of musical equipment, including four different models of record player. They call me a taxi, and minutes later I'm on my way.

Everything goes to plan until I arrive at the shop, which is closed. I only realise this as the taxi drives off into the distance. I look at my watch - it is 9.10am. I look back at the door, looking for a sign which tells me what time they open. There is no such sign.

It is a small shop, one among a parade of five shops facing

out onto a busy road. The parade consists of a greengrocer's shop, a cobbler, a butcher, and the record shop. These are all closed. However, there is also a newspaper shop, which is open.

I walk into the shop, and am surprised to find it both crowded with people and seemingly smaller on the inside than it appears from the front. It is crammed full of boxes of crisps and jars of sweets, as well as stacks of magazines and newspapers. I pick up a copy of 'OK Magazine', and a packet of cheese and onion crisps. Getting hold of the crisps is more difficult than I first thought it would be, as I have to negotiate my arm around a man wearing overalls and between two women standing side by side. I press my hand into the box behind them, and blindly grasp hold of a packet of crisps. I pull it towards me as carefully as possible, but as I do I hear the unmistakable sound of crisps being crushed. By time the bag is in view, having passed between and dangerously close to the combined buttocks of the two women, I feel sure that only a few crisps have survived intact. There are some things that can be repaired, but a crisp is not one of them.

I wait my turn in a slow-moving queue of people. To describe it as a queue is in fact misleading; it is more of a mêlée. The man behind the counter, a small man in his fifties, methodically takes money and places things into paper bags. Eventually, it is my turn.

He takes my flattened crisp bag and magazine, and without comment taps buttons on the till. He then looks at me. I stare back stupidly. He points to the display on the till. It tells me I owe him three euros and twenty cents. I fish about in my purse and retrieve a twenty euro note. He looks at it disdainfully.

'Do you have any smaller?' He says.

'Oh, yes - wait a minute…' I fumble about and find a five euro note.

'That'll be grand,' he says, and takes the note from me. I wait while he removes my change from the till. As he passes the coins to me I smile.

'Do you know what time the shop opens along the way?' I ask. 'The one selling record players...'

He passes the change to me. 'Well now, that depends.'

'On what?' I ask.

'On what time Declan gets out of bed. And, that depends on how much he had to drink last night.'

'Oh, right...well, what time does he open on an average day?'

'I'd say, if I had to say, mind - I'd say in about an hour.'

Just then someone shouts from the doorway of the shop, I turn to the voice and see it is one of the two ladies between whom my bag of crisps passed.

'No! He's opening now. I've just been to look. He's just opened.'

This news is met with a general sigh of contentment around the shop, and I realise, at that moment, that everyone has been part of this conversation - that everyone has contributed in some way. I feel obliged not only to thank the shopkeeper and the lady standing by the door, but to thank everyone for their help. I don't do this individually, of course, but with a general 'thank you'.

I am filled with the sensation that they are always here, in the shop - that they can never leave, but have to spend each day among the boxes - crushed together like sweets in a jar. They all watch me go, smiling, magazine and crisps in hand.

The record shop is, as reported, now open for business. That's what a sign, which has now mysteriously appeared, says on the door. I walk inside to the tinkle of a little bell. The shop, which is slightly larger than the newsagents, is completely empty, not only of people, but also of anything else. The shelves are completely bare, as is the floor space.

I am looking around at the blank walls, feeling perplexed, as a man appears from the back of the shop. He is wearing an

Irish rugby shirt, and he is strikingly handsome. I am taken aback by how handsome he is, and for a second I feel as though I'm on an empty film set, and he is the leading man.

'Can I help you?' He asks.

I look around involuntarily at the emptiness.

'Don't be put off by the empty spaces - all the stock is out the back.'

'Oh? OK.'

'Are you the girl looking for a record player?'

'Yes, how did you know?'

'Well now, I suppose it was you that woke me up this morning, about half an hour ago? Someone called asking after a record player…'

'Oh. Yes, that was me…'

'Well, I'm glad you woke me, or I'd be asleep till noon.'

'Did you have a rough night?'

'No - I have this condition. It means I fall asleep a lot, and I find it hard to wake up. They all think I'm a drunk.' He nods his head in the direction of the other shops. 'But I'm not. It's just easier to let them think that.'

'Oh.'

'Well, I'm awake now. What kind of record player are you after?'

'I'm not really sure. Just a basic one, I think.'

'Right you are then. Just wait a moment, and I'll bring one through…'

I wait alone in the shop for a couple of minutes, and then he returns with a small record player and a couple of black speakers. He whistles to himself while he plugs it all in.

'Why is all your stock out the back of the shop?' I ask. It just seems bizarre, and I have a compelling urge to know. He stops what he is doing and stands up straight.

'I'm selling up,' he replies. 'Everything is boxed-up now. I'm opening up somewhere else.'

'Oh - where?'

'Liverpool - I have family there. Have you ever been?'
'Yes, a while ago. It's very nice.'
'Is it? I don't think so. But I can make a go of it there. I've been here for a year, and it's been a real struggle. Also, there's a girl...'
'Ah...'
'Yes,' he says with a smile. 'I'm getting married next year. Over there.'
'Congratulations.'
'Thanks. I'm Declan, by the way...'
'And I'm Sandy...'
'It's a pleasure to meet you, Sandy.'

Declan demonstrates the small stereo to me, and I pay for it without any further searching conversation. I tell him it is exactly what I am looking for. In fact, I am just looking for anything that will play my record.

'How are you getting home?' He enquires. 'It's too heavy to carry.'

'Yes. Could you call me a taxi?'

'I certainly will.'

Declan calls me a taxi from the back of the shop, and while I wait for it to arrive he makes us both a cup of tea, as it transpires that it won't be here for twenty minutes. He pulls two stools out from behind the counter, and we sit together and drink our tea. My mug is in the shape of a frog. He asks about how it is I'm in Ireland, and I tell him some story about travelling around the country seeing the sights. Whatever I say, I can't tell him the truth, so this seems like a nice story to tell.

'Ah, it's a beautiful country, Ireland,' he says. 'The West Coast is lovely. I'll really miss it all.'

'Oh well,' I say. 'You'll have a new wife instead...'

He grins at me. 'I will that!' He says. 'Would you like to see a photo?'

'Yes please. What's her name?'

'Charlotte. There she is...'

Declan hands me a small photo of his girlfriend. She is pretty, but I expected as much. She has long blonde hair and a smiling face. She looks as if she is used to smiling. I hand the photo back.

'She looks very nice,' I say.

'She is...very nice,' he replies. 'She's like me...'

'In what way?'

'She falls asleep a lot. We have the same condition. We met in Liverpool, undergoing tests. She's not as bad as me, and I'm not that badly affected, really.'

'Oh, you said earlier. I've heard of this before. I saw it on telly once. Is it called "narcolepsy" or something?'

'No. Narcolepsy is where you just suddenly fall asleep during the day without warning, like someone switches you off or something. That's very rare. We don't have that.'

'Oh?'

'No. We have something called 'hypersomnia'. It's much more common. It means you get very tired during the day, need to have a nap sometimes. Also, you have a lot of trouble waking up in the morning, and when you do, you feel out of sorts, like you don't know where you are. You know, confused. In a while, me and Charlotte can wake up in the same bed and be confused together.'

He laughs at this and I laugh with him.

'You know,' I say, 'I feel like that all the time. Confused, like I don't know where I am.'

'Perhaps you're one of us,' he says, with a smile.

Just then a man appears in the door of the shop.

'Taxi for Sandy - is that yourself, miss?' He asks me.

'Yes. I have a stereo to take back to my hotel,' I reply.

'OK. Let me take it for you,' he says, and starts to collect up the speakers.

Declan watches from the door of his shop as we drive off. I wave at him and he waves back. He is a very handsome man,

I think, and at that point, very much awake.

As we journey back to the hotel, I think about all the different conditions there are in the world - all the millions of different people that have all kinds of conditions. Declan and Charlotte both have one called hypersomnia, and perhaps I just have a different one. But my condition has no name, and I would swap it with hypersomnia in an instant.

As we pull up at the hotel, I am struck my something else. Declan was able to talk about his condition - although he chose not to tell the other shop owners, he was able to talk to me about it. But I couldn't talk to him about what happens to me. I just wouldn't know how to begin anymore.

A long time ago I actually paid someone to listen to me talk about my condition. It was a disaster, and left me feeling worse. I have never spoken about it again - not with anyone. But at that time I wanted to talk about it with someone, wanted someone to understand and help me. This is what happened.

Time Two

Friday 1ˢᵗ June 2006

I entered Time Two terrified and confused, and although the terror subsided, the confusion stayed with me throughout. I simply couldn't believe what had happened - I had barely come to terms with the coma, and now this bizarre, impossible situation had been thrust upon me. More than anything, I felt as if I needed help.

I became desperate to find out what was happening to me - and to try to understand whether any of it had actually really happened at all. I was also worried that, come August, it would all happen again. I had no answers to give myself, and so I tried to seek out someone who perhaps would.

The hospital, when I left in March, had recommended a post-stress and trauma counsellor - someone called Dr Sharon Culpepper. She was apparently an expert at dealing with people like me who suffered various problems resulting from stress, and especially from trauma. She held a private practice in London, and they had given me her telephone number while I was at the hospital.

During the last week in May, after a particularly sleepless night, I called her surgery and booked an appointment with her secretary. I was told she charged eighty pounds an hour, and that she would tell me how many sessions I may need after she first met me. The secretary asked me a few background questions, and I told her about the coma and my accident. I could sense that she was writing all this down. I booked an initial appointment on Friday 1ˢᵗ June, at 10am.

* * * * * * * * * * * * * * * *

I arrived ten minutes early for my meeting with the doctor,

and sat in a small waiting room with a friendly Swedish receptionist and two goldfish, one of which had apparently murdered a third over the previous weekend. The killer had left no clues, and as neither surviving goldfish had come forward to admit to the crime, both had been allowed to live.

The receptionist told me all this during the ten minutes I waited to see the doctor. She, I think, was partly making small talk to put me at ease, but also I believe she was a bit bored. In response to the goldfish story, I replied that it would probably now be impossible to find out who the killer was, because the killer - being a goldfish - would have forgotten that they did it. The receptionist thought this was extremely funny, and laughed out loud for a good thirty seconds. When the doctor appeared at 10am exactly, the receptionist introduced me and also told her my thoughts about the goldfish murders and their memories, and again laughed loudly at the retelling of the story. The doctor smiled at her benignly, obviously used to her idiosyncratic ways.

Doctor Culpepper led me through to a small but well decorated office. There was a large brown leather chair for me to sit in, with a foot rest attached. The doctor sat in a more business-like chair and leant across the desk towards me.

'Well, Sandy - as you know, I'm Doctor Culpepper, but please call me Sharon.'

'OK.'

'Now, Sandy, can you tell me why you're here, why you've taken the time to come and see me?'

'Yes, well...do you know much about me? About what happened to me - my coma and everything?'

'Why don't you tell me in your own words?'

'Oh, OK. Well, on my eighteenth birthday I was hit by a car at Tottenham Court Road, and then I was in a coma for about thirteen years, and then I woke up.'

'OK.'

'And then I started to feel better, and I got a flat in

Greenwich, and enrolled on a course - you know, to study at college. And everything seemed to be getting back to some kind of normality - I felt as though I was coming to terms with everything, but then…'

'Yes.'

'Well, it's hard to explain...'

'Try telling me - just take your time.'

'OK, well…you know I said that I enrolled on a course, at college?'

'Yes.'

'Well - I did that in July.'

'Which July?'

'This July, I mean, next month. I mean, this is June, right? June 1st?'

'Yes, it is. It's June 1st today.'

'But I've already had a June 1st, and a June 2nd. I've done all this already. Last Time, when I came around from my coma, I carried on as normal until August 19th, and then I just went back to March again, and now I'm up to June 1st - again - and I think that maybe I'll get to August 19th and then start again, back to March. That's what I'm afraid of.'

Dr Culpepper looked at me without changing her expression. If she thought I was mad, she didn't show it. She changed the subject and asked me a few questions about my childhood and what kind of things I liked and disliked. Then, after a few minutes, we returned to the subject of time.

'I see. So it's like time is repeating itself?' She asked me, in response to my assertion that I had lived through this day before.

'Well - sort of. It's not the same Time, things are a bit different. But, well, yes - it's basically the same. I woke up in the same place, in March, and I suppose things are as they were last Time - but I've done different things. Gone to different places…'

'You can do that, can you?'

'Yes. So it would seem. I mean - everything's normal - you're normal, this place is normal. It's not as if it's some kind of weird nightmare. I can do normal stuff. It's just that I went round in some kind of loop - back to March - and I'm scared that it will happen again.'

The doctor took off her glasses and placed them on the desk. This seemed like a signal of some kind, that she was about to say something important. I waited for her to speak.

'Sandy,' she began. 'When people experience a trauma of some kind, bereavement perhaps, or an accident, they react in different ways. You've had a terrible accident, and you've been lost in time for thirteen years. Do you still feel lost in time - as if time is cheating, has cheated, you in some way?'

'Well, yes, I do. But...'

'Sandy, how did you feel when you heard that your mother had died?'

'Oh. I felt...sad, very sad. But I felt sadder the first time.'

'The first time?'

'Yes - the first time they told me. When they told me the second time, this Time, I didn't feel as sad because I knew that's what they would say.'

'Oh, so the first time was a shock, but this time you already knew?'

'Yes.'

'Sandy, do you think that these months will repeat again?'

'I don't know.'

'Do you not think that because you've had such a terrible shock - losing your mother and all that time in a coma, not to mention the accident - that perhaps you desperately want to get some of that time back. You've lost so much of your life - thirteen years - perhaps if you feel you've retrieved just a few months, then it would all be easier to cope with?'

'No, not really. I'd rather things had just carried on last Time. I was beginning to come to terms with things. I had a college course lined up and everything...'

'So you're certain that you've lived this time before. That

this is your second time living through June 2006?'

'Well…it's what has happened to me. I haven't imagined it. I don't want it to be real, but it is.'

The conversation continued this way for a few minutes more - with Doctor Culpepper offering me reasons why I might be imagining it all, and me basically just saying that it had actually happened. We reached a stalemate.

'Sandy, I'd like you to consider something,' she said after a long pause. 'I'd like you to come back and see me again - perhaps next week. I think that you have had a terrible shock, and that you are suffering from the result of that shock. I think, if you are willing to face up to the possibility that you may not have actually lived through these months before - that this is the first June 2006 for you, for all of us - then I can help you come to terms with all that you've lost. Would you be able to do that?'

I sat and thought for a moment. For a second, I believed her. It all had been a great shock. Maybe I'd imagined the whole thing - maybe the Time I spent in Greenwich was simply part of the coma. Maybe I should give it a try. But then I thought something else; something I knew to be true. The Time before really did happen. I really had been taken from that Time and placed here - forced to live these months again.

This was the first occasion I was certain of this, and I was also certain that this woman could not help me.

Because I was embarrassed to say no, I said I'd give it some thought and phone later to make an appointment. But I had no intention of doing so.

Later that afternoon, I lay on the bed of my Lancaster Gate hotel (this was the first Time I stayed there) and cried for ages. I cried because the doctor could not help me. The doctor could only help people who imagined things, help them to put things right in their minds. She couldn't help me, because my problem was a real one.

Time Ninety Six

Thursday 25th May 2006

Back at the hotel, I assemble the stereo, following as best I can the instructions that are taped to the turntable. In truth, it is a very simple task to put it all together, and within minutes the sideboard in my room has become its temporary home.

I take the record out of its sleeve and place it on the turntable. I then move the needle to the start of the record and wait. I can hear a crackle from the speakers, which makes me think that I have wired them up properly, as sound is obviously getting from the turntable out through the speakers. Then, suddenly, the room is filled with music. Not just music, but the music I have heard so many Times before. It sounds strange to hear it now, in a hotel room in Dublin, out of context. Usually it is in my head, but now it is all around me.

I remain standing throughout the short song. I have a pencil and a pad in my hand, ready to write down the lyrics as I hear them. I thought this would take a few listens, but the same verse is repeated three times - the rest of the song is instrumental. I write the verse down the first time, then listen a second time to make sure I have it right. I read through what I have written:

> *Please paint my heart with your love,*
> *You know I need you more each day,*
> *Please cover me with your embrace,*
> *Tell me that your love is here always.*

I can't see any obvious clue in these words. I read them again and again, but they are just silly, simple words; words about love. I flip the record over and play the other side. It is exactly the same as side A. I sit down on the bed and look at the words I have written on the pad, and then lean across and pick up the record from the turntable. I hold this in my other hand. I sit there looking at both, almost as if I am weighing them up, the pad in my right hand and the record in my left. I feel as if the record itself has the clue, not the song. The song is just to lead me to the record. I look at the label once more, and read out the name 'Richard Sturrock' aloud. This, I decide, is the only real clue I have.

I must find out who he is, and then go and talk to him.

Time Ninety-Six

Thursday 27th July 2006
4.20pm

I'm sitting in the lounge at Gatwick Airport, waiting to board my two hour flight to Venice - which has been delayed by three hours. I'm feeling a bit annoyed, but I'm in no hurry. I'm reading the last few pages of a book - The Falls, by Ian Rankin - a book which I hoped would have lasted the duration of the flight, but sadly I've read almost all of it waiting to board.

There are loads of frustrated passengers with me - one family has four or five children, all of which are misbehaving at the same time. They are annoying people around them, but this is because the people are already annoyed. As I mentioned, I'm feeling a bit annoyed as well, but I'm just interested now in finishing my book.

When I finish the final page, about ten minutes later, I close the book and place it on my lap. An elderly gentleman in a flat cap is sitting opposite me; he has a newspaper on his lap - a copy of the Racing Post. He bends down and picks up a small bag. He takes out a bottle of something - it looks like milk - and pours some into a plastic cup. He lifts it to his lips and holds it there for a few moments, then drinks the whole cup in one. He makes a face as if the drink was bitter, and then puts the cup back into his bag, along with the bottle. He catches me looking at him, and rather than look away, I smile.

'It's medicine,' he says. 'For my heart.'

'Oh...I didn't mean to stare,' I reply.

'Not at all - it tastes really horrible. But it keeps me alive!'

I ask him if he would like to read my book, as I'm finished with it. He says that he would, and offers to exchange it for his newspaper.

'The Racing Post?' I query. 'What's it about?'

'Oh. It's a racing paper - horse racing and dogs. Greyhound racing, it used to be very popular - not so much now.'

'Would I find it interesting?'

'I'm not sure.' He looks at me, as if seeing me afresh. 'No, I don't think so,' he admits.

Nevertheless, I ask for the paper, and promise to take a look at it on the flight. He gives a small shrug and passes it to me, and as he does so he smiles, as someone would to a small child.

In return, as agreed, he takes the book, and makes a show of starting to read it. Ten minutes later, we are finally boarding.

* * * * * * * * * * * * * * * *

Midway during the flight, I wander to the back of the plane to stretch my legs, and catch sight of the man in the flat cap. He is asleep, and the book has fallen on the floor between his feet. For a second, watching him sleep; the book on the floor, the medicine in the little bag, I'm struck by how old he is. He is tired, frail. He needs medicine to keep him alive. I wonder if this is what I really want - to grow old and die. Just to grow old and get ill and then die?

I search out the wrinkles on his face, the lines on this forehead, on his hands. I look down at my own hands. They are the hands of a thirty year-old girl - perhaps even younger. I look up at him again. I'm flying out to Venice, but I realise that this man is perhaps my real destination. If I escape from my life, I will start to grow old. I've never even been thirty-two.

I turn towards the toilet and fumble with the catch. I step in and close the folding door behind me. Once inside, I turn and look at myself in the small mirror. I see a pretty girl looking back at me. I know I am not glamorous, or even beautiful, really. But I am pretty, I'm sure that I am. But, if I start to age - what will happen? In forty years time, I'll be seventy! This seems to me an impossible thing, to be seventy years old, but if I were to succeed in all I've worked towards, my face would become as wrinkled as the man in the cap.

I sit down on the toilet. I have the gift of eternal youth. Why on earth would anyone in their right mind want to throw it away?

I run the tap and splash the tepid water in my face. I dry myself off and walk back to my seat. As I pass the man with my book, I steal a glance back. He is still asleep, his dreams full of horses and greyhounds; and of his wife, as she was when she was young, as she was before she died.

* * * * * * * * * * * * * * * *

Two things happened to me on the flight, and they both included the man in the cap. Firstly, and for the first Time, I truly realised that I can never grow old. Of course, I knew this already – but it had never hit me the way it did on this flight. When I stared down at his face, his eyes and his mouth, it was as if I knew what it was like to be old. At least I could sense it – had some idea about the enormity of it.

A decision that had been so clear to me – to escape from this prison of five months - was thrown into question. I felt my skin crawl at the thought of wrinkles, of my eyesight failing, of my memory fading away.

At that moment, as I stared in thought at the seat in front, old age seemed as if it were a sickness. It seemed unnatural, invasive – unnecessary. Why would I - how could I - choose such a thing? I had been young for so long – I had not lost my youth, but I had gained it. This is how I felt at the time, on that flight - but not for very long.

Secondly, I was intrigued by the Racing Post. I discovered what a form guide was and the science that went into picking horses and dogs – choosing winners from losers. I had believed it to be a random choice, like a bingo card or the lottery, but it seemed that I was wrong.

And during the flight, I realised something else – that I

already knew some of the winners. I knew all of the World Cup results. I knew that Italy wins the Cup, and that England gets to the quarter finals. I knew that Japan draws nil-nil with Croatia. I knew all these things. This, of course, was irrelevant if things stayed as they were. But if I were to escape, perhaps next Time or in the immediate future, a few well placed bets, during the course of the relevant Time, could change the rest of my life.

As with old age, I was amazed with myself that I had never really considered this before. It seemed as if I had discovered a choice. Stay young or grow old - but be old and rich. But I knew that money was no cure for age, and so I continued to stare at the seat in front, trying to fix onto these thoughts as they whirled around my head, mixed together with horses and football – a madness growing stronger in my mind that I was finding harder to control.

Although I was sure about my depression, I also became more and more convinced that I was going mad. I began to fantasise that I was in a race – that the finish line was my escape and that I had to reach it before my madness overtook me. Strangely, I felt completely sane about the realisation that I was going mad; given my circumstances, it seemed completely normal that this would be the case. In fact, I often felt amazed that I had hung on to my sanity for so long.

I knew something for sure: no amount of youth would be able to save me from my madness. My mind was peeling away inside this insanity that had become my life. In all things, I knew that I had to escape. This was still my goal.

* * * * * * * * * * * * * * *

When the plane lands, I sit quietly while everyone disembarks; and then I leave just behind them – leaving enough space to be almost alone.

* * * * * * * * * * * * * * *

Two months ago, I had flown back to England with a name - Richard Sturrock. The Internet had totally let me down, virtually unable to find any mention of a Richard Sturrock - and the few I did find seemed extremely unlikely to be the one I was looking for. So I began walking around jazz and blues record shops in London, showing the record to everyone I could find who may recognize it; but no-one did. No-one had ever heard of Richard Sturrock, or indeed The Blue Lounge Summer Jazz Quartet. Nobody had a clue.

That was until I spoke to Bob. I had been searching for weeks, and I was calling record shops in Manchester, asking them the same question every time, and always getting the same answer. It was nearing the end of July, and I felt that time was running out - that was until Bob stepped in and saved the day.

Time Ninety-Six

Monday 24th July 2006

Bob worked in a tiny record shop in Moss Side, next door to the largest fish and chip shop I had ever seen. Oddly, Bob hated fish and chips, and he complained about the smell of the frying fish more than once when I visited his shop. I made the trip to Manchester because of the conversation I had with Bob when I mentioned the record to him over the phone.

'Yes, I know that one,' he had said. 'It's a jazz record, isn't it? It was recorded in Italy.'

I couldn't believe what I was hearing, and almost dropped the phone when I heard the word 'yes'.

'I can't believe it!' I replied. 'How do you know it? I've looked everywhere…'

'Oh, it's quite rare. But I knew Richard when I was a little boy. He used to live across the road from me…'

Time Ninety-Six

Tuesday 25th July 2006

The very next day I arrived in Moss Side. A taxi dropped me outside 'Slater Road Records' at about eleven o'clock in the morning. It was raining lightly, and the pavement was covered in a thin sheet of water. The sun was trying to break through a bank of clouds and, looking up, I could see the day was promising to be a nice one. I reflected on how, each Time, most things seemed to be the same, but the weather was often subtly different.

A large blue and white fish and chip 'emporium' stood to the left. The awnings loomed over the pavement with so many shredded fingers, as if they were waiting to grab any passer by and pull them into the shop. A happy blue fish was the logo, smiling manically out into space - perhaps having seen so many of its friends fed into the fryer inside had driven it insane.

These were my thoughts as I pushed open the door to the record shop, and was confronted by a man in his late-twenties who I knew in an instant was Bob. I knew this, in the main, because he was wearing a black baseball cap with the word 'Bob' emblazoned across it in red. I found it hard to believe that anyone would wear such a cap; but this was Manchester after all.

I introduced myself to Bob as the 'girl on the phone yesterday', and he welcomed me to his shop with a wave of his right arm.

'So, all the way up from London?' He said.

'Yes, that's right,' I replied. Now I was here, I was suddenly unsure how to proceed.

'So, you were interested in that jazz record by Richard Sturrock,' he said. 'He used to live around here, as I mentioned on the phone. He gave me a call a couple of months ago, out of the blue. He told me about the record - even sent me a copy.'

'This was from Italy?'

'Yeah, he lives in Italy now. He had an accident - had a bad fall or something - here in England. His mum took him to Italy when he was ill - she's Italian. He never came back.'

He fumbled under the counter and picked out a disc. He showed it to me.

'There it is,' he said. 'Please Paint My Heart With Your Love.'

'That's it.'

'So - what did you want to know about it?'

'Not really about it, actually; about him…'

'Oh?'

'Yes - like, where in Italy does he live now?'

'Well - in Venice. In fact, I think I have his phone number or something…'

I could hardly believe that Bob was real. He was a mine of information, and I felt that if he came up with the phone number I would somehow be in his debt for ever. I thought to myself that he might like it if I were to wear a cap with 'Sandy' printed on the front for a day - to show solidarity or something.

Bob disappeared to the back of the shop and came back with a brown book. He flicked through it for a few seconds and then prodded something with his index finger.

'Here it is,' he said. 'Have you got a pen?'

Minutes later - after a reasonable amount of small talk - I was leaving the shop with a location - Venice, Italy - and a phone number. I was astounded that I had achieved so much. I turned back at the door and thanked Bob for all his help. I gave him a big smile.

'It's for a bet,' he said, instead of a goodbye. 'I'm wearing it for a bet - for one week. The money goes to charity…'

That afternoon I called the number. I called from my mobile phone - although I knew that it would be expensive to call Italy, that didn't really matter. I sat on a bench near Piccadilly Station, watching a pigeon greedily devouring a cheesy Quaver. I had thought over lunch about what I would say, but decided that all I really wanted to know, at this moment, was where Richard Sturrock lived, and if I could pay him a visit. The kind of conversation we would ultimately need to have would not, I thought, be very easy over the phone.

I dialled the number and waited. After a few seconds, a single ring tone sounded in my ear - the sound of calling someone abroad. Moments later the phone was answered.

A male voice came on the line. Deep - an English accent sounding foreign words.

'*Pronto.*'

I fell silent for a moment, unable to open my mouth. Then I forced myself to speak.

'Hello. Do you speak English?'

'Of course...'

'Ah - my name is Sandy. Sandy Glover. I'm calling from England.'

'Yes...'

'Well...this will sound a bit strange, but I need to talk to you about your song - your jazz song.'

'About my song?'

'Yes...'

'Do you have the record?'

'Yes.'

'You have heard it before - in your mind. Now you want to meet me?'

'Yes...' I feel tears starting to form in my eyes, and a lump growing in my throat.

'Yes,' I repeat, fighting to hold my voice even. 'I would like to meet you.'

'That would be nice. You know, of course, I live in Venice. If you have a pen, I'll give you my address.'

I already had a pen and paper to hand, prepared to make any suitable notes on the conversation.

'I have a pen,' I replied.

'Good. Then my address is '24, Calle Due Corti'. I'm near the railway station - come down the steps - the Grand Canal is in front of you - turn to the left. Walk for just two minutes until the first bridge, don't cross the bridge, instead turn left, walk for five minutes and you are there.'

'Thank you so much. When can I come? I...I don't have much time.'

'Of course... Come when you can. Call me when you arrive. I will be here.'

'OK. Well, I'll see you in a couple of days.'

'Good. Goodbye for now.'

With that he disconnected the call. I sat for a few minutes - dazed. I was all happening so fast. It was only when I stood that I realised that he hadn't told me who he was.

* * * * * * * * * * * * * * * *

On the train journey back to London, I sat for ages just thinking about all that had happened. I fought the temptation to phone back - to check that it was Richard Sturrock who had proffered the invitation. I was sure that it was.

I had no words to describe how I felt. It wasn't any kind of relief, or even joy. It was just the feeling that something different was about to happen. After so long of things being the same, I found I was actually scared of things becoming different.

Of course, things are often quite different each Time - but this Time I would perhaps find the answer to my quest. The rhythm of the train became entwined with my thoughts, my eyes closed, and my mind considered the days ahead.

I was about to follow a path - a path of my choosing - to wherever it would lead, and in doing so set wheels in motion so enormous that I could not possibly stop them. Giant metal cogs and springs suddenly filled my mind, pushed in on me, and it was as if I was looking out at the world through the inside of a clock. I squeezed myself past the sharp metal wheels, ticking at me with a strange, hollow sound, and managed to press myself up against the inside of the clock face. It was composed of a misty glass, and all around me were roman numerals, painted in black and gothic style. I peered out between the minute and hour hands, held either side of my face at five minutes to one.

Drops of water appeared on the outside of the glass - rain - and this obscured my vision even more. But, beyond the misty sheen of the clock face and the smear of the rain I could see a tree, and beside that a gate. It was like a gate to a field, pieces of wood hammered and screwed together in a haphazard way. And, I could now see, beyond this stood a man. He was calling to me - waving and smiling. I waved back, but I couldn't see his face. Suddenly a child appeared beside him, and took him by the hand. They both waved at me and smiled - calling me forward; asking me to join them. I squinted and stared, trying to see who they were. I felt certain that I knew them - I was certain that I should know them; but they were too far away, and it was growing dark.

Suddenly, I realised who they were, who they must be. I hammered on the inside of the clock, shouting to them to wait for me. But everything outside began to fade, turning to a dull grey and patches of creamy white. Slowly the man, still holding the child's hand, walked away from the gate. I stopped shouting, because I knew they couldn't hear me; that it was too late.

All of a sudden I felt resigned to this; having this reality as my life, hearing the moving of the cogs behind me. These cogs, the sound they make; it is always there. The ticking is real, methodical, soothing; but then erotic - so erotic, arousing me. That beautiful sound; so rhythmic, around me; stirring me inside. I closed my eyes, and I felt the sound sweep over me like a wave, caressing me, touching me everywhere, and laying me down.

I sat against the clock face, rested my head for a moment against the cool glass and then slid onto my back, my hands pressing outwards; palms down. The sound passed in rhythm over my body, on top of me, under my clothes, my hair, inside me. I was lifted up, gently, and then down, the waves passing through me and along me, each one reverberating in me with a shudder. I pressed my feet hard into the floor, pushed my thighs and body forward; I felt hands on me, my own hands - but no longer mine, each living a separate life, moving as one with the ticking of the clock.

My body felt alive - surrendered to the movement inside me. I moved my head to one side; eyes still closed, and as I did the clock gave an unexpected jolt.

I was suddenly awake, and I stared around me in confusion; my eyes resting on a platform sign beyond the window.

We had arrived at Watford Junction.

Time Ninety-Six

Thursday 27th July 2006
9.50pm Central European Time

It is later than I would have hoped, but I am finally in a hotel in Italy. Just over an hour ago, I caught the Airport Bus to the centre of town, and in fact I got off at Mestre Railway Station, which is just a single stop from the railway station in Venice itself. Mestre is not actually Venice, but it's akin to Greater Venice, being just five minutes or so by train or bus from the famous canals and bridges.

Across from the station there stood a large hotel. I jogged across five or six lanes of busy traffic and found the entrance, which was around the side of the building. I was fortunate that they had a couple of single rooms vacant, so I took one.

And here I am.

* * * * * * * * * * * * * * * *

I call Richard Sturrock while standing at my hotel window, looking out across to the railway station. The phone rings at the other end for a few seconds, and then it is answered.

'*Pronto.*'

'Hello again; it's Sandy Glover. I'm here in Italy. In Venice…'

'Sandy. It's good to hear from you again. Shall we meet…tomorrow?'

'Yes, tomorrow would be great. That would be great.'

'That's settled then. I am busy for much of the day, but perhaps you could visit me at six o'clock tomorrow afternoon, at my home. How does that sound to you?'

'That's great.'

'Fine; perhaps we could have dinner? You can ask me your questions.'

'I would like to. I have lots…'
'Good. So, I will see you tomorrow. Goodnight.'
'OK. Goodnight'

Seconds later, the line goes dead. I fold my phone in two and flip it onto the bed. I plug in the kettle and begin the process of making a cup of tea. Outside, in the street below, I can hear the sounds of foreign voices. They are a blur to me, so many voices talking in unison, mixed with the noises of music and cars and other sounds I cannot make out.

I stand for a moment listening, and then hear the click of the boiling kettle. Everything seems to be changing around me, and yet everything seems so normal. I can make a cup of tea, I can have a bath. Tomorrow, I will do some sightseeing. But at six o'clock I will meet someone who may know how I can escape from this life. Like the voices below, it all seems to blur together, the normal and the unusual; I can't tell them apart, and worse - I'm starting to feel gripped with confusion. I wish with all my heart that Chris were here; he wouldn't have a clue what to do, but it would be nice if he were here. He would make it all seem OK. He would help me, even though he wouldn't know how to. He would help me because he loves me; because he loved me - in some other Time; in some other Times.

Time Ninety-Six

Friday 28th July 2006

I have the day to myself in Venice, so I decide to do some sightseeing, even though I've been here before.

After meeting the scary Japanese man with Adam in Time Eighty-Two, I visited Venice for three weeks during the following Time, at his suggestion. He had told me to go to Venice, and he seemed somewhat keen that I did, so I just thought I'd follow his advice.

I had no idea what I hoped to find here, in Venice, and the three weeks turned out to be a bit of a pointless exercise - although the city itself is lovely and certainly worth a visit if you have the time - which I have.

* * * * * * * * * * * * * * * *

During that Time - Time Eighty-Three - I wandered aimlessly for days over bridges and along canals, half expecting someone to step out of the shadows at any moment with some vital piece of information for me. But nothing of that sort happened during my stay - in fact for much of the time I was bored and lonely. I was also annoyed with myself for the way I'd treated Adam during Time Eighty-Two, and a growing sense of guilt began to fester and take root in my thoughts.

However, I did enjoy walking around in the sunshine, and riding up and down the canals on the river buses. I even paid sixty pounds for a forty-five minute ride in a gondola, which although expensive was a lot of fun. I shared my gondola that day - it was a Sunday - with a girl I had sat next to on a river bus. Her name was Cindy and she was visiting her boyfriend, who was here 'working on an art project' (whatever that means). Cindy and the boyfriend were both from Alabama, and she was in Venice for a month.

'I'd love to go on one of those!' She said to me as a gondola passed the window of the bus.

So we did.

Cindy, adept at travelling abroad on a budget, was happy for me to pay and accepted without embarrassment. We both enjoyed the short trip on the canal aboard the gondola, sitting on and surrounded by the soft heart-shaped cushions. We had a cup of tea, or coffee in her case, in a small café near the Rialto Bridge afterwards.

She told me a bit about her boyfriend, and that she was worried that she would have to come and live in Italy to be with him.

'This project just goes on forever!' She complained.

'It must be important,' I said, unsure of how to best reply.

Cindy took a sip of her coffee and just smiled. 'Well…perhaps,' she said. 'But I think it's a heap of crap…'

I smiled back, but was taken aback by her bluntness. I wondered if she was always this candid about her boyfriend with people she had only just shared a gondola with.

'Oh? Is it?' I said.

'Well, yes. He thinks he's doing some great thing, but it's just in his head. You know what he's good at, what he's really good at?'

Feeling the conversation taking a turn for the worse, I was suddenly afraid to ask. I just shook my head.

'Fixing cars!' she said. 'He's great at fixing cars! That's what he's good at. He doesn't know shit about art! But his daddy runs some gallery out in Florida, and he's just desperate for Steven to 'join him in the world of art'.'

Cindy lifted a napkin from the table and wiped her face. It was hot, and she was starting to feel the effects.

'I love him,' she said, fixing me with her eyes. 'God knows I do. But…I want to go home.'

It was only then that I saw how sad she was, caught between two worlds - with neither offering her everything she wanted.

I felt that I should tell her that the same was true for me, but I didn't know how to. And when I opened my mouth to speak, I felt at once as if I couldn't; as if I had no words to say. I looked down at the round wooden table we were sitting at, the empty tea and coffee cups, the crumbs from the biscuits, and I knew I had to get up and go.

The whole scene suddenly seemed like a farce, something ridiculous and senseless, and as I looked up at Cindy - her eyes watching me for a reply - I felt a tightening in my chest as I searched for some empathy, some sympathetic emotion that I could draw upon for an answer. But I felt nothing for her - I did not feel concerned or have any compassion at all. She had walked onto my stage and was looking at me for understanding; for words of kindness and maybe advice. But I had nothing to give her, nowhere to go to find the words that I should say.

She was a bit-part in my play, this tragedy of mine, and I was the star. She had said her lines, and without fault, but I had no lines to say; just a blank page.

Instead I smiled at her, my eyes empty and cold, staring beyond her into the distance.

We said goodbye just five minutes later, and I never saw her again after that.

But being here in Venice now made me remember her again, and I find myself wondering what choice she had made - whether the choice had made her happy - if it had been the right decision.

Choices are so important. Life can change; can end, as the result of a choice. We choose to take the wrong flight, to cross the wrong road, to ride in the wrong car - perhaps to visit the wrong town; or to marry the wrong man. But how do we know what choice to make? Who will tell us? Who will tell me? And how can we tell each other, advise each other, when we can't make the right choices ourselves?

Before she fades from my mind, and my thoughts address

other things, my final contemplation is that I hope she is happy.

And also, thinking of her made me remember something else; that I'm not the only girl with problems; not at all.

* * * * * * * * * * * * * * * *

So I spend the day once again wandering the streets of Venice, as I did before in Time Eighty-Three. Apart from a lot of aimless meandering, I visit an art gallery with a selection of original watercolours by a Serbian artist, now living in Italy. They are full of bold colours and everything is larger than life. There is something about them that I like very much, but I can't quite discover what it is. After a while, I buy a catalogue to look at over lunch, and leave.

I also take a river bus out to Lido, and have lunch in a little café not far from the sea. After lunch I walk along the beach in the sunshine and sit for an hour or so staring out at the waves. Between staring, I flick through the catalogue I bought at the exhibition. The paintings look duller and less impressive in their miniature, reproduced form.

I leave Lido and the beach around 3.30pm - it is too hot to stay any longer, and I'm starting to feel as if I'm frying. I buy two bottles of mineral water from a tiny café along from the river bus stop. The brand is 'San Benedetto', and they each have a single bluebird in flight on the label. They are both very cold, and I drink one of them completely before the bus arrives. I put the other one in my bag for later on.

Time seems to move slowly throughout the afternoon. I drag my heels along with it, and look at my watch at least fifty times. I am just waiting.

Time Ninety-Six

Friday 28th July 2006
5.55pm CET

I stand outside the house that, perhaps, has the answers I need. It is in a row of seven or eight houses - a single terrace - facing onto a small square with an iron bench. Each of the houses is painted a pastel colour - one blue, another pink; but the colours have faded and the houses are slowly beginning to look like each other.

This blurring of colour reminds me of my feeling yesterday after the phone call, and this suddenly raises in me a sense of panic. But as quickly as it comes, it passes, and is replaced with something else. It's as if the houses are trying to trick me; that the effect is, in fact, one of dissemblance. I have to shake my head to remove these thoughts from my mind, but they leave a subtle mark on me, and make me feel wary.

The house, number three, has a purple front with four windows; each with black shutters. The door, which is also black, stands between the two lower windows. There is no doorbell and no knocker, and for a second I feel the urge to walk away; retrace my footsteps back to the canal and return to my hotel. But the urge passes, and I knock briefly, twice, on the door. It is 5.55pm, so I'm a bit early. This, strangely, also makes me feel nervous. I take a deep breath, and step back and wait.

Just seconds pass in waiting before the door is opened. I am greeted not by a man, as I expected, but by a girl wearing a smart suit. She looks at me for moment, as if confused, but then her face breaks into a smile.

'You must be Sandy,' she says; her accent is Italian, and she stumbles over the English words. 'I am so pleased to meet you. Mr Sturrock is expecting you, of course. Please come inside...'

I return her smile with one of my own, and walk into a small hallway with no furniture, but with a broom leaning against the left hand wall. Beside this is a doorway; open and leading somewhere. The girl steps back and signals me into the room with her hand. Somehow, the presence of the girl makes me feel more comfortable, and I walk in to a spacious living room; a sense of optimism growing within me.

* * * * * * * * * * * * * * * * *

Richard Sturrock is not at all what I had expected. I had tried to imagine what he would look like, but had only ever conjured up images of unattractive, often frightening men. However, this is not the case. He is handsome; more than that - he is very handsome. He is probably in his early thirties, blonde hair and blue eyes, wearing a smart suit like the girl, who stood now in the doorway smiling.

The room is larger than I would have expected from looking at the front of the house. It is decorated in modern style - pine chairs and pale walls. A painting of a small girl, crying and holding an umbrella, hangs on the wall opposite me. The painting reminds me of something I have seen before - perhaps another painting, or maybe something that has happened to me; maybe even before I was eighteen. For a moment, a sense of belonging takes hold of me - I feel that I have been here before, that it is right that I should come here; that it is somehow expected of me.

He walks across the room towards me, holding out his hand.

'Hello, Sandy. It's very nice to meet you.'

I shake hands with him, briefly. His hand is warm and he seems to study me closely as our eyes meet.

'It's nice to meet you too,' I reply. I sound nervous.

The girl is still smiling in the doorway. She is very pretty; tall with dark hair. She leans against the door frame, her hands resting in the pockets of her jacket. She looks across at me - smiling, but without feeling. I sense that she is apart from this, perhaps even aloof. She regards me politely, but without interest.

Richard Sturrock introduces her as Cristina, from Milan. He tells me that she is staying with him, for a few weeks. Cristina nods vaguely in his direction, and smiles across at me.

Suddenly, he steps back and claps his hands together.

'So, Sandy; let's go to dinner.'

* * * * * * * * * * * * * * * * *

We walk for only two minutes along a canal - one of the many leading to and from the Grand Canal, and then we arrive at a small restaurant with tables bunched outside. Richard Sturrock beckons me to sit and then goes into the restaurant. The wooden chair is not very comfortable, and I shuffle about, trying to find a position that the back of my legs and my bottom would like. A minute later, he returns with two menus and a couple of red velvet cushions.

'You will find it more comfortable to sit on this,' he says, passing one of the cushions to me with a smile. I dutifully place it between my bottom and the chair, and instantly feel happier about the dining arrangements.

He passes me my menu and sits down, opening his menu in front of him and studying it as if it were a book full of untold secrets. I gaze out across the small canal. On the other side is another restaurant. Outside there is a large table, seating perhaps twenty Orthodox Jews. They are loudly toasting each other's health, and one young man stands at the end of the table, waving a bottle in the air and trying to get everyone to join in a song. One or two people seem to reluctantly sing along, but soon the singing is as it began, a solo. It takes a few lines of a verse for him to realise that he is singing alone, and then he stops abruptly, makes a comment at which everyone laughs, and sits down to a loud round of applause. The people, dressed in black like priests, are all men, and although they appear as though they are very drunk, I have the feeling they are not.

The canal is beautiful; it is still light and the air is warm. Sunshine reflects off the windows across from where we are sitting, and I am glad that I brought my sunglasses.

Richard Sturrock discusses the contents of the menu with me, and he orders for us both. I choose a spaghetti dish, which he assures me is one of the best in Venice. His Italian is fluent, and he is charming almost in a textbook way. In fact, he almost acts like James Bond - like Sean Connery acted when he played the part. I wonder if Richard Sturrock is also playing a part, or whether I am seeing the real person.

He puts down his napkin, which he had been unfolding for a few moments, and smiles at me.

'So, Sandy - you wanted to speak with me...about my song?'

'Yes. Well, really...I want to know what it all means. Not the song, but why it's in my head each Time. You know, don't you? You know about...the condition I have? What happens to me?'

'Yes, of course. The song - it is there to guide you. It's as simple as that.'

'To guide me? To guide me to you?'

'Yes - to me.'

The waiter brings our drinks, and we sit in silence while he pours. I feel an urge to tell him everything, about the record shop and the saxophone player - everything. I am amazed that he understands me. I realise that no-one has ever understood what I am going through before - I have never been able to have a two-way conversation about it. I wait eagerly for the waiter to leave, and stare across at Richard, my eyes burning into him unashamedly. I think of so many things to say, so many things that have remained unsaid - locked up inside me for so long. But instead, I say the one thing that seems the most important - the most vital of all.

'Can you help me?'

'Can I help you? Help you leave this life? Return to how things were?'

'Yes.'

'Sandy, how much do you understand about what is happening to you?'

'I know I am going mad.'

He smiles, and waves his hand in a dismissive gesture. 'The whole world is going mad. Perhaps it is only us who are sane.'

'Us?'

'Yes. I am like you. I, as you put it, have your condition.'

'You are like me? You're trapped like me?'

'It is true that I am like you, but I am not trapped, not at all. Sandy, what is happening to you - happening to us - can be seen as either a curse or a blessing; what you choose to do with your time makes it so.'

'But...I hate what is happening to me. It's driving me insane. I have to get out - I have no choice.'

'You do have a choice.'

'But - I *feel* as though I have no choice; had no choice. And now, you tell me I do...have a choice.' I stare across the table at him. He sighs and smiles a tight lipped smile.

'You can never go back to the time before the coma - that is impossible. But I can help you. I can help you continue in this Time. Do you understand? I can help you grow old in this Time. If you are certain it is what you want.'

'So, you do know...how to end this?'

'Yes. But Sandy...you are here now, having dinner with me, in one of many Times. This is just one of many Times. I can show you how to continue here, past the day that you normally leave. You can continue on in this Time, carry on living here - you understand? But you must be sure. You will be giving up so much - what you see as a prison can be a glorious freedom. You can live out every fantasy, every dream... Which date do you return?'

'August 19th.'

'So, if you wish, for you there can be an August 20th. But there will also be an August 21st, and so on, until you grow old and die. So you must think clearly. I can show you how it is done - it is easy - but once it is done, it can never be undone.'

I sit and stare at him for a moment. His eyes betray nothing, but still seem locked onto mine. I think about what he has said; the implications of his words.

'I'm certain,' I reply. 'I really am.'

'You are certain, really? If you are, that is good. But you still have three weeks in which to decide.'

'Yes...'

'There is a place, a warehouse here in Venice. Inside there is a room, there are lots of tins of paint. It is used for storage. The corner of the room...'

'What?'

'It is...a space; just a space of some kind. I don't know. But, if you wait there at your...moment.'

'August 19th, 11.12am.'

'Exactly - if you wait at 11.12am, you will not go back.'

I look at him in disbelief. It seems just too simple, without effort.

'That's it?' I ask.

'That is it. I will show you tomorrow where it is. Then you can decide. But, remember, this is just one Time. You could choose the next Time, or the next. Make everything as you would like, and then...stay.'

My head is spinning by now, and I nod silently at him. The food arrives and he tells me about himself. He is from Manchester, and he was only seventeen when he had his accident. It was not his birthday. He was in a coma for thirteen years, just like me. He is now thirty years old; a year younger than I am.

As we eat, I ask him about his life in Venice. He says he loves Italy, but he says he lives here in order to guide people to the exit, as he now describes it. I ask him about the girl at his house, thinking she is perhaps the equivalent of my Chris, but he matter-of-factly tells me that she is a prostitute.

'Each Time, I am rich. My family accumulated a reasonable amount of money over time, and I inherited a great deal of money during my coma - over two million pounds. Here in Italy, there is an agency - a very elite agency. I stumbled across it at a casino once - in fact I was approached, while making large bets at the roulette table. This agency does not advertise, but offers its services to men who, like me, can afford to pay. They offer complete secrecy, which I have no need for, and also girls who are at the very top end of their business; girls who are so pretty it's amazing that they are - professional girls. I remember - I have memorised - the telephone number, and each Time I contact them with a proposition.

'I am here, each Time, for nearly six months, and so I simply hire one girl for that length of time. It costs me a fortune - you would be astonished how much - and for my money they come and live with me here. It is not always the same girl for the whole Time, but often it is. They are all very nice, friendly, and, of course, in bed they are eager to please. It is simple, and it suits me fine. I have not embarrassed you, have I?'

I realise that, despite myself, I am turning red.

'No, not really...'

'Do you not have any secrets, Sandy? Anything you would rather keep to yourself?'

I look across at him blankly. He takes a drink from his glass and smiles. He speaks quietly, but with authority.

'We all have secrets - every one of us. We are all ashamed of something - we are all ashamed...'

* * * * * * * * * * * * * * *

On the five minute train ride back to Mestre, I sit and look out of the window. We pass over a long bridge, so long it seems -

for a moment - as if it might go on forever. It's as if it would stretch away into the darkness, never ending as it trails through fields and towns and over mountains. I close my eyes and I can see the different views and vistas, the green of the fields and the deep blues and greys of the sea.

I watch the different people getting on and off the train - so many people I could meet, so many faces who smile; so many hands that wave.

But this is not my future; I will not let this be my future. This journey is about to end. I pull my bag close to my chest; I have had enough of travelling on this train; the track may pass on forever, but I will not.

A moment later, the train grinds to a halt in Mestre, and I almost trip as I hastily climb down from the carriage.

That night I dream that I am back on that same train. I have missed my stop and we trundle on into the night. Except where I am going, it is always day. Night does not exist there.

I look out of the window, and the sun comes up over ever more desolate views; churches standing in fields destroyed by bombs, villages empty of sound except for the bleating of sheep, driven mad by hunger.

I sink back in my seat, but I cannot take my eyes off the window. Now everything is desert; not even a tree or a patch of grass. I know that I must get off, begin the long walk back. But it seems so much effort, and the seat is too comfortable. I close my eyes and feel myself drifting off to sleep. The desert view is still in my mind, but is now replaced with a room, walls covered in panels and paintings. A single window lets light into the room, and suddenly I see that I am not alone. From behind a curtain steps a man - it is Richard Sturrock, and he is carrying a picture of his own. He smiles at me and hangs it on the wall. As he steps back to admire it, I can see it is the girl with the umbrella; the same painting on view in his home. He beckons me forward to join him, and I slowly walk to his side. He takes my hand in his, and we stand looking at the girl - the sadness evident in her face.

'Do you like this picture?' He asks, without turning to look at me.

'Yes. It's sad, but beautiful. I like it very much.'

'Yes, it is beautiful. You gave it to me, a long time ago. Do you remember?'

For a moment I am confused, and then I remember something. A dream or a memory, I am not sure which, but I am walking along with Richard Sturrock, and he has the picture under his arm. He is thanking me for such a wonderful gift.

'Yes,' I say. 'I remember…'

Then he is behind me, placing his hands around my waist, across my stomach. He leans into me, his mouth kissing the side of my neck.

'You are so kind,' he whispers. 'For giving me something so beautiful…'

I sit up in bed, and then fumble in the darkness for my watch. It has a button that makes it luminous. The time is 4.13am - too early to get up. I slump back on my pillow, and as I do there is a frantic knock on the door of my room. My heart jumps in my chest, and then I leap out of bed and fumble my way to the door.

'Who is it?' I ask, leaning against the door with my right arm. A voice shouts back, with a note of panic.

'Sandy! It's Lena! You have to leave now! There is a fire!'

I feel around on the wall for a light switch, and find one in the same place as in my usual room in Lancaster Gate. I switch on the light, and I am in my room in London.

'Lena, is that you? What's going on? I was asleep…'

'Yes, asleep. Of course, it is night time. But there is a fire, you must be quick. There is a taxi waiting for you, it is waiting downstairs. You have to leave…'

'OK, Lena - wait. I have to find some clothes. Wait for me…I'll just be a second.'

'Sandy! No time! Be as quick as you can, the taxi is

waiting, there is a fire! You must leave now…'

I pull on a t-shirt and jeans I find on the bed, and pull open the door to the room. Lena is outside; she is wearing a black cocktail dress, and looks very worried.

'OK, Lena - I'm here…'

'Good, now we must go, we must be quick…'

Lena runs along the corridor, and then suddenly stops. She turns to me and grabs me by the arm. She stares at me wildly, and for the first time I realise that this is not Lena, but someone pretending to be her. I try to break free, but she is too strong.

'Sandy, try to understand. You must leave now. Do you understand? You cannot wait…'

I know something is dreadfully wrong. I try to scream, but I cannot make my voice work. The sound gets stuck in my throat, and as I put my hand to my face, I feel that something terrible has happened. Where my mouth once was is now just a smooth layer of skin. The girl who has hold of my arm looks at me with pity. I stare at her, and then everything is grey, and then black…

I open my eyes, and I can see the distant lights from the railway station making patterns on the flimsy curtains in my room. The alarm clock beside me has red digital numbers, it reads 2.15am. I am shaking and covered in sweat. I lean across and switch on the bedroom light. I am in Mestre. I am awake.

I stand in the bathroom, splashing water in my face. I look and feel tired, but I'm scared to go back to sleep. However, I feel so tired that I have no choice. I walk slowly back to bed, and pull the sheets over me. I have stopped trembling, and, leaving the bedside lamp on, close my eyes and try to count sheep jumping over a wooden gate. The sheep just keep running off, darting and dancing in all directions. But it doesn't matter, because within minutes I fall into a deep, dreamless sleep.

Time Ninety-Six

Friday 28th July 2006
8.30am CET

I sit quietly at breakfast, thinking about the day ahead. I have arranged to meet Richard Sturrock at ten-thirty this morning, and he has promised to take me to the place that will act as a gateway out of this life. I cannot really understand how this could possibly work, or how the answer could be this simple. In fact, deep down, I have thought for some time that there was no way out at all; that I am condemned to this shadow of an existence forever, unable to truly live or even to die.

Richard Sturrock has offered me hope, and I am worried that my mind is becoming completely fixed on that promise; a promise of an exit from what has become of my life.

As I think about all of these things, I am reminded of the dream I had last night. I remember that he was in the dream, and that he was trying to seduce me. In fact, I was allowing myself to be seduced, and I then consider the possibility that this is what is happening now. Perhaps, because I wanted to believe him so much, I was allowing myself to take too much of what he said at face value.

My orange juice sits on the table in front of me, untouched. Little bits float on the surface, each a tiny piece of orange separated from the whole. I know, as I stare, that my thoughts are becoming this way, separate and disjointed.

I have so many memories, some from before my first Time, but almost all from afterwards. And this is a problem, because each of these memories bears no true relation to the next – there is no true sequence of time in my life. I cannot place any memory in order, one before the other.

There is one exception to this, and that is Chris. I can remember the first Time we met – the first occasion for me, and then every Time since then; every Time that has included Chris. All of this is clear to me, and these Times have been the happiest I have had. I regret the Times I have not spent with him – like this Time - and I often especially regret the Times that I spent with Adam.

I wonder what I should do, assuming that Richard Sturrock is able to offer me a way out. Should I just carry on this Time and see Christmas, grow older and older, or should I leave as usual and have another Time? I could set everything as I would want it, spend lots of time with Chris, and then stay in the next Time for ever; live and die, like a normal person.

Logically, I think I should leave next Time, just as Richard Sturrock suggested, but – at the same time – I am desperate to know if it would work. I need to find out if what Richard Sturrock is telling me is true. I feel that I can barely wait three weeks, let alone another five months.

I am confused about everything; I cannot make decisions any more. I need someone to make decisions for me. I wish I could call Chris and ask him what to do – but he doesn't even know me this Time, and nobody understands except me. That is, apart from Richard Sturrock.

In the end, I do drink my orange juice, slowly, and eat some cornflakes.

* * * * * * * * * * * * * * * *

I leave the hotel and step into a beautiful sunny day. The sunshine lifts my melancholy mood a little, and I begin to feel more positive about things. Perhaps today will be one of the most important of my life.

I trot across the busy road and jog into the railway station. I check my pocket for tickets - I bought ten yesterday from the little booth inside the station entrance, and I still have eight left. I can feel them; tiny pieces of card between my fingers. I slow my pace to a fast walk, and then – having found the right platform - stand waiting for the next train to arrive.

The platform is quite crowded – there are lots of families and some men wearing business suits. There are also many tourists, of which I suppose I am one. I am dressed in a white t-shirt with dark blue shorts and sandals; I am carrying a guide book and I have natural auburn hair; so I think I probably do look like a tourist. But I don't mind, and anyway, I am strictly here on business.

The train arrives after about five minutes, and I climb aboard and stand over to one side next to the opposite door. The train is crowded already, and there are no seats left vacant. However, as the journey takes only five minutes, I feel happy to stand. My feeling of wellbeing is becoming stronger, and I find myself quite looking forward to meeting Richard Sturrock again. I still feel slightly unnerved by his antics in the dream, but I think that perhaps he is, in reality, a fairly interesting person. I find myself wondering if it might be fun if he were to show me around Venice after today – he must know every alley and canal by now.

The sun, low and bright in the sky, passes the window as we travel over the long bridge to Venice. This brings back another part of my dream, where I was on a train travelling to a place where there was only day, and never any night. I wonder to myself if a land which has no night would be as bad as a land which has no day. I think that it would.

During one Time, Time Forty-Eight, an elderly Chinese lady told me how she had been considered an intellectual during the Cultural Revolution. We both had tickets for a puppet show in Beijing, but on entering the auditorium we converged on the same seat. The show was a sell-out, and we had both somehow been sold the same ticket. After a pointless discussion with a seemingly fourteen year-old usher, we both decided to forgo the show and instead have tea in the 'excellent tea shop' across the road (it wasn't just 'excellent', as described by the lady; it was actually called the 'Excellent Tea Shop').

The Chinese lady, whose name was Lee Tan, was from a province in China called Hunan, which was quick to adopt the teachings of Chairman Mao, and slow to remove them after his death in Nineteen Seventy-Six. She told me all this while we were drinking traditional tea, seated on stools either side of a tiny plastic table.

Lee Tan spoke excellent English, as she had been a young English teacher at the time of the revolution. She was branded an intellectual and a subversive almost straight away. She had no children at the time (she now has a son, who teaches English in Beijing), but her husband was sent away for 'compulsory re-education'. Amazingly, they were reunited some years later.

She was arrested during the first days of the terror, and her students - themselves terrified - testified against her, saying she was a friend of the Queen and other bourgeois imperialists in England. This and other evidence, including a 'pen-pal' relationship with Charles Dickens, was accepted as fact by the Red Guards who oversaw the trial, none of whom could read at all, and one who was only twelve years old.

Lee was sent to work in a factory making 'shoes for the people'. These shoes were of the poorest quality Lee had ever seen, and the factory was instructed to make five thousand pairs a day.

'They were terrible shoes!' She said. 'We all had so many to make each day. And there were no nights, only days…'

When I asked what she meant she explained.

'We ate, slept and worked at the factory – on the factory floor. Always there were inspirational talks playing over the speakers, and the lights were never off, never even dimmed. It was always light, bright light to make the shoes; all the time.

'Sometimes, we had to work for ten days and nights in a row, and then we could sleep for twelve hours. Of course, it was impossible to stay awake for so long. We would try to snatch a few minutes' sleep, one at a time, when the foreman was not watching. There were three foremen, who each took turns to watch over us. But most often, there was only one particular foreman, a stupid man whose name I forget; I have chosen to forget.

'One girl, Li Na, she was sent to make shoes because of her religious beliefs. She was a very religious girl, very religious. She would pray all the time. She would sing hymns, quietly, beneath her breath.

'Well, often there was only this one particular foreman watching us girls. We were locked into a single wing of the factory, there were ten of us, and we were locked in so we could not escape. It was a huge wing for so few of us - perhaps made for sixty workers!

'We were considered the most subversive of all, and therefore the most dangerous. The foreman was often locked in with us, although of course he had a key. Li Na was very pretty, and this foreman liked her very much. He liked her face, her body, you understand? So, do you know what she would do?'

I shook my head, transfixed by the story.

'When we were forced to work for so long, when we were all so tired, Li Na would lead the foreman into his office and be with him for an hour. She would do all things to him, things that people then would not even speak of, and sometimes they would be gone for as long as ninety minutes. As soon as Li Na closed the door of his office, we would lay down on the floor and sleep.

'When she had finished with him, she would open the door and bow, saying 'thank you, sir!' very loudly. This would wake us up, and we would stand up and work as if nothing had happened. She did this for us, so we could sleep. I think, because of her, we survived. She was a very kind and religious girl. She believed in God very much. So, you see, there were no nights, only days.'

Lee sipped her tea gracefully and told me all this without

passion or anger; it was simply what had been. But she would talk about nothing else from that time in her life.

I felt I understood what she meant; the blurring of days into days, and for me, the blurring of Time into Time.

Her suffering had been worse, of course, but it at least had an end - and she had, one day, found peace.

* * * * * * * * * * * * * * * *

I am forty minutes early for the time I'd agreed to meet with Richard Sturrock, so I sit on the steps outside the station in Venice and drink a can of Sprite. I like Sprite because it tastes like lemonade. The sun is becoming warmer, and the canal is shimmering with natural light. People pass in front of me both walking and standing on boats; some of them are slowly wending their way forward in gondolas, but most squashing onto water buses which stop outside the station.

I am feeling a bit tired; but also excited. I cannot sit still for long, and so I walk down the steps and, turning right, walk along the Grand Canal. Everything seems beautiful in Venice, and the sunshine further lifts my mood.

The dream from last night still plays on my mind, and the shadow it casts makes me feel as though something is not quite right. But my positive mood is winning me over, and I turn around and walk with confidence in the direction of Richard Sturrock's house.

* * * * * * * * * * * * * * * *

He is waiting for me when I arrive; standing in the doorway of his home. He is wearing a pair of jeans and a sweatshirt - much more casual than yesterday. I am taken by surprise at this sudden change of dress. I had imagined that he always walked around in a suit, but of course I had no reason to believe this was the case.

In fact, I realised - as I looked at him and smiled a hello - that I knew very little about him at all. He had not avoided my questions yesterday evening, but had instead somehow made me not want to ask any. He made me talk about myself, and was able to deflect investigation away from himself. He had done this in a way that was not obvious; skilled perhaps. Maybe, I thought, he has done this before.

Richard shook my hand and gave me a kiss on the cheek. This brought back my dream to me, and I resisted the urge to pull away.

'So, Sandy, how are you this morning?' He said with a smile.

'I'm fine,' I replied.

'Good, I'm glad that you are feeling well. Are you ready?'

'Yes, I'm ready.'

'Good. Let's go then.'

For the first few moments I find myself walking just behind him, almost trotting to keep up. Then he slows his pace and I naturally step alongside him.

'It's not far,' he says. 'Not far at all.'

We walk for a few minutes in a straight line, following the route of the small canal beside which we had dinner yesterday. But today we are heading in the opposite direction, towards the edge of the island. Soon I can see the end of the canal, disappearing into the sea beyond. We pass by a stone bridge, and a small water bus passes underneath as we walk by. A little girl, standing at the front, waves at us. Only I wave back.

'Another five minutes and we'll be there,' he says. 'Just five more minutes...'

'Ok, that's fine.'

'It's a very simple route - I can mark it on a map for you, if you like. But, whatever you decide, you will remember the route easily. Could you find where you are now?'

'Yes, no problem. I know where I am.'

'Good. It's good to know where you are.'

We walk on for another couple of minutes, and then we reach the end of the canal. There are two green metal benches facing the other side. Someone has left a newspaper on one of them. Richard sits on the other one, and beckons me to sit down beside him.

'Are we there?' I ask.

'Not yet...'

'Oh...'

'Sandy, I need to talk to you before I show you what I have learnt - what it has taken me so long to discover. Once I show you what I know, you will be able to leave at will. Whether this Time, or the next, or any Time in the future, you can just make sure you are there on the correct day, the correct moment, and that Time will last until death.'

'Yes...'

'But you must be absolutely sure you realise what you are giving up. We are a special people. You and I, we are special. There are so few of us, just a handful, but we are incredible, because we are immortal. We can live forever, do whatever we choose, and then just begin again. We can live on into eternity; death has no hold over us. If you choose to leave - choose to leave us - then you can never return. You can never again capture what you once had. If you decide to leave, then you must understand this fact.'

'Yes, I do understand...'

'But, please, Sandy. You have time to think - other Times in which to think. Think carefully, that is all I ask.'

'I promise...'

He smiles at me and stands up.

'Good. Then I will take you now. Please forgive my lecture, but these things are so important...'

'That's OK. I will give it all lots of thought. Like you said, I have three weeks...'

'Of course...'

We walk away from the bench and follow the edge of the island along to my left. I can see bigger boats out on the water, and a ship in the distance. There are warehouses on my left-hand side; they look deserted and neglected. Then, a moment later, we pass two warehouses that have been converted into art studios. People are working there, creating art as we walk along. Then we turn inland up an alley and walk for another minute. The sounds of the sea are behind us and we stop at a green door on the right side of the alley. Richard pushes on the door and it swings inwards. We step together into an empty space, dark and strangely cold. Richard switches on the light, and the space becomes a redundant carpenter's workshop, with benches and posts still riveted to the floor. There are still copious amounts of wood shavings scattered all over the brick tiles, and discarded off-cuts of wood leaning in haphazard piles against the walls. He takes a few paces forwards into the room and then turns around to face me.

'This way,' he says with a small smile.

I take a step forward and then suddenly stop. A feeling passes over me like a wave; a feeling I remember from before. It is an overwhelming feeling that I am being watched, that I am naked and exposed, and someone is examining me - as if I am uncovered to somebody.

I remember this feeling from my hotel, the lobby of the hotel in Lancaster Gate - but this Time the feeling is stronger; so strong that I feel short of breath. The sensations are the same as before - powerful, invasive - wonderful and terrifying at the same time.

Richard has realised that I have stopped and so he stops as well. He turns to me again, looking concerned.

'Are you OK?' He asks.

For a second I can't speak, but then the feeling begins to pass, and I nod at him.

'Are you sure? Do you need help?'

I shake my head.

'Well, OK then, Sandy. If you follow me, it's just around this corner.'

He moves away again and stops at the end of the room, before an open wall leading away to the left. The feeling has left me now, and I run my hand through my hair, press my palm onto the back of my neck. I am sweating, even though the room is cold. I shake my head and walk forward. Richard waits until I am just behind him and then walks away through the open wall. I follow him.

We are now standing in another room, a smaller version of the last. Richard starts to explain about the history of the building - how it was once a family business that closed when demand lessened for the specialist furniture they had once produced. As I stand and listen, I begin to feel more at ease and I try to dispel the confusion which is the aftermath of my feeling.

He tells me about the hundreds of businesses like this in Venice, almost all family concerns going back generations. He speaks with authority and with knowledge, smiling all the time, as if he knows that I need to calm down.

As I relax, I start to take in the surroundings in a new light. There is a high ceiling and grey brick walls. This room has no equipment, but just the same discarded wood and shavings, waiting in vain to be swept away. But it is a nice room - I could even imagine it transformed into a modern apartment for a rich couple and sold for a fortune by a property developer.

Richard continues to talk, and then points out the tins of paint in the corner. There are about twenty tins of white paint, some of them are opened. They are scattered about, surrounding a steel ring attached to the floor. This appears quite new, as if it has been put there recently.

'So,' he says. 'Over there, in that corner with the paint...That is where you must stand.'

He walks over and stands facing the wall, his feet in amongst the tins of paint.

'This is the place'. He says this quietly, almost to himself. He still has his back to me, but I hear him speaking, his voice echoing off the wall in front.

'This is the place. This is the place…'

He turns to face me again.

'What's that?' I ask, in a whisper. My mind and voice are now full of fear.

'It's OK. I'm not going to hurt you.'

He is holding a knife, a large knife. I step back towards the wall. He comes towards me.

'I'm not going to hurt you'.

He pushes the blade into my stomach, through my white top. I gasp as he pulls it out. Then in, then out, then in – this time he holds onto the handle, pushes deeper. He leans towards me and whispers.

'You don't understand! None of you – you never understand! This is all I have. This is all I want…'

I start to feel cold, an awful cold, creeping up from my stomach to my chest, and across my arms.

He begins to stroke my hair as he speaks.

'Nothing matters, only this. Only killing; that's all that matters. That's the greatest thing of all; the only thing worth having - to be able to kill.'

I feel cold all over now; a terrible, empty cold. He is still speaking, but I can't hear him anymore. My mind is filled with memories; so many memories. Not just from different Times, but before that.

I am a little girl. I'm sitting on a swing, and I'm crying because I've hurt my knee. My tummy starts to hurt as well, and my mummy is smiling at me. She wants to make me better.

I am standing at the side of the road, outside my home in Bexley. Cars pass by, and I am trying to count them, but there are too many. I keep losing count, and this makes me cry. My mummy bends down beside me. 'Never mind,' she says. 'Just start again. Just start again…'

I am with Chris, and we are holding hands. I am happy.

I am with Adam, and we are talking to the Japanese man. He is saying 'You go Venice!' This time he is not just pleading, but he is warning me. He points to Adam, but looks at me. 'You take boyfriend!'

I look down at myself; I am wearing a red England top. I look at the badge, and at the little gold star. Now I am the star. I float away from the top, and into the air. I reach up toward the sky - climbing higher, higher...

Time Ninety-Seven

Saturday 18th March 2006
11.35am

Oh my God. Oh my God. Oh my God. Oh my God. I say these words over and over in my mind as I awake. I feel stunned, as if I have been pushed over and hit my head. I feel sick, but I have no strength to vomit. I just lay staring up at the ceiling – I stare, but my eyes are closed; my eyelids clamped down in a refusal to see the light. They cannot admit that I have woken up.

But I see the ceiling in my mind; I remember it so well from the Times before. On the ceiling in my mind I can see images, pictures of myself, covered in blood. I feel the knife in my stomach – still there. I am too weak to move my hand down to check. I can see the blood everywhere, draining out of me, as if somebody has carelessly left a tap running. This is still happening - I am still bleeding, the knife is still inside me; everything is as it was before.

I know I am awake, but not properly. I am still asleep – in a way – and so what has happened is still with me. I force open my eyes – try to dispel the scene in front of me. As I do the light floods into my retinas, cleansing the blood away, bringing the white of the ceiling into focus.

But I can still feel the knife. It's ghost is like an intruder inside me. I want it out. My skin twitches around it. I want to reach down and remove it, but I can't. No energy. I close my eyes again – I feel so tired. I am so tired. The blood has gone, but the knife remains. It is a reminder of what has happened to me, of what is.

I have been murdered.

* * * * * * * * * * * * * * *

Later that day – much later – I feel as if I have cheated death. I am elated, but frightened at the same time. I remember with clarity what has happened, and this - all the memories of my death - is what frightens me.

But I learnt so much last Time; there is so much more to remember, and this gives me hope.

These are the things I know for certain:

1) Richard Sturrock is completely insane and wants to kill me. He has killed me.
2) He knows where I will be this Time - at the end.
3) He has told me the correct location to escape.

I don't know how I know the last thing, but I am certain it is true.

I feel as if a picture is beginning to form - once out of view and in shadows, it is slowly being bathed in light, until it becomes clearer and clearer. This Time has taken on a new meaning; now I am in a battle.

It is a battle that I must win, and this gives me the greatest hope of all - it is a battle I believe I can win.

Richard Sturrock has reached the place of madness - a place that also awaits me in the future, and not the distant future. The undeniable fact that he is completely mad is his weakness - he is surely no longer able to think with clarity. I can almost see inside his mind - a mind filled with killing and death - and I can imagine how his days must be crowded with these thoughts.

I can imagine these things because he and I are the same - we walk down the same road. But the difference, and the only difference, is that he has almost certainly walked down it for longer than me.

I believe that his obsession is only with killing, but his confession about his need of the services of prostitutes worries me. I want to believe that he killed me and left me when I died; I don't want to think about anything else happening to me - to my body.

The thought that he may have touched me afterwards makes me feel queasy - like seasickness. However, I cannot dwell on these things because I cannot change anything now, and anyway, my instinct tells me that I was simply left for dead. But I am not sure about that; not certain.

I remember him touching my hair, whispering to me like a lover; this is one of the last things I do remember. This plays over in my mind, and I have to force myself to think of other things. And my instincts tell me that nothing happened. I must trust my instincts, I tell myself.

But, do my instincts work when I am dead?

These are pointless questions, and I am stupid to spend time thinking about them. But for hours they play on my mind, until one thing rises to the surface of my brain - a simple and pure emotion that helps me refocus my thoughts: revenge.

Murder of any kind always seemed to me wrong - I did not believe I was capable of it, and I did not think it justifiable under any circumstances. But what happened to me has left a mark so deep that I cannot reach the bottom, and time itself is ruining me as a person - driving reason away and leaving nothing of value in its place.

So, if revenge will help me to think, to get beyond what has happened, then I can accept it with open arms.

With revenge in mind, I formulate this plan: I am going back to Venice to escape, and while there, I am going to kill the bastard.

Time Ninety-Seven

Friday 24th March 2006
10.00am

I am out of BUPA and safely installed in my hotel at Lancaster Gate. I spend the next few days eating, building up my strength and mulling over my options.

I badly want to go and see Chris, to spend time with him and have him hold me and tell me everything is fine. But I don't think I have the mental energy to strike up a relationship with him from scratch - to pretend that I'm not familiar with every inch of his body, to act as if I don't know him better than any other person in the world.

Instead, I go for long walks in Kensington Gardens to help me think. I watch normal people walk around and I feel jealous of them. I also wonder if any of them are like me - if there are many others in England, living the same kind of life as me. Now that I know that there are others, the world has become a different place to me.

I think and think about my predicament - about the possibilities. I have changed as a result of what has happened. I feel more serious about things, and my thoughts feel sharper; more focused. I am absolutely certain that I want to escape - there is no longer any doubt in my mind. And I am sure that Richard Sturrock intends to play some kind of 'cat and mouse' game with me. This is not a game I want to participate in; not with his rules.

And, I am certain of this: this Time, I am going to be the cat.

Time Ninety-Seven

Tuesday 28th March 2006
5.10pm

I am going to spend two hours before dinner searching the Internet; turning my decision to fight back against Richard Sturrock into reality. I am going to book myself onto an intensive self-defence course, and try to find one that will empower me the most for the task in hand.

Lena logs me on to the computer and leaves me to browse. I search for ages and find lots of different classes, but nothing suitable. However, after an hour I find two courses - both in America - that seem as if they might be the kind of thing I am looking for. One is in San Francisco, California, and the other is in a place called, eccentrically, 'Truth or Consequences' in Southwest New Mexico.

Although I am fascinated by the idea of visiting a town called Truth or Consequences, I e-mail for more information on both classes and then go off to have dinner.

I eat at the hotel - which is rare for me - but I just can't be bothered to go out, or to make anything in my room. I have steak and chips - not very imaginative but very tasty. After a strawberry cheesecake for dessert, I go back to find Lena to get the password for the Internet computer again. A couple of minutes later, Lena is again logging me on. It is now 7.55pm.

I am surprised to find that one of the sites I e-mailed has replied already. Someone called Sandra has responded to my e-mail personally, asking me to call her to discuss the suitability of the course, and so she can explain more fully the nature of the commitment. I am impressed by the seriousness of her reply, and so I decide to call from my room straight away.

I begin the call lying on the bed in my room, one hand

resting on a glass of Sprite. But forty-five minutes later - and still on the phone - I am now standing and pacing up and down, as far as the telephone lead will allow. I have been asked a hundred questions, and I have asked a hundred of my own; each question and answer leading to another, and leading me further down the road to committing myself to this course.

It is expensive; but I have the money. It is residential and takes eight weeks; but I have the time. And, in every respect, it seems perfect. It is possible that I may be taken for a ride, but my instinct is crying out, by the end of the call, for me to commit. However, I tell Sandra that I will sleep on it, and promise to e-mail in the morning if I decide to join the course. She thanks me for my time, and then I hang up. I finish my Sprite - which is now flat - and have a bath.

In the bath I consider the things Sandra has said over the phone, but I have already decided to go. I cannot believe I would find anything more suitable, and if Sandra is not lying to me, then it should be ideal. The next course starts on May 19th, which is about seven weeks away. This gives me plenty of time to prepare myself - to get myself fit - but I wish that it would start tomorrow.

Time Ninety-Seven

Wednesday 29th March 2006
9.30am

I e-mail Sandra confirming my intention to come - to commit to the eight weeks of training - and Sandra replies that same day with various details, including a link to a map of Truth or Consequences. There is also a map of Southwest New Mexico, and the town is marked upon it with a black dot.

The house I will be staying at is just over a mile outside the centre of the town - a town of seven thousand people. I still find it hard to believe that a town exists with such a strange name, but further research proves to me its existence, and leads me to find out a great deal about a place that would be my home for two months. These details are not important, apart from to say that the town is named after a popular American radio show of the 1950's.

Over the weeks that follow, I engage fully in a regime of fitness and stamina building. The hotel does not have a gym, so I join a fitness club in Queensway about half a mile along Bayswater Road. I spend almost every morning there - sweating and running, drinking bottled water and getting fitter and fitter. I start eating more healthily and drinking bizarre vegetable juices - but I am less successful at this. All the drinks taste like crap, and after exercising all morning I need enormous amounts of food to assuage my hunger. I try to eat enormous amounts of good, wholesome food, but it is not always available, and so I eat what is easily accessible.

I also do something that turns out to be of great value. I bet on the World Cup.

Time Ninety-Seven

Friday 14th April 2006

After meeting the man in the flat cap on the flight to Venice during Time Ninety-Six, I consider seriously for the first time what a good idea it would be to place bets on the World Cup. I know nothing about betting, and all that it entails - but a single evening's research on the internet tells me everything I need to know to win a very large amount of money.

This, of course, will only matter if I am able to stay in this Time - Time Ninety-Seven - but I intend to do that very thing. I will place the bets here in England, fly to America for my course, travel on to Venice and kill Richard Sturrock, and then leave the cycle of Times by way of the 'exit' already shown to me. This is my plan, in a nutshell. What could be simpler? What could be simpler?

* * * * * * * * * * * * * * * * *

The World Cup begins in about two months, and Italy are 9/1 to win. I have a long and fruitful discussion with 'Plastic Bobby' on an independent gamblers website, and he answers the many questions I have about placing my bets. I find out a number of useful things.

I discover, amongst other things, that there is a maximum amount you can win in any one day with a single bookmaker. This is, on average, about one hundred and fifty thousand pounds. I had asked Plastic Bobby if I would have any problems collecting my money if I registered with a number of different bookmakers and placed the same bet. He said that as long as the bet was accepted, and that it was unlikely that I could have had any influence over the result, or that the result was not deemed 'suspicious' in any way, then they would pay without question - even if it was a fairly large amount of money.

He explained that bets are made, on both sides, in good faith. If punters (which I learnt is the term for people who bet) thought that a bookmaker was going to give problems when paying out, then they would simply bet elsewhere. He told me that many millions of pounds a day are gambled on websites and in bookmakers all over the world, and that they could well afford to lose every now and then.

He also explained to me how to register with a site, and how to take advantage of the free initial bet, usually of between ten and a hundred pounds, that they offer as an incentive to register.

Plastic Bobby is intrigued by me and my seemingly sudden impulse to bet, and he ends our web chat by asking me if I have any good tips. I tell him that maybe I have, but that I don't want to type them on-line. Perhaps I have been reading too many American spy novels, but somehow I feel I should keep this information to myself - or not publish it too widely.

However, Plastic Bobby has been very helpful, especially as I am obviously such a novice, and I wonder if it would do any harm to pass on some information to him. But, at the same time, I think 'why should he believe me, anyway?'

Plastic Bobby takes my reluctance to pass on my tips as a cue to end the conversation, and says that he is fine with that and wishes me well. The fact that he doesn't push me at all makes me suddenly have an idea. I think for a second, and in response I quickly type this:

Listen - Plastic Bobby - I do have a tip for you! Call me now on this number - 09785 334546. This is my mobile. Please call...

For a few seconds nothing appears on the screen, and I think that maybe he's gone. Then suddenly he replies:

Is this a premium rate number? A scam?

I reply again quickly:

No, it honestly isn't. It's my mobile phone. You've been a great help, and I have a good tip. Call now.

Again a few seconds without reply, and then:

OK.

Literally seconds later my mobile phone rings in my bag, and I have to scramble to fish it out. I push the little green button and say hello. A voice replies to me, a woman's voice:

'Hi - is that San555?'

This is the name I used on the site. The voice sounds as if it belongs to a middle-aged woman, perhaps from the Midlands.

'Hi. Is that Plastic Bobby?'

'Yes, it is.'

'Thanks for calling. I thought you were a man...'

'No. My name's Roberta - my friends call me Bobby. You said you had a tip?'

'Yes - Bobby, do you have a piece of paper?'

'Yes - is this straight? Is this a real tip?'

'Yes, it really is. Just write this down, and then you can bet if you want...'

'OK...'

'The World Cup is in June. England beat Paraguay 1-0 in their opening match - Paraguay score an own goal. Then England beat Trinidad 2-0 - both goals scored in the last ten minutes of the match. Then they draw 2-2 with Sweden - that's the last group match.'

'Right...'

'Are you writing?'

'Yes, but...'

'OK. Then England beat Ecuador 1-0 in the last sixteen -

David Beckham scores, and then England lose to Portugal on penalties in the quarter-finals. The final is between France and Italy. Italy wins. Italy wins the World Cup.'

'Right…'

'Have you written that all down?'

'Yes…'

'Good… Bobby, you've been great! Thanks for all your help. Good luck with everything. Bye.'

And with that I hang up. I switch my phone off, and go to bed.

I am ready to enter the gambling arena.

Time Ninety Seven

Saturday 15th April 2006

In the morning, I throw my phone away. I feel strangely paranoid about the whole thing, as if I have a great big secret that, if discovered, will get me into lots of trouble. The phone was a 'pay as you go', with no contract. That same morning, I simply go into the Vodafone shop near Oxford Street and buy another one.

Plastic Bobby was invaluable help, and in the afternoon I register with fifteen separate bookmaker's websites, and in each case transfer twelve thousand pounds to the relevant accounts. I had considered betting on England to beat Paraguay 1-0 in their opening match, or on the England - Sweden Match to end 2-2, but in the end I place the same bet of twelve thousand pounds on each site, getting odds of either 9-1 or 10-1, depending on the site. I bet on Italy to win the World Cup - that is all.

I place the bet from each of my new betting accounts, and the bets are taken without question. It is that simple to bet, that simple to lose a fortune - or in my case, that simple to win one.

I have ten bets at 10-1 and five bets at 9-1, so I work out - using Windows Calculator on the Internet computer - that my overall winnings will be one million, seven hundred and forty thousand pounds exactly, and also my stake money back, which is one hundred and eighty thousand pounds. This seems as if it is a good amount of money to have for the future; my future - my future with Chris.

* * * * * * * * * * * * * * * *

Plastic Bobby, whose actual name is Roberta Saunders, lived

with her husband and two children, both boys, in a small terraced house in Wolverhampton - not far from the centre of town. She loved to gamble, and knew a great deal about it - but she found it difficult to make money at it. She was not a bad gambler - never chased after money she had lost, and she never lost a great deal - but she never really won that much either.

Bobby bet on horses. She had no interest in football; and, although she kept the information given to her by Sandy in her 'betting drawer', she forgot all about it by the time the World Cup began.

Her husband and sons (aged 12 and 10) all loved football, and her husband was a lifelong Wolverhampton Wanderers supporter. They planned to watch the World Cup together, and bought some plastic flags and St George Cross hats for the England matches.

It wasn't until England won their first match 1-0, the victory brought about by a Paraguay own goal, that Bobby remembered what Sandy had told her. That evening, after dinner, she pulled out the sheet of paper from her betting drawer and read what was on it.

She put the paper back, a bit perplexed, and decided to wait and see what would happen in the second match.

The second match (against Trinidad) ended exactly, of course, as Sandy had predicted. Bobby could hardly believe it. She read and re-read the sheet of paper over and over again. It wasn't just the fact that the score was correct - the girl who had given her this information had told her the goals would be scored in the last ten minutes. She was right. It seemed impossible, but the piece of paper seemed to hold, so far, accurate information about the results of matches that had not yet happened.

Try as she might, Bobby could find no logic in this. But, and this was undeniable, the girl had been absolutely right so far. And right in a way that could not possibly be a coincidence.

Bobby spoke to Dave - her husband - about the paper and the information she had been given. He was sceptical, but even a great sceptic like Dave could not deny that the information had so far proven to be true.

Bobby and Dave had very little money, although they were not really poor. He worked as a mechanic - for a large firm in Birmingham. Bobby worked part-time in a supermarket - on the tills - and in that way they got by. But they had very recently taken out an extension to their mortgage, twenty-five thousand pounds, to enable them to pay off some existing debts, and have the kitchen renovated. The whole family agreed that the kitchen was in desperate need of renovation. There would also be enough left over to buy a second-hand car. The Vauxhall Astra, which had been in the family for twelve years, was near to death.

Bobby suggested they should risk a small amount of this money, which was sitting in their joint account at the moment, on the next England match with Sweden. After some discussion, Dave reluctantly agreed to risk one thousand pounds.

On Tuesday 20th June, the whole family sat down around the television that evening to watch England play Sweden in their last group match. England dominated the first half, and went in 1-0 up. It seemed unlikely that Sweden would get back into the match for a draw. But they did, and as predicted, the match ended 2-2. Bobby and Dave looked at each other as the final whistle blew. They were dumbstruck. Once again, the result had been correct, down to the score.

Bobby had bet one thousand pounds with Ladbrokes on a 2-2 draw. She had won nine thousand pounds. Just like that.

Bobby and Dave sat up much of the night considering the possibilities. They sat at the dining table with the piece of paper between them. She explained over and over again the possible options, but in the end Dave decided to leave it all to Bobby.

'You're the expert,' he said. 'Bet as much of the money as you like. Bet the whole loan if you think it's right.'

In this way, Dave was absolving himself from responsibility, should it all go wrong. This was because he was scared. But, nevertheless, he was right - she was the expert.

Bobby, without betting the nine thousand pounds she had won earlier in the week, bet twenty thousand pounds on David Beckham to score the first goal against Ecuador, at odds of 8-1, and five thousand pounds, at 3-1, on England to win 1-0. She spread these bets over three bookmakers.

When David Beckham scored the opening and only goal from a free kick during the second half of the match against Ecuador, Bobby let out a scream of delight so loud that it could be heard outside in the street. She stood with her arms in the air as Victoria Beckham hugged Cheryl Tweedy in celebration on her television screen. If she'd have been at the match, she would have hugged them too.

At the end of the game she was exhausted. It finished 1-0. England had made it to the quarter-finals, and she had won one hundred and seventy-five thousand pounds. It was more money than she had ever had in her life.

The piece of paper told Bobby that England would lose on penalties to Portugal, therefore it was also the case that the match must have been a draw after both ninety and one hundred and twenty minutes of play. No score or scorers were mentioned, so the most lucrative bet was a double - to bet on the score being a draw at ninety minutes, and still a draw at the end of extra time - after one hundred and twenty minutes of play. If the match was going to end in penalties, then a draw was the only possible outcome.

Dave took Bobby's word for it as she bet one hundred and fifty thousand pounds of the winnings on a draw at ninety minutes, rolling into a draw at the end of extra time. She spread this as ten fifteen-thousand pound bets at ten different bookmakers. The odds varied slightly across the bookies, but they averaged out at 2-1 for the draw at ninety minutes, and evens to remain a draw after extra time. If she won, then her winnings, including her stake return, would be nine hundred thousand pounds.

Bobby wrote the figure down five times on a piece of blank A4 paper:

> 900,000
> 900,000
> 900,000
> 900,000
> 900,000

She stared at it for a long time, resting her right hand on her face. It seemed an impossible amount to win.

* * * * * * * * * * * * * * * *

But she won. The match ended 0-0 at ninety minutes, and stayed the same until Portugal won on penalties. When the match was over, Bobby stood up and went into the kitchen to make tea. She stood in front of the fridge, but she was unable to decide what to do next. She had forgotten how tea was made.

Dave and the two boys came in and sat at the table, and she just went and sat with them.

'How much have we won?' asked Dave.

'Lots,' she replied.

'How much is lots?' asked Scott, her eldest son. Bobby couldn't decide whether to tell them the full amount. She was planning to bet with most of it, and so could possibly lose it again. She didn't want them to be disappointed, especially after England losing on penalties. They'd had enough disappointment for one day. She decided, there and then, to keep back one hundred thousand pounds.

'We've won a hundred thousand pounds,' she said.

'No way!' said Dan, her youngest boy.

'Shit! Really, Mum?!' said Scott. 'Can we go to America?'

Dave just smiled at her, a proud smile, and he knew she had won more. When they were alone later that evening, Bobby told him it was nearly a million.

'But I'm going to bet with most of it. Whatever happens, we'll keep a hundred thousand,' she told him.

'That's a good idea,' he replied. 'But you do what you reckon is best…'

The next morning, after breakfast, Scott tapped his mum on the shoulder as he passed her.

'Mum?' he said. 'Are we going to win more?'

'Yes,' she replied, in a matter of fact way.

* * * * * * * * * * * * * * * *

The semi-final places were settled - Italy would play Germany, and France would play Portugal. On Friday - before beating Ukraine in the quarter-final, Italy were 9/2 to win the Cup. Today they were 3-1. Bobby had a choice. She could just bet now on Italy - bet it all and take odds of 3-1 - or bet on the semi-finals and then again on the final. She could even do an accumulator of all three matches, but she thought she may have to spread the bets too thinly and too wide.

In the end, she knew that a simple bet of eight hundred thousand pounds at 3-1 would win her a further two million four hundred thousand pounds. It was the simplest option, would allow her to complete the transaction now, and seemed as if it was more than enough money to win; enough to change their lives forever.

She worked through the accumulator odds and knew there

was more money to be won. But, and she didn't like this, she was starting to feel greedy.

Also, she remembered the girl's voice when she talked over the phone about the final - 'Italy wins. Italy wins the World Cup…' This was not a tip - not a belief. The girl had been absolutely certain.

She needed to simply make the bet and wait for the final. So she did. Spread across twenty bookmakers, she bet eight hundred thousand pounds on Italy to win the World Cup outright. It took about two hours on the computer, and then it was done.

* * * * * * * * * * * * * * * *

On the day of the final, Bobby explained to all her family that they had over one hundred and twenty-five thousand pounds safely tucked away in an on-line account, and that if Italy beat France that evening, they would have won a further three million two-hundred thousand pounds.

Nobody knew what to say. They were all speechless, in the truest sense of the word.

After moments passed, Bobby spoke first.

'Let's just watch and see.'

* * * * * * * * * * * * * * * *

That evening, every ball was kicked by Dave and the boys, every French attack met with silence, every Italian assault met with screams and cheers. When France took the lead, depression settled over the living room.

'Don't worry,' said Bobby. 'There's a long way to go yet…'

When Italy equalised, the living room erupted into frenzy. Bobby was the most subdued of them all. She felt in control, as if she were a puppeteer and the players her puppets. It was a strange feeling, but a pleasant one.

In time, the match went to penalties. The tension filled the room like water, dripped down from the walls and covered everything in a terrible dampness. It made everything muffled, no one could speak; not even look at each other.

Eventually, Grusso stepped up to win the match for Italy. Dave turned his back to the television but the boys crowded in, faces almost touching the screen. Bobby closed her eyes, and waited for the commentator's voice.

She never heard that voice - seconds later it was drowned out by her sons screaming and shouting 'Mum! You've won! You've won!'

She stood up and hugged them - she hugged them all - the boys and Dave; her family.

'Yes,' she said. 'We've won. We've won...'

* * * * * * * * * * * * * * * *

Everything moved so fast over the next few months - time melted away as if it had no grip on them. They bought and moved into a house a few short miles north-west of Wolverhampton, towards the A442. It was a beautiful house - Victorian - five bedrooms and in a quiet street. Dave started his own firm of mechanics. He oversaw his business, and only worked three days a week. He enjoyed it, and was successful. The boys were happier than they had ever been.

Bobby gave up gambling on-line, but once a week gambled where she most enjoyed it - at the horses. She always took a limited amount of money with her - usually about four thousand pounds, and she never bet more than that. She usually came away about even.

The piece of paper had weeks ago been framed and hung on the wall of her study in their new home. Whenever Bobby looked at it - took it down from the wall and held the frame in her hands, as she did often - it was as if it did not belong there; neither in her hands nor on the wall. But where did it belong?

Although it was written in her own handwriting, it felt as if it belonged to another time and place; another place altogether. When she held it, it seemed as if it were not real; as if it were not real at all.

But all around her, the carpets and the walls, the high Victorian ceilings and sash windows, the beautiful garden with its own apple tree - the house in which she stood, her house, bore witness to its reality.

And this paper had given so much to her - and to Dave and the boys - so much more than just money. Her family loved her and she loved them, she had before and she loved them now; they knew that.

The money had not made them love her more. She felt their love for her - the same; unchanged. She was still a mother and wife to them, competent and reliable and loving. She had their love and their respect. And that was enough - more than enough - but now she saw in their eyes something she had not seen before. It was something extra, something else; she was to them now something she had never been.

She was something beyond what she had been before, and the knowledge of it made her happy every hour of every day.

She was a hero.

Time Ninety-Seven

Friday 19th May 2006
3.56pm Mountain Daylight Time

The taxi drops me off at the end of a long road. It's nearly 4pm. There are few houses here on this street - just one or two scattered here and there, with large barren spaces in between. They are nondescript - typical American middle-class houses. I had imagined that the road would be lined with millionaire mansions - all gates and hedges. Instead, the taxi has left me in Middle America, outside a moderate brick house with a small front lawn. The number, impaled into the grass on a large black board, at once decorative and clumsy, reads '10680'. I pull the confirmation booking out of my jeans pocket to check. The address is 10680 Harvest Avenue. This is the right place, assuming I am in the right town. And surely I must be - how many other towns are there in America called 'Truth or Consequences'? Not many, I reckon.

I ring the bell and wait. I am standing on a wooden porch - the door directly in front of me. Beside me is a rocking chair, and beside that a bath chair, with a red tartan cushion. They both face out towards the road. It is hot today, and I am beginning to sweat. The taxi had air-conditioning, but the heat and the strong sun are starting to make up for lost time.

Moments later, I hear a voice behind the door and slowly it swings open. A lady in a floral dress, perhaps in her early forties, smiles at me and asks me who I am.

'Sandy,' I reply. 'Sandy Glover.'

'Sandy!' she says, in a strong southern accent. 'How lovely to meet you! You must be so tired! Please, come in…but we must be quiet. The teacher is asleep.'

'Oh. OK…'

'We must be careful not to wake him. He is conserving

energy, for the demonstration this evening...'

The house, so average from the front, is like the Tardis. It is huge inside, and I soon realise that this is because an enormous extension has been built stretching out from the back of the house. It has made it appear perhaps three times larger - but it goes straight back, so it's invisible from the front. I am guided into this extension, and into a large sitting room.

'Sandy, please take a seat. You are the first to arrive. There will be others, some joining this evening. After dinner, the demonstration will take place. Then you can decide...if this course is for you.'

'Good - I'm looking forward to the...demonstration.'

'That's great - would you like a drink?'

'Yes, please. Do you have lemonade?'

'We do. I'll be right back...'

Inside, the house is modern. It is simple - utilitarian even - but definitely pleasant. There are no decorations to speak of, no photos or paintings, just carvings and furniture in light wood. I am shown to my room, and it is beautiful. A wardrobe and a single bed, all pine and white, and a large window looking out to the back of the house.

There is a garden, perhaps two hundred yards long, with a small fish pond at the bottom. When I look later, there are no fish. The lady in the dress, who is called Sandra, leads me out to the garden and asks if I would like to sit for a while to 'rest and enjoy the air'. I say that I would, and pull up a chair underneath a large shady tree. She brings me another glass of lemonade and a book to read. It is called 'Raise High the Roof Beam, Carpenters' by JD Salinger. As I look at the silver cover, I remember that he wrote 'The Catcher in the Rye', an American classic, which I had read a long time ago.

I sit back in the shade; read my book and drink my lemonade. So far, I am having a nice time.

I have been keeping fit like a maniac during the weeks before my arrival here, and I am probably the fittest and the healthiest I've ever been. But I am still feeling nervous about whether this course will be too much for me. I wonder if perhaps I will just lag behind, become a burden on the others here, and that I will be told - in a friendly way - that maybe I should just call it a day. I don't want that to happen.

My instinct tells me that I'm doing the right thing. It tells me that I'll do very well, and that it will all be a worthwhile experience. But I'm still plagued with these thoughts, and they begin to encroach upon my rest in the garden.

The character in my book is feeling hot, and so am I. But the shade is nice, and I'm too sleepy to move. Travelling always tires me out, and the trip out from London - changing in California to reach New Mexico - has taken sixteen hours in total.

My body is feeling listless, but my mind is awake. It is awake to the possibilities of these eight weeks - of what they may mean for my future. I want to believe that I will do well - that I will learn skills that will help me in my quest. But the nagging doubts are surfacing with venom, trying to smother the confidence I have in myself. But what can I lose here? Some money, some time? Why am I so worried about failure?

I really have no idea why I am feeling so concerned. Perhaps I am still depressed; perhaps I'm just a bag of nerves. And who would blame me? I start to 'feel' my breathing, it is shallow and fast. I sit up and take deep breaths, and for a moment I reach a point where I think I may pass out; or even begin to hyperventilate.

But the moment passes and slowly my breathing calms. I close my eyes tightly and breathe; breathe. I am tired and I am nervous; that is all. Nothing else is wrong. After a minute I feel better again. I feel normal. I will be fine. I will be fine.

I finish my lemonade and start reading again. The character has found the air-conditioning and turned it on.

That evening at dinner, there are six of us, including Sandra our host. There are three men, then Sandra and me, and then one other woman. She is about twenty-five, with black hair and brown eyes. She engages me in conversation over dinner, asking where I am from and other such questions. She tells me her name is Sarah and that she was married, but not any longer.

'My husband - my ex-husband,' she says, 'he had no idea who he was. He thought he knew who he was, but he had no idea. Not really…you understand?'

I do not.

'He would always want to be what he couldn't be, and the things he was, he neglected. He just became bitter, I suppose…'

I begin to get a bad feeling about this whole thing, and wonder if I should maybe just grab all my bags and make a run for it.

'His name is Teddy. He's a really nice guy, but he just can't be himself. He doesn't know how to be. It's sad, I guess…'

I nod and smile in a non-committal way. I think: 'I can't stand two months of this! I just want to learn self-defence.' By the end of dinner, after talking with the other guests in turn, one of whom may as well have asked me up to his room he was so obvious in his intentions, I am absolutely ready to leave.

That is until I see the demonstration. After that, all the other guests combined could not have dragged me away.

* * * * * * * * * * * * * * * *

'I will teach you how to kill. But you must never kill.'

The 'Teacher' is sitting, cross-legged, on a small cushion against the wall, and we all sit in front of him, in a kind of semi-circle.

'This course is very expensive, and very tough. After tonight, you can each leave, each of you if you choose, and you will not be charged…not even for dinner.'

This raises a smile in each of us, already tuning in to being a disciple.

'There are few people who have mastered the skills I will teach you. Perhaps you will master them yourselves…perhaps not. But - you will learn.'

We nod.

'This is not a religious teaching. This is not religion. I am a Christian - but that is not part of what I will teach you. So, understand, this is not mysticism of any kind. If you are looking for enlightenment, you will not find it here.'

We nod again, but one or two look disappointed.

'However, what you will learn will enhance your life. You will have strength in your bodies - more than you ever knew was there. These eight weeks will be more than just a beginning, they will make you strong. I must demonstrate now, and then you can decide if you wish to join the course. Even if you decide to leave, please feel free to stay overnight if you wish - if that would be more convenient. But - I hope you will all choose to stay.'

He smiles at us, each in turn, and we smile back. But he is not pretentious, not at all. He is self-assured beyond anyone I have met before.

What followed next was unbelievable, and - to use the well-worn phrase - you had to have been there to get the full flavour of it. This is what happened.

* * * * * * * * * * * * * * * *

The Teacher (Who's real name is Mark Salter) walked to the door and welcomed a new man to the group. He was dressed in jeans and a biker jacket, and was well over six feet tall. He was covered in muscles - abnormally so - and he described himself as a 'professional wrestler and fighter', who had played the circuit in New Mexico for seven years.

'I won shit loads of awards,' he drawled. 'And I been on

television, and won, more times than y'all had a piss this year - excuse me, ladies.' He nodded to Sarah and me.

'Damn,' he continued. 'I spent seven years in the ring, and there ain't no bone I ain't broke in some poor bastard's body - excuse me, ladies - and I can't get near this guy!' he nodded towards the Teacher. 'Damn, one day I'm just gonna run him over in my truck!'

By this point, I was beginning to think this was an elaborate set-up, but I sat wide-eyed for the next few minutes as the wrestler made a serious, and I mean truly serious, attempt to tear the Teacher to pieces. He lunged and punched and kicked, not slowly as you would think by his weight, but with speed and dexterity. He flung himself at the Teacher with every fibre of his body - this was not acting - and the Teacher dodged and weaved and deflected his blows, even pushing some back on him so that he seemed, at times, to feel the weight of his own attack.

Minutes later, now armed with a baseball bat, the wrestler tried again, swinging with absolute ferocity - swearing now without an 'excuse me' - and crashing the bat down upon the Teachers body. But the Teacher was just too quick - incredibly so - and even when the bat seemed, at least twice, to make contact with his head, it just appeared to glide off to the side, as if it were a rolled up newspaper being flicked away.

After just a couple of minutes, I could not understand how the Teacher was not dead, let alone still standing. But standing he was, his eyes staring ahead at his attacker, watching his every move, pre-empting every strike with a move of his own.

It was exhausting to watch, and terrifying, and in the last few seconds - when the wrestler had really lost his temper (he seemed close to tears at this point) - I sat with my hand over my mouth as - in a last-ditch blaze of fury - he lunged his full weight at the Teacher, trying to drag him to the floor by his hair and neck. But, in a second, he was free from his grip - the wrestler tumbled forward onto the floor and the Teacher stepped over to the far wall, just watching and waiting, his eyes never leaving his attacker.

The wrestler began to cough, uncontrollably for a few moments.

'I'm sick of this shit!' he said, his voice barely audible. 'I'm not doing this no more! You hear me!'

The Teacher stepped out of the corner - just a single step towards him.

'That's fine,' he said. 'Then we are finished.'

'You're damn right we're finished!'

At that moment, as if moving to an invisible cue, Sandra came into the room (she must have been listening to everything behind the door). She asked the wrestler - who she addressed as 'Steamer' - if he would like to come with her and get a drink.

He looked up at her, confused for a moment, and then nodded. He stood up, avoiding our staring eyes, and followed Sandra out of the door. The Teacher sat down where he had been before the demonstration. He looked across at us, smiling - but only slightly.

'Steamer is a good man, but he gets a bit upset when things aren't going his way. He'll be fine, because I pay him five hundred dollars for this.'

We all nodded - I was transfixed.

'But...' he continued, the smile dropping from his lips. 'I could have killed him at any time; at any time. Now, let's all go to the sitting room. Sandra has laid out some drinks...'

* * * * * * * * * * * * * * * *

That night I decide that I will stay - after the demonstration of the Teacher's abilities I feel that I have no choice. He is truly gifted, and I am certain that even a small percentage of the skills he has obviously mastered will give me a vital edge over Richard Sturrock.

Another reason that convinces me to stay is the departure that same evening of Sarah, the crazy divorcee, and Marlon, the man intent on getting me into bed the moment he saw me.

After the demonstration and during drinks, Sarah gave a long speech about how she felt that she needed 'something more spiritual and less physical' at this stage of her life, and was gone by 10pm. Marlon just left without a word, and we only found out he had gone, and was not in his room or something, when Sandra announced to the remaining three of us that he was on his way back to Corpus Christi (an eleven hour drive) in his Chevrolet.

So, as I lie in bed this evening, I am pleased on two fronts. The 'worst' two people in the group have left, and the course looks as if it may be worth the forty-five thousand dollars I will pay in the morning.

I drift off to sleep in my comfortable bed, feeling content that I have made the right choice.

At breakfast the following morning, the three of us sit around a small pine table eating cereal, toast and fruity yogurts. My two fellow course members are Josh, a forty year old fitness and self-defense instructor from San Diego in California, and Latham, a twenty-eight year old professional boxer from Chicago.

For Josh, this course is a way to improve his fitness and skills; he is from a wealthy family and teaches fitness classes because he enjoys it. Although the course, he admits, may not be totally what he needs, he thinks that there is a lot he can get out of it.

For Latham, the course is simply a way of avoiding punches. His philosophy is simple; avoid getting hit and you win fights. I know nothing about boxing, and I am sure he is right.

And then there is me. I am here to kill the man who wants to kill me - again - and therefore prevent him from stopping me escape from this prison of five months that is driving me insane with increasing rapidity. Do I tell them this? No. I tell them I was hoping to start a self-defense class in London, and I am here to learn the skills I would need. This seems simpler to explain and they, of course, believe me without question.

During breakfast, I accidentally flip a segment of grapefruit up into the air as a result of spoon pressure - applied while struggling to release it from a grapefruit half. It flies a good six feet into the air and lands directly in a teacup on the coffee table about ten feet behind where Latham is sitting. Both Josh and Latham watch the segment land, and are full of praise and compliments for my grapefruit flinging skills. This piece of grapefruit produces a great deal of humour during our first breakfast, and an atmosphere of comradeship begins to develop. However, my only reservation is a tiny pulsating fear that there is - possibly - an opportunity here for them to develop instead a battle for my affections.

I hope that is not the case, as I just cannot be bothered.

* * * * * * * * * * * * * * * *

After breakfast, the three of us meet with the Teacher, who now wishes to be called Mark, to confirm our corporate desire to stay and therefore to pay up the forty-five thousand dollars agreed. I write a cheque, as do the others, and Mark places them inside a small blue folder between a row of books on a shelf.

We spend the next hour discussing the programme for the next eight weeks. Mark does most of the talking, but we chip in with relevant questions. Afterwards, we all file out into the garden and have a drink. I have tea, but the rest drink coffee. The sun is already very warm, and I close my eyes to the glare - sipping my tea by sense of taste and touch.

Sandra shows us around the rest of the house - my home for two months - before lunch. There is a huge library - possibly about two or three thousand books, mostly paperbacks. Sandra tells us that we can borrow as many as we wish while we are here, and if we particularly like any we may take them with us. I - being a lover of books - browse for a few minutes amongst the rows and rows of books waiting to be read. Already, after a quick look, I can see three or four books I would like to read during my stay.

The house is modern and really lovely - it is a very comfortable place to spend two months. My room is simple but it has everything I need. When our tour is finished, and just before lunch, I return to the library alone and choose two books to take back to my room. They are 'The Secret Life of Bees' by Sue Monk Kidd, and 'Enigma' by Robert Harris. I place them carefully, one on top of the other, on my bedside cabinet, alongside the book I am currently reading. This came with me from England ('Deception Point' by Dan Brown), and I have only thirty pages left to read.

Seeing the books beside my bed makes the room feel like mine. I am beginning to imprint myself upon it - *my* clothes in the wardrobe, *my* shoes by the door. This gives me a sense of belonging, strangely more than I would normally have. This 'need to belong' is something I recognise that I crave, perhaps something everybody craves, and already I feel as though I belong here.

As I walk back downstairs for lunch, I can see how easy it would be to become attached to a group of people, or a leader of some kind. Even if all that they promised was that you could belong, that you could be part of the group; for many this would be enough to stay.

So many people live their lives each day and are lonely, and so who would give up the gift of belonging, to return to loneliness and feeling apart?

This afternoon, we start our training with a number of exercises - this all lasts just over an hour. Mark has a laser pen, which emits a powerful but concentrated beam of light. Although the room is quite bright, you can still see the light clearly.

We have to stand in a line, the three of us, facing a bare grey wall. We are in another room built as part of the house extension. It is at the back of the house, with French windows leading out to the garden. Light silk curtains are drawn, which keeps the sun from shining in too brightly.

Mark tells us to stand with our legs slightly apart, and to place our left hand behind our back, as we will only need our right hands. He instructs us to do this, even if we are left handed - which none of us are. He shines the light onto the wall in front of each of us, and we have to try to touch it with our right hand. We are standing about three feet from the wall, so we can just touch the wall with the tips of our fingers.

The light shines in two colours - white and red. If it is white, we must try to touch it. If it is red, we must try to keep our hand and arm still. It is a simple exercise, and we are all much better at it after the hour is up. During the final session, I get thirty-eight hits out of forty. My arm hurts a bit by now, but I am pleased with myself nevertheless.

Mark explains the value of the exercise after we have finished. He tells us that it is to improve our reflexes - our hand-to-eye coordination - but also to show us how quickly it is possible to make measurable progress. He tells us that by the end of the eight weeks, we will all be astonished at the progress we have made. He assures us that we will succeed, and that we will be, in effect, different people. I can't wait.

Time Ninety-Seven

Friday 17th June 2006

During the first couple of weeks of training I had the panicky feeling about four more times. On every occasion it happened not when I was training, but when I was resting or reading in my room. But, as the training has started to take hold of me - change me - I seem to have left the panic behind. Instead, I feel calm and in control. My reflexes are as fast as lightning, and Mark is full of compliments about my progress.

'You're really good, Sandy,' he says regularly. 'You're good now, but you're going to be great…'

I feel as if I am.

Time Ninety-Seven

Sunday 19th June 2006
8.30am MDT

It's exactly one calendar month since I started my training. We are still a group of three - with Mark making four - and we now train about six or seven hours each day, but not on Sundays. Sunday is our day off.

Mark still sets us 'homework' to do - which is a few exercises and some reading which all takes about a hour, but other than that we are free to do as we please.

Mark and Sandra - who is his wife - visit their church each and every Sunday without fail. It is just over a mile away, and they always walk. It is an 'Episcopal' church, which - I have learnt - is the same as the Church of England. Although Truth or Consequences is a town of just over seven thousand people, it has sixteen churches. The Episcopal Church, which is called St Paul's, is one of the smallest.

By this, Mark is not talking about the size of the building, but instead the size of the congregation.

'There's just around fifty of us,' he told us over breakfast, in response to a question from Latham about his church. Latham was Catholic, although he said his attendance at mass these days was 'sporadic'.

'What do you do, at your church?' I ask, struggling to cut a grapefruit into equal halves.

'Oh, we worship God. We take communion. Listen to a sermon. We pray,' Mark replies.

'Is it…fun?'

'What do you mean by fun?'

'I don't know really. I don't know a lot about church. Do you enjoy it?'

'Yes. I enjoy it.'

I decide to go along and see what it's like. I ask Mark if he would mind taking me along. He tells me he would be delighted.

Time Ninety-Seven

Sunday 19th June 2006
10.30am MDT

The service began thirty minutes ago, at ten o'clock. I'm sitting next to Mark, with Sandra sitting on the other side of him. We are seated in a pew, and because each pew only holds about four people (or perhaps five small people), we have the pew to ourselves.

The whole church is painted white, and six fans - attached to the ceiling - only succeed in blowing warm air around the building. It is hot.

The church would probably seat seventy or eighty people, so it's fairly small, I think. Including me, and the vicar, there are forty-seven of us. We have sung two songs, confessed our sins, and now we are listening to the sermon.

It is essentially about kindness, and I couldn't disagree with any of it. It fact, it is very interesting, and for the first time I find myself thinking about kindness as something corporate, rather than something individual. The service goes on for another thirty minutes after the sermon. Most of the congregation takes communion, and pretty soon after that it is over.

I ask Mark about the sermon after the service ends, and he replies by saying that Jesus was always kind to people, even if they didn't deserve it. I say that surely everybody deserves some kindness. Mark smiles at me, and tells me he'll have to think about that.

I have a cup of tea with the others in a small hall at the back of the church. Mark introduces me to almost everyone as his 'star pupil', and I cannot help but be pleased. Every time he says it I have to suppress a wide smile, and replace it with a smile more suitable.

Everyone seems genuinely pleased that I am there, and they

ask me lots of questions about my life in England. I tell them a few bits and pieces - about Lancaster Gate and living in London and so on.

One man - Harry, who is about sixty years old - tells me that he was in London during the late 1990's, and asks if I was living in London then. I stare at him for a moment, perhaps a moment too long, while my mind invents some crap story about living in Scotland or something. He glances across at Mark for a second, and then looks at me again, smiling. He seems unnerved by my sudden silence, and I realise at that moment that I'm staring at him, and have been for a few seconds.

'I was in a coma,' I say. 'I was hit by a car when I was eighteen, and I was in a coma for thirteen years. I missed most of the 1990's. Sorry…'

Harry looks at me, his face still frozen in a smile. He seems shocked, and his mind is obviously searching for a worthy response. He removes the smile from his face.

'Well, I'm very sorry to hear that,' he says. 'That must have been awful…really awful. Have you recovered now?'

'Yes, thank you. I'm fine now…'

'Well, that's good. That's good…'

Mark, who had heard the entire exchange with Harry, turns to me as we walk back from the church.

'You didn't say anything about what happened…about the coma,' he says, looking at me with a mixture of sympathy and puzzlement.

'You never asked,' I reply.

Time Ninety-Seven

Sunday 19th June 2006
3.15pm MDT

Mark and I discuss my coma, and he is certain that it will have no impact on my training.

'You're doing really great,' he says. 'I see no reason to stop now.'

I tell him I feel as fit as can be and that I would really like to complete the course.

'Well, that would be the right thing to do, I think. We are already half-way through the training,' he replies.

'Let's carry on,' I say.

'OK,' he says, scratching his chin. 'Let's carry on.'

* * * * * * * * * * * * * * * *

Later that afternoon, I sit in the garden alone and read a book. It is a good book (The Mosquito Coast, by Paul Theroux) but I can't concentrate, and my mind wanders back to the church I visited that morning. I realise that I enjoyed it very much, but I can't work out what it was about it that I liked. It brings to mind, all of a sudden, the paintings by the Serbian artist I had seen the day I was killed. In the same way, I had liked them but I didn't know why.

There was no one thing about the service that I had particularly enjoyed. The church was too hot, I didn't know the tunes to the songs, and the cup of tea at the end was absolutely horrible. But something about it as a whole made me feel happy. Not even happy, really, but just content in some way.

Placing the book on the grass and closing my eyes, I realised what it was that had injected this small measure of contentment into my life. It was a strange realisation, and feeling sleepy with the warm sun on my face, it felt almost unreal.

Cut adrift as I am, and floating from Time to Time as I do, I often feel as though I am lost. But sitting in that tiny white church, visiting a world that in so many ways seemed so alien, I felt for once, almost at home.

I mumbled to myself, 'almost at home...', and then drifted off to sleep, the sun warm on my body, like blankets; like a sleeping bag.

Time Ninety-Seven

Saturday 15th July 2006

It is the last day of my course, and the previous four weeks have passed in a blur. They contained some of the most intensive training of all - sometimes we worked for eight or ten hours a day. I now know all about pressure points, how to make someone fall over, how to hit someone in such a way that they cannot hit me back.

Mark has been keen to emphasise the dangers of using force of any kind.

'Using force against someone makes them use force against you. Using a weapon of any kind potentially arms them…'

We have listened to what he has said to us, and spent eight weeks of our lives following his instructions and exercises; and it has been completely worthwhile. We agree - the three of us - that we have learnt a great deal from coming here to 'Truth' (as people who live around here call the town). For myself, I am not totally convinced that I have enough strength and skill to deal with Richard Sturrock at his most insane (although I'm sure that Mark could), but I feel myself in a much better position to try.

At the very least, I have more confidence; more certainty in my abilities. Mark tells me that I have reached 'a very good place' (in his words). My body shape has changed a bit - I have more muscle tone - but all in all I look pretty much the same. I have lost five pounds in weight.

But the main change has been to my reflexes - my ability to react to danger; to duck out of the way of an attack. During the final two weeks, Mark has been attacking us with rubber poles, actually made of some kind of foam, and we have been trying to avoid being hit. We were all amazed at how quickly we could move, how we could see where the pole would land and get out of the way.

'Don't jerk your body,' Mark would say. 'Just try to step away - try to step to one side.'

In the final week, we all mastered this - perhaps the hardest thing we had learnt. I found that, no matter how fast Mark moved the rubber pole - how fast he swung it at me - I could just step backwards or to the side; out of its reach. Also, it was possible to actually step forward beneath the arc of the swing, and from there deliver a blow of one's own to any assailant.

'From this position,' Mark would say. 'You could finish the attack within seconds. Remember, you are always in control - you decide when to end the fight...'

* * * * * * * * * * * * * * * *

After dinner, I lie in my room, gathering the will to pack up my rucksack and bag. As I lie there, watching a strange New Mexico-type insect crawl across the ceiling, I mull over the idea (which had been growing in strength for some time) of asking Mark to join me in my 'project'. He would not need to know any details - just that he had to incapacitate Richard Sturrock at the appropriate time. He could be a mercenary. I would pay twice as much as I had paid for the course. Perhaps he would be willing to, for the money; and because we now know each other; because we are - have become - friends.

I decide that tomorrow - after breakfast - I will ask him, and just see what he says.

Time Ninety-Seven

Sunday 16th July 2006
8.45am MDT

The following morning I sit at the breakfast table - our last breakfast together - with Josh and Latham, and we are joined this morning by Mark and Sandra. Josh and Latham had posed no problem romantically - which was a relief - and I realise that I will miss them both quite a lot.

But not as much as I will miss Mark, and watching him eat breakfast with us - cutting up his toast into four equal triangles - I know that I will never ask him for his help.

The eight weeks have been more than just a course; I have learnt things that I did not even know existed. I have learnt that I am a remarkable person, that I have talents hidden inside me; abilities there all the time but just asleep. How much more could there be to me?

Everyone should have to do this course, I think to myself. If only for the self-confidence it brings - the wonder in realising one's own abilities.

I have learnt how to fight, how to size-up situations, how to defend myself, how to attack. I have learnt that I am an amazing person, capable of so much. I have learnt about God.

And I know that to ask Mark to help me fight against Richard Sturrock would somehow cheapen all that has gone before. It would make him think of me differently - perhaps as someone with a vendetta of some sort - intent on some kind of revenge. I don't want him to think of me differently. I don't want him not to like me.

That afternoon, I am the last to leave. Josh left straight after breakfast, and I gave him an affectionate hug goodbye. We exchanged e-mail addresses and promised to stay in touch. Latham left about an hour later, and we said a similar goodbye, both agreeing to e-mail from time to time. Perhaps, I thought, if I stay in this Time, then I would.

I go back and take a last look at my room, its whiteness, and try to remember it for the future. I am determined not to forget what it was like here - the room and the house, the garden where I read so many books, where I played so many games of skittles with Josh and Latham during the evenings. Who won the most games? I think it was me, but I'm not sure even now.

My bags are waiting at the bottom of the stairs, and Mark is waiting with them, along with Sandra. They have called a taxi, which will be here in five minutes or so.

As I descend the stairs, it seems for a moment that they are just waiting for me to go - the last to leave - so that they can get on with their normal lives. But as I reach the bottom, I realise that this is not the case. Their eyes seem genuinely sad to see me go, and as I shake hands with them and we exchange brief hugs, I am touched by their warmth.

I have felt alive in this place; in this house. I thank Mark for all I have learnt, and for letting me come with him to church.

'We were pleased to have you Sandy, both here and at our church,' Sandra says, and I notice, to my surprise, that she is beginning to fight back tears. 'Please don't forget what you have learnt...' Her voice trails away, and Mark holds out his hand for her to take.

'I won't,' I say, and find, in response to Sandra, that I now feel tearful myself. It doesn't take much, at the best of times, to make me cry, and within moments tears start to roll down my face. 'I'm sorry,' I say, wiping my face with the back of my hand. 'It's silly...'

'It's been a real pleasure having you here in our home, Sandy,' Mark begins. 'You were one of the best pupils I've ever had...'

'Thank you,' I reply, making an effort to steady my voice.

The taxi is still not here, and rather than stand in awkward silence, we move out onto the porch, with Mark carrying my bags out behind me. He lays them down on the porch, and we all look down the road - looking for the taxi that will take me away. But, as yet, there is no sign.

I don't want our time together to end in awkwardness, so I suggest that I wait out on the street, 'so I'm ready when the taxi arrives'.

At this Sandra takes my hand, and wishes me a pleasant journey. I think she is saying a final goodbye, and is about to go back into the house - perhaps she was - when she suddenly takes hold of my arm, gently, in her other hand.

'It's nice to have girls on the course,' she says. 'We don't have many girls here…mostly men…' She looks at me, more tears forming in her hazel eyes, and I am suddenly gripped by her sadness, overpowered by it - a sadness that until this moment had been hidden from me.

'We had a daughter,' she continues. 'She was a beautiful girl; at least she was to us. She didn't think that way…she died six years ago now - took some drugs. She died at the hospital over in Socorro - they couldn't help her here in town, at Sierra Vista. They moved her out to Socorro General. We went to the hospital in town when we got the call. They never said they'd be moving her, never told us. We got there - she was gone, out to Socorro. We never got to say goodbye…'

Mark gently takes his wife from me, unravels her grip from my hand and arm, and begins to lead her inside. By now she is crying freely, the tears flowing out of her eyes, but not the pain and guilt. That was stuck inside her.

Mark sits her down on the bottom of the stairs and comes back out to me, just as the taxi appears at the end of the road.

'I'm sorry…' begins Mark.

'No, please…' I say, wiping more tears away.

'Sandra gets upset sometimes, you know…she took the call from the hospital. They said afterwards they had told her on the phone that our daughter, Debbie, was being moved. Said that she must have forgotten, what with the shock…'

'Oh...'

'They didn't tell her shit. They're just lying to cover their own backs...'

'I'm sorry...'

The taxi beeps its horn twice, and breaks the spell between us. Mark leans over and kisses me on the cheek, his face breaking into a smile.

'You have a great journey back to England, Sandy! It's been wonderful to meet you, really wonderful...'

I smile back at him, and give him a big hug. Sandra comes to the door as I unwrap myself from him, and she too gives me a hug. She is now smiling too, but the pain is still etched on her face.

As I climb into the taxi, Mark and Sandra stand on the porch and wave. I wave back with vigor, and try to smile, although I still feel tearful. Not just because of the pain and grief that they have suffered, but also because I am leaving.

I don't want to leave at all. I want to stay here, where I am safe. The taxi moves away, and I turn around and look out of the back window. They are still standing there, waving me away. I give them a final wave, unaware of whether they can still see me or not, and then turn to face the front of the cab.

During the long journey to the airport, I am surprised at how 'all at sea' I feel. I am aware that the course had given me a temporary anchor, and following a set of rules and routines had given my life a sense of pattern, something so often missing. I begin to see why some people join the army - perhaps it is nice, in a way, to have a set of rules to follow.

I suppose I also have to follow a set of rules - but I don't know who sets them, and the rules are crap.

* * * * * * * * * * * * * * * *

At the airport, I use an Internet computer (the keyboard is covered in spilt coffee) to find out how far Socorro Hospital is from Truth or Consequences. I discover, to my great surprise, that it is over sixty miles away.

In an instant, I can imagine the terrible drive that Mark and Sandra must have endured - finding their daughter had been moved sixty miles from home, driving all that way, a journey spiked with silence and raw emotion, to find only that she had died. They must have wondered, during the drive home, where they had been on the road when she had passed away. Perhaps stuck behind a lorry, the driver unaware of their urgency, or maybe sitting at traffic lights or at a junction.

Although the knowledge of their personal tragedy has overshadowed my stay, I still feel uplifted by what I have achieved. I stretch my arms behind my back and, still stiff from the taxi ride, stand up and straighten my spine. My fingers are sticky from the coffee-covered keyboard, so I set off to find a toilet to wash my hands.

In the sink, I wash my face as well - the cold water stinging my eyes, which are still sore from the crying. As I wash away the soreness and the coffee, I know that this section of my journey is over. The most difficult part, the most fearful, is yet to come.

I have never had this dream before.

Everything is blue; a beautiful blue. I am in a room; a room with a cot. There are pictures on the walls - animals, tiny bears, Andy Pandy in his trademark stripy pyjamas. There are teddies on a shelf, books on the floor, blue blankets in the cot.

I am standing, and I am wearing nothing. I am naked, but I am not cold. I am not ashamed, because I am alone.

But then Chris is beside me. He holds my hand, and I am still not ashamed, because he has seen me like this many times; so many times.

He speaks to me, but I cannot hear him. Instead of words, a memory flows from his mouth. I remember the times I have cried myself to sleep, the sadness I have felt. The nights that have failed to give me any rest, but instead have emptied me of tears. I have cried so often in my sleep. I have felt the loss, the frustration, the hopelessness of everything. I have slept on a bed of onions.

But Chris is not here just to show me memories; he is here to show me the future. Holding my hand still, he leads me to the end of the cot. He beckons me to look in, but I can't. I plead at him with my eyes not to make me look. I couldn't bear the emptiness that I may see; the pile of blankets, the little doll, the fluffy tiger.

But Chris guides my eyes with his, and as I look I see Jack, my baby, lying asleep amongst the blankets. Chris smiles at me kindly, and I know then that this is my future. This is the reality that awaits me. It is what should have been, should always have been.

More than that, it is what shall be; what I have always known would be.

Time Ninety-Seven

Monday 31st July 2006

I have been back in England for two weeks; tomorrow it is August. Whether I will ever live through a September remains to be seen, but this Time, I will try my very best to make that happen. I have written out a plan of campaign; a plan that I believe gives me the best chance of success.

This is my Plan of Campaign:

1) Fly to Venice just a few days before 19th August. This gives me less chance of accidentally meeting Richard Sturrock before the 19th.
2) Make sure I know where to go to get a knife in advance. I may just get a carving knife from a kitchen shop, or something like that.
3) Keep my level of fitness up. Keep doing my exercises as I did in New Mexico.
4) Stay in Mestre, away from the centre of Venice.
5) Arrive at the 'place' just a few minutes before 11.12am on August 19th - ready for anything.
6) I must remember that Italy is an hour ahead of us, so I'll need to be there for 12.12pm local time, which is 11.12am here in England.

I look at my plan every day, and it still amazes me that I have a plan at all; that I have got this far. All of this has happened during the last two Times, and it seems to have happened so fast that it feels as if I am running to keep up.

But I will run as fast as I need to, because I am sick of all this - this madness I call my life. I am absolutely sick of it.

* * * * * * * * * * * * * * * *

A week ago, I collected up all my winnings and deposited them in a newly-opened building society account. I was unable to open the account I wanted on-line (or even understand what type of account I wanted to open), so I decided to go face-to-face with a financial advisor at a building society near Marble Arch tube station.

The advisor (a bleached blonde in her fifties) was very helpful, even before she realised how much money I had available to open the account. I had transferred the entire amount already into my current account, so I had about one million nine hundred thousand pounds at my disposal.

After she realised how much money we were talking about, she became even more helpful and her attitude changed almost imperceptibly. I had become a 'valuable customer'.

Eventually, after forty minutes of discussion and debate, I opened a 'ninety day notice account' with a 5.75% interest rate. I'm sure if I had shopped around I would have found something even better, but this account seemed simple to manage, and the interest alone would be in excess of one hundred thousand pounds a year. This was enough.

A further fifteen minutes saw the forms being signed, and a transfer (one million eight hundred and fifty thousand pounds) made from my current account into my new savings account. The whole process, including the walk down to Marble Arch, took about ninety minutes.

Afterwards, I went for a stroll in Kensington gardens, and I wandered over to the Diana Memorial Fountain. I sat on the grass and ate a strawberry ice-cream I had bought along the way. Some of it melted too quickly, and a blob fell onto one of my shoes. I remember thinking that I could afford to replace them a thousand times over with the interest from my account alone.

But, as I bent down to wipe my shoe, I was unexpectedly besieged by the sensation that I was being watched. The feeling gripped me - literally took hold of me, so much so that for a moment I couldn't move at all, and I was stuck bending over with my right hand on my shoe. Then, as my recent training kicked in, I shot upright and spun around. My eyes searched my surroundings, darting from tree to tree and person to person and then, within seconds, rested on a man with straight black hair walking briskly away towards the road. For a few seconds I hesitated, deciding what to do - wondering if my imagination was working overtime, my nerves shredded as they were. But my instinct is never wrong. It is never wrong.

And then he was running, and so was I. A squirrel leapt up a tree and onto a branch - convinced I was chasing after it, but I passed it just as the man turned right onto the road and out of my field of vision. Twenty seconds later I arrived at the road, and heading off to the right I scanned the street in front of me, trying to catch a glimpse of him. But he was gone; just gone.

I stopped and looked around me, trying to work out where he could be hiding, as he must have turned off and headed back into the gardens somewhere; perhaps crossed quickly to the other side. There were bushes and trees everywhere, and I felt a sense of embarrassment as I searched the locality - looking behind, and in, the various places I felt he could be hiding. But I couldn't find him. What did he look like? He was too far away to tell, but he was wearing a suit, I think - or at least a smart jacket. But beyond that I had no idea.

I walked back to the hotel, watching out for him all the time. But he had vanished into the sunny day, just become part of the warm air. In truth, I am convinced he was hiding somewhere, somewhere clever, and just waiting for me to go; to give up.

But whoever he was, he was spying on me. My instinct told me this, and it has never been known to lie. But who was he? Who is he?

Time Ninety-Seven

Sunday 13th August 2006
7.25pm Central European Time

Two weeks later, and I am now here in Mestre. I am waiting; just waiting.

I arrived yesterday, amid chaos at the airport due to some kind of strike action. It was hard to find a taxi, and I had to wait for nearly an hour in the heat.

I feel as though, because of all the training I have done this Time - all that I've achieved - I should be brimming with confidence, perhaps almost looking forward to the challenge. But I don't feel that way at all. I feel sick all the time.

Last night as I took a walk up to the town centre, a clown came up to me and asked me for money. He was collecting for some kind of charity, but spoke only Italian, so I'm not sure what the charity was. He walked up to me from behind, and so I didn't see him until the last minute. When I saw him, almost beside me holding out his can, I nearly jumped out of my skin. Every muscle in my body tightened, and I know that I must have looked at him with staring and fierce eyes - full of fear. I gave him twenty euros, and his face showed his gratitude.

'*Grazie per la vostra bonta*,' he said, and gave a little bow as he walked away. I smiled at him weakly as he left and as I strolled back to the hotel, trying not to rush, the palms of my hands were so sweaty that no matter how often I wiped them on my shorts, they wouldn't go dry.

* * * * * * * * * * * * * * * *

I'm sitting in Brek, which is a pizza restaurant. It's actually part of a small chain, and it offers made-to-order pizzas along with dozens of other things to eat. It is very popular amongst the people who live around here, and I've been here on a few occasions before.

The décor is modern and subdued, and it is always crowded. I've been sitting here, hogging this two-person table, for over an hour. I'm mulling the plan over in my head, tossing the options this way and that. At all costs, I want to avoid confrontation of any kind with Richard Sturrock. However, I think this is unlikely. I feel sure that he will be waiting for me on August 19th, and (although I feel terrified by the thought) I will have to fight him.

Whilst I believe that I can hold my own this Time, I fantasise that he has been run over by a car in Mestre, or fallen into a canal and drowned, perhaps losing his footing and hitting his head on the side of a stone bridge while walking home one very dark evening. But I know, in truth, that he is alive, that he is not far away, and that I am now just waiting to face him - the man who has become my nemesis.

My table is full of the remnants of food - a three cheese pizza, a bread roll, a fruit salad, a cake with little currants in - all of these lay partly eaten in front of me. My mineral water and my lemonade are just empty bottles. The place is now getting very crowded, and I am aware that I am taking up a much needed table.

I am literally just getting up to go when a man sits down on the chair opposite me, filling the empty space at the table. He has no tray and no food. He smiles across at me; a smile familiar in my memory. He is wearing a dark blue jacket and a white shirt, along with a light blue silk tie. He folds his hands in front of him. He is Japanese.

'Good evening, Miss Glover,' he says. 'I see you are very well…'

* * * * * * * * * * * * * * * *

I smile back at him in an involuntary way, but my mind is

turning cartwheels to figure out who he is. He doesn't speak again, but just looks across at me, smiling. He is waiting for me to remember.

Moments later, my memory serves up an image of the World Cup; of Adam and the Japanese football supporter. It is him. For a second I feel scared, in fact almost horrified, and I put my hand over my mouth in shock, just like someone would in a play or a film. I can't speak. I just stare back at him, waiting for the next thing to happen.

'Shall we order more food?' he says. 'I'm feeling very hungry, and then we can stay and talk.'

I nod at him, and he gets up and takes a black plastic tray from a large pile nearby. The shock is wearing off, and I consider just getting up and running out of the restaurant. But instead, unable to truly engage my brain, I just sit and wait for him to come back.

A few minutes later, he returns with a tray packed with food. He picks up the remnants of my meal and tips everything into the bin. Then he sits down again.

'Have a chip,' he says, pointing to his tray.

'Who are you?' I ask. My voice, annoyingly, sounds a bit wobbly.

'Ah! You remember me…at last! No football shirt today!'

'No.'

'My name is Hiroshi Murakami. I am from Tokyo, in Japan. You have been?'

'No.'

'Ah! That is a shame!'

'Yes.'

'So, Sandy - you are here in Venice…to leave, I think…'

'What do you want?'

'To help you, of course…'

'Why?'

'Why? Because you may need my help, I think. Do you believe you will defeat Richard Sturrock?'

The question takes me by surprise, and I realise then that he knows all about me, about my plans. I feel confused, but the man, Hiroshi, does not seem threatening in any way. And Brek is crowded with people, so I decide to listen to what he has to say.

'Yes. I think, this Time, I'll defeat him. I've been training…'

'I know. You are very fit and strong. I would not want to fight you…not at all,' he smiles at me. Then, as quickly as it came, the smile leaves his face. 'But you will not defeat him. He will kill you and perhaps worse. Maybe, this Time, it will be even worse for you. But he will certainly kill you, and he will use your body. Yes…he will do those things.'

Again he takes me by surprise, this time by his bluntness. I continue to stare at him across the table, the food beginning to grow cold between us. I suddenly feel cold myself, and wrap my red cardigan around my shoulders. I begin to take in what he has said.

'Richard Sturrock is a madman,' Hiroshi continues. 'He has the strength of someone who is completely mad. He has been driven insane by…all this…' He gestures with his right hand, palm upwards, at the restaurant and the people around us. 'He is not responsible for what he has become. He lives for almost the same length of time as you, about six months in his case. Do you know how many Times he has lived?'

'He could have…touched me? When I was dead?'

Hiroshi just looks at me. He seems unwilling, or unable, to answer.

'But…all the blood…' I say quietly.

Hiroshi lowers his eyes. He looks as if he is being forced to talk about something shameful, and he seems almost contrite.

'Sandy, I do not know,' he replies. 'But I believe he may have, yes. He has done so before…to others. I know this…'

'But…you didn't see…'

'No, I was not there.'

'So, perhaps…'

'Yes, perhaps…'

The silence hangs between us for a moment. Hiroshi looks up from the table. He has a sad look in his eyes; they appear mournful.

'I am sorry for all this, for all the things that have happened to you. You must leave this illusion of life. Five months is not enough time. You will be driven mad, like Richard Sturrock has already been...'

'How many Times has he lived?'

'He has lived so many Times. Richard Sturrock, I believe, has lived for nine hundred and twenty-eight Times, including this one.'

'Nine hundred...'

'Yes. He was mad many hundreds of Times ago, I think...' He pauses for a moment, and then spreads his hands out on the table, palms down, fingers apart. 'Sandy, I can help you escape. Richard Sturrock will be waiting for you on August 19th, and we cannot allow that to happen. We need...what is the word in English? Ah, of course...a pre-emptive strike...'

* * * * * * * * * * * * * * * *

Two hours later, we are in a bar opposite Mestre Station. There is a television in the corner, showing a programme about the First World War. People are sitting all around us, drinking coffee and speaking in Italian. We are both drinking tea. Hiroshi has outlined his plan to me; a simple plan. But if it works, it will be very effective.

The plan, in a nutshell, is for Hiroshi to wait for Richard Sturrock to leave his house, to follow him, patiently waiting for the right moment, and at that moment, for Hiroshi to use his '454 Casull Handgun' to blow Richard Sturrock's head off his shoulders. Hiroshi assures me that his gun is more than capable of that.

'At point blank range,' he tells me, chewing on a bread roll, 'it would blow the head off a sheep. I know this, because I have tried...'

Hiroshi wants to have a 'dry run' tomorrow, and then to execute the plan the following morning.

'He does not know I am here in Venice,' he says. 'But he may suspect soon, so we must act quickly. Tomorrow, we will meet for breakfast, at your hotel. I will try to answer any questions you have about all of this...about everything. I know so little, but perhaps more than most. So, think about what you would like to ask and tomorrow I will explain as much as I can.'

Hiroshi stands up and rubs his eyes with the palms of his hands.

'I am tired,' he says. 'I must go to bed now. My hotel is nearby, and I will walk. Goodnight Sandy - and I will see you tomorrow.'

With that, Hiroshi turns and walks out. The barman wishes him a good evening, and without turning round, he waves in response.

* * * * * * * * * * * * * * *

I have so many questions to ask, but already what Hiroshi has told me has left my head spinning. Hiroshi is like me, but I think I knew that anyway. But he was in a coma for just four years, and so each Time he lives - is awake - for nine years before being taken back, before returning. He has nine years awake to my five months.

'You can live a life in nine years,' he had told me that evening. 'Eventually I will leave - live and die. But not yet...'

When I asked how many Times he had lived, I expected him to say a low number. Perhaps six or seven - something that would equate in length to the amount of time I had spent awake. But, to say the least, his answer surprised me.

'Oh, quite a few Times,' he said. 'One hundred and forty-five.'

I couldn't believe it.

'One hundred and forty-five!' I replied. 'One hundred and

forty-five multiplied by nine years! That's over a thousand years!'

'Yes. But Sandy - remember - you too have lived over a thousand years. But you have spent most of it in a coma. You have, shall we say, slept through most of your life; your lives. I have not. I have been awake…'

* * * * * * * * * * * * * * * * *

I lie for ages in my hotel bed, unable to sleep, twisting and turning beneath the quilt. I am worn-out, but my thoughts are full of the things of this evening. I cannot pull the curtain of sleep across my mind, so I get up and run a bath.

However, as soon as the bath is full, I suddenly feel myself overwhelmed by a wave of tiredness. I stand looking into the water, the artificial light in the bathroom glaring unnaturally at 2.15am. I gaze at myself in the mirror over the sink; I look tired. My skin seems pale, and I rub my cheeks with the palms of my hands.

This evening has answered so many questions, and given some solutions, but I feel uneasy about the course of action I have agreed to. I don't feel troubled by the fact that someone will die (although I do feel guilty about my lack of concern), but instead because the plan seems almost a slight upon me. It seems a slight upon my new abilities; my new strength.

I have spent two months in training to enable me to confront Richard Sturrock, and now someone this evening tells me that all that effort has been worthless. But I cannot believe that.

I can't believe that Hiroshi could really know that much; how could he really know about the weeks spent toning and sharpening my reflexes? Do I need his help? Would I be a coward to accept it - to let him do my dirty work? Or should I just be grateful that he can, perhaps, help me escape?

And why on earth should I trust him? Why should I trust him at all? Is he now my friend; my ally? Or am I still alone?

I turn around, walk out of the bathroom, and climb back into bed. I imagine the bath in my mind, still the other side of the wall, waiting for me to step in; to submerge myself beneath the warm waters.

I imagine it will turn red; like my blood. I imagine that it will overflow and drown me while I am asleep. I imagine it will grow cold during the night - but colder and colder until it turns to ice. I feel, more than anything, confusion; confusion and tiredness. I snuggle down under the quilt, open my eyes for a second, and close them again. Then I am asleep.

Time Ninety-Seven

Monday 14th August 2006
8.01am CET

Hiroshi arrives wearing another smart suit; this time grey with a white shirt and a green tie. He smiles at me as he sits down; pulling a napkin from the table and flicking it open in front of him. He lays it on his lap.
 'So, how did you sleep? Well, I hope?' he says.
 'No - not very well…' I reply.
 'Ah! That is a shame. But it does not matter today. Tonight you must sleep well, so you are ready to execute our plan tomorrow.'
 'I'll do my best…but I didn't sleep badly on purpose.'
 'No, of course not…'
Hiroshi pours the milk meant for the tea into a glass and drinks it. His eyes are searching the table for food, but finding none.
 'It's a buffet…' I inform him.
 'Ah! So the food is not here, but instead all around us!'
 'Yes, that's it…'
 'So, please excuse me…'
He gets up and wanders about for a couple of minutes collecting various edible items; a boiled egg, some toast, a bowl of peaches. When he cannot carry any more, he returns to the table and lays down his spoils.
 'There is not much food here…for breakfast…' he says, looking at his collection with a self-pitying stare.
 'I suppose…' I reply.
 'No matter - we will eat more later on in the morning.'
Hiroshi starts peeling his egg. His English has improved vastly from when we met in Germany during Time Eighty-Two, but it is still a bit quirky.

'Your English is very good…excellent,' I say, pouring tea for myself. 'Much better than when we first met…'

'Yes. You mean when we met in Germany. I saw you once before that. For me, it was many hundreds of years ago. It was in Hawaii, at Pearl Harbour…'

'Oh? Yes, I think I remember seeing you… It seems a long time ago for me too…'

'Yes, a long time ago. But, thank you, my English is much better now. Of course, I have had time to learn, but before meeting you I have helped others. I speak German and Italian. I also helped someone from Norway very recently, but fortunately they also spoke English. This was good, because the language is ridiculous! Norwegian, I mean. I tried to learn a bit, but…my goodness! What a strange language!'

'Is it?'

'Yes! I learnt a bit, as I said… But now I only remember one sentence.'

'Oh? What's that?'

'*Min strøk ødelegger.*'

'What does that mean?'

'My coat is ruined.'

'Oh? That's useful, I suppose…'

'Yes. Perhaps if one day I am in Norway, and my coat is…'

'Ruined?'

'Precisely…!'

'Have you killed anyone before?'

Hiroshi places his half-eaten egg on a saucer in front of him.

'Yes,' he says, his face struck with seriousness. 'But never without reason…very good reason. I will kill Richard Sturrock because there is a good reason to do so.'

'Me?'

'Yes,' he says quietly, while retrieving his egg.

'Have you killed Richard before, in other Times?'

'Yes.'

'Has he ever killed you?'

'Yes.'

'Oh?'

'So we both know, you and I, what it is to die…'

'Yes, I suppose…'

'It is not any fun… How do you say this in England? Not exactly a picnic?'

'No…it isn't.'

He begins buttering the toast, lifting layers of butter onto each slice. He has finished the egg.

* * * * * * * * * * * * * * * *

During the thirty minutes that follow, I fire endless questions at Hiroshi; questions about my life, and about him. He seems to vacillate between smiling and shrugging his shoulders, while doing his best to give me answers I might find acceptable.

I ask him about the gun, and how he had managed to get it into the country, or where he had bought it. I too had considered such an idea, but - even with access to the Internet - I was at a loss where to start. Hiroshi told me that he had bought the gun here in Italy, in the south of the country.

'I always buy the same gun from the same person, every Time I think I will need it,' he says. 'This Time, I bought it three months ago, and then stored it in a safe deposit box in Verona. I picked it up just two days ago. It is hidden in my luggage; in my room. I always leave it in the same safe deposit box in Verona. I don't know why. It's just it's been OK before. Never any problems…'

'Is it easy to buy a gun - here in Italy?' I ask.

'No, not really. They have very…what is the word? Not strict…'

'I'm not sure…'

'In Japan we say '*kyuukutsu*'… Ah, yes! Tight! Tight controls on gun sales,' Hiroshi says with a grin. 'I like English! It is good to practice…'

'Your English is great…'

'Yes...getting better all the time. So, I buy from a man in the south of the country. I finally met him after nearly six months of enquiries. This was during the first Time - the first Time I needed a gun. Now it is easier. You have the money - he has all the guns in the world! Every gun on the planet! He runs a farm, and the basement...full of guns!'

'Guns scare me...'

'Yes...me too! I have a 454 Casull Handgun - very powerful! When you fire, your arm is sore for a whole day!' He doesn't sound very scared. 'This afternoon,' he continues, 'we will go through my plan. There are three things that must happen.'

'Oh?'

'Yes, three things. Number one - Richard Sturrock has to be killed. Number two - you must not be implicated in any way. You have to continue to live in this Time, you do not want to spend the next ten years in prison, I am certain!'

'No.'

'However, number two is easier to achieve than you might think... And, number three, if I am captured by the police, then it must be after August 19th - it must be after you have escaped from the cycle. I need to stay with you until then...'

'Oh? But I know where the place is. I could definitely find it on my own...'

Hiroshi looks across at me, seemingly unsure about whether to say something. He runs his hand through the right side of his hair, smoothing it down. He has black hair; shiny. It was the first sign of nervousness or embarrassment that I had seen all morning.

'Sandy,' he begins, placing his hands flat on the table, and then immediately lifting them off again and placing them on his knees, 'you will still need my help...you will need my help to leave, even at the last moment. This life...it is a sickness. It can be a sickness...'

'But why...?'

'Do you remember the place, in the warehouse? Do you

remember the ring attached to the floor? I put that there. I always put the ring there…'

'Yes, I remember. It was bolted to the floor…'

'Yes. It is hard work…'

'But what is it for?'

He looks at me with a nervous smile; his discomfiture showing in his eyes.

'So,' he says, 'that is where I must chain you up…'

* * * * * * * * * * * * * * * *

When you live a life like mine, you grow accustomed to people saying strange things. And even the most ordinary thing that somebody says can seem strange, dependent on the situation. This is especially true during the last few hours of a Time. For example, someone could offer me an opportunity to win a holiday, or ask me to sign-up for a credit card. If they did this on August 19th, it would seem especially bizarre. I would think 'why would I want a credit card? I have enough money, and anyway, I'm leaving in under an hour…' This is the sort of thing that might happen, and also the kind of thing I might think in response.

So when Hiroshi tells me he wants to chain me up, my mind simply accepts the idea as yet another weird proposition; just like being offered a free holiday with only thirty minutes left.

However, I look across at him with questioning eyes and wait for him to explain. But he just sits there looking at me, and after a few seconds I realise he is waiting for me to speak.

'Why do you want to chain me up?' I ask, almost with a sigh. In truth, I am becoming bored with all of this - this strangeness. I understand what needs to be done to Richard Sturrock. I can accept the need to kill him, and even accept that Hiroshi is completely stoical about the probability of blowing his head clean off his shoulders. I can accept all of this, because there is some logic to it. But it seems that as soon as I have come to terms with something - some weird idea or occurrence that is mixed into my life - then I am faced with another for me to assimilate. This is the latest in a very long line.

'Because otherwise you will run away…' Hiroshi replies.

'Run away from what? From you?' I ask.

'No, not from me. You will run because you will not want to leave…when the moment arrives. I know about these things…you must trust me.'

'Trust you to chain me up?'

'Yes. Unless I chain you to the place, the place where you can escape, you will step out of the room at the last moment. Or you will run far away during the final minutes.'

'But why? Why - if I really want to escape?'

'Because your mind, Sandy, is in a state of confusion.' He raises a finger for emphasis. 'Part of you wants to escape, but another part, a stronger part, will want you to stay. This…life, as I said…it is a sickness. It makes you sick - in the mind. And, in the end, during the last few moments, you will not be able to think…not at all. Your thoughts will be enveloped in the sickness. You will do anything to get out of the room. If you had a knife, you would cut off your own hand to be free from the chains. Believe me, you would do it. Sandy, you must allow me to chain you to the ring. It is the only way. If you do not, there is no point in pursuing our plan any further. The choice, of course, is yours. But, you must…'

I stare across at him, this man sitting in front of me; this strange but yet normal man. My mind, working fully at the moment, is bursting with 'what ifs?' What if Hiroshi is as mad as Richard Sturrock? What if he chains me up and then sets fire to the warehouse? What if he wants just to kill me as well?

These are just a few of the possible outcomes, and I am at a loss to know what to do. But I do know something. My instinct, which I have relied upon for such a long time, is unhappy about my attempts to escape. But more than that, it is as if my instinct is changing, becoming more powerful; more suggestive.

I have had dreams during this Time and the Time before – vivid dreams; erotic dreams - dreams about time, about eternal youth, about how great it is to live as I now do. These dreams are telling me to stay; to leave things as they are. These dreams are stronger this Time than they were the Time before. Perhaps next Time they will be stronger still.

I hold my stare for a moment longer, and then blink. My eyes feel tired. I am tired – tired in lots of different ways.

'OK,' I reply. 'Chain me up…'

* * * * * * * * * * * * * * * *

During the remainder of breakfast, and for a great part of the morning, Hiroshi answers more of the questions I have about our common situation. He shrugs his shoulders when I ask if there is any reason; any purpose behind the life we now lead. The life I am hoping to leave behind.

'Something has happened to us,' he replies, not very helpfully. I wait for him to continue, but he appears to have nothing else to add.

'But why us? Why not everybody? How many of us are there?'

'Well, why the whole world is not affected, I do not know. It happened about the same time, when you were eighteen years old - when I was thirty-four. We all passed into a coma within days of each other - in Nineteen Ninety-Three. I awoke in Nineteen Ninety-Seven; you awoke in March this year. And around and around we go.'

'Yes…'

'There are, I believe, dozens of us - but no more than that. Not hundreds. I have helped six people before, and I have met some others, like Richard Sturrock. Some are happy…with what they have. They are the ones awake for years, like me. Others have only a short time, like you. They are not happy. Sometimes, after a while, they are still not happy - but they have been driven insane. Then they believe they are happy. And for them, that is enough...'

Time Ninety-Seven

Monday 14th August 2006

That afternoon we head across the bridge to Venice on a number seven yellow bus. We are on our way to have our practice - our dry run. Hiroshi sits reading a newspaper, seemingly engrossed in an article on page two, and I just look out of the window. But I see nothing, for instead my mind is reliving our earlier conversation.

We had discussed a whole range of other things, and although Hiroshi had few concrete answers, or even strong opinions, there were two things that he was able to answer. These were questions that always buzzed around my mind, and it was good to hear an answer. It was even good to be able to pose the questions; to find anyone who could listen - who would understand.

I had asked Hiroshi what happened to me when I passed from a Time; when I was taken. What happened to the Sandy left behind?

'I mean,' I said, 'I could be walking along the street, or perhaps with Chris, and then…well, you know. So, what happens to the 'me' that is left? Does that Time just end? Or do I just stare vacantly into space for the rest of my life? Is everything reset back to March, for everyone, or do things carry on with another Sandy? What happens?'

'We all return at different times,' Hiroshi replied. 'And we return just a few days apart. You return on August 19th, and I return on August 21st - two days later. If you were to go around again, decide to have a Time Ninety-Eight, then I could watch you return, and then I would return myself two days later. So, you see, the Times continue…for others. August 21st is actually quite late to return, so I have seen others - been with others - when they have left a Time.'

'So what happens to them - to me?'

'You die.'

'Die?'

'Yes - you must have thought that was possible. You just die.'

'So, I could be with Chris, and then...'

'You will just collapse and die. When you are taken, that which is 'you' - your consciousness, your being - leaves both your body and that Time. The body left is just a shell.'

I thought about all the Times I had been with Chris; all the Times that he had seen me die. Of course, I had considered this was possible, but it just didn't seem likely. It didn't seem fair. It was ghastly; macabre. But there it was.

Another question answered by Hiroshi was done so with the aid of a prop. I asked him how it was possible that Richard Sturrock had lived over nine hundred Times, and me less than a hundred. If we had both gone into our respective comas in Nineteen Ninety-Three, then surely we would have lived the same amount of Times? And Hiroshi had lived over a hundred Times himself.

When I put this question to him, he reached inside his jacket and produced a small block of wood. Not much bigger than a mousetrap, it had a brass winding handle attached to the side, like on a music box, and three coloured rubber bands stretched across the top. These were connected by a number of small screws and levers. Hiroshi placed it on the table in front of me; it looked at once both complex and primitive.

'What's this?' I asked.

'An explanation,' he replied. 'Imagine each of these rubber bands is a person. The blue one is you, the red one is me, and the yellow one is Richard Sturrock...'

'OK.'

'So, when I turn the handle, the bands will stretch to the end of the block and then ping back and catch on the lever on the other edge. Then they will stretch again and repeat. Each stretch of the rubber band represents a Time, a Time through which we live...'

'OK.'

'So, notice there is only one handle. On the side of the block, one handle; one force that drives all the bands.'

I nod my head.

'When I turn the handle,' he repeated, 'the bands all stretch towards the end of the block.' He pinched the small handle between his thumb and forefinger and began turning. All three bands began to stretch, and when they reached the end of the block they snapped back again. Hiroshi continued to turn, but this time only the yellow band stretched forward. It once again reached the end and then pinged back. As the handle continued to turn, this happened three more times. And then the red band joined the yellow band on its short journey, both snapping back together. Next, all three bands stretched out along the block, and all snapped back at the same time. With that, Hiroshi put the block back on the table.

'Time, for us, is not the same as for others,' he said. He waved his arm around the restaurant as he said the word 'others', seemingly encompassing everyone there and the rest of the world. The wave was dismissive, and for the first time I saw that they - the 'other' people - did not really matter to him any more.

'Time, for us, is not...'*sonchi*',' he said. 'Continue? No. Continuous...Is that the right word?'

I was unsure, but I nodded.

'So, each August we are, in effect, reset back to Nineteen Ninety-Three; but some of us experience further Times before others begin their next. Richard Sturrock, in fact, lives ten Times to your one. Let us say you both have a Time One, then in August you both return. Richard Sturrock will then have another nine Times before you once again awake in March Two Thousand and Six, and then you will have your Time Two - back in synchronization with Richard Sturrock - but it will be his Time Eleven. And this is a pattern; always followed…'

Looking down at the little wooden block, I found that I understood what he meant completely. It made perfect sense to me, and that in itself surprised me.

'So,' he continued, 'if Richard Sturrock has realised the pattern between you and him, he will be waiting for you, perhaps for me; and that is bad. But I think he may not yet know the pattern. However, if he finds you this Time, he will learn. And then you will be in danger in the Times that follow. But in This Time - your Time Ninety-Seven - I think we have the element of surprise…'

He looked suddenly around the restaurant, as if he thought we were being overheard. He appeared worried, perhaps perplexed. He turned to face me again, resting his hands on the table in front of him. His face seemed a little paler; a bit tired. But in his eyes shone determination, and in that moment I saw the strength that he had gathered through a thousand years of life.

'We will not fail…' he said with a smile. And I believed him.

* * * * * * * * * * * * * * * *

The dry-run takes only twenty minutes. We walk quickly to a small apartment building about five minutes from the railway station, which means it takes us ten minutes to walk from the bus station on the other side of the Grand Canal.

Hiroshi leads me to the back of the building, and then up a flight of wooden stairs attached to the outside of the rear wall. They seem old and worn, as if many people had made this journey before. We alight on the roof, and step onto a wooden terrace, made from the same wood and seemingly at the same time as the stairs. I am amazed to see the terrace has a brilliant view of Richard Sturrock's house.

'You must look as if you belong here,' Hiroshi tells me. 'That you belong out here on the terrace. Relax - read a book.

But watch for Richard Sturrock to leave his house. This house beneath us belongs to an English couple - I came here for dinner once. But at the moment, they are in England, and the property is empty.'

'So they don't mind me being up here?'

'They will never know. Now - tomorrow, I will wait close to Richard Sturrock's house; somewhere he will not see me. I will be hidden, and I will have no view of his front door. You must be my eyes. When you see him leave, you must phone me with your mobile phone. Tell me if he is heading towards the canal or away from it. That is all. Then, hang up and go back to Mestre. I will meet you in Brek later that evening.'

'That's all I have to do?'

'Yes - but you may have to wait for many hours. You must not fail to see him when he leaves his house. Your role is not as easy as you may think. Perhaps we will be lucky, and he will leave his house in the morning. But, maybe not...'

'Yes...'

'Tomorrow, we will travel here separately. You will come here, to this terrace. I will be in position by 8am. Please be here at the same time. He will not leave before that.'

'Why separately?'

'Because, if anything were to...go wrong...if people were to see what happens, if I am seen, then you must not be implicated. You must not be seen with me. If we are not seen together, it may still be possible to escape this Time. But if not, you may have to go around again.'

'I want to leave now...'

'Of course, I understand. And if all goes to plan - which it will - then that is what will happen. But, we must have...contingency...'

He looks at me, and then gives me a little smile. 'Are you sure,' he asks, 'there is nothing you would like to do differently? Perhaps, during one more Time?'

I remain silent for a second, gathering my thoughts. 'Yes,' I reply. 'I would have started a relationship with someone. But it's OK. I can do that after I leave; after I escape.'

'Oh?'

'I love him,' I continue, surprised by my own candidness. 'And he can give me something back that I lost - someone who existed in another Time; he can make them exist again.'

'I don't really understand...'

'People exist over and over again, don't they? The same people - I meet the same people over and over again; Time after Time. Well - this one only existed once. Chris and I, we made him. But, like everybody else, he can exist again. Chris and I, we can create him again...'

I stare at him, willing him to agree. I am sure that I am right - my instinct tells me I am right. But Hiroshi has an instinct too, an older one than mine. Surely he will agree with me - tell me I am right. That is all I want, at this moment; to be right about that.

'Ah...I do understand,' he says, placing the fingers of his right hand on his lips. 'These things...they are...not for us to know. But, I believe that you are right. If you feel it to be so, then it is probably what will be. I think that is so...'

His answer is acceptable to me; more than that. I suddenly feel a surge of emotion, and I fling my arms around him and give him a hug. He puts his arms around me too - but loosely; embarrassed. Sensing his awkwardness, I slowly pull away.

'Thank you for doing this...' I whisper, my eyes full of tears.

'You are most welcome,' he replies, giving me a little bow.

We make our way back down the stairs, and he holds my hand; helping me down the last two steps.

Time Ninety-Seven

Tuesday 15th August 2006
10.35am CET

I have been here, on the terrace, for over two and a half hours. Already, I am feeling very hot - there is no breeze today; none at all. I am not really very high up, perhaps thirty feet, but I can see people going about their business along one of the smaller canals. One man carries a big chair; he is holding it upside down by the legs. He has to keep stopping to rest, and the effort makes him sweat profusely; he is constantly wiping his face. I'm finding him, and the others, a distraction from my task.

To anyone looking up at me, if they should choose to look up for whatever reason, I am playing the part of a sun worshipper - a tourist with a holiday home, enjoying the beautiful weather. I am sitting on a little bench, and I have bought magazines and towels with me for effect. Regardless of the importance of the job I am doing, I am bored. I have been bored for over an hour.

The boredom is making my mind wander, and I find myself constantly trying to bring it back - to refocus it on Richard Sturrock's house, his door, any movement; any sign of life at all. A life that Hiroshi and I hope will be extinguished today.

Nothing is happening at all, and the boredom is starting to numb my mind. I can't read my books, of course - I must just look at the house, waiting for the front door to open.

Ten minutes later, it does.

I am folding one of the towels into a neat square, trying to get the sides exactly equal (a self-imposed challenge), when the door opens on Richard Sturrock's house. He steps out into the street, and turns to lock his door. He is wearing a white short-sleeved shirt and black trousers. He looks a bit like a waiter in an expensive restaurant. I drop the towel and fumble with my phone, hitting the speed dial button with my thumb. I hold it to my ear, trembling, and it rings.

'Yes?' says a voice; Hiroshi.

'He's leaving the house. He's walking now - towards the canal…'

'Thank you.'

The line goes dead.

I stare at my phone for a second. That is it. I pack up my towels and books, and walk, like a tourist, down the wooden stairs and back along the street. Fifteen minutes later, I'm on a train back to Mestre.

Time Ninety-Seven

Tuesday 15th August 2006
6.35pm CET

So now I'm sitting in Brek, once again surrounded by food. But I feel too nervous to eat. I feel too nervous to eat much, anyway. I've had half a pizza and some chips. Hiroshi said he would meet me here at 6.45pm, if everything has gone well. I hope that's what has happened; that it has gone well. If it hasn't, I have no idea what to do next.

I just wish he'd have called me - told me that everything was OK. But he hasn't called, and so I don't know what has happened. I'm fed up with waiting - waiting for Hiroshi to show up, waiting for Times to end, waiting; waiting.

I just want to know what has happened, but I don't. I just wish I did, that's all.

* * * * * * * * * * * * * * * *

Earlier that day, Hiroshi had passed under the bridges and along the tiny streets with absolute certainty of where he was. He had walked these streets so many Times; seen landmarks that never change - a post-box or a blue door with tiny white flowers painted on the frame. They were walking in the area of Venice known as Cannaregio - a lovely part of the city, Hiroshi thought. It was full of character, but never full of tourists.

He walked under a bridge he had passed beneath a hundred times before; and in the distance Richard Sturrock strode purposefully on - his white shirt clearly visible before a backdrop of grey buildings and walls, and further still, the blue of the canal.

He was walking, it seemed, to the edge of the island, perhaps just for a walk, perhaps to catch a bus out to one of the smaller islands - Murano or Burano. Hiroshi didn't know, and he didn't care. He was now focused entirely on the task ahead; just that one thing. He had already forgotten Sandy; the reason he was committing murder. At that moment, in his mind the only thing that mattered was not losing sight of Richard Sturrock. That was all.

Five minutes passed before Hiroshi turned the corner at the edge of the Island. Richard Sturrock had turned right and, once out of sight, Hiroshi had to jog to keep up. He slowed his pace to a walk as he turned the corner. The white shirt gleamed in the sun about one hundred yards ahead, still striding away, but the gap had closed. To the left stood the Isola di San Michele, just four hundred yards away out in the canal. The island was known simply to the locals as 'Cimitero' - the Cemetery.

Richard Sturrock was now heading past where the buses stop for the smaller islands, and then he suddenly turned inland again, walking away from the large canal. Hiroshi would have liked to, once again, break into a jog; but this time there were a few people about, and he was keen not to be noticed. And anyway, Hiroshi now knew where Richard Sturrock was going. There was a brothel just a few streets from the alley that he had disappeared into. Hiroshi was sure he was going there. He slowed his pace to a gentle stroll. He would let Richard Sturrock get ahead. Now he knew his destination, he was happy to keep a good distance from him. He would slowly arrive at the brothel; time was now on his side. He would wait.

* * * * * * * * * * * * * * * *

The brothel was a large grey house with a white door; pots of red flowers - in full bloom - stood on each windowsill. Hiroshi walked past the house, close to the wall, and turned down an alley three doors along. He turned right into an even smaller alley, and from there he walked parallel to the street with the brothel, and turned back onto it a hundred yards further down. He sat down to wait on a stone step, which had been carved from a single block, and formed the entrance to a now disused shop.

He waited in silence, unnoticed and in semi-darkness, for forty-five minutes, and then Richard Sturrock appeared from the white door; opened and closed by unseen hands. He walked away in the direction he had come, back towards the edge of the island. Hiroshi crossed behind him and followed his route along the parallel alley. He walked fast; making two strides for every one Richard Sturrock was taking. Before the end of the alley there was another, smaller alley - a slight shortcut - that ran diagonally and came out a little further down towards the bus stops. Hiroshi walked quickly to the junction of alley and street, just in time to see Richard Sturrock turn into the alley opposite. Hiroshi had been right; he had chosen to use the shortcut. He stepped across the street, and entered the alley.

Now just twenty yards ahead, Richard saw the light from behind him - pouring into the alley from the sunny street - darken for a second. He knew someone else had walked into the passageway.

One second after joining Richard in the alley, Hiroshi pulled the gun out of his inside pocket, leveled it at Richard's head, and fired. It was a simple act; there was no fuss, no exchange of gunfire like in a film. It was as if Hiroshi was taking out a handkerchief to wipe his face in the heat. It was performed in a normal way; almost mundane. To Hiroshi, there was no violence in this; it was a means to an end - that was all. He thought of Sandy as he pulled the trigger, of the terrible death he was saving her from. But he was not happy, and he did not feel he was doing either a good or a bad deed. He felt nothing beyond success - a simple satisfaction in knowing that the task was finished, and that everything had gone well.

The bullet missed Richard's head by a couple of inches, but instead entered through the back of his neck and powered its way out the other side. The impact was immense, and his head - his whole body - flew forwards in an unnatural, cruel way. Blood shot from the front of his head and neck like someone had thrown a glass of redcurrant juice, in anger, at the wall in front of him. He was dead before his body crumpled to the ground, making no sound but a dull thud.

Richard had not heard the loud noise from the gun that killed him, but in the moments before he died, he had been aware of a number of things.

Firstly, he had known he was going to die. As soon as the light disappeared from the entrance to the street, he had known someone was behind him, and he had known he was going to be killed. He knew for certain that Hiroshi was with him in the alley, and if he had had a second longer - just a moment more - he would have shouted out his name, the word 'Hiroshi', as loud as he was able.

Secondly, he knew that Sandy had enlisted Hiroshi's help so she could escape. He had wanted to kill her again - this Time to watch her fight for her life - and he was disappointed that the chance would be gone forever. But, and this was almost his dying thought, he did not hold any grudge against her, and he hoped that she would find happiness by following the path she had chosen. She was now out of his grasp, and her suffering would no longer bring him any pleasure; for her to suffer no longer had any point; it would have no meaning.

But his final thought was one of pleasure; immense pleasure. He saw himself again, once more back in his house here in Venice, another beautiful girl in his bed at night; another chance to live. He could not be destroyed, not this way. He had lost Sandy, but there would be others.

His song would continue to play, to be sung. He would rise again.

Hiroshi knew Richard Sturrock was dead the moment he fired the gun. The noise of the gun would bring people to the spot, he knew this, but not for a few minutes. Nobody would run to the sound of gunfire. That was not how things were.

Placing the gun back into his jacket pocket, he walked back out of the passageway and across to the alley opposite. He walked along and passed behind the brothel, continuing as far as he could, and then turned right out onto the street. He glanced behind him to see if anything was happening, but there was not a soul in sight. He continued, strolling now as a tourist, looking at the buildings and doorways as he passed, and just seven minutes later he was crossing the Rialto Bridge. People were now everywhere, all around him, but he was still as invisible as when he had been alone.

He walked through San Polo and all the way down to Dorsoduro. He continued until, minutes later, he reached the southern edge of the city. He walked along to a bus stop, and then he was lucky to straight away catch a bus out to Guidecca, just five minutes to the south.

The bus was almost empty, and Hiroshi stared out across the beautiful Canale Della Guidecca, separating Guidecca from the centre of Venice - now bathed in sunshine and shimmering so brightly that he wished he had brought his sunglasses. Nobody saw him as he lifted the gun out of his pocket and calmly dropped it over the edge of the rail. It gave a small splash as it disappeared into the canal, the white of the splash swallowed up in the waves made by the bus.

The gun was gone. He had left no fingerprints at the scene. It was less than thirty minutes ago, but already he was nearly in Guidecca. He looked up at the sky, and felt some kind of relief for the first time. Perhaps, one day, he could be caught for this crime. But, he was certain, not within the next few days. Not by August 19th - and that was all he needed.

He sat down on a brown plastic seat. He felt OK, but he was hungry. He patted his jacket pockets; but there was nothing there that he could eat.

Time Ninety-Seven

Tuesday 15th August 2006
6.44pm CET

Hiroshi arrives a minute early, and this evening there is plenty of food. I have to resist the urge, when I see him walking towards me, to stand up and run over to him. But he smiles at me as he walks to my table, and I know then that everything has gone to plan.

He sits down and grabs a slice of pizza off my plate. 'He is dead. The gun is gone. I was not seen,' he says, and then takes a bite out of the pizza.

'So, everything was OK?'

'Everything was perfect. I was lucky. He was not. He did not know the pattern; he was not expecting me. He is dead. I will not be suspected. Nobody saw me, the gun is miles away, I did not touch him - there are no fingerprints. We are in the clear. Trust me - I have done this before...'

I feel relief spread through me like warmth, but am at a loss for what to say next. I want to say 'thank you', but I feel it would sound so trite; perhaps almost seem insincere. Instead, I just say the first thing that pops into my head.

'He must hate you.'

'Hate me?' The statement takes him by surprise. 'No, I do not think so. He understands me, why I do what I do. Very few people understand me...understand what we are. But that is not important. Now you are able to escape. And you must now be certain, over the next day or so, that you definitely want to escape. I think that you must, to avoid becoming the man I have just killed, but you must be sure. Once you have done this, you cannot return to this life...these lives. You will have only one life, and you will one day die.'

'I'm sure, Hiroshi... I'm sure.'

'That is good,' he says with a slight smile. 'Because I do not want to, one day, be pointing a gun at you. So, I must explain what we have to do now…'

Time Ninety-Seven

Wednesday 16th August 2006
8.55am CET

I am tired. I look down at my toast and marmalade. The toast has gone cold, and the little pot of marmalade is impregnable. I have trained in New Mexico for two months, I am as fit as I have ever been, strong; but still I cannot open the little pot. It looks back at me – the small gold lid like a single eye – and it reminds me of my frailty, my weaknesses; my humanity. It, like so many on breakfast tables in hotels around the world, has had its lid tightened by sumo wrestlers – grunting and sweating as they turn it tighter and tighter; each turning until exhaustion, and then passing it along to the next. It is impossible to open.

I rub my eyes with my left hand; my right propping up my chin. I am tired because again I have not slept well. I am scared.

* * * * * * * * * * * * * * * *

Last night, before I went to bed, I went for a walk. Hiroshi had gone back to his hotel – he does not want to see me again until Saturday, just in case he is implicated in some way in Richard Sturrock's murder. He does not think that this is likely at all, but he wants to 'be on the safe side'. Hiroshi likes using English expressions.

But my walk, which lasted only ten minutes, left me shaking back in my room as I tried to pour myself a cup of tea. Nothing happened that should have made me feel that way, but somehow the darkness in the streets, the faces I did not know, the world; all of it seemed too much to cope with. The great distance of time that awaits me, that I will commit myself to in just a few days, seemed to stretch out before me like an endless path. Mingled with the streets of Mestre, it beckoned me forward, offering freedom, but at the same time promising aging and death.

I am used to being thirty-one. How can I not be thirty-one? How can I allow, even force, my body to age - to waste away; to decay? It seems as if this is the true madness.

The streets around me last night, the people, they were all busy in the darkness of the late evening; all engaged in things that were not a part of me - driving cars, planning for the future and putting children to bed. It all seemed so ordinary. The normality of it all! Absolutely everything was normal. Is that what I want - to be normal? Is that what I really want? Because now - at the moment - I am special.

And these feelings overcame me, and after just a few short minutes, just two streets from the hotel, I turned around and made my way back. I walked close to the walls of the buildings and kept my eyes down to the ground, so I would not see, could no longer sense, the life which awaits me.

* * * * * * * * * * * * * * * *

When I went to bed, at about midnight, I lay awake for ages thinking. I couldn't switch off my brain, and when finally sleep overtook me, I dreamt that Hiroshi was my enemy. I dreamt he had locked me in a room, the key hanging in the corridor just out of reach, because he had decided to keep me, like a pet. And each day the room would become smaller, the walls would move towards me - just a tiny amount each day, such a small amount that you could never notice, perhaps not even realise. But as the years passed the walls would one day crush me, leave me with no room at all, and eventually - unable to move at all - I would simply starve or suffocate.

When I awoke from this dream it was only 2am - I had only been asleep for a matter of minutes. I couldn't get back to sleep at all - not for the remainder of the night.

* * * * * * * * * * * * * * * *

And so now I'm barely awake. I can't eat because I'm so tired. I actually feel a bit sick - through tiredness, nerves - I don't know. I'm going to have a bath, and then perhaps have a nap. I just can't keep my eyes open. Maybe I'll sleep this morning.

I look out of the window of the hotel restaurant; a lorry is blocking the view, but when it moves, the sun streams into the room. It is a beautiful day, and this afternoon I may go out somewhere; perhaps to a park. Maybe sit in the sun and read a book - finish my copy of 'Strangers on a Train'.

But this morning - sunny or not - I'm going to spend in my room, hopefully asleep. I have no plan beyond that. I have no plans until Saturday.

Time Ninety-Seven

Saturday 19th August 2006
9.00am CET

Hiroshi meets me outside my hotel at 9am. It is only 8am in London, so I have three hours and twelve minutes left in this Time. It seems inconceivable that I will continue beyond that; that I could remain here for lunch, let alone see tomorrow. It seems impossible.

Hiroshi is carrying a brown leather bag, and he is dressed in a light blue short-sleeved shirt and grey trousers. He smiles at me, but he seems nervous. This makes me in turn feel more nervous than I am already.

'How are you feeling?' he asks.

'OK. A bit scared…' I reply.

'Please do not worry. Everything will be fine. Have you had breakfast?'

'No…I had some orange juice, that's all.'

'That is good. It is best that you have little to eat.'

'Oh?'

'Yes,' he looks up at the sky - it is a brilliant blue, as it has been for days. 'So, shall we go?'

We take the train from Mestre station. Once we arrive in Venice, Hiroshi stops to buy a newspaper. I wait patiently for him as he then buys two cups of tea from a small stall. He beckons me to follow him with a smile, and we walk down the steps at the front of the station. Just five steps from the bottom, he stops and sits down. I sit down next to him.

'Sandy,' he says, without looking at me. 'This will be difficult for you…for both of us…'

'I'm still sure…' I reply

'Yes, I know that you are. But…' he searches for the words, and then seems to give up. He looks across at me, at the same time passing me a cup of tea. 'Sandy, you have had...dreams. These last few nights...bad dreams, perhaps?'

'Yes, most nights...'

'And in these dreams, I am a bad person?'

'Yes.' I take a sip from my tea. It is too hot. Not enough milk.

'I have become worse, I believe? Perhaps done worse things?'

'Yes. You locked me in a room, a few nights ago. Last night...'

'Yes, I understand... These dreams, they are trying to warn you about me. Tell you not to trust me. This is because part of you, a very strong part now, wants you to continue with things as they are. This part of you will become stronger over the next couple of hours, but in the last thirty minutes; perhaps the last hour, it will take you over.'

'By then...I'll be chained up?'

'Yes, but it may not be enough. It may not. There is a wall within reach of the spot. You may try to harm yourself. But remember this. Whatever you do...to yourself...whatever you offer, however you plead or beg...I will not unlock the chains. This evening, you will thank me. It may seem unlikely, even now. Even now you are beginning to hate me; to fear me. But very soon - even today - you will thank me. Remember that.'

'I'll try.'

'Sandy...I have some tablets. When I chain you, you must be honest about how you feel at that moment. It will help me to judge how you will be...in the last few minutes. If I have to, I may ask you to take some tablets. They will help you to be calm.'

'I'd rather not...' I look down at my tea, as yet not touched apart from a small sip. He smiles.

'Your tea is not drugged. I will do nothing to you without your permission. You have my word...'

'I'm sorry...'

'Please, it is OK. Now, it is nearly a quarter to ten. Let's take a walk, and we will walk near the place. I will only chain you when it becomes necessary. But, that may be sooner than some in the past...' He looks me up and down, at my body. 'You are very fit, very strong. I have no desire to fight you. I think, perhaps I will lose...very badly.'

He smiles, and I force a smile back. But I feel sick.

Time Ninety-Seven

Saturday 19th August 2006
11.05am CET

It is five minutes past eleven, here in Italy. Five minutes past ten in London - just over an hour to go. Contrary to Hiroshi's predictions, I still feel quite calm. He keeps talking to me, asking me questions; all kinds of questions. And I answer him, as best as I can, but my mind is elsewhere. He is very nervous now, and we are walking along the edge of the island, close to the spot where I will be chained - never more than two or three minutes away. He is also close to me - his right arm almost touching my left, as if ready to grab me at any moment. Probably, he is.

'Sandy,' he says, 'you are doing very well. Your training, in America, it has helped you, I think.'

'Maybe…'

'But, I think it is best if we make our way there now…to the place. I am not sure, if you ran off, that I could catch you…'

'OK…'

'So, let's take a slow walk there now…'

Time Ninety-Seven

Saturday 19th August 2006
11.14am CET

I have set my watch to the time in London, which is 10.14am. It is 11.14am here in Venice, but that does not matter. That is not real. What is real is that I have just an hour left.

I have felt the sensations for hours, the sharpening of senses that I always get during the last morning of each Time. I am in the room now - the one with the paint. I've been here before, with Richard Sturrock. Hiroshi has opened his bag and taken out the chains. They are not thick, perhaps an inch across, and are made - he tells me - of 'strengthened steel'. They are silver in colour, I think, but in the dimness of this back room, they look dull and old.

Hiroshi runs them through the ring cemented to the floor; once, twice, and then brings the two ends together. He holds them in his right hand, the manacles held tightly in his grip. I have skinny wrists, but they look very adjustable.

'So, Sandy - could you please place your hands through here...' he asks, holding the manacles up to me, and smiling; an uneasy smile. He says this in a natural way - as natural as possible, as you would perhaps say 'Could you pass me that book on the table?' or 'Which bus do I need for Tower Hill?'

But his voice is shaking, and his smile, unconvincing, hides something barely beneath the surface. It is fear. He is frightened of me. I realise this only at that moment, and within that moment I want to kick out at him. To force him to the ground and then run as fast as I can back into the morning air, the sunshine; into the breeze that would cool me down.

But I hold out my hands towards him, and I know then that I cannot do it; that I cannot put my hands through the silver holes myself. We have gone beyond that stage - I cannot help him anymore. Hiroshi stares into my eyes, and seeing for himself what I now realise, he quickly pulls my hands through the holes and tightens the manacles around my wrists. They snap shut and the sound resonates through my body. It is like a door slamming in a house during the night - it alarms me; makes me feel afraid. He steps behind me and clicks the padlock shut on the chains. He then stands up and takes a step back. He is still smiling, but the smile is now just painted on. Beyond it are so many emotions; more than I can count. I am squatting on the ground; I am like an animal chained in a cage. I look up at him, my eyes boring into his. I cannot smile. Not now. What do I feel - anger, rage, hatred? Yes, all of those things. But I know, still, that he is helping me. He wants to help me…but why? Why? Do I know why? Did I ever know? I can't remember.

The walls are painted white, but they appear dim and dark; there is hardly any light in here. The tins of paint are still scattered about - they are mostly white too. There is nothing else, just a few shelves, and a few pieces of wood - that's all. Is this where I have to live now? Is this what Hiroshi said…what we agreed? That this is now my home? I can't believe that is true, but I'm not sure. I'm not sure.

'So, there we are,' he says, taking a further step back. 'There we are…'

Time Ninety-Seven

Saturday 19th August 2006
11.44am CET

Everything is different now…everything is worse. I am chained up. He has chained me up. Did he say he would do that? I can't remember. But I'm trapped, and he's looking at me. He's sitting on a box, with his bag on the floor. It was the bag that had the chains - that's why I couldn't see them! He had them hidden away! But…he told me…about the chains. I'm sure that he did. He told me something…something…

The room is getting smaller - like in my dream. But it's faster; I can see the walls closing in. Still slowly, but I can see them. This room, it is going to kill me! He has chained me here, and he wants me to die! Why couldn't I see that before? I've been stupid! He just wants me to die!

Suddenly he speaks. His voice sounds loud, rough - like sandpaper. It makes me jump.

'How are you feeling?' he asks.

'I feel sick. I'm going to be sick. I need air…'

'Try to take deep breaths. We can't go outside, not yet…'

'I need to…'

'I have some lemonade, here in the bag. Would you like some?'

'What?'

'It is nice lemonade. It is your favourite. You like lemonade, don't you?'

'I…feel sick…'

'Do you remember, Sandy? Lemonade is your favourite drink. Try to remember. Would you like some now?'

I try to look at him, but he is out of focus. He seems miles away, talking to me across an enormous distance. 'Yes,' I reply. But my voice is starting to sound strange - not me.

Talking is an effort. Everything is an effort.

'Ah! Good! Well done, Sandy! Here it is...'

He rolls the can across the floor towards me. I expect it to take forever to reach me, because he is so far away, but it reaches me in seconds. I can't believe it! It reaches me in just a couple of seconds! Hiroshi is not far away; not at all. He is in the room with me! He is near me. He could step forward and touch me!

I shuffle backwards, as far as my chains will allow, towards the back wall. My eyes stare at him - I hate him now! I hate him! I kick the can away, and it spins and collides with an empty tin of paint, making a dull clunk.

Hiroshi looks back at me; he is looking more worried. He sighs and pushes his hands through his hair. He bows his head, as if in prayer. He won't look at me, not anymore.

Time Ninety-Seven

Saturday 19th August 2006
11.53am CET

What is the time? My mind is alert now, alert to what is happening to me. It is 10.53am, in London. Less than twenty minutes left - only twenty minutes left in this Time. But I'm here in this room - I remember - because I can stay in this Time forever! Until tomorrow, the day after; until next year! That will be two thousand and seven! A different year, not two thousand and six - not this one.

But this is not what I want. Not at all! How did I get here? He tricked me! He told me it would be for the best. But he is killing me! He's chained me up - he's chained me up in this room! He's going to kill me! How can I get away? How can I? My mind is straining, searching for an answer.

I look at him - he is still not looking at me. He won't look at me - he just looks at the ground. I think that he's happy if I am not talking. But I have to talk, have to persuade him to let me go. I have so little time…now it is 10.55, in London. So little time…

'Hiroshi…'

He looks up. 'Yes?' he replies.

'I want you to…let me go.'

'I can't do that. There's not long now, just a few minutes…'

'But I want to go home - you said that you wouldn't act against my will. But you are. You've chained me here. I want to go - back to the hotel. I want you to let me go.'

'Sandy, remember why you are here. Try to remember. You remember your boyfriend, and the baby. You remember them, don't you? Try to remember…'

'I think so…but I want you to let me go…'

'I can't…'

'Please…'

329

'I can't…'

'I'm dying…'

'No, you are OK. Try to relax. It will be alright…'

'No, it won't! What do you want?'

'Nothing…just to help you - that's all.'

'You're not helping me! What do you want…to let me go?'

'Nothing…'

'Do you want me?'

'No.'

'Let me go…you can have me. You can have me if you want. I don't mind…'

'No. Sandy, I will not let you go. It is 10.57 in London. Just fifteen minutes more and you are free…'

'I want to be free now! Let me go!' I am starting to shout, and suddenly I am sick. I vomit out in front of me, and again against the wall. My stomach is empty, and I feel the acid in my throat. I start to convulse, and I can feel my head moving forward - quickly, back and forth - but I cannot stop it. Hiroshi is there, in front of me. I think he is going to help me, to clean my face, my mouth, but instead he grabs my head, and places a pad over my mouth. For a moment I cannot breathe as he forces the pad into my mouth, and then there is tightness behind my hair. A hair catches and is pulled out; it hurts for a split second. It is a gag. I stare at him, wide-eyed.

'Breathe out of your nose,' he says. 'Breathe out of your nose…'

I can't reply. Only think. What is happening? Is he happy? Is he sad; angry? I continue to stare at him, searching his face for an answer. He understands my look; my stare.

'Sandy, I do not want to drug you, it would be better not to - we are so close, just a few minutes more. But you must not shout, must not scream. People may come, they may hear you. I don't think they would, not here, but I'm not sure, and we cannot take the risk. The scarf around your face, in your mouth…it will stop you shouting, that is all. Also…there is…something on the cloth. It smells nice…it will help you relax. You will feel OK; it will make you feel a bit happier. But you must try hard to relax - to calm down. Please, Sandy, it will be easier...'

I can smell it now, beneath my nose. It is strong; sweet. I try not to breathe it in, but I have to; I have to breathe. It fills my nostrils each time - the smell. It is so sweet - like sugar; like candy floss. It is pink. In my nose, in my mind, it is pink; just pink.

Time Ninety-Seven

Saturday 19th August 2006
12.11pm CET

I can see my watch - it is 11.11am. I have only a minute left, and then this Time will end; the end of Time Ninety-Seven. Hiroshi thinks that he has won - that he has claimed some victory over me. But he is wrong, because in just a minute this Time will be over. I am not meant to stay here; not made to stay here. I am made to live forever - Time after Time, stretching into infinity. That is my destiny, not this.

Only thirty seconds. Hiroshi is looking at me now. He is smiling. He stands up and stretches his arms. The sudden movement startles me - he has been still for so long; for minutes, hours, days, I don't know. I don't feel pink any more, but I feel very tired. My mind feels exhausted. I still want to pull away; to escape. But the strength has drained out of me. I can't fight any more. Perhaps he is right, perhaps I will stay here, not be taken back to another coma; another Time. But how can that be? I don't know. I can't think…

Just ten seconds. I watch the second hand sweep around the face of my watch. I know Hiroshi has started to come towards me, but I can't take my eyes off the watch. Five seconds. I close my eyes - I can't help it. I'm waiting for the blindness, the deafness, the silence, and the pain in my head - that terrible pain. I count down in my mind - four, three, two, one…nothing has happened. Perhaps I have counted too quickly - I should start again - but surely five seconds have passed now…

I look at my watch, blink, screw my eyes shut, and look again. It is 11.12am and eight seconds. Nine seconds, ten. I am still here. I open my eyes and look up. Hiroshi is standing over me. He bends down and removes my gag, and wipes my face with the same scarf. Then he unlocks the padlock and pulls the chains through the ring. He tries to unlock my wrists from the manacles, but he drops the tiny key on the floor. He says something in Japanese, to himself, and quickly retrieves it. Moments later my wrists are free. He places his arms under mine and lifts me to my feet. Only then do I realise that I was sitting down.

He asks me how I am feeling, and I reply that I am not sure. He smiles.

'You will be amazed,' he says. 'You will feel better…normal, in just a minute or two. This will pass, all of this, it will pass…'

I look at him, confused. I know who he is now. I know where I am. Things are rapidly coming back into focus - so fast I can't control them, cannot order them. But, above all things, I feel confused. This is because I am still here. Why am I still here? How can I still be here?

I watch him as he moves away from me; across the room is his bag. He retrieves it and carries it to where I am now standing. He drops the keys into it, and then, after winding up the chains, he drops them in also. He clasps the bag shut, and gives it a little pat, as if to say 'well done'. He turns to face me.

'So,' he says with a smile. 'Shall we go?'

Saturday 19th August 2006

12.15pm CET

We walk out together into the sun. The air is warm, and I feel dizzy, like I have woken from a deep sleep. A few steps take us out to a narrow path, and then a wider one. We pass an iron bench - it has a swan engraved on each arm. I want to sit down but Hiroshi wants us to walk on. He walks slowly, and I keep pace with him.

'Where are we going?' I ask.
'Where?' he replies. 'We are going to get a cup of tea.'
'Oh?'
'Yes. Would you like a cup of tea?'
'Yes.'
'Me too. Perhaps we could get some food as well. Are you hungry?'
'Yes. But I've been sick. I need to clean my teeth…'
'Ah! We can buy some toothpaste and a toothbrush in a chemist. There is one just along here, not far from here…'

We walk together, in this way, as if everything is normal. As if everything has been normal. And I still can't take in what has happened. I was so desperate to escape from the chains, but now everything has changed. In London, it is 11.20am now, and I am still here.

The desperation has gone. The desperation, the terror I felt while I was chained, it has gone. It has left me, and a realisation of my new reality is beginning to take its place. This man walking beside me - he is not my enemy. I turn and give him a little smile, the most I can manage, and suddenly he reaches out for my hand, my left hand, and I place it in his, without thinking. He gives it a little squeeze, and then relaxes his grip. But we are still holding hands when we reach the chemist. We are friends now. All of this, it is so strange, but it is all so normal.

Saturday 19th August 2006

8.35pm CET

I spend the evening with Hiroshi, and we talk about what has happened.
'This is all over for you now,' he says, munching on a bread roll. 'You will never see Richard Sturrock again because, well, he is dead. Here…he will be dead forever. And after tomorrow, you will never see me again…'
He raises a fork in the air as if for emphasis. I realise what he means, of course.
'Yes,' I reply. 'You return the day after tomorrow. What time?'
'What time do I…go back?'
'Yes…'
'10.26am.'
'Exactly 10.26am? No seconds?'
'No, exactly 10.26am, no seconds...'
'That was the same for me. 11.12am, no seconds…'
'Yes. It is always that way, for everyone like us. Strange, isn't it? Someone, I think, is very precise…'

We talk for ages, about his future, my future, and there is still so much that I don't understand. Tottenham Court Road, the record shop and the song - so much I still don't comprehend. But it is all drifting away; it is becoming the past. Already I am growing accustomed to this new reality, at once so bizarre and so ordinary.
This is where I will live and die, and here I will live with Chris, and here there will be a Jack. Here I will live and we will live. It is impossible but true. There will be no more Times, just this. There will be only this.

Saturday 19th August 2006

11.40pm CET

I sit on the end of my bed - a large double bed - and comb my hair. I can feel the hair pulling on my scalp - perhaps I am pulling too hard; perhaps I am not concentrating enough.

I pull out a hair by accident, and I feel the same tiny pain that I felt this morning. The sensation takes me back to the room with the paint, the scarf around my mouth, the fear and confusion.

But was I confused? How did I feel then? I put down the comb on the bed beside me, and for the first time since this morning I start to cry. And these are not big tears, there is no sobbing; but instead a gentle trickle of tears fall down my face.

Did I know what I was doing; what I have done? Oh, God, what I have done is irreversible; so completely final. I have lost so much. But I have gained so much more. Surely I have.

But I can no longer live as I have lived. The decisions I take, the choices I make each day, they will follow me forever. It is a massive responsibility, and one I am so used to being without. It is a burden totally unfamiliar to me.

I lay down on the bed, fully clothed still (I even have my sandals on), and stare up at the ceiling. It is whitewashed, recently I think, with a fresh coat of paint. Adam would know. Chris doesn't know much about paint. Neither do I. We have that in common.

My mind is wandering now. I close my eyes and watch the window-and-kaleidoscope world beneath my eyelids. It's funny, but there is so much to see when you close your eyes.

But it's not what I can see, or the absence of things, but a sudden feeling that strikes me as extraordinary. I am going to sleep on August 19th, 2006. It is bedtime. This, I feel, seems stranger to me than returning, once again, to March. But yet it all feels so very normal; so exceptional, but yet so commonplace.

I begin to drift off to sleep, laying still on the bed and not in it. I feel incredibly tired now. The tears have stopped. I reach out for my glass of water - pull it towards me and take a gulp. It is left over from this morning, and it tastes stale.

I am now getting older - like the water; getting staler. I can actually feel myself aging - or at least I imagine I can. Slowly, slowly, slowly, but yet with a steady, plodding pace, I grow old as if nothing in this world could be more ordinary. And the vastness, the terror of this realisation, is anesthetized by a single emotion that is crowding out everything else. It is an emotion that helps me to fall asleep with the trace of a smile upon my lips. I am happy.

Monday 21st August 2006

11.20am CET

Hiroshi is leaving in six minutes. He is going back. We are standing on a concrete block in Guidecca, leaning on an iron rail, looking across to Lido. There are a few boats about, and a bus; but there is no-one around where we are, no people. Hiroshi wants it that way.

'It is not nice to see someone die,' he has told me. 'It can be most unpleasant...'

But here I am with him, waiting for him to do just that. I have promised to walk away exactly one minute before the end of his Time. We stand watching the boats in silence. I know exactly what is going to happen to him, and I can see in his face that he is afraid.

'It's silly, isn't it?' he says. 'I have done this so many Times before, but each Time, well...'

'Yes, I've done it too, remember? It's terrifying...'

'Yes, terrifying...'

'What will you do...next Time?'

'Ah! I will practice my English. I think...Perhaps I will go to Australia! I have never been. I would like to visit Sydney, I think. There is so much I can do...I have nine years...'

'Yes...nine years.'

'This is better than five months; I think you will agree...'

'Yes...much better. But, maybe one day...'

'Certainly one day, I will become as you are now...truly free. But, not yet...'

'No...'

'Then, I must fight Richard Sturrock for myself. For my own benefit. That will be a fight to remember...'

'You will win, I'm sure...'

'Yes. I will win.'

Only three minutes remain now, for Hiroshi. He sighs to

himself.

'It has been nice to meet you,' he says. 'Very nice...'

'It's been lovely to meet you. Thanks for everything...'

He waves his hand in a dismissive way. 'I hope that you enjoy your life,' he says, smiling, but his eyes betraying the fear he is feeling.

'And I hope you have a nice...Time,' I reply with a smile of my own. 'Nice Times...'

'Yes...Sandy, I would like to be alone now. You understand.'

'Yes, I do understand.' I lean across and give him a kiss on the cheek; a farewell kiss. 'Goodbye.'

'Goodbye Sandy.' He turns to face the water, and then, as I am about to walk away, he turns to face me again. 'You are right about your baby. You will see him now...soon. He will be born. I am sure of it...'

I feel tears forming in my eyes, but for some reason, I do not want him to see me cry. 'Thank you,' I say, forcing out the words. 'I am certain too...' And I am certain, I really am. I just know it; know that it will be.

He turns away again, and this time he doesn't look back. I walk away from the rail and towards the grass and buildings behind me. I see someone a few hundred yards away, dressed in black and walking slowly. She seems old, and perhaps she is in mourning. She is too far away to tell for sure, and moments later she disappears between two buildings. Everything is empty again; no people. It's as if she were never there.

Most of the buildings seem derelict, as I approach them, and I realise that Hiroshi must have come here before - other Times - to die. It is a part of Venice 'earmarked' for development, but never developed. I look back at him. He is still standing by the rail. His black hair is waving in the breeze, and I can see his tie blowing about over his shoulder - flashes of blue and gold. I look at my watch. Just fourteen seconds. I feel somehow terrible watching him, as if I am intruding on his most personal act. But who more has the right to see this than me - than one of us? So I continue to watch as the seconds pass...six, five, four, three...

Hiroshi steps back from the rail, raises his arms in the air as if he is trying to grab something - some heavenly rope to pull him upwards. I glance down at my watch, just one second. I look up and as I do, Hiroshi's arms fall down by his side and he stands there, unmoving, until his legs collapse from under him, and he slumps to the ground, no longer alive, with one arm pointing out beyond the railings and towards the water.

Immediately, I turn and walk away. I do not want to see this. I don't want to remember him this way. I want to remember him with life, not as a pile of clothes on the ground. I quicken my pace, feeling an urgency building in me to be somewhere else. Not here. Despite the heat, I am shivering.

Twenty minutes later I'm on a bus back to San Marco. Each time I close my eyes, even to blink, I can see Hiroshi's body lying on the ground. But I know this will pass, that other things will happen to fill my thoughts; happier things.

Once I reach San Marco, I'll walk to the Rialto Bridge. There's a really lovely restaurant nearby, just away from the Grand Canal, and I'll have an early lunch. I ate there once with Hiroshi, just once; but he liked it very much.

Wednesday 23rd August 2006

10.00am

And now I am back in England. In fact, for the moment, I am back in my hotel at Lancaster Gate. I returned to England yesterday, arriving at Heathrow at about seven in the evening. From there I took the Heathrow Express to Paddington, and then a couple of tubes to Lancaster Gate. Lena is here, my room is here, everything is the same as always, but yet it is different; it is August 23rd.

I have never been this far before, and these dates, these months, September, October; even the sound of them in my mouth is strange and alien. These months, these novel months, they are now for me to live in. It's as if they have been away, somewhere in the distance, and now they have returned to greet me like long lost friends. November, December…Christmas…it seems so long ago, these months, the sound of these words.

I am walking in Kensington Gardens now, and it is hot as it always is in August. But, and I can hardly believe it, summer will now pass and be replaced by autumn. And then winter, and then spring. I am wearing shorts and a t-shirt now, but today I will buy a coat for the winter. I cannot wait to wear it, to plunge my hands deep into its pockets and pull the collar up around my neck. And I need a scarf - a warm one. I will wear them in the winter, when it is cold; when perhaps there is snow. I cannot wait to wear them. I cannot wait.

This afternoon, I am going out to Gravesend to rent a flat. Gravesend isn't very attractive, but there are some very nice apartments by the river - new developments. And, of course, this is where Chris lives. It is all part of my plan; my wonderful new plan.

Wednesday 23rd August 2006

8.30pm

It has been a successful day. On the way back from Gravesend, on the train, I mapped out in my head exactly what I need to do between now and Saturday. Saturday is the day I will meet Chris for the first time; the first time for him. I have just two days, and there is a lot to do.

I have met countless people during my life so far, and I can think of so many of them with little effort. I have an urge to find them all, discover how they are doing now. But after making a list earlier today, and slowly and reluctantly crossing off those I could not find before Saturday (Saturday is when I start afresh), I was left with just three names. Three people I would like to see again, people who I would like to have some impact on now, perhaps just to say goodbye.

These are the three people I would like to see again:

1) Lena
2) Adam
3) Chris

Lena I have seen already, she is here at the hotel, but I am going to write a letter to the manager of the hotel. The letter will say how wonderful she is as a receptionist, how helpful and kind. It will highlight her excellent customer service, and how great she is at her job. I am sure the letter will have no lasting impact on her life, but it will be written as much for me as for her - a kind of farewell. Strangely, although I like her very much as a person, we have little in common, and I don't really want to see her again. That may sound unkind, but I am just being honest.

So I will leave the letter for the manager when I leave

sometime next week, and move into my executive two-bedroomed fully-furnished apartment in Gravesend. I have paid the deposit in full, and am now just awaiting the completion of various pieces of nonsensical paperwork. This would normally take longer, but when you have over two million pounds, and make it clear you can easily look elsewhere for a property, things move faster.

I will also leave a letter for Lena; I will give it to her myself as I leave and kiss her on the cheek (even if she will be surprised and embarrassed). The letter will contain a cheque for twenty thousand pounds. This will be my parting gift.

As for Adam, I have a special plan, which morally I must execute before Saturday. This plan I have already set in motion, this afternoon. I called the firm that he contracts for (I couldn't remember the number but I did remember the name), and asked where he was working this week, posing as a previous client. I said I had some of his tools and that I had promised to deliver them at the end of this week. The man on the other end of the phone, while being a bit grumpy (or possibly just tired) gave me the information without question. Adam is in Hampshire, and so will I be tomorrow.

And that just leaves Chris. Chris I will marry and have a child with; a baby boy... Jack.

Thursday 24th August 2006

4.30pm

Adam is working on a two-week contract, which he started this Tuesday. I expected him to still be in Birmingham, but that job finished at the weekend, and now he is here. He is working in a large hotel and conference centre called Heckfield Place. It is in the middle of Hampshire - in the middle of nowhere, in fact. There is a small town nearby called Hartney Whitney, but my train came into a town called Hook. Everywhere around here seems to begin with an 'H'.

Adam is staying at the hotel he is working at, and now so am I. I have seen him already - he is with a team of six men. They are plastering and painting a huge conference room on the ground floor. When I saw him it made me smile; involuntarily. He didn't see me, but I suppose it doesn't really matter if he did; he wouldn't know who I am. He wouldn't remember.

I last saw Adam in Time Eighty-Four. He looks the same now; just the same, but I try to look at him as if for the first time; look at him anew. He is quite handsome really, I think. And when I saw him, at that moment, I felt sure that he would find someone who would love him again, someone to replace the wife who had so cruelly left him, and someone to replace what he had, once, found in me.

After seeing him this afternoon I went for a long walk in the grounds of the hotel. Seeing him in the flesh had unnerved me somewhat, and made me doubt whether I would carry out my plan. But walking in the beautiful grounds, listening to all the sounds around me, I became certain that I needed to do this. I needed to 'draw a line' under all that had happened between us. And anyway, I reflected, I am here now in Hampshire, and the train journey had taken forever. It would be a waste of a long journey to simply do nothing.

Friday 25th August 2006

9.20am

I have already checked the train times, and I'm hoping to be on a train back to London by 11am. Then I'll be off to Greenhithe, which is where Bluewater is. It will be a day of travelling.

I have had breakfast, but I feel so nervous that I had difficulty eating much. I try to fathom out why I feel this way; indeed, why I feel the need to do this at all? But it just somehow seems right - the correct thing to do. I believe that I owe something to Adam - I'm not even sure what - but I feel as though this small act will in some way repay him for his...what? His love? His attention? I'm really not sure, but at the same time I am in no doubt that this will act as a full stop - that I will leave Adam here in this hotel and I will never see him again. This is the right thing to do. It is the right thing.

I dressed quickly this morning (red England top and jeans), but spent a while on my make-up. I wanted to look nice, to look attractive. That is important, in my plan, that everyone in the room thinks I look attractive. That is the part I am playing; the part of a pretty girl. Not tarty, of course, or cheap or any of those well-worn phrases or ideas, just pretty. A nice girl; the sort of girl you would like to take home to your parents. 'Hi Mum and Dad,' you would say. 'This is Sandy. She's a nice, pretty girl.' That's what I want to be today.

I stay in the breakfast area for a few minutes more, and then go in search of the toilets. I stand and check myself in the mirror, and apply the final touches to my make-up. I am looking as good as I can; as good as I want to look. Before I turn away, I lift my right hand up to my hair, and notice that it is shaking. I place both hands out in front of me - they are both shaking; trembling, and for a moment I consider just abandoning the plan, grabbing my things (all packed and ready to go in my room) and heading off to Hook station in a taxi. But, putting my hands down by my side, I shake my head quickly to dispel the thought. Just five minutes, I tell myself, it will all be over in five minutes.

I leave the toilets, my nerves reaching a crescendo, and walk slowly towards the entrance to the conference room. I stay close to the wall, trying not to look suspicious or strange, but keen not to be seen either by Adam or any of his workmates. There are four Internet computers directly opposite the door to the room, situated a few feet away. I quickly cross and sit down at one of them - they are all vacant. I look up, my face hidden behind the monitor. I then slowly sit upright, so my eyes lift above the level of the screen, and look ahead through the door. Immediately I see six men in a room, three are painting and two are plastering. One is stirring a large plastic bucket of paint in the centre of the room. It is Adam. The men are all talking at the same time, arguing about something, but in a friendly way. Everything is in place, and I know that now is the time to act; to execute my plan.

The feeling I have is like when you are waiting to go in to see the dentist, and then suddenly, unexpectedly, your name is called. I feel that sickening fear, knowing that I must act now, but I am able to force myself out of the seat, and then I stand still for a second.

I am in view of the door, so I have to move. I am trembling. I look up at the ceiling just for a moment, and then look back at the entrance - at Adam - and smile. I walk forward and, with the plan in motion - irreversible from this point - I feel a burst of confidence and walk smiling through the door. Three of the men see me immediately and stop working.

'Hi,' says one of them, paintbrush in hand. 'Are you OK?'

But I do not see him; I just look straight ahead at Adam. He has seen me and drops the stick into the bucket. It stands almost upright - the paint is obviously still thick. I stop in front of him, smiling. The other five men are watching now. They know something is about to happen; we all do.

'Adam.' I say, holding my smile.

'Yeah?' says Adam, smiling back. He is confused; he is wondering where he has seen me before - if he has seen me before, if he knows me at all.

'Adam.' I say again, and then take his face in my hands, gently. I kiss him on the lips, move my hands around to his back, and lift my left leg up, slightly, touching his thigh. He is nervous; perplexed, but he doesn't resist. He kisses me back, and as he does I lean into him - press my body up against his; push myself against him. We kiss for maybe five seconds, and then he begins to pull away, and as he does I pull away too, making it appear as if our parting was natural. I slowly pull myself from him, and lean to kiss him on the cheek. I do this quickly, and then turn my left cheek against his. I whisper to him, into his ear, quietly so only he can hear - so he knows these words are just for him.

'It's OK, Adam. Everything is going to be great...'

And then I pull away completely, but slowly, and turn around and walk out, back through the doorway. The other men look at me, smiling, but their faces are almost as perplexed as Adam. This is because they see something in me; I know this, something of my strength of character, of my certainty. They don't view me as crazy or cheap, but rather as a pretty, normal girl behaving in a surprising way. This, for them, is the most bewildering - and the best - thing of all.

I walk away from the room, and I don't look back. I will never see Adam again, not from this point. But I hear something behind me, an unmistakable sound that rises and ripples through the air. It is a round of applause.

* * * * * * * * * * * * * * *

It was probably because it was such a strange thing to happen (they say we always remember unexpected events) that news of Adam's kiss spread like wildfire amongst his peers. It seemed that within a few weeks every contractor in the painting and plastering trade knew about Adam's brief liaison with Sandy. Of course, no-one knew her name – least of all Adam – but what had happened between them, just for those few seconds, elevated him somewhat amongst the people with whom he worked.

And so it was three months later, when Adam was attending a 'hopeless' party (a party with virtually no single girls) that he met Fiona.

To say that the party was totally hopeless would be a misconception, because there was at least one single girl there - Fiona, who had very recently (two weeks ago, in fact) split up with her boyfriend of almost a year. The boyfriend was someone Adam knew vaguely, because he also worked in the hotel and large building painting trade. It was in this way that Fiona had heard something of Adam's exploits (they had been exaggerated somewhat by now) and she was therefore, despite herself, intrigued to see him at the party.

Adam was considering, for the third time, the best way of leaving without offending the host (it was a friend's birthday party – someone who took birthdays very seriously and would possibly be affronted if he left so early) when Fiona caught his eye. She smiled, just for a second, and then looked away. Then, almost immediately, she looked across at him again and walked over to where he was standing, by the wall.

'Hello,' she said. 'It's Adam, isn't it? I've seen you before, a few weeks ago, at that big hotel near Liverpool Street. You were working there…'

'The Regent…'

'Yes, that's it. I was meeting my boyfriend, my ex-boyfriend…'

'Oh?'

'Yes...' Fiona suddenly felt embarrassed by what she had just said – 'my ex-boyfriend' – and to cover her embarrassment she just said the first thing that came into her head, the only thing she really knew about Adam; the reason she had, in all honesty, approached him.

'I've heard all about you,' she said, her face breaking into an awkward smile. 'Heard you're a bit of a ladies man...'

'No.' Adam replied.

The smile dropped from Fiona's face like a stone.

'Oh,' she replied, 'I just heard...'

'No.' Adam reiterated. There was a slight, awkward pause. 'This girl came up to me when I was stirring some paint. She kissed me and then went. That's it. I didn't even know her. Everything else you've heard...'

'Hmmm...why do you think she did that?'

Adam suddenly found himself smiling. Perhaps it was the memory of the kiss, the strangeness of it all, and her words to him that he had never told anyone - or perhaps it was this girl, this girl smiling at him now, who seemed so interested in him. He looked at her and sized her up in his mind. She was plain - that would be the best word to describe her - plain. But, she was not unattractive, not at all, and she had, he now noticed, the most beautiful eyes.

'I don't know, perhaps I'm irresistible to women. If I am, women do a good job of hiding it...'

Fiona smiled back, but didn't reply. She couldn't think of anything else to say, really. She looked down at her drink, held in her left hand (she was left handed) and then back at Adam.

'Well...' she started to say.

Adam looked at her, and felt something in his stomach turn. He felt sick, all of a sudden. He was hot, the room was too hot, and, he realised, the music was too loud. And he didn't like the music; it was hardly music at all. Not like the music he loved when he was a boy, not at all. Everything was changing, he was getting older, and life was passing him by.

His life, so far, had been a disaster. What had he achieved? Nothing really – just a failed marriage; and that was hardly an achievement. He looked at her again, the girl standing in front of him. He didn't even know her name. Perhaps he should ask her name?

'You know what?' he said, without a trace of a smile. 'You have the most beautiful eyes I've ever seen…'

Two years later, Adam and Fiona were married. She was just a year younger than him, but the last two years had made her feel even younger still. She was happy, and so was he. She realised - with a sense of surprise - that she had never really been happy before. At least, not like she was now.

The night before the wedding, Adam dreamt about the girl in the England top, the one who had given him that kiss. Sometimes, even now, someone would mention it; that kiss. Adam felt guilty, even in the dream, seeing another girl on the eve of his wedding, but this time they didn't kiss, or anything like that.

They were in the room again, at Heckfield Place, and this time she bent down and helped him stir the paint. She took his hands and they stirred together, moving the paint round and round. She smiled at him as they did this, and she said, as she had before, 'Everything is going to be great…'

When he woke up, it was the morning of his wedding. As he dressed, the dream played on his mind, even though he had a million other things to think about. He couldn't remember her face, the girl in the dream, and he realised this was because, for most of the time, he had been looking down at the bucket of paint.

He had been watching and they made the paint turn, it was stiff and they had to push hard, but together they the stirred it round, round and round, like the paint itself was a large white wheel.

It was an effort, but the harder they pushed, together, the

faster it went. Patterns appeared in the paint, a few at first, then many; like little spirals, little wheels. And so around it went, faster and faster, little wheels within wheels, it seemed; wheels within wheels.

Saturday 26th August 2006

5.40am

Last night I moved, for two nights only, into a small hotel in Greenhithe called 'The Abbey Hotel'. It's only two miles or so from Bluewater, and in that respect it's ideal, but it's actually more of a guest house than a hotel. This was far from clear from the website.

My room in Lancaster Gate is huge, and I am used to that amount of space, but the room here is tiny. I have about a million skin, hair and face products, and they are all jostling for place on the tiny bedroom cabinet and the even tinier bathroom shelf above the sink.

I slept quite well last night, and was deeply asleep when the alarm went off at 5.30am. It took me a good ten minutes to surface, and now I am up and out of bed. Now begins the task of making myself as beautiful as possible. This is of the utmost importance, because it is for Chris.

I spend the best part of the next two hours trying on clothes and getting ready. Last night, I whittled it down to three outfits, but now I can't decide between two. But, in the end, I plump for the light blue dress with shoulder straps. It is quite low cut and knee length, but it is not tarty; it is instead chic (after all, it cost nearly two hundred pounds!). It is, to sum up, simple but effective. My make-up is on, my hair blow-dried to create gentle waves – everything is ready. I am ready.

I look in the mirror, one last time. I look as good as I can get.

Saturday 26th August 2006

9.30am

The taxi drops me outside the side entrance to John Lewis, the department store, and I quickly step inside - through the revolving doors - and out of the heat. I almost skip through the doors, as I still hold a bit of a fear due to getting my hand trapped in one once. This was during one of my many Times. I am not surprised that these events still affect my present, but my future – the real future that I now have – is no longer dictated by them. I am free.

I think for a moment of Hiroshi – of whether he will one day choose the freedom I now have; if he will fight Richard Sturrock one last Time for his own sake. Or if he will remain in the cycle of Times, nine years after nine years, thousands and thousands of years upon countless years more, until, like us all, he slips into a raging insanity from which he will never return.

I pass through the bedding section, see a beautiful cushion I would like to buy, and this snaps me out of these thoughts. I shake my head to remove Hiroshi from my mind. I make a decision to concentrate now on my task ahead, to concentrate on Chris. This is why I am here, after all – for Chris. Everything is now for Chris.

* * * * * * * * * * * * * * * *

Bluewater opens at 9am on Saturdays, but Chris is rarely behind the counter at Waterstones bookshop before 10am. As he always tells me - always told me - he has 'things to do'. These 'things' include making tea for everybody and straightening up piles of books that will be messed up again within hours of the shop opening. So, as always, and now for the last time, I will wait until just past 10am and then I walk into the shop. That way, I know he will be there, behind the counter to the right of the door, and that the shop will be virtually empty.

Of course, this is the first time I will meet Chris on August 26th - in fact it is the first ever August 26th 2006 for me. I have had many August 19^{th}s - ninety-seven to be precise - but never an August 26th.

I am aware, therefore, that I am entering unfamiliar territory. In some respects, it is all new, but as I walk through John Lewis and out into the main body of Bluewater, in other ways it is all dreadfully familiar.

And this dread is yet to leave me - the dread of familiarity; a spoken phrase or a place I see can hurtle me back to the past, make me believe that I am once again trapped in the cycle of Times. I am getting this sensation now - the sale signs all too known to me, the shop fronts and the staff the same as they ever were.

But, and it is a big but, it is all counterpoised by that which is new. For example, a shiny red sports car is on display at one of the large seating areas. I am not sure what it is promoting, except perhaps itself (people are still struggling with the signs and hoardings), but I have never, ever, seen it before.

Again, while walking along Thames Walk I pass the Virgin Megastore, which has a completely new display in the window. This includes a large inflatable man in a black suit playing the guitar. I have, I am certain, never seen him before; never.

So much is new, and this all points to my freedom; to the incredible reality of it.

From John Lewis it is a very short walk to Waterstones - if you simply walk straight up Guild Hall, you would be there in two minutes. So, with time to kill, I walk the other way around the 'Triangle' (Bluewater is like a big triangle), which will take me much longer to arrive at the same spot. Including

Virgin Megastore, I pass a number of other shops with changes, and each change, each new thing that I see, builds in me a confidence that I did not believe I would be able to feel.

At 9.50am, I stop in the toilets to touch up my make-up. Looking in the mirror (watched all the time by a strangely over-inquisitive cleaner) I add a couple of touches to my lipstick and play around a bit with my hair, but other than that everything seems pretty much intact. With a forced smile to the cleaner (which is not returned) I step out of the toilet ready to execute my plan.

I am now outside the toilets on Thames Walk (the ones next to 'Next', if you see what I mean), which is a five minute very slow walk to Waterstones. I take a deep breath and set off. I expected to feel quite nervous by now, like I did yesterday, but I feel improbably calm. My sense of confidence, rather than diminishing, appears to be growing.

As I walk along, passing after a minute or two the 'Yo Sushi' restaurant with the rotating counter, I start to run through the plan in my head. This is fairly pointless, because I will do as I have always done before - talk to Chris at the counter and then faint (or pretend to faint, anyway). This has a 100% success rate. This time, of course, I *must* be successful. This lunchtime, I want to be drinking tea with Chris, and this evening, I want to be having dinner with him at La Tasca. I cannot accept the possibility that this may not happen. It simply has to.

After walking as slowly as is possible without seeming silly, I arrive within a few steps of Waterstones at exactly 10am. I can already see the window display offering '3 for the price of 2' on selected books, and as I tentatively step closer I see the pile of John Grisham books from which I originally chose. It seems just so long ago.

And, slowly, I turn my head to the right, and then I see him.

My heart does actually skip a beat, or at least it seems that way, when I see him standing behind the counter. He is alone, staring into space, thinking in the way that he always does, and seeing him there creates an enormous feeling inside me; a feeling of everything crashing into place.

He is there, as I knew he would be, as my instinct told me. My former life, that ghastly muddle of a life, those five months in which I spent over forty years, has passed away forever, but my instinct - which has guided me for so long - seems to be still intact.

And the force of it here, in this instant - almost speaking to me in an audible voice - causes me to wobble for a moment on my feet, and I have to lean forward and steady myself on the glass in the window. I step back out of sight of Chris, and lean back, as unobtrusively as possible, against the wall.

I am suddenly and momentarily gripped with a fear, a terrible fear, that when I look again he will be gone. That he was just there for the moment, for a matter of seconds, and then like a ghost he will disappear into the gas and air that surrounds us all. But beyond that fear, everything is well. More than well - I feel ecstatic! He is there, and I know - I *know* - that everything will now turn out well.

This is not just an idea, it is a certainty. Everything today will go to plan, I will faint and he will catch me. We will have lunch and then dinner. We will become a couple and he will move into my new flat. We will marry, one day soon, and I will get pregnant and give birth to a baby. My baby, the baby I had before, the baby lost in time but still waiting - not on an Island in Hawaii, as in my pitiless dream - but somewhere else; like all of us who come back to this same place Time after Time, he has been waiting and he will be born to me. And we will be happy, myself and Chris and the baby, my darling baby; my Jack.

All of this unfolds before me - in my head and before me - as if I could reach out and touch it, feel it between my fingers and on the palms of my hands - it is there, my future; my certain future.

And all of this passes, but the mark it leaves is so strong that I feel…and words fail me at this point…but it is a feeling more than wonderful.

I step away from the wall, run my hands gently through my hair. I walk along towards the entrance; walk beside the glass window, and see him standing there still - as if he himself is frozen in time, still staring into space - waiting for me.

The bookshop is almost empty as I walk in, my hair and make-up immaculate, my body still toned from the weeks of training, my beautiful summer dress almost shining under the lights of the shop. I feel as if I am shining myself. I feel fine, full of confidence.

I stroll over to the pile of books, and choose three copies of 'The Broker' from the pile. I hold them in front of me; like a gift. Before I turn, I can already feel Chris watching me. Then I turn and I see that he is. He seems a little embarrassed, as if I have caught him doing something naughty, and he looks away and pretends to be doing something with the till.

He is the love of my life - my whole life. Every single bit of it that has any meaning at all. And he doesn't even know me, not at the moment. But, this time, over the weeks to come, he will know me very well.

I walk towards him, and put my three books on the counter. He looks at me and smiles, and I have to stop myself from just throwing my arms around him and pulling him over the counter towards me; my Chris.

But I don't do that, not at all. Instead I smile, I just smile. But the best smile I can manage.

'Hi,' I say. 'I wonder if you can help me…'

The End

Acknowledgements

I am indebted primarily to two people; with their help and support this novel has been completed.

Firstly, my grateful thanks go to the love of *my* whole life - Katie, my wife - who has supported me throughout the year it has taken me to write this book, and also for the expertise she has used and the time she has spent in designing the cover.

And, secondly, I would like to thank my agent and great friend, Anna Drew, for all her help and support, and especially for her unrivaled sense of humour.

In addition, I would like to thank my children for their contributions: Zac, who switched lights on and off and banged on various items (mostly books) while I was trying to write, and Luca, who asked about five million questions.

Finally, my thanks go to anyone who has read this book. I hope that you have enjoyed it.